Seducing the Rabbi

a novel

Jala Pfaff

BLUE FLAX
PRESS

This is a work of fiction; any references to real persons, places, or events are used fictitiously.

All rights reserved.

Copyright © 2006 by Jala Pfaff and Blue Flax Press.
www.jalapfaff.com

Cover design and layout copyright © by Jala Pfaff, Sanjay Rajan and Blue Flax Press.

Portions of some Alan emails by Joel Schwimmer.

Author photo by Michael Grasseschi.
ahophotographics.com

This book may not be reproduced in whole or in part by any means without explicit permission.

ISBN: 0-9772558-0-8

P.80 excerpt & p.136 excerpt from "The Meme Machine" by Susan Blackmore (1999). Reprinted by permission of Oxford University Press.

"Penis in a bottle" article, from the October 04, 2001 edition of Boulder Weekly, reprinted by permission.

Lyrics of the song "Alfalfa's" written by Vince Herman of Leftover Salmon, reprinted by permission.

Originally published by Blue Flax Press in 2006.
www.blueflaxpress.com

Printed in the U.S.A. on recycled paper.

To S, who makes things possible.

Seducing the Rabbi

So many men, so little time.
—*Mae West*

Sigh no more, ladies, sigh no more,
Men were deceivers ever;
One foot in sea and one on shore;
To one thing constant never.
Then sigh not so,
But let them go,
And be you blithe and bonny;
Converting all your sounds of woe
Into Hey nonny, nonny.
—*Shakespeare, Much Ado About Nothing*

Too much of a good thing is wonderful.
—*Mae West*

Prologue

Could I be more excited? I, Aviva Goldberg, ABD (All-But-Dissertation) and professor-to-be, was in the passenger seat of my darling Brandon's tiny Toyota (those long, strong legs of his severely origamied), holding hands sweatily with this love of my life as we approached on Highway 70 the city I'd be living and teaching in for the next who-knew-how-many years. We'd left behind the big, bad, dirty East Coast two days ago, and my lower back was feeling every minute of it. Our mission was to get me settled, and then Brandon would also be starting a new job: hydrologist with an environmental consulting company about four hours' drive from me, on the Western Slope. (See, I was already proudly throwing around terms I knew nothing about, like "Western Slope" and "Front Range.")

"Can I have the chips?" asked my sweetie.

"But of course!"

I reached into the back seat to locate the mylar bag of what I knew to be only leftover salt dregs (but hey, if he wanted 'em, he could have 'em). As I was rummaging around—slimy peach pits, part of an avocado peel (one of Brandon's adorable habits was to eat avocados as if they were apples), used undies (let's not talk about that)—I heard Brandon go "Ooooohhhhhhh!" Last time I'd checked, he hadn't been on the verge of experiencing sexual release, but I'd never heard him produce that sound in any other context. What could it be?

Empty-handed, I turned back around in my (unbelievably uncomfortable) seat, to see an enormous double rainbow over a quaint, almost fake-looking (it was *that* beautiful) town, its mountain backdrop something from a movie set.

We'd reached Boulder, Colorado, and my life was about to be perfect. My wild days were far behind me; I was ready (well, maybe in a couple of decades) to get married and do all that wonderful domestic stuff (well, other than having kids). As we eased down the exit ramp into town—my new town!—I noticed several cars sporting the same bumper sticker: *Keep Boulder Weird*.

"Brandon, *mon cher*, what do you suppose *that's* about?"

ð

I came out of my reverie about Alan (oy, *Alan*!) as I heard the beginning of one of my favorite Christine Lavin tunes, to which I was compelled to sing along. It was the one where she sings of discovering "Rocky Mountain splendor" and the (all-natural) Rocky Mountain High.

Christine Lavin, ever since I first heard one of her songs on the radio and became an instant fan, has always been an unwitting prophetic influence in my life. (And we also have certain things in common, like we're both a bit on the short side, and we both salivate over Harrison Ford.) The most obvious way in which she proved prophetic for me is that I heard this song when I was getting ready to move to Colorado for the first time. Rocky Mountain High, it was to be indeed. In more ways than one, although not in the drug sense—not for me, anyway, although as for the rest of Boulder...*sans commentaire.*

I forgot about Alan for about three minutes while heavily involved in belting out (off-key, I'm afraid) the lyrics, my voice cracking on the high parts. Some people have claimed that I'm easily distracted, but I don't agree: I think it's just that I tend to digress because I think *parenthetically*, which is, I believe, a sign of an extremely active and creative brain—one which can entertain multiple levels of thought with ease. I bet Einstein would've agreed. (Being Jewish myself, I of course always like to mentally align myself with other Jews, preferably those famous for their intelligence, if not their looks.)

Alan is Jewish. Mmm... What delicious memories (a few of them; the rest of our time together was usually frustrating as hell). A bicycle racer, opera lover, sometime player of a decrepit violin with one missing string which he never bothered to replace, and one of the most physically active people I've ever met (even considering that this *is* Boulder), he had the most beautiful thighs. The first time I saw him in his "little biking clothes," as I call them, I almost died. And it was very hard to do the polite thing and tear my eyes off that…bulge, package, whatever you want to call it. I think all the extant words sound clinical, ridiculous, or just plain gross. So why hasn't anyone invented any new words? Or if someone has, why haven't they stuck?

This subject is of particular interest to me, as I am a Linguistics professor. In terms of my teaching and research, I'm multidepartmental: primarily Linguistics; but also French, the occasional course in Anthropology, Psychology, even Computer Science (if it's a topic in Artificial Intelligence—say, handwriting recognition, or neural nets). In terms of my personal life, I'm multiorgasmic. Unfortunately, this doesn't count at all toward my tenure-building dossier. If it did, I could go directly into early retirement. At the risk of sounding arrogant (*qui, moi?*), I will say that although I'm extremely knowledgeable about many things, there are also lacunae. Often these have to do with pop culture, ensconced as I am in the ivory-look (we only do faux ivory these days; real would be too un-P.C.) tower. For example, you know the white bumper sticker with the colorful teddy bears strolling across it? Well, I spent *years* blithely assuming that was some daycare center's logo, when "*duh, dummy*" (as I was finally, bluntly informed) it signified The Grateful Dead. Another example: I didn't know until very recently that lesbians wore purple (as a *statement*, I mean). When someone finally told me about it (my students—they were inquiring blatantly about my sexual identity), I was like, *Oh shit!* Purple has always been my favorite color—I wear it almost every day.

Now, why am I teaching French as well as Linguistics? *Well, why the fuck not?* That's the reason my African-American colleague Colleen gives whenever she's asked why she has a doctorate in Yiddish Studies, and it's what she snapped at me, too, the first time I met her and was foolish enough to ask.

Another way in which Christine Lavin proved prophetic was that when I first moved to Boulder (my then-current boyfriend, Brandon, driving me all the way out here from the East Coast—just shows you what a mensch he was), and I mean literally the first *day* I'd arrived in Boulder, we saw a flyer up on Pearl Street announcing that Christine Lavin herself would be appearing that very night at the Boulder Theater. Being recent Christine Lavin fans, we immediately bought tickets. (I said Brandon was a mensch, and he really, really was. So what *else* was he like? Well, I'll be telling you little things about him now and then, but I can start with a couple of them now: I used to love to make word games out of his name, one of my favorites being "brand;" I'd give him about a two-second warning that he was about to be *branded*, then the uproarious giggling chase around the apartment would begin, ending in my breathlessly pinning him to some surface a few minutes later and tugging his jeans down far enough to give his fabulous butt a good solid bite. How fabulous was this butt of his? Well, his sister-in-law used to appraise him, torso to toes, in *far* too interested and close a manner, concluding every time: "Brandon's bustin' out of his jeans again.")

That evening, outside the lovely, cozy venue (which, all these years later, I still prefer to any other concert hall), Christine did her thing, twirling her baton at intermission—one of those leftover girly-girl things that we all once did but that most of us are too embarrassed to admit to anymore. Afterwards, I decided to buy one of her tapes, since it was one I'd never seen for sale before on CD. I got into line for an autograph on my happy purchase. When I met Christine and told her the usual stuff (true, though) about how much her music had affected my life since I'd discovered her, she asked to whom she should write the autograph, and I told her I wanted it to be to me and my boyfriend Brandon, since we both loved her work. She got this look on her face and said, "I don't think I should autograph *this* one, then—this is really a *cynical* album, about how true love never lasts and never even *was* in the first place... I would hate to *jinx* you guys!" And then she let loose her trademark high-pitched wacky giggle. Of course I told her, no, no, go right ahead, *we're* not superstitious, *we're* such a strong couple, *we've* been together years and years, there's no danger in *us* splitting up...

Yeah, right. My sweet Brandon was long gone by the time Alan ever came into the picture.

When I first met Alan, he had been, for several months already, on this extremely unfortunate (for me) new kick where he'd decided he wasn't going to have casual sex ever again. He swore he'd either be in a very,

very serious relationship to have sex, or else he'd just be celibate—he claimed he didn't mind. Maybe it was because he was about to turn forty. I'm starting to get the impression that men and women start to kind of *switch places* around then. There's no end to the jokes about "older" women wanting sex—and at times having to be very aggressive about it, too. And around that age, men seem to lose interest in sex and simultaneously get scared of women, preserving their virtue—or simply their energy. And then later in life—even worse. Women grow facial hair, men breasts. Much of this, of course, really does have a biological basis, hormone changes and such. But still. Awful is awful. (I'm permitted the tautology—I'm a linguist.)

I'm not forty; I'm thirty-five, but that's close enough! From what my girlfriends and I see and hear and talk about with other women these days, the pattern is real. Another cruel joke of nature: we women with our raging I-want-sex hormones, and all the men wilting right and left around us. And the Boulder men spending hours a day on their "road bikes" (remember when those were just called *10-speeds*?), and suddenly discovering male bonding and the pleasure of "just going to sleep tonight." And some of them (which is *really* not fair, what with the attrition rates of modern-day hetero, single men) even riding so much that that *vein* or whatever it is develops that *problem* and they can't even get it up anymore. So you see, our gripes are justified.

A final Christine Lavin coincidence is this one song where she lectures tongue-in-cheek on not trying to call your lovers by their real name when in the heat of passion, since at that moment you're liable to be a bit out of your head and call them by last week's—or maybe last night's—guy's name. This song would also prove prophetic, and has, as you will see, a great deal to do with my story.

β

Alan is a strange one, or, as those even stranger Brits would put it, an odd wanker. (I love Briticisms.) Every time he and I got together to do a bike ride—a mellow one, as I'd *never* have been able to keep up with him on a "real" one—we'd spend half our time goofing off, me poking him in the side of the butt (you know, where that delicious little indentation is), him pretending to get back at me by pushing me, but really ending up kind of holding on to me instead...and on we rode. If it was summer we'd usually end up lying around in some grass somewhere relatively isolated and...I don't really know what to call it, as someone well beyond the age, experience, and vocabulary of a teenager: rolling around together. Grappling. Making out. But, of course, never *screwing*. Never *doing it*. (Sorry—again, the lexical dilemma. Though the frustration level was surely the same as any adolescent's.)

If it was winter, we'd end up back at his place, an Alan-created disaster area which disgusted me to no end and which confirmed the theory that men are only bears with furniture, but where we at least had the privacy of his own little rented room (his bicycle racing earned him just about enough to cover rent for one room plus a hot plate, and bike repairs. Alan did not aspire to more). There we'd do basically the same stuff as out in the grass in the summertime; sometimes serious, other times much less inspired, depending on how tired we were after our bike ride (which, for him, was often his second or third ride of the day, depending on whether he'd also been playing rugby, Ultimate, squash, or hockey that day, in addition to his *serious* ride). But, of course, we never had *intercourse*.

You may be wondering why I didn't apply to be the "girlfriend" to whom he'd referred when discussing his hypothetical future sexual activities. We weren't suited for each other in that way, somehow...and we both knew it.

There were too many things he wasn't that I wished he were: well-groomed, well-dressed, more materially ambitious, less socially inept, less nerdy. What I liked about him was his athleticism; his irresistible spicy, musky odor; his body (in spite of that "tribal member" hair, in quantities and places which would cause great embarrassment to me if seen with him on a beach); his inherent intelligence; his crashing on his bare mattress and cranking up his stereo as loud as possible after a ride to listen in rapture not to head-banging grunge but to Madama Butterfly; and—perhaps also—the challenge of trying to "nail" him. Anyway, there were probably plenty of reasons that I didn't seem to him like a real candidate for girlfriend either... I wasn't athletic enough, for starters.

But what Alan and I did share was an amazing attraction for each other's body. Rarely in my life, my horny and, may I say, sexually rather full life, have I felt *that* degree of animal attraction. It's purely a chemical, hormonal, brainstem kind of thing. You're embarrassed to be seen in public with the guy, with his cheap, uncool K-Mart jeans and perpetually tape-repaired glasses, but your body screams for him. Merely thinking about him in his little biking clothes, his body powering that bicycle sixty miles in a single session, makes you warm and wet instantly. Lying on top of him (clothed or mostly clothed) is such a heady experience that you almost swoon, and it is there, on top of his iron body, inhaling that *guy* smell, that for the first time you actually understand what the word *swoon* means, and why such a lexical entry does in fact need to exist.

And it wasn't all one-sided. No, I believe I've mentioned that the feeling was mutual. Now, there've been guys who've told me my body was really great, but there've also been plenty who thought I was merely average-looking or worse, even one Brazilian who proclaimed me "not bad in spite of" my large breasts. (Most Brazilian men seem to feel strongly for one of the African ideals of beauty, that of small breasts and a large behind. Knowing this, I tried not to take his comment too personally, although it still wounded my ego—and later I also thought to wonder about what it implied about my *derrière*.) There do seem to be some fundamental truths about Jewish women, at least in my opinion: we seem to really enjoy sex, and aren't shy about it either, and we seem to be a bit more on the zaftig side—more voluptuous, more generous. And as for Jewish men, well, in my experience they're a bit better-endowed. Just look at porn star Ron Jeremy.

I continued to be infuriated and disappointed that Alan wouldn't change his mind about the "casual sex" thing (it wouldn't be *that* casual anyway—my god, we'd known each other several years already.) Yes, I am embarrassed to admit that for *years* this had been going on, countless hard-ons for him in his black Spandex shorts while out riding with me, which obliged him to wait before he could dismount in comfort, and which afforded me no end of visual joy and titillation. (Those little biking shorts should be required clothing for all men, all the time.) I loved his slightly sheepish expression when he got the inevitable "stiffy" (silly Brit terminology), although he somehow wasn't at all humiliated by this event, as most guys seem to be. (They usually look simultaneously proud and embarrassed. I think the closest similar expression guys get is when their dog is taking a crap somewhere public, and an attractive woman walks by.) One mysterious and fascinating thing for me is that, in my experience, Jewish guys are agonizingly, painfully self-conscious in ordinary daily life. But in the sack, they're relaxed with their bodies, unabashed sensualists.

My girlfriends, of course, knew all about Alan and the weird shenanigans going on between us. It was during just such a *tête-à-tête* that one of my best friends and I got on the (at first somewhat guarded) topic of *how many* lovers we'd had. Little did I know at the time what this conversation was going to lead to and how much it was going to affect my life the whole coming (sorry) year. Georgette had just annoyed me by cracking up while reading about my astrological sign in the college newspaper she'd found when she'd arrived at the Trident coffee shop. "Oooo, just wait till you hear this!" she'd hooted.

"Okay," I'd sighed, knowing there was no escape. "Let's have it. But you know I don't believe in any of that crap."

She'd waved away my protest. "'Characteristics of Scorpio: If the soul wobbles while it's incarnating, then there will be either odd sexual proclivities or else a tendency to focus on sex to the exclusion of all else.'" She whooped and hollered and banged her hand down on our table while

I tried my best to roll my eyes as much as is possible without doing any actual ocular damage.

"So, Georgette…how's *your* love life these days?"

She instantly sobered. "Don't even ask. I haven't met a decent guy in…how long has it been? No, never mind, don't answer that. I think I'm giving up."

"Georgette! Don't say that. So you're between relationships at the moment, no big deal." Georgette embodies one of the Boulder archetypes: an aging quasi-hippie, she helps organize the Boulder Farmers' Market (which is where I met her, come to think of it) and at 39 has very long, straight, needs-a-good-cut hair and a fondness (which I'll never understand) for "vintage" clothing, including once (I counted while she giggled) four petticoats. Where one finds such things as petticoats to buy, I don't even want to know. Most of the time she looks like she stepped out of one of those sepia photos where people had to hold their breath and sit really still for a long time while the box camera's shutter slooooowly closed.

Anyway, we compared notes and memories about past guys we'd had, and I think at one point we both started feeling slightly paranoid that we were each looking at the other funny, as if unconsciously judging and thinking *slut!* or whatever the modern, feminist equivalent of that term might be. I revealed that I had at one point in my life actually kept a *list* of guys I'd slept with: names and nationalities, as there had been quite a smorgasbord of internationals on my sexual buffet table. (Although, come to think of it, none from either the land of *smorgasbords* nor, surprisingly, the land of *le buffet*.)

My other best friend is Therese, who can be a bit prudish; Georgette is the one I have to share my juiciest secrets with. Therese is so the opposite of Georgette, it's not even funny. No, actually, it *is* kind of funny. Therese is Ms. Corporate America. She works at one of these hi-tech places that surround Boulder like hungry sharks (I never remember which one, because it's just a bunch of initials—is it ELO? TLC? PMS? Whatever). She lives in this totally suburban house and she grows peonies. She can tell you what week or even day of the year each variety will bloom. She's a year younger than me but has been married to this really boring guy for what seems like forever (I do remember *his* name—barely. It's Harry. Harry plays golf. Enough said.) What I love about Therese is, she isn't even aware of how quirky and funny she can actually be. Like, this one time, she was leaving for work in the morning, wearing her business suit and tennis shoes. While she got her car keys out, she put her pumps and one of those gold-foil-wrapped Power Bars on top of the car. Well, of course she drove off having forgotten they were there. A ways down the street, another car signaled her to stop and the guy goes, "Yo, lady! You just lost a shoe—and a harmonica!" She only ever did find one of her pumps. And it must have gotten run over, because she said the heel was all *accordioned*. She simply pulled, though, and it came right back out. (Of course, a single shoe did her no good.)

There was the time she spent about a week with strange, heavy-headed, headachy symptoms and was certain she'd developed encephalitis. She consulted me about it three or four times a day, growing ever more concerned, until she finally decided to see a doctor and made an appointment for the following week. "But what are you going to say?" I asked her. "That I think I have encephalitis, of course!" she responded indignantly. The mystery was solved a couple of days later—and fortunately before her appointment—when she discovered that she'd accidentally bought decaf instead of regular beans.

Once she found a strange ball in her backyard. She was out having her morning coffee before work, still a bit fuzzy-brained. She figured some neighboring dog must've left it on his rounds, and she bent to pick it up; it looked like a cool toy, with little prickly things all over it. In her hand, as she was about to pitch it over the fence, it uncurled itself, pointy pink rodenty nose sniffing her hand. She screamed, dropped it, ran into the house, and peered at it through the glass. But Therese being Therese, curiosity quickly overcame fear. She placed it in a shoebox, poked airholes in the top, and drove to her nearest Humane Society, making herself an hour late for work, just to find out what it *was* and to save the creature's life. (It was a hedgehog. Hedgehogs do not live in Colorado, so it must have been someone's lost pet. She wouldn't leave until the Humane Society people reassured her to her satisfaction that they would take good care of it and find a nice new home for it.)

There was also an incident involving a little white mouse she found out by the dumpsters (this was before she got married and before she and Harry bought their house) and which she "rescued," certain it must have escaped from some cruel lab where cruel scientists had been performing cruel experiments upon it and its siblings; upon reentering her apartment she remembered she had a cat and realized she had nowhere safe to put little mousie. She thus had to construct a swinging trapeze shoebox contraption (those shoeboxes really are such useful things) suspended from the ceiling lamp via multiple shoelace pulleys, at which point she called to inform me of her current situation/progress and asked me, in her slight Austin accent, without even saying hello, "Ave, hwhat do hwhite mize eat?"

I have digressed. The important thing is that Georgette and I actually admitted how many lovers we'd had in our lives to date (or rather how many we thought we'd had, plus or minus two, which seemed to be about as well as we could do, memory-wise). And lo and behold, we'd actually had about the same number, which, in spite of our belief that we embodied the modern, liberated, marriage-scorning woman, nonetheless reassured us that *we must not be sluts*.

The idea first came up the next time I was with Georgette and Therese at the Starbuck's near campus. We'd just enjoyed a great laugh over the latest Darwin Award, a guy who'd electrocuted himself while repairing his girlfriend's defunct vibrator; and I'd shared my day's favorite bumper sticker, *Fuck Art, Let's Dance*—we'd come out split as to whether Art was the concept, or a person.

At the table nearest us was a Hare Krishna dude with that really funky hair (the close-cropped do except for the little spiky parts in back), mesmerized by his portable DVD player. What's up with that hairstyle, anyway? I mean, what sort of statement is that supposed to be making? You'd think the hairdo alone would keep more people from joining. He was watching one of the Terminator movies, his religious book on the table now forgotten, open to the chapter *Absolution for Accidental or Unavoidable Violence*. Besides the haircut, I could never be a Hare Krishna because of the clothes—those bedsheets they wrap around themselves might be good at hiding flab, but those peach and orange colors just would not suit my skin tone. On the other side of us was a guy whose laptop cover bore a shiny sticker: *Ask Me About Chloroplast Implants*.

I hadn't talked to Therese in a few weeks. She started off by saying, "So, you guys, guess what I saw on the way here?"

"What?" Georgette and I asked simultaneously.

"This guy dressed up like a ninja, even including that forehead bandanna thingie with the Oriental characters on it, screaming like a banshee, hacking watermelons apart one by one." We stared at her.

"What, with a knife?" I asked finally.

"No, with, like, a *samurai sword*." We waited. "Like, as big as his whole body."

"Where?" asked Georgette, alarmed. I was frightened too. Was Boulder at last becoming less safe?

"Eben G. Fine Park."

"Oh," I said. "No wonder." "Oh," said Georgette at the same time. "Eben G." We all nodded, absently, relaxed. "Where'd he get watermelons so early?" Georgette mused aloud.

"I wonder if they were organic," I added.

"So, Ave..." Therese said. "How's your love life?"

"I don't have anyone at the moment. I'm between men—a free agent once again."

"Who was that last one, again?" she asked, laughing.

"Who knows? I don't even remember. They're all kind of blending together," I answered, hoping for more laughs (although what I'd said was a truer statement than I would have liked). "They're all alike. Jerks. Ever since Brandon..." I willed myself to stop, knowing that both of them had to be tired of my laments about how I'd never meet anyone else like my ex. I could sense their relief that I'd cut short my whining.

Suddenly Therese remembered the infamous Alan, and asked about him. "He's *gooooone*," I told her in a tone that was only semi-exaggeratedly mournful. Then I couldn't resist: I added, "I *laid* him first, though." The shock on her face was even better than I'd expected.

"No *way*!" she gasped, "Ave, you did *not*!," hoping, you could tell, that I really had, so she could hear the whole story. She knew how long I'd been lusting after Alan, thought him cruel for teasing me, and also thought I was nuts for going along with it for so long, and (must admit it), even enjoying it.

Vicariously speaking, all three of us had Alan that afternoon. Lucky Alan (or poor Alan—I'm not sure which way he'd think of it). I could tell Therese was getting wound up to start a small speech about how "amazing" it was that I'd had so many...lovers? Relationships? I wasn't sure which word she'd use. (Secretly, I'm pretty sure she just thought I was a slut.) This caused Georgette and me to lock eyes, both of us immediately recalling the conversation we'd had together about the *lists*. I could tell Georgette was wondering whether or not she could safely say something about it in front of Therese, whether Therese knew about it.

"Aaaaave... Ave! Earth to Ave!" came Therese's voice now as if from far away.

My name is Aviva, Ave for short (pronounced like "Abe," as in Abe Lincoln, except *v* instead of *b*—which is the whole spiel I have to go into every time I'm introduced to someone, and it gets to be a real drag). I personally think my name's pretty cool, even if I get sick of explaining it...although I always wonder if everyone thinks it sounds a lot like the word *vulva*. It's the fault of those two *v*'s. Not many words have two, so one is almost forced to make the connection. Volvo. Vulva. Vivid. Vivacious...Aviva. Aviva...Vivacious vulva—quite frankly, not an inaccurate description.

Aviva Goldberg: my parents could hardly have gotten more Jewish without calling me Yentl. There was a time, in my teens, when I longed more than anything for a "normal" name. I wanted to change mine to Melissa, or maybe Jessica. But my great-uncle Moishe refused to give me permission, and by the time I was old enough to forgo a guardian's signature, I had started liking being Aviva. According to my now-dearly-departed Unkie Moishe (hey, don't blame me—it was a childhood nickname that stuck), my parents weren't at all religious, so I've always wondered why they picked this name for me. And I can't ask them; they died before I ever knew them—well, I guess technically I knew them briefly, but I sure as hell don't remember. *Their* names were Robert and Evelyn, so what hat did they pull Aviva from? It's probably better I'm an only child; god knows what handles any poor siblings of mine might have ended up with. (I feel sure that if I'd had a brother, he would have been Jedediah.) As the story goes, Robert and Evelyn won one of those free cruise things (lucky, huh?). However, their planned idyll was rudely interrupted by the engine failure of the small plane they were using to check out the island-hopping scene (pretty unlucky, huh?). Since I never knew them other than photos (apparently I have my mom's hair, my dad's eyes, and both of their noses), it's hard for me to call my feelings "sad." It's more like simply curious. And maybe it's also why I never take baths, only showers.

When I introduce myself, people always say, "Oh, Aviva—that's a *beautiful* name!" a little too enthusiastically; do they actually think the opposite? If all those Lisas and Cheryls and Stephanies really think Aviva is such a *beautiful* name, then why aren't they out there naming *their* kids interesting, *beautiful* names? Because how much do you want to bet they'll name their own kids John and Megan and Ashley and Mike and Kristen? Although Boulder names, of course, can get a *bit* more exotic: I've met a Rain and a Ravyn, a Savannah and five Sierras. These are little girls who were born here, named by their parents (or at least by their mothers; somehow I suspect it's always mothers who do the naming).

Then there are the Boulderites who have renamed themselves. They get really deeply into these Boulder/California things, *teachings* or *explorations, journeys* or *paths* or *healings*, and somewhere along the *process*, it's either required, or else they feel the pressing need, to *transform* themselves. Part of this transformation involves transferring money to the teacher, and part of it involves, apparently, renaming yourself. So you meet a lot of adults here who tell you with a straight face that their name is Joy Om or Satsunder (rhymes with "fat thunder") or Rising Moon Woman or Healing Stick or some such. (This reminds me of a very funny thing Therese and I once discovered: approximately every other dog in Boulder is named Cody. Not kidding. If you want to be wicked, go up on one of the hiking trails on a nice spring or summer day, where most of the dogs are off-leash, and just yell "Coooooooodyyyyy!" Guaranteed to be fun.) If I ever have a kid, which I'm not planning to do, but just in case, if I change my mind, I am *definitely* not naming it Ryan or Brian or Cindy. Nor Cody. Although I'd probably also pass on Wolf Tracking Lightly.

There are a couple of places in town that would be ideal if one wanted to go meet people who have had *transformations*, and who have renamed themselves—many of them several times. Well, and who not only have renamed themselves, but know what their names were during their previous seven lifetimes, all of which they keep meticulous track of and would be happy to describe to you in excruciating detail, and which they paid someone to map out for them when the moon was full.

The first two places that come to mind are the coffeehouse Penny Lane, and the Solstice Institute. Penny Lane's claim to fame is that those infamous good-time boyz of the Beat Generation—Kerouac, Ginsberg—apparently hung out there, back when it was still on the opposite side of Pearl Street and when smoking was still allowed. Some things about Penny Lane haven't changed, though—like you just absolutely cannot go in if you are not, superficially at least, hip enough. The guidelines change with the times, of course. Current requirements include unwashed dredlocks, preferably extremely long and matted; at least two piercings above the neck; and a visible tattoo.

The other place is the Solstice Institute. I think they actually *do* celebrate solstices, and perhaps other related phenomena as well, but the only time I've been there was when a guy I was dating invited me to go to the Barefoot Boogie. You pay three dollars, kick off your shoes, and in you go to dance to New-Age spacey non-rhythms; do backbends over Swedish medicine balls on the sidelines; sit in your own little corner and chant; walk the large, carpeted room backwards while gesturing to the heavens (well, to the ceiling—for all its celestial denomination, it is about the most ordinary building you could imagine); and, if you are one of the brave many (I wasn't), to do Contact Improvisation.

My date, who looked so much the Stiff White Boy, turned out to be actually quite experienced and talented at this. It looked pretty damn weird to me, even for Boulder: so you're kind of dancing around, and someone near you is too, and then somehow (psychically perhaps? I never did determine this), you suddenly begin bouncing and rolling off each other. Kind of an unrehearsed and less talented version of Cirque du Soleil. It's one of those things that if you think about it while doing it, trying to plan, it doesn't work at all. You end up knocking heads, jabbing the other person in tender places, and pulling muscles, maybe even breaking a rib. However, done well, I must admit, it is a kind of athletic, sweaty, (albeit bizarre and overly intimate) ballet. Who started this, I wonder? Did it begin in the mosh pits and then somehow spread, herpes-like, to the New-Agers?

Therese had just commented on how many guys I've "been through." Sounds like "eaten my way through," like a rodent in a silo. I really don't feel it's been like that. I've just had lots and lots of mini-relationships. And of course I've been in love—who hasn't?—but those loves ultimately didn't last.

Amazingly, Therese took this moment to ask me something she'd never dared before, probably squeamish about what the answer might be: "So…um…how many have there…*been*, actually?"

I could feel Georgette's eyes boring into me, sparkling with hidden amusement, wondering if I'd "come clean" to Therese. I debated about whether the truth would shock Therese overly, finally decided to just go ahead and tell it like it was.

"A nice, even thirty," I said boldly, meeting her gaze.

She exhaled, but was still afraid, as I could tell from her face and her next question:

"In your...*life*, you mean? Or...?"

What did this woman *think*?! That there'd been thirty in the last *year*? The last *month*, for god's sake? That I was a *total slut*?

"*Yeah*, in my *life*," I couldn't help retorting a bit defensively. "And I know *other people*" (pointedly not looking at Georgette) "who are similar, other women I mean."

I know Therese; I knew she must've been shocked. She herself had been with less than a handful of guys in her life—like I said, she's a teensy bit prudish. (But one doesn't hold these things against one's best friends.)

She tried to cover up: "Hell, Ave, it's just that you're so damn *attractive*. I think it's *great*!" (I think that's a *beautiful* name!) "I wish *I* could have that many guys after *me*...!"

I smiled. Therese, Therese, Therese...

I noticed that Georgette was conspicuously silent. Suddenly she went overboard, trying to throw Therese off the track of herself as a target: "It is *so* true! Our Ave is so popular with guys. Hell, I bet if she wanted to, she could get *another* thirty anytime. She sure as hell gets dates more easily than *I* do. Yep... Within a year from now, I bet she could *double* her current track record!"

A deep, somehow very full silence. Georgette and Therese were staring at one another, eyes shining, smiles beginning on both their faces. I couldn't believe what they were hinting at, needed to squelch this insane line of thought immediately. Therese you could tell couldn't bring herself to enunciate it, but Georgette is far less shy.

With a huge grin, she said it: "What do you say, Ave? A bet? Thirty more, in a year—think you could do it?"

In my defense, I'd like to say here that I was actually more than a little shocked at the idea. I've never (well, okay, *rarely*) gone after a guy in that *guy* way, just to add that notch in the belt. I have to admit I was sort of intrigued by the challenge, by the possibilities...but I also felt a bit sick at the idea. Now, a total extrovert would interpret that as mere stage fright, but I think it might've been the lingering double standard, the stuff we modern women still unconsciously half believe—that we're sluts if we have "too many" lovers, that we have to be in love if we're going to have sex...and all that garbage.

More silence. Then I thought: what glory for women everywhere!

What an eloquent turning of the tables on those preying bar guys! What a lot of beautiful naked male bodies I could add to my "collection"! What a lot of...um...guys. Damn. Oy. Um...Really? Double my current, lifelong tally? In just one year? Were they nuts?

Then I thought, at least three-quarters of their desire to have me take on the bet was probably vicarious. Georgette was surely totally turned on by the idea, while Therese was slightly disgusted and turned off, and only turned on deep down, on some Freudian level that she, by definition, wasn't aware of. But they both had the same eager, oooo-aren't-we-being-naughty look that they'd surely had as little girls stealing cookies before dinner, or sitting on their just-constructed mud pies and getting those cute little frilly panties completely filthy. That wet, cold mud on their little-girl *tucheses*, that giggle when they felt it soak through to the skin and knew their mommies would be mad as hell and that their pink panties with the ruffles on the back and the tiny satin bow on the front would be ruined and would sag coolly, deliciously, gravelly, all the way home.

Should I not accept the challenge in the spirit of those universal little-girl tendencies? (Or at least those adorable *tucheses*?) I should. No, I shouldn't. I should! I should?

"Oh my god, she's actually *tempted*! She's *considering* it!" shouted Georgette gleefully, uncontrolledly, attracting the attention of even the noisiest of the other patrons. Therese looked a bit shell-shocked (again, or still?). They waited for my verdict.

"Lemme think about it," I mumbled finally, as quietly as possible, suddenly absorbed in reading the *beaucoup de* propaganda covering my paper cup of grande-decaf-vanilla soy-double-latte-with-one-and-a-half-squirts-of-chocolate-and-cocoa-sprinkles-on-top.

t^h

I went to the public library to do my usual book exchange (I devour at least three novels a week) and my liquid exchange (go pee and then refill my omnipresent water bottle from the fountain). After dumping my return books in the chute, I went inside, past the sanseveria plants (according to houseplant guides, "commonly known as mother-in-law's tongue"—presumably because they are long and sharp), to a computer. I usually haunt the Boulder Bookstore, reading a page or two of the newest fiction, then keep checking here for whatever I liked (which I wrote down in a little notebook while I was at the bookstore—quite the geeky thing to do, I know. But it is the only affordable way to be as avid a reader as I am).

No luck at all today. I'd checked for: *My Lead Dog Was A Lesbian*, *Stepford Husbands*, *Cybersex*, and *Throat Sprockets*, none of which, it appeared, the library had chosen to acquire, at least not as yet. I had my doubts for *Cybersex*, ever, liberal even as the Boulder Public Library purports to be. Boulder in general loves to tout itself as ultraliberal, hang its Tibetan prayer flags and to "Celebrate Diversity!" but just try painting, oh, say, a Bhutanese flying phallus on the front of your house and see how fast the cops show up.

Next to me was a homeless guy playing on-line chess. On the other side of me was a high-school-age girl trying a Google search on *wete dary alergys*. I didn't tell her about her misspellings, although it reinforced my already very strongly-held opinion that that generation is, to borrow a lovely antiquated phrase, going to hell in a handbasket.

In L.A., everyone is writing a screenplay. In Manhattan, everyone has a shrink. In Boulder, everyone is allergic to wheat and dairy. I must be, too, but who can resist homemade pasta, fresh Parmigiano Reggiano, Brie, focaccia? I'm sure I'm doing some sort of irreparable damage involving ketones, bad cholesterol, good cholesterol, and/or antioxidants, but brown rice pasta tastes like cardboard, and soy cheese takes you immediately back to nursery school, because it tastes, smells, and sticks to the interior regions of your mouth exactly like Elmer's Glue.

I browsed New Fiction and found a couple of promising-looking novels. I got in line behind a grandmotherly type checking out, anomalously, and in my opinion, over-excitedly, a video whose cover sported a bland, smiling, chunky blond man standing in the middle of a winter marsh, and entitled *A Moose For All Seasons*.

Outside, there was yet another of those pesky creek festivals going on. Every couple of months there seems to be one: Boulder Spring Fair, Boulder Arts Fair (some junk, some good stuff), Boulder Crafts Fair (totally cheezey junk), Boulder Kids' Festival (to be avoided at all costs), Renaissance Festival (total weirdos and freakazoids—best to flee the entire area).

I passed a teenage boy wearing a T-shirt that said *Chicks Hate Me*, which made me grin, even though I tried to hide it (unsuccessfully). Then a couple more teenage boys in shirts that said, in small script over the left breast, *Wifebeater*. What the hell is that about? I admit it, I'm out of the loop.

A booth charging fifteen dollars to read your aura. One to balance your chi. A build-your-own-pyramid kit, two hundred bucks. Kites. *Your name written on a grain of rice!* Candles—always so many candles. Tie-dyed Phans for Phish. Bad pottery. Good pottery. Hippie skirts, made in India: sizes S, XS, and XXS. Ugly wood carvings. Photography featuring "Authentically Ethnic" subjects. Ten-minute, ten-dollar massage. Water filters. A big tent with people doing polka or something equally strange, vaguely embarrassing, and outdated—clog dancing? Square dancing?

Psychic readings. Tarot readings. Runes readings. Five-minute pencil caricatures. Magnet therapy. A booth handing out information about recycling: paper handouts printed on non-recyclable fluorescent colors; these mostly end up in the trash cans at either end of the festival area.

Russian pocket pastries made by the Russian Pocket-Pastry Man. Local wildflower honey. Henna temporary tattoos. Petitions to be signed, children's faces to be painted, dogs to be tugged back as they tried to smell everything at once. Hippie jewelry, beads, hemp clothing…

Shiatsu for your toe neuromas.

I had to go home and recuperate.

There have been plenty of Only In Boulder Moments in my ten years in this quirky and wonderful town. I remember one of my first: On the bike path, I rode through Settlers Park tunnel (they spell it without an apostrophe, which irks me; I'm a Punctuation Nazi—god, did I really just use the word Nazi?) and out the other side, where the path was lined with high brush and there didn't seem to be anyone around, though it was broad daylight. All of a sudden a male voice came shouting from the impenetrable weed mass: "Goddess bless!"

Ironically, having just moved from D.C., some incensed weirdo suddenly shouting at me out of nowhere was not nearly as much of a shock as it would be to me now. I merely held my breath and started pedaling faster. My nervous system was primed for this sort of thing: people randomly yelling at you, saying *fuck you* as soon as *thank you*. (Literally, my second afternoon in Boulder, walking down the sidewalk, I remember some guy coming towards me had *looked me in the eyes*. My system had prepared for fight or flight—then as he'd passed me, me with clenched fists, he'd said...*hi*.)

Apparently a happy hippie, lying blissed out in nature, was randomly spewing out blessings in case anyone was passing by.

Boulder Moments are always benign—well, as long as you're not that woman who was murdered in the alley, and if you're not Jon-Benet

Ramsey, and if you ignore the frat boys on the Hill throwing flaming sofas off balconies.

χ

I hit the Alan jackpot on one of the last nights before he was due to leave town (for a warmer clime, where he could bike eight hours a day all winter, instead of the paltry two or three that Colorado invernal afternoons could offer him). He came over and we rented a French video, When The Cat's Away (*Tout le monde cherche son chat* in the original, which sounded much better, being a tongue-twister and having a punacious *double entendre*). The French word for pussy (the non-feline kind) is *chatte*. I knew Alan had spent a few months biking through France (show me one cyclist dude who doesn't dream he'll be in the Tour de France one day, never mind the odds) and wondered if he'd had any *chatte française*, that being back in his casual-sex days, and if so, who the lucky bimbette was.

The movie was mediocre. It was certainly nothing to make Margot cry or anything—as they say *en français*. Anyway, all video rentals were just an excuse for Alan and me to get smoochey together. But that night...

We had been groping as usual throughout the film. We were just *inhaling* each other. We didn't have enough hands. As always, once things heated up, Alan somehow lost all nerdiness, ditched the coke-bottle glasses, and became Mr. Stud (albeit Mr. Unwilling Stud). This time, though, perhaps because he knew he was leaving soon—or maybe the lava had finally just gotten to the boiling point inside him and he couldn't stand it anymore—I sensed a hint of weakness in his resolve and decided to exploit it as far as I could.

I started playing unfair. I didn't actually take off my underwear (he never "allowed" that), but I kind of moved it to one side and sat on him as far as the angle of the futon-couch would allow, and let him feel *ma chatte* purring. At the make-or-break moment, this time, he hesitated. And we know what that means, don't we? That's right: he who hesitates is *perdu*.

As was Alan's resolve. I often replay the wonderful memory in my mind these days: I came when even *I* was least expecting it, several times. Maybe it was just all that anticipation, or maybe it was just that he was so damn *good*.

I prefer to believe the latter; anyway, it gives me something to fantasize about, running the slick, hot reels of memory past my longing, grieving brain—for, contrary to all I hoped, he did then leave town, he did say he wouldn't slip up again in his determination, and once he left, he didn't call. *Adieu, mon cher.*

⊙

Spin class. Monica: so cute, so blond, such the little biker fiend. She's a great leader, though, very fun. I'm just jealous, 'cause she's a *real* cyclist—in Alan's league—the kind that does "group rides," something I can only dream about. I own a piece-of-shit mountain bike, used, ill-fitting, whose crank shaft (whatever that is) is rumored to be dying. These people have four or five different "road bikes" as well as several dozen mountain bikes, a new one for each *type of ride*, for each different fucking *mood*.

Anyway, Spin class really is a fabulous workout, and maybe someday I can even aspire to an actual group ride, if I do enough classes. The whole concept is so weird, though—such a modern-society phenomenon. I mean, can you imagine some rural farmer a hundred years ago showing up for Spin class, where he would put four hundred calories' of effort into producing nothing and getting nowhere?

I have a great strategy for visualization while I'm in Spin class. Visualization is the thing nowadays, you know? Everyone's doing it—rather like the Spin class motto: *The world is spinning. Are you?* When I start feeling fatigued and it's no longer enough to be looking around out of the corner of my eye at the couple of cute guys in class, legs, thighs in those little Spandex bike shorts, spinning fruitlessly but oh so beautifully, then I start my visualizations.

I imagine that Alan is just ahead of me on his bike, in those racy (sorry) little cycling clothes of his, and that if I can go just a little faster, work just a little harder, keep up on the whole sprint instead of only about 2/3 of the way, which is when I usually bail out of nausea and fear of looking like an idiot from passing out by merely riding a stationary bike…

"How tough can it be?" asked a new class member with a smug smile as he got on his bike a couple of weeks ago, in answer to the instructor's concerned question "Have you spun before?" Later, after class, we stood in line together at the water fountain. "So what'd you think?" I asked him conversationally, one Spin-masochist to another. "God, it fucking killed! I'm never coming back," he said as he shoved past me to the water.

Push it, push it!—there's Alan just up ahead, gotta catch up, come on come on, there's that unbelievably cute butt, let's go, there's those hard thighs, you're almost there, those adorable fuzzy legs, that's it, just a little further, those lean, chiseled triceps...

The only problem with this technique is that often I get quite aroused, and then it's even harder to keep up, because my instinct is telling my body to get down on the floor and *be supine, now.*

3

Went trail-running running today. Well, I guess it's not really *running*; technically it's only jogging (the dividing line being the ten-minute mile), or, on the really grueling parts of the Enchanted Mesa trail, what I do could be more accurately referred to as "barely moving."

I was thinking a lot about the proposed challenge. Pros: I love sex, and it would be fun to try to seduce all those different men. Cons: weirdos, and worries about diseases (even with condoms). Also, how would Therese and Georgette keep track of the number of conquests, or would they simply agree to believe me? Had the honor system ever been utilized before for such an irreverent, downright *slutty* cause?

I struggled up the last steep section and finally reached Deer Leg, where it levels out after the previous brutal forty minutes of gradual uphill. Deer Leg is what Therese and I call this part of the trail since the time we saw, in that exact place where the views start getting nice (marred only by a grotesquely huge house here and there), the lower part of a deer's leg, chewed off at the knee. There are supposedly plenty of mountain lions in the woods around Boulder; there's lots of evidence and photos in the paper, as well as the occasional missing Fifi and Fluffy from the yards of the fancy foothills mansions. However, I've never actually seen a mountain lion around here. I'd *love* to see one. Like a giant-sized version of my kitty, Baby. I'm sure it would be terrifying, but I have this idea that it'd be so cool it'd be worth the fear. Of course, there *was* that runner who got killed by one out in California somewhere...

I glanced to my left to check out the view and could hardly believe my eyes—there was one of Boulder's famous double rainbows! These occur several times a year and have a special significance for me; I tend to see them whenever I'm trying to decide on a big issue. The first day I arrived in Boulder, there was a double rainbow over the entire city as Brandon and I neared on Highway 36. Ever since, I decided to take this particular atmospheric phenomenon as a sign that I should proceed with whatever it is that I was wondering about.

This time, I knew exactly what the rainbows meant: I was to take the bet. Boys, beware!

I stood in line at the Trident reading today's handlettered sign: *For pastry: You must have one dollar or one goat to exchange.* I obtained my Hippie Mocha and found a table.

A cell phone rang next to me. Suddenly the Trident Vacuum Cleaner Woman, who, like Elaine's co-worker on Seinfeld, never swings her arms as she walks, rushed over and chastised the guy whose phone had rung: "Excuse me, but you'll have to leave now. We have a sign posted on the front door—didn't you read it?—it says 'No Cell Phones. Sensitive Bio-Electrical Equipment In Use.'" The guy just stared at her in horror, and off she stalked, arms immobile. The dude stashed his phone as quickly as possible and looked at me.

"*What* bio-electrical equipment?" he asked me, wide-eyed.

"Human bodies, maybe?" I guessed. He stared at me in bewilderment. I looked away. What could I do? He obviously wasn't a regular.

A full year stretching ahead of me in which to fulfill the terms of the challenge felt luxurious. We'd agreed on my deadline being the Bolder Boulder, a 10k running race always held on the Monday morning following Memorial Day weekend. I had plenty of time.

I skimmed the Boulder Weekly. Under *Recreation* was "Five Animal Chi Gong." Was that something like Tai Chi? I'd nearly died of laughter once when a guy I was dating demonstrated the pose Repulse Monkey.

Under *Other* was the announcement "Healing Clinics: Receive an aura and chakra healing and communication about what you are working on as a being," offered by the Psychic Horizons Center.

I saw that Naropa would be hosting a talk called "Journeys Through Nine Dimensions." I wondered how they'd arrived at the number nine. Perhaps the same way the Beatles had? There was also "Recovering the Indigenous Feminine: Women's Rituals and Initiation." Did I have to be "indigenous" to participate properly? Indigenous to where? Was she talking *aboriginal*? I wondered if this was the person I'd heard about recently, who, for a mere two thousand-dollar "donation" per woman, would lead a group into the mountains to each sit naked on her own rock for "nature reinitiation."

I checked out all the males on display within my view. I was in the back room, away from the noise of the espresso machine. There is an ever-changing art installation on these brick walls; this week's exhibit involved apparently termite-munched wooden chunks of varying sizes, hues, and textures.

The men: the first thing I noticed right off was that there were an awful lot of guys sitting at tables together. This would be more normal on the evenings when the Trident got incredibly crowded with university students studying at midterms (read: opening their books for the first time) or right before finals (read: opening their books for the second time), but tonight was relatively slow—there were even a few empty tables. The next thing I noticed was that almost all the men I was checking out—as they got up to go to the bathroom, or settled down balancing a coffee drink or a little white teapot—appeared to be very, well, *small*. In fact, they pretty much all seemed to top out at about 5'2".

I suddenly realized, really staring around the room now, that I had accidentally stumbled onto what was apparently an underground and previously unsuspected (by me, anyway) *tradition à Boulder*: Tiny Gay Men's Night Out At The Trident. Now, don't get me wrong; I'm not homophobic. But this situation certainly wasn't going to suit *my* purposes. Plus, maybe I felt subconsciously offended that something unbeknownst to me has been going on here, considering, as all regulars do, the Trident theater to essentially be my own living room.

As I was leaving, a diminutive man with a pink shirt, green plaid pants, and a *monocle* was coming in, disproving the belief that gay men always dress better than hetero guys.

ë

I bike along the Creek path, as usual getting very irate over the *bloody tourists* and other idiots whom you suddenly find on the wrong side of the path in the worst possible places—like the Broadway underpass. I pass as close as I dare to these imbeciles, so close we can both feel the sudden rush of air whooshing only centimeters between us. The editorially much-discussed phrase "On your left" is unknown to the tourists, who pay no attention; and apparently unheard by the inebriated and stoned folks—thus, even when used properly, is useless.

As usual on any summery day in Boulder, people are wading in the creek near the public library. This is Grand Central for people with dogs, grandmothers with young charges, free spirits with no charges, new mothers keeping a watchful eye on the precious offspring, and tourist types too. Someone is always trying to eat their lunch in business attire, while someone else's canine insists on doing the classic rolling wet splattery shake after every retrieval of the tennis ball or stick. Someone's kid always gets too close to the quasi-rapid in the middle, causing great consternation among all attending parental types. Some baby's legs are always being dipped, to the baby's obvious delight, for the first time into this running snowmelt—something I've never understood. It is *painfully* cold to even put your *toe* in there. I can hardly talk myself in up to the ankles even on dog days when it's a hundred and four degrees.

When and why did these huge, long, baggy shorts become so popular for all swimming-scene males? What ever happened to the, as a Japanese acquaintance of mine puts it (and very funny it sounds, too, in his accent) *tiny tiny Speedo*?

At first I thought: maybe men want to hide whatever it is they've got. But then I started thinking, well, thanks to Seinfeld we've all learned about cold-water *shrinkage*, and thus perhaps what they're trying to hide is the fact of it suddenly becoming such a tiny little thing… Although men are wearing this type of shorts all the time now, not just for swimming, so there goes my hypothesis (also an extremely funny word when pronounced with a Japanese accent). This current style must be a godsend for those who don't have much to start with, thwarting as it does any and all attempts by keen female X-ray eyes like mine to visually navigate the eternal mysteries of *that stuff*.

So, *can I just say* (as a friend of mine always announces very loudly) I'd like to see a return in men's fashions to something a bit more revealing, thank you very much?

á

Bike ride on the path again. In the tunnel between Settlers Park and Eben G. Fine, I barely miss colliding with two homeless types, one of whom is reverently holding aloft a stick deodorant. The other guy appears to be just as worshipfully gazing up at it, mumbling loudly yet incoherently.

As I pass through the park, avoiding the numerous Mexican and Hmong picnickers, voluminous barbecue smoke, and the ubiquitous Frisbee game, something odd catches my eye. Outside the always-gross bathroom with the always-flooded floor, I stop to pretend to adjust my bike seat.

It seems to be four couples—pairs of women—each woman facing her female partner, hands on the other's shoulders. I wheel my bike a little closer, scrutinize them. Okay, my best guess is it's the Anorexic Hippie Lesbians' Society. Each woman rapturously blesses the other with some wild gesticulations, there is a reverent kiss on the lips, then the women all form a circle, interlocking arms, and begin to (rather gracelessly, considering they're women) move clockwise while chanting something.

It also appears to be Topless Skinny Male Guru Day. There are several such long-gray-raggedy-bearded shirtless sages perched meditatively in the lotus position on large rocks in the creek. They bear the most uncanny resemblance to that poor Monty Python dude who'd held his tongue for decades, only to be tricked into saying something stupid and prosaic when discovered at the very end of his extremely observant, ascetic existence.

Ž

Today I'm out for my usual four-mile walk along the creek path. By the way, lest you think I'm some kind of super-athlete, let me assure you that by *Boulder* standards, I'm out of shape, have way too much body fat (the percentage of which any Boulderite can instantly cite you their most recent statistic), am not the least bit "cut," lack the six-pack or even a two-pack, and am extremely wimpy, as I do not participate in the following sports: ice climbing, kayaking, or expeditions to summit K2. Having stated that, let me also tell you that whenever I travel to other parts of the U.S., everyone I meet asks sincerely if I am going to be in the next Olympics, and if so, which sport, so they can watch me on TV. If this doesn't give you an idea of what Boulder is like compared to the rest of the country, then nothing will.

Near the Red Rocks trail, the usual band of Pirate Kids are out, doing something with plastic swords and treasure maps that costs their parents a hundred and fifty dollars a day. A Saab parked at the trailhead bears a bumper sticker I've seen before: *Eddie would go.* This is about the only bumper sticker I've ever seen that even *has* punctuation, let alone *correct* punctuation. As always, I wonder: who is this Eddie? And why would he go? (I always note the modal verb.) And whence shall Eddie travel? This type of sticker, where you have to understand the context in order to get it, really bugs me. Frequently, the reference is to pop culture, which came from TV, which I never watch. Okay, okay—I used to watch Seinfeld reruns (until I moved to an apartment which doesn't get reception due to the interference of our signature mountains, the Flatirons). And E.R. And way back when, Northern Exposure—I've never gotten over that gorgeous D.J. And way, *way* back when, Thirtysomething. Before I even was. But enough confessions already.

My seven years of graduate-level Linguistics training is what makes me think about stuff like verb modalities while perusing such commonalities as bumper stickers. I haven't mentioned much about my job yet mostly because I'm pretty burned out and bored by the whole thing. Not by linguistics *per se*, nor by the French language, *bien sûr*, but rather by the whole spiel—about grading policies, about not cheating or plagiarizing, that kind of crap—that I have to spew out semester after semester. And I'm sick of the same predictably stupid questions (you know how all these teachers nowadays like to say *There's no such thing as a stupid question* in this sugary, encouraging kind of voice? Well, that is complete bullshit) asked at the same exact moments during my lectures, year after dull year. I'm also tired of the blond sorority types who insist that I give them passing grades because otherwise their lawyer daddies in Aspen will sue my Department and get me fired. I'm *so* sick of frat boys' pathetically transparent excuses delivered on waves of stale beer breath at 2 p.m. I'm weary of so much bimbette anatomy on display—how many pierced bellybuttons must I see each semester?—and jealous of such perky young braless A-cup titties (I'm a heavy D).

Moreover, lacking the typical computer-geek husband, I sure as hell can't live in Boulder on this salary much longer. Teaching university classes is hardly the prestigious, rewarding job it must have been at one time; I can only imagine. One of these days I really must do something else, something practical—like go to law school. Eddie would go.

♀

Tonight I'm supposed to have dinner with my friend Donald (who's not Jewish, in spite of his dweeby name) and his newest girlfriend. To tell you the truth, I haven't been extremely impressed by the previous few. We'll see what Lizzie is like.

Donald and I go back a long way. He's one of the most verbal guys I've ever met, which of course is lots of points in his favor. His vocabulary is, I'd even go so far as to say, *almost* as good as mine. We play viciously competitive games of Scrabble in public, usually at the Trident (made especially challenging by the Trident's ancient donated set, missing a certain portion of its consonants) which draw admirers from surrounding tables—but no one else even *tries* to play with either of us, as Donald and I always spontaneously invent at least one esoteric rule for each match. For example: only words related to sex; or, you can steal one letter at a time from your opponent's rack (its back facing you) per turn; or, you're allowed to have as many letters at a time as you can physically fit on your rack, however you manage that. Even our pre-game rule-making process itself is mysterious, impromptu, and different every time.

I almost always win by about three points, although Donald tends to start throwing a small tantrum toward the end of a game when he can tell he's about to lose, upsetting the board and all its letters, such that no one can tell for sure who would've definitively won. Also, to be fair, we often get chased out by the Trident Vacuum Cleaner Woman when we're on our final, winner-determining round.

Donald constantly tries to sneak in fake words (best if he can use up all his letters at once, of course) that he then enjoys arguing loudly and tirelessly for, like QUOBELOLT, DRUAVENTORES, JETHRA, and OILMUTHR. I suspect his motivation for this is to wear me out mentally, but it's actually way more amusing to see these "words" appear on the board and to hear Donald's subsequent wholehearted arguments for them than it would be to just play the game straight (well, I guess you can hardly call the way we play "straight,"), so I never actually try to prevent him from doing it, though I have to lodge some token protests each time (which he equally expects). In its own way, it's a dance as ritualized as—but way more fun than—the pre-bedtime *toilette* of any long-married couple.

I'm waiting out in front of one of my favorite restaurants, The Med. It's early summer...you can tell because temps lately have been in the nineties or hundreds every day. Ah, here they come now—I'd recognize Donald's swagger and his huge, hard thighs anywhere (he loves telemark skiing—*Free your heel, free your mind*—more than anything on earth, possibly even more than playing Scrabble with me). The chickette on his arm is of the dark-curly-hair variety: going for a bit more of an ethnic look this time. Young, as usual.

"Hi," I say a bit desultorily, if anyone's noticing—which Donald is, although it just went right over Lizzie's head.

Actually, *I* also have dark curly hair. The requisite Jewish Look, I suppose you'd call it. Brown eyes. Prominent dark brows. My nose perhaps considered by some to be too big, but I know it gives me character. Just slightly on the zaftig side, as I've mentioned (and do you have any idea how depressing it is to find that your waist size, in inches, is keeping exact pace with your age in years?), especially as concerns the word *busty*. I hate that term. I'd prefer curvaceous or voluptuous, although those sound quite outdated. Who's the last woman who was called voluptuous? Marilyn Monroe, maybe?

Lizzie goes inside to check with one of the many interchangeable hostesses, who all resemble underage prostitutes. What is it with this place, anyway? Good food, good prices, good atmosphere...but someone's affinity to hire only anorexic young women wearing too much makeup and cheap Victoria's Secret clothing.

Two really rugged-looking guys (rather like Donald) pass us on their way inside. One of them says to the other: "Oh, dude, I forgot—I gotta show you my prairie-dog wound!"

Inside, we order Mediterranean tapas. I can't help but notice smugly how Lizzie mangles all the French. (I'm so mean.) Donald and I are, as usual, flirting (even right in front of Lizzie); it's just something between us... We've always been attracted to each other, but it's like we've known each other for too long now; that window of opportunity closed without our taking advantage of it. Lizzie seems to be noticing, and tries to change the subject by interjecting: "So, hey, movies... You know, Spike Lee I just do *not* get. Did you guys see Summer of Sam?"

Donald appears stunned that someone else is present at our table, but recovers quickly. "No, not yet," he responds, "I missed it when it came out. I want to rent it, though."

I say, "Yeah, I saw it. I thought it was awesome."

Donald asks, "What was that guy's name, again? I mean his real name? Like Goldstein or something?"

"Yeah, something like that," I say. "I know—that is so weird. When's the last time you ever heard of a Jewish serial killer, anyway?" I laugh.

Lizzie, with supreme earnestness and this look of *I-need-to-pretend-to-like-this-Aviva-chick-because-Donald-obviously-thinks-very-highly-of-her* on her face, leans forward and admonishes: "Well, the *Nazis* were Jewish, and *they* sure killed a lot of people!"

I drop my water glass right into my baba ghanouj. Is this woman for *real*? I wait for her to say something like "Oops, duh, I mean...!" But she doesn't.

So...okay. Obviously she's a moron. Plus she can't even tell I'm Jewish. (She did give me the usual "Oh, *Aviva*: that's a *beautiful* name!" during the introductions, but didn't ask its origins, apparently lacking sufficient curiosity, and I didn't offer any gratuitous explanations.) After her unforgivably ignorant comment, I ice her permanently out of my attention, treating her civilly but like something distasteful you'd rather weren't there, like a pile of dog shit next to the picnic blanket.

It turns out she has somewhere to go right after dinner (hurray!), so Donald and I are left alone to wander the Pearl Street Mall in all its tourist-filled, money-saturated summer Saturday nightness.

The Zip Code Man is here, with one of the biggest circles of onlookers of all the buskers. He looks Jewish, come to think of it. Too bad Lizzie's gone—we could have sicced her on him as an additional Pearl Street Mall performance art piece. Wonder how he would have reacted. Nah...he seems too nice, somehow. He probably just would've responded "40334" or something.

I'm feeling so silly (in large part, no doubt, thanks to the sugar rush from a huge cup of Ben & Jerry's Chocolate Fudge Brownie with just a *dollop* of hot fudge, which had zero chance of prematurely cooling) that I insist Donald become part of Zip Code Man's act. I force Donald to raise his hand and, blushing but proud, he steps into the chain-link United States outline as a representative of Montana, his home state. He's looking even cuter than usual out there, big burly unshaven sparkly-eyed guy in the midst of a bunch of little kids and old ladies. In fact, he looks downright *virile*. (Not to be confused, of course, with the word "viral," as one of my students did recently in a paper.)

I get kind of horny watching Donald out there, his feet spanning an entire state-and-a-half (he's encroaching on Idaho), so I start flirting again as we walk back to where his car is parked, poking him (but he's not ticklish, damn it), grabbing his itty-bitty-boy-titties (don't guys have the most adorable, grabbable pecs?) and his (as a Korean colleague once accidentally said) "lovely handles"—what tiny amount of them I can find, anyway. Donald responds by also getting more personal—even, at one point, grabbing my right bun. (Brandon and I, in our own shared dialect, called them Tocks, as in "Man, I really hurt my left Tock when I wrecked on my bike today.") When we get in his Subaru, Donald pretends to reach over to make sure my seatbelt's fastened and "accidentally" grabs my breast. And doesn't let go.

I feel my breathing suddenly change, the temperature increase. We find each other's eyes and both suddenly blurt out, "Have you ever thought about—?" We laugh.

"*Oh* yeah," he purrs as he leans over and kisses me. Mmm—he tastes great. He tastes like sex. I sometimes tell my lovers this, but they never really seem to know what I'm talking about. Donald does. He instantly responds, "So do you."

"What if we...you know?" I ask him.

"Are you serious?" He's disbelieving but eager, if I can interpret his tone correctly. (Which, being a linguist, I am pretty confident of.)

"Would it ruin our friendship, do you think?" We have a two-minute pseudo-debate à la Jerry and Elaine in which we both tumble over each other rushing to provide reasonable explanations of why that's probably what would happen to *most people*, but *we're* too aware and mature and intelligent for that to ever happen to *us*, and if we both want to, then why the hell not, blah blah blah. We drive the rest of the way to my place in silence, an unknown condition for us. We head into my bedroom hand in hand, not a way that we ever walk together.

Once we reach my bedroom (where he's been a million times, but never as my lover), Donald starts disrobing immediately. I'm amazed by this, reminded once again how different men are—they're not shy no matter what they look like; they strip down so matter-of-factly, like they're just uncovering their functional parts to do the job at hand.

I lie there and watch in the darkness. Donald looks extremely white. Nice build; average penis, almost erect. I'm used to more body hair; I seem to attract the more hirsute among men. Donald has only a little brown wisp under each arm and on his abdomen. Beautiful thighs, my god. They are literally *chiseled* and look as solid as they ever have in jeans or shorts, which are the ways I've always admired them. Michelangelo would've used him as a model. More guys need to take up telemarking.

He kind of lunges toward me and strips my leggings and underwear off in one quick, unexpected move: not my style. I frown, my ardor diminishing. Then I grab a Donald thigh in each hand. They are so rigid they make me instantly wet again. Lucky thing, as Donald fumbles in his pocket for a condom (was that for Lizzie?), parts my thighs (not quite as lapidarian as his, I'm afraid) and plunges right inside.

He feels good—good but not great; could that be because I'm somehow so *aware* of this, like I'm viewing this scene from outside, now that it's really happening? I come during his last few, weaker thrusts, just before that always-so-sad sudden and inevitable shrinking back down to a two-inch, limp, used, worn-out nub.

We are two very agile people in the verbal department; we start our usual banter right up again, not mentioning the fact that we just had sex and are lying naked next to one another, post-orgasmically. We joke about dinner, then get into an argument about Lizzie—how can he go out with someone that stupid, is what I want to know. Why the hell should I care, is his response. We often debate like this, which is a little disappointing (the fact that we're debating *now*), but then, what did I expect—instant true love?

He gets dressed. We do our usual parting ritual—a big bear hug where he lifts me off the ground—while still bickering about Lizzie and her (as I put it) *Fascist worldview*. And then he's gone.

It doesn't occur to me until after I've already brushed my teeth, washed my face, turned out the light and settled my black silk eye bag comfortably over my sleepy lids, that Donald himself was the *first of the thirty*. No reason not to count him, after all.

This is gonna be cake, was my last thought as I drifted off, with a smile.

ù

Date: 05 JUN 01 23:14:05
From: allpedalnowork@yahoo.com
Subject: coulda been worse
To: profaviva@yahoo.com

Aviva,
How are you? How's Boulder?
Had some fun getting back from the East Coast (was visiting the parents) to CA. (CA weather is great for cycling, by the way!) No delays on the flight segments for once (though there was some bad turbulence at one point—however, for some reason, there were a lot of nuns on board, and I figured that was excellent, because their total combined praying activity was probably helping to keep the aircraft aloft), but because of cascading bad luck, it still took me 12 hours from door to door. I had 20 minutes to catch the airport bus after our flight arrived, but the baggage delivery was just slow enough to make me miss the airport bus by one minute, forcing me to wait 15 minutes for the next

one, making me miss my train by two minutes, making me wait 90 minutes for the next train, which happened to pull in in 43 minutes instead of the scheduled 40 minutes, which made me just miss my bus, meaning a 60-minute wait for the next bus…but I took a different bus that I only had to wait 30 minutes for, but which had as its nearest bus stop a spot half a mile from home.

I was pissed because I had about 120 pounds of hockey equipment and other stuff to carry, and even though the bus driver was willing to let me out in the middle of the road a lot closer to home, he had to renege on that deal when too many people were waiting to get on at the last stop—so I had to get out at the last **real** bus stop and get ready to walk half a mile uphill in the gutter of a busy road (no sidewalks out here in blue-collar land) in traffic carrying 120 pounds on my shoulder—when miraculously a full-sized shopping cart appeared right on the sidewalk ahead of me.

So I was able to blithely roll my stuff home in the cart in style, under the adoring and might I say even envious scrutiny of the coterie of SUV-driving spectators passing me by.

Alan

♍

This morning while I was in the shower I thought I found a white pubic hair. I froze in panic. My god, isn't it bad enough all the gray hairs I'm getting around the temples? And zits, still (usually just one a month, around PMS, but *always* in the worst of places: on the end of my nose so I look like a Halloween witch; in the middle of my forehead like a third eye; right under a nostril so it looks like a booger and people smirk at it surreptitiously). The curse of being in your thirties, I've heard it called: gray hair and acne at the same time. But…gray pubes? Already?! No—this is too much to ask a woman to bear.

Luckily, upon closer investigation it did indeed turn out to be a pussy hair—a silky, perfect, white one—from my cat, Baby.

y

More and more I've been noticing this student. He's in both the summer seminars I'm currently teaching: Hebonics and Yinglish, and The Semantics of Humor.

Steven is pretty attractive. Sure, it's totally not kosher to sleep with your students, but hey—I'm on a mission. As long as he can be trusted to be discreet... The biggest problem with sleeping with one's student is that sooner or later they always starts bragging about it—of course, only to their closest friends, but how long does interesting gossip take to spread around a campus? A lot of my colleagues have been found out this way.

The only thing I don't really like about Steven physically is that about a third of the way through the semester, he shaved his head. When I asked him why (I hadn't even recognized him the first time I saw him bald while I was taking roll), he said it was because he'd lost a bet with his dad, and refused to comment further. Amazing. People are so weird.

I was insanely curious.

In any case, on the positive side, Steven's shorn head did make his eyes look more vivid...and, if I could get past the fact that it made him look like a skinhead, it was starting to look a little bit sexy, now that I was more used to it. How would it be, though, to reach up to his head right before orgasm, like a phrenologist? Would the shock be enough to prevent the orgasm from occurring, or would the novelty be a sudden turn-on and make the orgasm better than usual?

ô

Steven made an appointment with me for office hours on Thursday. He said he needed to ask my advice about the political correctness of some of his Hebonics examples. *That* will have to be interesting…

I was grading papers tonight at Starbuck's, a place I normally try to avoid, like a good BIBA citizen. Here in The People's Republic of Boulder—as they say, a few square miles surrounded by reality—BIBA stands for Boulder Independent Businesses Alliance, fighting chains like The Gap and The Cheesecake Factory, which, in spite of the BIBA, have nevertheless managed to infiltrate the Pearl Street Mall.

I saw James come in, this Buddhist guy I met when I went (once) to a drop-in Zen meditation hour.

"Hey, James."

"Oh, hi, Aviva. How. Are. You. Doing?" He asked this very slowly and like he *really* meant it, his eyes boring into mine. I'd forgotten how *now* he was. "Are you still practicing your meditation?" he asked me. Like so many modern American Jews, I am a "Jewddhist" wannabe. I get really fired up every now and then, do more reading about Buddhism, am blown away as much as anyone by the Dalai Lama, swear I'm going to meditate just five minutes a day…do it once or twice the first week, and not at all by the second. Hey, what can I say? I read my Pema Chödrön now and then, but stop short of purchasing a *zabuton*.

"Yeah... Um, how about *you*? How's *your* practice going?" I asked.

"Actually, I just got back from a weekend retreat. It was really good. Really, really good. I really got a lot out of it. I highly recommend it. Highly."

"That's nice..." And what the hell are you doing in Starbuck's, I thought.

"Actually, I'm just on my way home. We're having a big group dinner tonight, vegan of course. You'd be very welcome. Aviva. Very. Welcome."

I took a new look at James. I *was* out of groceries at my apartment. And I did need a Number Two. James was a little on the stringy side—too much brown rice, not enough protein—but sort of cute, in a lean, ascetic way. Was he flirting at all? Even all these years of development of primate social mores wasn't helping me. He said my name a lot, but maybe that was just because his speech patterns in general were strange. He seemed sort of asexual... Was I jumping the gun here? Would I be jumping James?

We walked to his place, chatting about the differences between zazen and TM, and why the Corpse Pose really is the most difficult. I thought he was starting to warm up a little. By the time we sat down at the huge wooden dinner table with about fifteen other hippies, he made an effort to sit next to me. I also caught him—I swear—taking a glance at my boobs, camouflaged as they were in a gigantic loose purple T-shirt (so good luck).

Skye and Sunflower, looking radiantly (yet vacantly) ecstatic about something—wouldn't it get tiring to be that ecstatic all the time?—led us in a Prayer to Goddess. We all had to hold hands and say what we were grateful for about the food tonight. Jewel went on about how she was grateful to everyone who had helped bring this food to our table: this included the farmers, the crop buyers, the delivery people, the salesclerks, the managers (okay already...the no-butter spelt Apple Brown Betty was getting cold!)... I got out of it easily by simply saying I was grateful to have been invited to dinner, and looked up at the next person while trying to smile mysteriously radiantly.

Later, after some yellow squash-quinoa-and-tomato stuff (the girl on my other side didn't serve herself any of the casserole, and when I asked her why, she replied: "I'm currently not consuming any members of the nightshade family"), everyone helped clean up. Most of the hippies retired to their "sacred spaces" with sticks of sage and solemn intentions. James asked me if I wanted to see his sitar. *Mais bien sûr!*

We went into James' messy room (he's still a guy, Buddhist or not). He showed me his sitar, his zither, his Andean panpipes, and his didgeridoo. Not to mention his berimbau and a bass ukulele he'd found at a garage sale. I asked him if he'd play the didgeridoo for me. He said he'd like to, but he couldn't right now, because he might disturb some of the people meditating. "Oh," I said, disappointed. I'd always wanted a private didgeridoo concert. I once got a private bassoon concert, and that was pretty cool. There's nothing for the libido like a guy playing an esoteric instrument just for you. And if a bassoon had gotten me wet, I wondered what the didgeridoo might've accomplished.

James was staring at me meaningfully. We embraced suddenly, and he pulled me down onto his mattress (unmade, of course). I tried not to notice the random zigzaggy pubic hairs stuck here and there to his unbleached cotton sheets. They were black and extremely corkscrewy. Then my attention got completely diverted—James had found my nipples (how, through all those yards of cotton?) and knew what to do with them. How come it never feels that good if you try to do it to yourself?

James slid his hand down my belly and when he reached the top of my pubic hair, he *killed* me by just making this happy little noise, "Hmm!" And then he sighed. From what I could tell in those acres of burgundy corduroy, James had a rather wonderful-looking erection. I was just about to ask (as softly and seductively as possible) about condom availability, when he groaned and rolled away from me.

"What? What's the matter? James?" I half straddled him, my knee grazing his stiff crotch. He groaned again.

And then: "I can't."

"What?! Why not?! Yes you can! Look!" I gently wrapped my hand like a hot dog bun around the…well, the hot dog.

"No, I mean, I know. I mean, I *can't*. Because…you know…I'm a Buddhist."

"But Buddhists aren't… I mean, they don't… Really? Are you sure you…?" I was getting wistful; I could feel his erection going away already.

"Sorry. Aviva."

I sighed. *Let it go.* "That's okay, James." What else could I do? I'd have to accept this reality; if Pema Chödrön, Zen leader (I've always thought that should be an oxymoron), had taught me nothing else through her simple yet profound books, it was that: Let It Go. I wondered if this type of situation had ever happened to her. Maybe not since she'd gotten the crewcut.

I must admit, James did have a wonderful bedside manner, for a guy. He hugged me and asked me to please spend the night anyway with him. What the hell, he *was* awfully sweet, he smelled nice—like natural musk with an overlay of jasmine incense—plus it was really late by now, 3:26 a.m. in fact, according to his clouds-and-chimes triangle-shaped clock.

I settled down, snagged a buckwheat-hull pillow for myself, sighed a few more times, remembering the promising shape I'd perceived but which, alas, was not to be... And next thing I knew, the chimes were chiming. James was not in bed.

It was only six a.m. Jesus. I felt like shit—sleep-deprived as well as abstemious. The damn clock kept chiming. I didn't see any obvious way to turn it off. Perhaps if you ignored it, it would turn itself off—a clock koan?

I dressed and hesitantly tiptoed upstairs. There were sixteen bodies in lotus position, facing east, palms upturned. Before I could decide what to do, there was a loud collective breath, and then: "Ommmmmmmmmm mmmmmmmmm..." It sounded pretty cool. I was tempted to join in but didn't want to break any possible group meditation rule. And my knees would never make it into lotus. I didn't know what else to do, so I sat there on the top step, quietly, and tried to sort of doze without actually falling asleep again. Pretty soon, everyone stopped om-ing and James came over and very gently touched my shoulder, in a brotherly sort of way, a signal to forget the almost-sex stuff from the night before.

Too bad. Sometimes morning sex can be really fun, when I'm still half-asleep and sort of zoned already... Although I can only *have* morning sex is if the guy is enough of a morning person to have the energy to do all the work himself. All this crap about "nothing says I love you to a man like a blow job in the morning"—well, as a very southern-accented African-American nurse once said to me about my chances of running in the upcoming Bolder Boulder when my leg was swollen up to elephantine proportions from a Look-Mom-No-Pads rollerblading accident: "Honey, you can just fo-*get* about that!"

At breakfast, which was lots of granola with vanilla soymilk, James seemed sheepish, perhaps a little contrite. And well he should! I was too tired to be properly indignant, but I was sure I would be later. Not only had he cheated me out of a really delicious night (never had the lack of red meat in a vegetarian household bothered me before), he'd also unwittingly given up his rights to the Number Two spot on my list.

I noticed one of the hippie dudes out on the patio, serenely contemplating a glass of clear yellow liquid which steamed in the early-morning sunlight. I don't usually drink chamomile tea unless I have a stomachache, but it sounded preferable to granola, so I asked the table at large: "Can I get some chamomile, too?"

One girl followed my gaze languidly, then snorted and corrected me: "No, that's Govinda, like, doing his morning thing, you know?"

I looked at her in confusion. She explained: "You know?, he like, drinks his urine first thing in the morning?, so he can, like, go into this really sweet trance for the rest of the day?"

The kitchen screen door suddenly slammed and some bearded guy came in and sat at the table. He was carrying something, which he set down near his breakfast bowl. It was a spoon. A really dirty spoon. I mean dirty as in real dirt—like black, garden kind of dirt. He'd set it right on the table, though, instead of pitching it into the sink. Tiny moist black dirt balls rolled a little ways, besmirching the otherwise clean table. Was he repotting a plant right before breakfast? No one else was paying any attention. *My* curiosity, on the other hand, even at this ungodly hour, was uncontainable.

"Hi, I'm Aviva, nice to meet you. Um...so where were you just now?"

"Outside." Ah—a man of few words.

"What were you doing with that spoon?" Were they short on garden implements here, couldn't afford hoes or whatever those things were called? How poignant!

"Digging my grave," he responded nonchalantly, and then continued in the same tone of voice, "Could you please pass the Silk?" Conversation went on all around us as if this guy had said nothing more noteworthy than *Looks like it's gonna be really hot out today.*

I was trying to proceed delicately. In Boulder you have to constantly be on your guard to be politically correct, but not only that—you also have to be constantly up on what's the latest P.C. terminology for everything. Like, god forbid you should accidentally slip up and talk about the cat you *owned*, instead of properly describing yourself as its *guardian*. Maybe I hadn't heard him right? It *was* early.

"You were *digging your grave*?"

"Yeah. And I *said*, could you *please* pass the soymilk?" There was an edge to this Buddhist's voice now. I thought I should tell him to practice patience, but first I wanted to find out what was going on. I passed him the carton, then persevered:

"Is that...something...that you've always *wanted* to do, or...?"

James, next to me, finally noticed my expression. He explained to me, gently, as if to a four year-old: "Aviva, among certain lineages it is a Buddhist tradition to dig part of your own grave every morning. This practice allows you to contemplate your own mortality, and to then live more fully in each moment of the rest of your day because of it."

Huh. "Is that kind of like T.S. Eliot, then?" I tried.

Blank stares all around.

"'I have measured out my life with coffee spoons,'" I quoted.

But inwardly I was thinking, Well, *damn*, that's sort of a cool, if morbid, idea. Although those of us who rent an apartment and have no land, what are *we* supposed to do? Taking our trusty teaspoon out into the communal yard and starting to dig a hole, however small at first—where? By the dumpsters?—would have a posse of Mexican landscapers after our asses in no time.

ç

Riding low on my James failure and sleep deprivation of the previous night, I nevertheless pull off a great teaching day (self-rated), and am waiting for Steven at the appointed time, out of breath from the three flights of stairs. At this altitude, you can get an aerobic workout just carrying a heavy backpack up to your office, never mind climbing actual Fourteeners.

I leaf through the school newspaper. Have to try to keep up with the kiddies' current tastes, at least to some minimal degree, or else risk total embarrassment. The key is to demonstrate familiarity with key words; you don't actually have to know who or what the hell the students are talking about. I learned this the hard way, several years ago, when I admitted ignorance in front of my students as to the existence of some band called Smashing Pumpkins. I check out the page where the week's musical events are listed; this is the crucial section to simply browse every couple of weeks or so. An advertisement for one of the local on-the-Hill dives today features weekend bands and album release parties for Afterbirth, Dilated Peoples, and Butthole Surfers. It seems unbelievable to me that in the not-so-distant past, band names tended toward the sweet and cute: The Monkees, The Beatles, The Beach Boys.

Under Dance Activities, I see that there is going to be a "Hemp Hop," and also advertised is a course in Whirling: "Pause; breathe; revive; and then, Remember & Remember & Remember. Whirling! Bring a full skirt. A donation of $10 is suggested." It notes that the instructor has trained in the Shattari method with a Sufi master.

There's a photo of some students streaking across the fountain area outside the student union building. I think I recognize the slogan-painted flanks of one of them as those of an activist undergrad I taught in a previous semester.

Steven is finally here. His head looks particularly shiny in the fluorescent lights of my office. Did I say office? I meant asbestos closet. No, really—this "office" used to be a storage closet, and the asbestos threat is very real; you're just not supposed to do anything to disturb it—say, by climbing the walls. Fortunately, the urge to do this comes only about ten times a day.

Steven pulls up a chair and brings out a folder.

"So, Steven, what can I help you with?" Relieve you of your possible virginity?

"Oh, well, I just wanted to, you know, make sure, like, these examples I chose don't, um, you know, like, *offend*...anybody." By *anybody*, of course he means me. This is, after all, a Hebonics and Yinglish seminar. And as far as I am aware, I am the only Jew in the department, probably here because they need to avoid a potential anti-Semitism lawsuit. This university spends a great deal of its time and money dealing with (including trying to suppress, and trying to hide) discrimination lawsuits of all stripes. Steven's examples for his Hebonics and Yinglish syntax paper are:

1. "Oy vey!! Sciatica I'm getting now!!"
2. "What?!! Are you meshugge?! Pasta I can *always* eat!!"
3. "Sweetcakes!!! Prune juice we need too!!!" (yelled to spouse who's leaving to go to the store)

Suppressing a grin with great difficulty, I ask him sternly and professorially if his examples were taken from real discourse. He assents. So I remind him (without asking where he'd found any such real-life discourse) that anything that is an example of real discourse is of course game to be subject to linguistic analysis, and that matters such as propriety or potential offense are completely moot, but that he might want to lose some of the exclamation points. He brightens—I guess he'd been worried I'd get offended or (much more likely) that I'd make him do more work, finding new examples.

Enthusiastically, he says, "Oh, that's right, duh, of course, I remember that now—anything from real intercourse—" He turns four shades of puce, almost but not quite all the way to the top of his head—"I mean, *dis*course, is valid for linguistic investigation." I have to bite the inside of my cheek to keep from laughing.

I remind him about the Multidepartmental party this evening, and say I hope I'll see him there. He blushes again, scarlet, maroon, cadmium red, then mumbles *thanks* and practically runs out the door, offering me only a split-second of enjoyment of the sight of his lovely young rear end.

13

I arrived a bit late to the party, being held this time at the Linguistics Chair's house, one of those fabulous huge places being taken over by vegetation on the south side of Boulder Creek, the sort of quasi-mansion in which any academic living there is able to only because their spouse is a software developer or a systems architect. The fact that the Ling Department was hosting this party meant that we had decided the theme, rules, and prizes. (Every time the School of Engineering hosts it, we all have to build parachute contraptions for launching eggs off the roof.) Our theme this time was an Ugliest Word Contest: everyone had to show up with a sign around their neck on which would be written the ugliest word they could think of. All the linguists present would later judge the best entry. So we're a total bunch of geeks, what can I say?

Right off the bat I saw several soon-to-be disqualifications: VEGEMITE for being a proper noun, who was chatting with BRUSTWART—truly an ugly word (for a rather nice part of the anatomy), but foreign languages were disallowed. Hell, you could probably win this contest with almost *any* German word. On the sofa were PUS and EXPECTORATE. On the floor, sitting cross-legged in a half-circle in front of the stone fireplace, and all balancing paper plates heaped high with nachos, hummous, and guacamole, I spotted RECTUM, PALPITATE, and PLACENTA (as one of the linguists, I knew that PLACENTA would be eliminated quickly from the running: while it brought to mind an ugly image, its phonetic realization was actually rather lovely). In a fantastic coincidence, SMEGMA (always sounded to me like a little-known Greek philosopher, buddy perhaps to Testicles) was cuddling up to SCROTUM against the pantry doors in the kitchen alcove.

I had thought hard about my word, as I could quickly tell so had the other linguists. I apparently wasn't the only one who'd realized that they'd earn bonus points during the judging for choosing a word (the opposite of the case of PLACENTA) which had a beautiful *signifié*, but which sounded ugly. I'd chosen BOUGAINVILLEA, and the Ling Chair was PULCHRITUDE. As I walked around, I realized that a lot of these words would make great band names: e.g., FECAL MATTER (phrase: disqualify), LIPOSUCTION, EXOSKELETON.

Someone's kid (also dressed up for the party: EARWIG) was careening around out of control, supercharged from all the adult attention and all the sugar he'd just consumed. Being the only kid there (high-level academics aren't usually breeders—we tend to produce monographs rather than homo sapiens), a lot of this attention was unwitting: most of us were observing him the way we'd observe a rat or any other alien creature in Psych Lab, part of our brain storing info in case we had to write up the research results immediately after the party. The kid, to the great consternation of his quadruple-Ph.D. parents, was tunelessly screeching out, "Oh, oh, oh, Nat King Cole was a merry old soul, a merry old soul was he..."

A couple of boring-looking guys accosted me and started chatting me up (a Brit phrase I love—it's just so descriptive. So many Brit expressions are. Once I accidentally used the American term "fanny pack" instead of their "bum bag"—I got a *really* interesting reaction). These guys had to be from the Business or Law school. To demonstrate how totally lame and pathetic they were, their words were PETUNIA and DOODAD. I shook off the duds, headed for the kitchen. On the way there, I saw a rather cute redheaded guy. I've never slept with a redheaded guy...Do they have red pubic hair too?

Then, I spotted it: a bald pate!

"Steven, hi! Glad you could make it." I checked his chest: SELF-FLAGELLATE. Oooh. Not sure about hyphenates; I'd have to make a note and check with my fellow geeks later. But I liked it, I liked it. (Not to mention that it made me think of the term "self-abuse," and boy, could I picture that...) I couldn't help but notice that Steven was looking ravishable in tight black jeans and a long-sleeved, cuddly dark green polo shirt.

He saw me and stammered: "Hi, um…" It was the usual Appellation Anxiety (entire Linguistics theses have been written about this phenomenon): when a student encounters their professor in a social situation, they can never figure out what to call them; "Professor" doesn't quite work, but then neither does a first name. The way out is to simply skip over it in the initial address, and then stick to the second-person-singular subject pronoun thereafter.

But just as I was looking forward to having an informal, hopefully flirtatious *tête-à-tête* with Steven, another guy butted in and stood in front of me. He was wearing DOUCHEBAG, but other than the excellent word choice, he didn't seem to have much to recommend him. For starters, he was wearing a necklace composed of about fifty small white skulls strung together. He appeared to be one of my least-favorite types: a Goth. They dress only in black, have dyed matte-black hair, wear black lipstick (boys and girls both), and are really, really pale. A lot of them even wear white pancake makeup at all times. The Goth Look is distinguished from the Heroin Waif Look by very little as far as I can tell, but I guess there must be some subtle distinctions I'm unaware of, since they can recognize each other and stay separate. It's as mysterious to me as how the gangs in L.A. tell each other apart.

Anyway, *monsieur le* Douchebag looked vaguely familiar—maybe I'd met him at some awful, enforced-attendance faculty shindig, over a table of Ritz crackers? I was trapped now; might as well be polite and hope to get another chance to talk to Steven later. The Goth's word being such a good one, however, was worrying me—because a date with *me* was one of the prizes. (If a woman won, she got a date with one of the very few unmarried male Linguistics adjuncts—although I had to wonder if that date might turn out to be awfully disappointing; how many of them were possibly actually hetero? Probably about as many as the male students in the Dance Department.) *I* had actually volunteered for this, figuring it might help me check another guy off my To Do list.

"So, what department are you?" I asked him.

"Writing." Look out! The Writing ones are always the looniest.

"Really? Have I met you at one of the New Faculty meetings, or…?"

"I don't know, but you look kind of familiar," he told me.

"Yeah, so do you." I felt like asking him if maybe I'd known him in his pre-Goth days. But modern society, as far as I know, still hasn't come up with a polite way to ask a stranger: So, how long have you been a Goth? Instead, I asked: "So, what have you written? Anything I might know?"

He looked really excited. "Maybe! I have two books published so far…it's gonna be, like, kind of a series, you know? The ones I have out already are called *How To Mongoose-Proof Your Cabin*, and *How To Make Trays*. I'm working on the third, which I think I'm going to call *Removing Nails From Wood*."

Suddenly, the redhead approached. I decided to pretend to know him.

"Hey! Hi! Heeey!…" I called to him, but was ignored. I squirmed away and followed him, out of the kitchen and into one of the three living rooms, this one sunken, with incredibly high ceilings and golden bamboo-paneled walls, though in terms of square footage it was quite small. It was like being trapped inside a Honey Nut Cheerios box.

I tapped the redhead on the shoulder. "Hey there. Hi. What's your name?"

He must not like the ethnic look—he wasn't looking super pleased to find me there. Or maybe he was gay? (I always prefer to think they're gay rather than they're not attracted to me—saves on ego wear-and-tear.)

"Jim." Ugh—one of my least favorite names. His cardboard sign, however, was much better: DUODENUM. So, he'd at least be in the running for a date with *moi*.

"Jim, nice to meet you. I'm Aviva."

"Oh, *Aviva*?" he gushed. "Wow, that's a *beautiful* name!"

Damn. Definitely gay. I repeated that it was nice to meet him and set off to find Steven again. But was grabbed by the elbow. It was a colleague—apparently it was time for the judging. Oops. I'd forgotten to make any notes, but that was okay—I have a really good memory. Not to mention I was planning on nominating SELF-FLAGELLATE for first place.

Lisa led me to the solarium. On the way, I overheard a bit of conversation between two extremely attractive women about my age. They were gorgeous, both with long hair, clear skin, and aesthetic features. One, WEEVIL, had sort of burnished brown tresses (one of those great antiquated words); the other, DUNDERFUNK, had shining silver—literally, silver—locks (wow, locks and tresses both: how Brontëesque). I wondered if an experimental foray into lesbianism would count on my list.

WEEVIL was saying, "Jesus, I am so fucking HSP today! I'm *sick* of it!"

The other one looked sympathetic and responded, "Yeah, I know. It's like, we're going to end up having to live in a fucking *bubble*!"

PMS I was plenty familiar with; was this some kind of new variation? As I was all but dragged past them, I asked, "What's HSP?"

"*Highly Sensitive Person*," they responded in unison, in a tone of voice that let me know I *really* should've already known that.

The glass room was filled with flowering cacti. And my colleagues. I whipped out my little notepad that I always carry and pretended to make a few last-minute urgent notes. (In reality, I was sketching little 3-D cubes.)

Judging time. The nominees were, on my part: SELF-FLAGELLATE (however, it made me nervous because I could hear some dubious murmurings due to the fact it was a hyphenate), CORNHOLE, and PERIODONTIST.

The next reporting party, Jenny (wearing BELCH) had chosen BARF, BUNG, and BILLABONG (the latter ending up disqualified after some discussion, its origin being foreign, and its current usage apparently also limited to proper nouns, e.g., casinos).

Then one faculty member (whom I won't embarrass by naming here, but his evening pseudonym was BETTY) had on his list only several (admittedly ugly) proper names, to wit: BUBBA, BERTHA, and BOB. Obviously, he was clueless. Not to mention (okay, I will name him) that *his* real name was Ralph, so I didn't think he had much room to talk when it came to ugly names. It also occurred to me that it would've been semantically more interesting and appropriate if it'd been Ralph who'd chosen BARF.

Lisa's favorites: PUSILLANIMOUS, PUG, and PERIPATETIC. (Note the proclivity, in voting, for alliteration.) Lisa's own sign read PREPUCE, which, once I noticed it, I urged everyone to vote it second place.

Then Chris (wearing URETHRA) spoke up for DOUCHEBAG (was I going to get stuck with a date with a Goth, after all?), SUCCUBUS, and LABIA. Ouch. I always *had* suspected Chris of misogyny.

The Chair's choices were, as to be expected, superb: PUD (a bit risqué for a woman of her age and stature, I must say), UPCHUCK, and USURP.

Another guy who apparently either hadn't known about, or hadn't paid attention to, the rules, had chosen some great *phrases*, but of course all had to be disqualified. He argued that some of these could be considered, rather, compound nouns—but was swiftly and loudly outvoted by the rest of us. I'm sure that going through the Chair's mind as well as everyone else's was disgust at a member of a Linguistics Department who didn't know how to identify a compound noun—this guy's days, especially tenureless as he was, were numbered now, although he seemed blithely unaware of it. He had offered: ROTARY CLUB, PUTT-PUTT GOLF, BOWEL MOVEMENT. Chris The Misogynist confessed to him, with fraternal affection, that he himself had wanted to vote for PAP SMEAR, but hadn't because it was, well…um, a *phrase*. Chris' voice died as he realized he'd put his foot in his mouth.

Lisa started cracking up. We all looked at her.

"What?" I asked.

"*Rotary Club*—that's their nametag, not their contest entry!" We all dissolved into embarrassed giggles.

Jane offered, stiffly (everything she did and said was stiff, and she wasn't even a Brit): MUCUS, PRAWN, and SPIGOT. Not bad. I was impressed with stiff ol' Jane.

Michael, the newest member of the adjunct faculty (who clearly knew his place, as he'd waited until last to speak), had TUBA, TUBER, and SHIBBOLETH. I was curious about the similarity of the first two words—randomly present at the same party?—I said I'd have to ask someone in Statistics about that.

Michael responded, "I know, I felt the same way. But it turned out they were the identical twins, from Anthropology."

Poor Mr. Phrases didn't seem to see the humor in that, and while the rest of us were greatly enjoying Michael's answer, the doomed one piped up: "Well, can I enter PUDGY instead of my phrases, then?"

No one bothered to answer. The poor sod. I felt sorry for him, but was grateful it wasn't *me* who'd soon be applying for part-time positions at community colleges in Armpit, Louisiana.

g

In my office, waiting for Steven. The fact that he's made another office hour appointment is definitely causing me to suspect that he's *interested*. I feel like I'm in junior high. I'm uncomfortable, keep fiddling with the elastic waistband of my leggings. Back in my twenties, I never used to be bothered by things like waistbands; it's like my whole stomach area has just sort of...e*xpanded*. (And no, I'm *not* pregnant, in spite of what that evil woman in the Safeway line asked last week.) Seriously, I am so sick of that overused and untrue phrase in all the clothing catalogs: "comfortable elastic waistband." What the hell is *comfortable* about an elastic waistband, will someone please tell me? Is it the way it digs in mercilessly, shortchanges the natural breathing process, causes painful intestinal constriction, bloating, and gas? And by the way, everyone who feels tempted to point out that if I were a little less *zaftig*, I might find elastic waistbands comfortable, can just go out and shoot themselves right now.

If there's any cosmic justice, I'll come back as a guy—they're two-dimensional, you know—they buy their pants via one measurement down and one across, without even trying them on.

But who wants to be a guy? Their orgasms are so feeble.

One of my other students just left. I cannot, for the life of me, discern whether said student is a male or a female. "Its" name is Chris, which doesn't help me at all. Chris favors the unisex skateboard style of baggy clothing, wears his/her hair to the shoulders held back with a "retro" hairband, has delicate features that could belong equally gracefully to either sex, big silver hoop earrings in both earlobes (ah, what nostalgia for the old days when there was significance in the act of a man wearing a single earring in the right versus the left ear) and purple lipstick, and is extremely slender—there is zero visible body shape to go on. It looks exactly like a boy trying to pass as a girl, or else a girl trying to pass as a boy. It would be extremely un-hip to admit to any other student that I can't tell, and extremely un-P.C. to ask the student. Androgyny is very trendy right now amongst the high school and undergrad populations. From what I overhear amongst my students, it's also currently quite trendy to be (or at least to *say* you are) bi. Man, am I a dinosaur or what?

Today's band names in the paper: House of Pain, Cherry Poppin' Daddies, Badly Drawn Boy, Del Da Funky Homosapien, Insane Clown Posse, Swollen Members, Buried Alive, Death Threat, Ozric Tentacles, Slim Cessna's Auto Club, Atomic Bitchwax, and the Hate Fuck Trio.

Last night, SUCCUBUS had won. He turned out to be (very luckily for me!) a gorgeous guy I'd seen a few times around campus but never met, an Iranian working on his Master's in Computer Science. (Most of them don't introduce themselves as "Iranian" to Americans anymore, since both Iran and Iraq consistently have such a bad flavor to Americans from the news, and since the average American is typically not even aware that they are two different countries and different cultures. They usually call themselves "Persian" now. Every time I hear that, I'm tempted to ask about things like Persian Cold Wax for the bikini line, and whether it really was they who invented Venetian blinds and were they still angry about the misnomer.)

Reza was definitely my type: in my opinion, tall-dark-and-handsome never goes out of style. We went out to the Trident for coffee after the party as our "date." Reza said, "You know what, Aviva, there is something I am always wondered. May I ask you it?"

"Sure," I answered, paying more attention to the way his dark-blue dress pants bunched up at the crotch than to the conversation. Are Iranians circumcised?

"Well, you are Jewish, right?"

"Yeeees...," I said warily, waking back up—any question that starts that way, when spoken by a non-Jew, usually does not bode well.

"So, why you Jewish are worshipping the rabbits?"

"Worshipping *rabbits*? No, no, you must have some other religion in mind. Jews don't worship any rodents...that I know of. Maybe you're thinking of, I don't know, that Biblical scene where there's that ram or whatever? Or maybe the Hindus, who believe that *cows* are sacred?"

"No, I am sure I heard they are rabbits. I am sorry. Must be mistake."

Weird. But he was so cute, that hair so incredibly black and thick and shiny, it looked like a healthy winter animal pelt; those eyes so richly dark, like espresso; that I was willing to overlook some intellectual strangeness. After all, I didn't want him for his *mind*.

He changed the subject, apparently sensitive enough to sense that perhaps Judaism wasn't his area. "Aviva, you are linguist, yes?" You had to hand it to this guy, he was great at making small talk. Either that or he had no one to talk to and had been saving up questions since he left Tehran.

"Yes..."

"Maybe you can explain to me the word 'idealist'? I am hearing it and not understand it."

"Well..." What a strange date this was so far. More...*verbal* than I'd expected. After thinking for a moment, I asked him, "Well, do you know the Indigo Girls?"

"You mean the music group, the singers women?"

"Exactly. Well they have this one song that goes, 'There must be a thousand things you would die for... I can hardly think of two.'"

He processed. "Oh, I think I understand. You are idealist. I am not idealist."

"Right. In the context of the song, and taking into account deixis, that's exactly correct. So you understand it now?"

"Yes. Thank you. I understand now."

O-*kay*.

For something to do, I looked around the café. The guy at the next table was minding his own business, absorbed in a book, *Teach Yourself Telugu*. I could hear the barista having fun practicing his fake British accent on customers: "Yes, yes, what *is* it that you re*quire*?"

I decided I'd better take over the lead, or we'd be going nowhere. And damn, was Reza attractive! I couldn't believe my good fortune. What would I have done if I'd gotten the gay redhead? I wouldn't have been able to find out the answer to the redhead question, that's for sure.

"So, Reza, are you glad you won the Word Contest?"

"Well, you know, your neighbor's chicken is a duck."

"*Excuse* me?"

"Your. Neighbor's. Chicken. Is. A. Duck," he repeated, enunciating carefully.

"No, I know. I mean, I *heard* you. I just have no clue what you *meant* by it."

"Oh, okay, now I explain!" It crossed my mind that his sounded a lot like a French accent; Farsi and French must share a lot of phonemes. It was a *very* cute accent for a guy to have. "You see," he continued, "I like you, I think you very attractive. This I think *before* I win contest. But once I know I am contest winner, I think maybe you *not* so attractive. You understand?" he smiled, as if he hadn't just blatantly insulted me.

"*What?!* You're saying suddenly you don't think I'm attractive?"

"No, I think maybe now you attractive, again." He winked. Reza was now staring at me with—it looks the same in every culture—lust. "You know what, Aviva? I have hard one."

That, needless to say, was when I decided that the time had definitely come to take care of Number Two on my list. So! A Persian it would be. A strange conversationalist, but hopefully…

He *was* a good lover. This was in spite of some kind of sex-on-a-chair fetish of his that seemed to excite him tremendously, but that I couldn't really get into, as it required way too much work on my part. And he was prepared (is there a Persian Boy Scouts faction?). He called this morning to say thanks for the "date" and that he thought I was definitely a duck and could he see me again?

I quacked at him but didn't tell him I had twenty-eight guys to go before I'd be available again.

In fact... I now grabbed a piece of scrap paper from the corner of my desk and had just started to make some calculations, when there was a cocky knock on the door. Steven must've gotten lucky at the party after I left. He had that *look*—of pride or whatever. Are guys just so relieved each time that they've managed to get it up once more, or what?

Steven was wearing an awesome T-shirt: *The Center For Body Controlology*. I gave him what I hoped was a dazzling smile. As a Star Trek character, now would be the time to tell him, in a robotic voice: "Welcome, Number Three. Resistance is futile. You will be assimilated."

Steven sat down. "Hi, um…"

"Hi, Steven. Did you have a good time at the party last night?"

"Yeah—yeah, I did. Yeah!" There was definitely a little spark of something there that he was trying to hide. I wondered whom he'd gone home with. Maybe one of the HSP women? Or were they gay? Oh, who the hell can tell anymore? He looked down at the piece of paper I'd been writing on. "Oh, I'm sorry. I didn't mean to, um, you know, like, interrupt your work or anything."

Yikes! I glanced down. Nothing incriminating; just a few numbers.

"No, no, it's fine. I was just...preparing some material for a course I might teach next semester...ah, Mathematical Modeling in Linguistics. So, what can I do for you, Steven?" Wasn't that exactly what I asked him before? I'm in a rut.

"Um, okay, well, I'm, like, a little confused about some of the pronunciation stuff? You know, the phonemes and stuff?"

"Could you be more specific?" I love being pedantic.

"Well, like, remember when you were talking in class about those words like 'Karen'?"

"Oh, okay, you mean the Yinglish /a/?"

"Yeah, right, exactly. Could you go over that one more time with me?"

"Sure, no problem. But, Steven, tell me what you know, first."

"Well, there's like, the name *Karen*, and...let's see...wasn't it, like, anything with an *r*, something like that?"

He was obviously a bit clueless. I gave him the condensed form of the lecture I'd given that day in class: that in Yinglish, the /ar/ combination was pronounced differently than in non-Yinglish dialects, as in the words *Karen, apparently, parents*.

He said, "Oh, yeah, right, I remember now, thanks. Actually, you know what? I realize why I wasn't totally, you know, mentally all *there* that day in class. I mean, I don't want you to think I wasn't, like, paying attention, you know? I mean, I, like, *totally* always pay attention in your classes..." He was turning red again. Studying the line of demarcation between his rosy face and the very top of his shaved white noggin, I remembered I'd been wanting to see if I could get him to talk about that.

"Steven, um, I know it's none of my business, but I'm really curious..."

"Yeah?"

"Can I ask you again why you shaved your head? I'm sorry, I'm just *so* curious..."

His fading red returned in great strength. "Um…well, it's kind of, you know…personal."

"Oh. I'm sorry, I shouldn't have asked."

"No, no, it's okay. I mean—really. I mean, I *will* tell you…sometime. Maybe not right now."

Hmm. Yes, perhaps some other time, in some other more *private* kind of moment—one that I must try to arrange, sooner or later.

Steven leaned closer to me. "You know what, um… I wanted to tell you, you know, one of the reasons I, like, took this course is because…I mean, because I'm really interested in the topic, you know, and of course I'm just starting my Master's in Linguistics… And I'm also, you know, really, like, interested in Jewish stuff, you know… In fact, I even, like, have a Jewish relative, so I guess that kinda makes me, like, in a way, pretty much Jewish myself, huh?"

"Really? Who in your family's Jewish?" He didn't look Jewish—or was it just the shaved head?

"It was, like, my father's uncle, I think."

I had to smile. "Well, I hate to break the news to you, Steven, but technically you're only Jewish if your mother was Jewish."

His happy expression disappeared. "What do you mean? How come?"

"Well, it comes from ancient times—you know, it was always obvious who the *mother* of a baby was, but who the *father* was…well..."

He blushed a little bit again after a moment of contemplation. "But what about genetic testing? I mean, they do that for paternity suits now, don't they?"

"That's what I mean, it'll probably change sooner rather than later. But so far, the law still stands—well, as far as I know. So…I'm afraid you can't really say you're Jewish." He looked a bit bummed. So I added, "Some people, though, hold the theory that anyone who *feels* Jewish must actually *be* Jewish, so those people are encouraged to explore that—you know, to convert."

"Con*vert*?!" He looked really alarmed. Maybe he was one of the rare American Caucasian males who wasn't circumcised and it had suddenly occurred to him what he'd have to do. But statistically speaking, he almost surely was—circumcised, I mean.

"Well, I'm not saying you *have* to convert. Just that you *could*, if you wanted." He still didn't answer. I changed the subject: "So what was the other reason?"

"What other reason?"

"Didn't you say something like, *one* of the reasons you took my course was because you had a Jewish relative…?"

The blush, yet again. "Oh, yeah…Well, the other reason was just that I'd heard, you know, that you were, like, really good. At *teaching*, I mean." His face looked like one of those fluorescent crayon colors, the kind that we deprived older generation had to grow up without. I thanked him for the compliment, and asked if there was anything else. He said, "No, no, that's it… Except…"

"Yes?"

"Um, I was wondering… I mean, I think it's, like, not kosher—" He turned vivid vermilion; I had to laugh, remembering the time I had just gotten to know an African-American man, and the color *I* must've turned when, discussing family professions, I'd said to him without thinking, "Oh, so you're kind of the black sheep of the family, then?"

"What's not kosher?" I asked.

"To, um…what's the word they use? *Fraternize* with your professors?"

Now it was my turn to blush. "Steven, are you…asking me out?"

By now, we were both as crimson as my correcting pen. (You know that fad going around right now that claims that red ink is too *traumatic* for the poor little students? Well, that is total bullshit.)

"Um…yeah. I am." He gave a small nervous laugh.

"Well, indeed" (did I really just say *indeed*?), "one *is* supposed to wait until one is no longer in the relationship of…" (this syntax was getting ponderous; as a linguist, I ought to do better) "…Let's just say, you're right, it's not kosher. *But* that's only because of these new rules from the last few years, you know, what with the P.C. climate and the potential for litigation, all that stuff…" I hoped he'd catch my (ridiculously obvious) subtext.

He did catch it. "So, let's say no one knows and everyone's okay with the situation…"

"Right." I looked him in the eye, willed myself not to blush again.

"So," he said, "what about this weekend?"

I had too much to do this weekend, to get ready to leave for a Linguistics conference in Austin, but we made an appointment (okay, okay, a *date*) for next Sunday, to do a little mountain biking. I reminded Steven I wouldn't be holding classes this coming week because of the conference. He gave me a little smile (I'd like to say of sweetness or good will, but it was more like complicity) at the door, then took off, and I was left to muse about all we'd talked about.

It's funny: I'm Jewish, legally (as concerns, say, potential citizenship in Israel) as well as culturally (my family and heritage). Yet I actually know next to nothing about the religion— the ritual stuff, the Hebrew prayers, what the different holidays mean, whether observant Jews feel anything special for the order Rodentia. Yet a person who *isn't* Jewish, if they want to convert, would have to really learn all that stuff and, I think, even take a test on it or something. To tell you the truth, I don't believe in conversion anyway, especially as concerns Judaism. It just doesn't compute. It's like me saying, hey dude, I think I'll convert to African-Americanism.

ñ

Lying in bed that night, feeling a bit...shall we say, *horny*? I alternated between fantasizing about palpating Steven's shaved head, and remembering Alan's tremendous and unusual skill: Alan of the Thousand Ways To Make You Come. He was able, just by rhythmically moving *any* of his body parts on my mound of Venus (I love that term—it sounds so...*historical*), to bring me to orgasm, and incredibly fast.

He'd obviously spent a great deal of time practicing this amazing talent, too, because the man was *fine*. His knee, his hipbone, his pec, his shoulder, a rib, big toe... I honestly think that within a few more years, if he keeps working on it, he'll be able to make a woman come just by looking at her.

ę

My plane stopped in Dallas, Austin-bound. Most of the people from the previous flight were now gone, with an almost entirely new set of passengers. I was getting a bit hungry (as usual, the airline had proclaimed innocence and ignorance when it was time for me to get my vegetarian lunch), and therefore less tolerant as hypoglycemia began to set in. I could tell we were now *intra*-Texas: lots of big hair, lots of makeup, homogenous ethnicity, louder voices, cowboy boots with suits, bigger people. I took out a novel I'd brought along, *The Girls' Guide To Hunting And Fishing*, and buried my face in it.

The man who ended up sitting on my left, in the aisle (as usual, my reservation of the aisle seat—closer to the bathroom—had apparently vanished into cyberspace immediately after I made it, along with my veggie lunch), had just barely made it onto the plane, dashing my hope of that seat remaining empty. I always seem to end up trapped in the middle, a bad place for a claustrophobe suffering from low blood sugar.

He was a tall, big-boned type, big sombrero which he showed no sign yet of intending to remove, expensive-looking just-shined cowboy boots, brand-new Levis (I keep forgetting to research how it happened that some nerdy Jew ended up getting involved in the manufacture of blue jeans in the Wild West), an ironed denim shirt the exact color of the jeans, and of course the string tie (is that like the most useless piece of clothing ever?).

As the plane began to taxi out, I heard him say, "Justy Willis, ma'am, haddie do." I didn't look up from my book. "Ma'am?" I wondered whom he was addressing—one of the flight attendants? "Wha, little lady, we could at least howdy before we shake! Haw haw haw!"

I glanced up, irritated. He was looking at *me*. The last time someone called me *ma'am*, it was some sixteen year-old employee-in-training at Starbuck's; before that, it was probably one of the greasy guys at Jiffy Lube. "Gawlly, little lady, s'like a cat scratchin' on an anvil, tryin' to git ya ta talk to a fella."

Jesus. And it's even harder to be polite when I'm hungry. But it looked like this character wasn't going to give up anytime soon. "Hi," I said as unenthusiastically as possible.

He reached out to shake my hand—too hard. "Justy Willis, ma'am, an' ah'm mahty pleased t' make yer acquaintance."

"I'm Aviva."

"Yer a *what*?!"

"No, that's my *name*. A-vi-va," I enunciated for him.

"Well now, ain't that a interestin' name! Ah thought ah'd heard all kahnds, but this here one just about tayuks th' cayuk."

I was getting ready to kill him and he'd obviously only just begun. Just my luck to get a *cowboy*—and a loquacious one—next to me all the way to Austin. I'd better change the subject. As I learned long ago, a guy will happily talk about himself exclusively during an entire conversation—and not even be aware of it. There was a linguistic study done once: men and women on first dates were taped in conversation, and later were queried as to what percentage of the conversation they *thought* they had dominated. Women guessed fifty percent but had actually used only about ten; men estimated twenty but had really taken almost ninety.

"Don't you think you'd better fasten your seat belt? The flight attendants are going to yell at you," I told him.

"Ah don' care if it harelips the gov'ner! Ah cayn't abahd them thangs. If them purty little stewardesses want ta yell at me, wha, ah'll just have ta turn on some a that ol' Teg-zus charum!"

I winced involuntarily at the word "stewardesses," and wondered how long this guy would last on the faculty at my university, where you can be fired for saying "mankind" instead of "peoplekind" (yet where the most egregious discrimination is subtle, takes place daily on a large scale, and always goes unpunished). He persisted. "Missy, now tail me, whatcha fixin' ta do in Austin?"

"*Tail* you? Oh…gotcha. I'm going to a Linguistics conference."

"What's that? Ya'll stand aroun' an' talk different langages an' all? Haw haw!"

Haw haw indeed. "No, it's an academic conference—people presenting papers, that sort of thing."

"Now where'dja get such a name as Aviva, young lady?" God, what was up with this "little lady" and "young lady" (where the first syllable of "lady" rhymed with the word "lie") shit? He was maybe five years older than me, at the most.

"It's Hebrew."

"Hebra! Why, I thought all them Hebra folks' done got barned up!" He looked at my face. "'F'y'll excuse th'expression."

Someday, when I'm rich, I'm going to donate a lot of money to the Anti-Defamation League—towards education of the frigging *masses*. "No, the *Jews* didn't all die in the *Holocaust*. About *six million*—but not *all*."

"So, whatcha readin' there? Girls' Guide to Huntin' an' Fishin', huh? Wha, that's wunnerful, little lady, ain't a whole lotta girls that's innerested in them kinda *may*un-ly activities. Fact, ah kin tayuk ya—"

"No, no, that's just the *title*!—that's not what it's *about*."

"Well now, missy, s'far as ah'm concerned, a tahtle of a book's usually a fairly good indicaytor of its contents, 'few pardon mah sayin' so."

"No—I mean, yeah, I know—but this is a *novel*. It's fiction. The title's probably just kind of catchy."

"S'it good?"

"I don't know," I answered pointedly. "I was *just starting* it."

"So ya'll gonna be at this—what is it?—taycher's conference? Yer a taycher? What grade dya taych? Kindergarten? Them littl'uns sure is cute, ain't they?"

"No, I'm a *professor*," I corrected, disgruntled anew. "At a uni*ver*sity."

"A perfesser! Well, I'll be durned! You don't look old enough to be a per*fesser*," he said with a big wink.

"I'm older than I look," I said dryly, and opened my book back up.

"So, whadja haf'ta do ta get ta be a perfesser? Ya'll haf'ta get one a them pie-eytch-dyes an' all?"

"Yep, sure did." Aaaaackkk! I was starting to sound like him; already

I could sense the dissolution of the high-vowel-preceding-nasal distinction, as well as my diphthongs lengthening. It flashed through my mind that one of us linguists should've used the word DIPHTHONG in the contest.

"Ya know, ah never did see the point in all that edjacayshun, mahself. Ah usetah live in Useton, ya know, when ah was just a little tahyuk an' all. Ah went ta school, an' they passed me along when they got sick a seein' mah face. Fact is, ah kin make more moneh in one die than y'all in one year with y'all's college degrees an' all, if y'll pardon mah sayin' so. Fact is, mah friends all know that ol' Justy here's got himself enough moneh ta barn a wet dawg."

Well. What was I supposed to say to that? I said nothing, hoping to discourage him from further conversation.

"Fact, ah'm on mah whay raht now to close a big ol' bizness deal on a bunch a steaks on th' hoof. Deal's tighter n' two coats a paint. Guy ah'm buyin' 'em from, he's tighter n' a power line after a blue norther. Yayup, he'll squeeze a nickel till th' buffalo scrayms. But he's all hat an' no cattle, if ya get mah drift." He winked. "Cotton an' cows, ma'am, s'the way a Tegzin lives. A course, cayn't fergit th' *awrl*! Haw haw haw!"

I remained silent, looking down at my book, very rudely I must say. To no avail.

He continued, "Ah got mahself a coupla ranches outsahd a Lubbock, one in Muleshoe... Also got me a carpet 'n' tahl factory over to Santone, an' a trash dump outsahd a' Amarilla... Where you hayl from, little lady?" I was starting to understand why some linguists are able to specialize wholly in Texan dialects. I was amazed at how little actual direct phrasing there was; how fascinating, if extremely irritating, to communicate in almost pure simile and metaphor.

"Where am I from? Oh, lots of different places."

"Now, Miss Aviva, far's ah know, yer only born in one place—less a course you were born *again*! Haw haw haw!"

"But where I was born had nothing to do with where I grew up, so..."

"*Are* ya born again, missy? I shore do hope so. Cuz if ya haven't tayken th' Lord Jayzus Chrahst as yer personal an' only sayuvyer, then we got us a big problem hayr!"

"Well, Jews don't—" I started.

"But just one minent, girlie! Cuz you shore are in luck today. Ah kin tayl ya awl about Jayzus. Fact, if ah'd had mah way, ah woulda been a televangelist. Now them people *rilly* make a difference in th' world. They's *ril* Amurkins. Git folks *cryin'*, they're so happy to fand Jayzus! An' raht there on the tay-vay, too. With millions a folks watchin'—more'n you kin shayke a stick at. Mike a lot uh moneh too."

I sighed audibly. Must maintain my academic demeanor...think of something linguistic... I was pretty sure I could successfully predict that this guy would first-syllable-accent the words *umbrella* and *insurance*. I also recalled a phonics-for-kids textbook draft I'd had to review once. It had been written by a Texan couple, and I'd given my professional opinion that it would only work within that state, as they'd spelled out all the words with their own peculiar pronunciation.

The same trick: change the focus back to him. "So how come you *didn't* become a televangelist?"

"Well, seein' as how ah was the only payunts-wearin' kid in th' famly, ah had to be a mayun an' tayuk over th' rayuns on th' fam'ly bizness. My Pop shore do preshate mah personal sacrifahce. But hayul, this is the good lahf. Ah kayent compline."

"So you have sisters, or are you an only child?"

"Shucks, missy! Only chalds are fer Chinamin. Ah've got mahself fahv sisters."

"Five! Wow. What do they do?"

"Wayul, they shore do lahk t'go shoppin'. An they've got themselves some prahz roses, yayus they do. Sigh, Miss Aviva, cayun ah treatcha to a fancy dinner tonaht? I'd shorely lahk t' show ya a little Tegzin hospitaliteh."

An appalling thought occurred to me: this man with the repulsive accent, this man who could not be more different from me than if he'd come from another planet (and I'm not talking just Mars vs. Venus here), this man I couldn't stand for one more minute...was a man. A presumably fully-functioning, sexually mature adult male human being, of an appropriate age. Which meant...he could be Number Three. Torturous as it would be to listen to that accent much longer, nevertheless he actually wasn't bad-looking, he filled out his "jayns" nicely, and he was no serial killer (unless you counted bovines). The sex might even be okay if I could just get him to shut up.

"Thanks, Justy. I'd love to go to dinner tonight."

k

Justy picked me up at my hotel in a cab, which took us to an Indian restaurant, as I'd requested.

He said, "Wayul now, you clayn up ril good, Miss Aviva. Ah shore do wish ah had mah motorcycle here in Austin. Then ah could rilly show ya a good tahm. You kin probly gayess, ah never wayur a helmet. Ts'fer sissies. Anyway, 'f'nit comes mah tahm, then the Good Lord kin jus' call me on up ta that big ol' corral in the skah."

It was going to be a long night.

The driver had brought us to an almost empty place called the Taj Mahal (I read somewhere that there's an Indian restaurant called Taj Mahal in every medium-sized or larger city of the world). I asked for the *palak paneer*, spicy; and the cowboy told the meek waiter that he wanted a "sta-yuk, rayer, biggest one ya'll got." The waiter was so horrified he couldn't speak for a moment. Then he managed to squeak out, "Sir, I am sorry, so wery sorry, sir, this is being one hundred percent only, wegetarian restaurant, sir." Justy looked bewildered. The waiter said, "I am giving you few more minutes to decide, sir." He withdrew, visibly shaken.

I hissed at Justy, "Hey, you know, I think cows are *sacred* to these people. You can't *eat* one—can you imagine how offensive that would be?"

"Hayul, cows are saycred ta me, too! They're mah lahvlihood. Haw

haw!" Justy replied, slapping his knee. "What was that wayter tryin' ta tell me, anyhow? Ah cayn't make heads or tayuls a that thick accent. Why'ont these people learn ta speak Amerkun?"

"It's a vegetarian place. No meat."

His blue eyes got big. "Wul ahlbedayumd! No mayt! How kin ya call it a mayul, if there's no mayt?!"

"Jeez, keep it down. You'll just have to order something else... what else do you like? ...There's eggplant, potatoes. *Dal*—that's lentil stew..."

"Yer th' doll, little lady! But them *vegables* not a *mayul*, them's jus' th' *fixins*. Ah guess ah'm 'bout as bad off as a rubber-nosed woodpecker in a petrified forest. What're we gonna ayt, if there's no bayf?"

"*I'm* a vegetarian."

"Well'n, I guess yer happier n' a rooster in a hen house. Plenny a vegables hayur."

"Can you just decide on something? The waiter'll be back in a second."

The waiter did, indeed, choose that moment to come back, a wary look on his face as he approached the Stetson. I guess these Texan types never take their hat off. What about in bed? Do they keep the hat *and* the boots on? Actually, that image, strangely enough, got me kind of excited. A man wearing nothing but the hat, the cowboy boots, and a big erection... Oooh. I decided I'd have to keep thinking about that.

"Sir? You have decided now, sir?"

"Ah'll tayuk the...the lennil stew. An' some tayters." Justy gave a sigh that spoke of great deprivation.

"Wery good, sir, just one moment it is taking, please." The waiter backed away submissively.

Justy leaned across the table toward me. I thought he was about to whisper some flirty endearment. Instead he said, "That mayun shore has got himself a big nose. Look like he got whupped with th' ugly stick! Now look hayur, missy. The Lord Gawd gave mayun dominion over all livin' thangs, here on Gawd's grayn earth. So that mayns we're meant ta ayt 'em. An' if that ain't in th' Bahble, wha, ah'll eat mah churt."

By now I was too food-deprived to try to argue. He continued, "'Sides, little lady, ah need mah red mayt ever' day, cuz ah'm a *mayun*." He winked again and leered at me. I pictured him: hat, boots, erection. Hat, boots, erection. This would get me through dinner.

He relaxed about the lack of animal flesh available for consumption once he got a couple of Kingfishers in him. "Ya know, Miss Aviva, ah come from a *drah* county. So drah the trees are bribin' th' dawgs."

Okay, I *almost* laughed at that one.

When the bill came, he grabbed it and said, "Now, don'tcha go worryin' yer purty little head 'bout any a this," and picked out one gold card at random from the immense stack of them I could see in his wallet, glowing in the candlelight.

I'd been waiting to use one of the Texan phrases I'd looked up on the Internet in my hotel room to impress him with. Now was the perfect time. I said, "Thanks... You know, I'm so broke, I can't pay attention."

He stared at me for a second, then burst out laughing. "Wha, missy, yer quicker n' a duck on a June bug!"

å

Tex was all too happy to comply with my request to see him in just the very top and bottom cowboy accoutrements. I surveyed him critically, then asked him to also put on his belt, with the big, shiny silver buckle. It was a strange, yet amazingly erotic look. He had one of those wonderful, big, long, sturdy erections ("big as Texas"?), that was so hard it even curved upwards—the undauntable kind.

Tex grabbed his doffed "churt" and starting swinging it around his head, lasso-style. "Let's go, honeh! Off mah butt an' on mah feet, outta the shade an' inna the heat!" He then proceeded to produce from his "churt" pocket one of those Maxx condoms—you know, the extra-large kind. He waggled his eyebrows and opened his mouth to blab some more.

Need you ask? I gagged him with his own "churt," which got him even more excited—he thought I was into S&M; in reality it was just so he wouldn't talk. I figured, what the hell, he could still *grunt* if he needed to.

Then I rode him. At one point he motioned that he wanted the gag out; I took part of it from his mouth to hear what he wanted to say. "Honeh girlie, this ain't mah *first* rodeo! Oooo-weee!" He grabbed my hair, got stuck in some of the tangled curls, and laughed. "Looks like a cat's been suckin' on it!"

"Jesus!" I gasped, and came.

"Now don'tcha be takin' the Lord's name in vine, missy... Oh my Gawd, does that feel good... Oh, Gawd, Gawd, *yay*-us...!" I stuffed the shirt back in.

At the last moment, he got so excited he tore the gag from his own mouth and shouted, "Rahd 'em cowgirl! Yeeeeeee-haaaaaawwwwww!"

U

Toward the end of reading the paper I was presenting at the Semantics conference (my talk was titled *Is Tony A Twin?: A New Look at the Tiger's Stripes in Possible Worlds Theory*), I suddenly, unwittingly, got a mental picture of The Cowboy as he was getting ready to leave my hotel room.

I actually laughed out loud, then had to quickly squelch it, since I noticed that the escaped giggle had caught the attention of most of the two hundred attendees who'd all been drowsing off. (Most professors go to conferences for two reasons—to sleep around, and to catch up on their sleep.) They all jerked up their nodding heads and glared at me—how dare I laugh? This was, after all, serious business.

Tex had been moving a bit strangely as he went about picking up his clothes (the ones that he wasn't wearing, that is—although the belt had had to go pretty early on; too uncomfortable against my tender flesh), almost limping. "Is something the matter?" I'd asked, sprawled comfortably, limply, and very nakedly (for some reason I'm never self-conscious immediately after sex), across the king-size bed.

"Now, missy, ah'll be allraht. Little lady, you are a wahldcat! No, ah'll be fahn... Ya'll just gave me a little hitch in mah gitalong."

ŕ

What a relief to be back in Boulder. I decided to walk to the gym; it was a beautiful day out.

Crossing Ninth Street, I narrowly missed being hit out of nowhere by the kamikaze rollerblading guy who always comes zooming suicidally all the way down from Chautauqua Park (*avec* ski poles and *sans* helmet). As I approached the Pearl Street Mall, the Buddhist in the saffron robes who always walks all over town monotonously beating a drum passed me, doing his thing. He doesn't have the kind of expression on his face where you could ask him why he does this. The Mall was starting to take on that summertime look: lots of flowers, lots of mediocre singers with their guitar cases hopefully open, and tons of tourists.

I thought about the irony portion I'd be teaching in the Semantics of Humor class. I already had a few notes, including a local newspaper article about the recent university student riots at the beginning of the semester: "...it is understandable when the students riot during midterms." Another was from my last trip to Safeway, where they had these big signs up all over the place announcing that "for *our customers'* convenience," they'd installed "safety devices" on their shopping carts, which prevent the carts from being removed from the Safeway parking lot. So many of the excellent examples of irony to be found in this country exist purely due to litigation fears—for example, there's my new vacuum cleaner, which came in twenty little parts in a box and whose instruction sheet admonished: "Caution: Assemble vacuum cleaner before using." Then there were a couple of wonderful little facts I'd recently discovered: that it costs money to declare bankruptcy; and that I don't make *enough* money to qualify for low-income housing in Boulder. Then there was this pill I was supposed to take for a couple of days when I had a bladder infection. Supposedly it would turn your urine orange, which was nothing to worry about. On the information sheet, it said, "Do not be alarmed if your urine turns orange, unless you have not taken the drug which turns your urine orange."

I walked by the hip-hop clothing place, seemingly out of place here, yet very popular because of all the highschoolers. I recalled the time Therese and I had gone into the place, intending to buy her then-current boyfriend some snowboarder pants for his birthday because he was starting to get really interested in the sport (in spite of being much too old and constantly and loudly jeered at: "Hey, dudes, check out the *poser!*"). Therese and I had gone in and started looking around, feeling incredibly out of our element. The gangly, pimply, sullen teenager who was "working" there ignored us until finally Therese had to go right up to him and say, "*Excuse* me. We'd like some *assistance* here?"

He reluctantly drawled out, "Yeeeeah?" Like, do I *have* to?

She explained that we were looking for snowboarder pants for her boyfriend. He looked her full in the face then, took an estimate of her age, and actually smirked. Teenagers—I hate 'em. If I ever have a kid I'm going to have to send it away between the ages of ten and twenty-five.

He led us to the appropriate rack, all pants so large, they had to measure about 50" x 30". They appeared to be made for giants. Therese and I started giggling, imagining Wendell looking such the *poser* in his genuine pants. Therese grabbed a pair and held it up against her body.

"I don't understand," she said. "What holds them up? The waists are so *huge*. I know that's the style, but..."

Our assistant didn't interpret it as a rhetorical question, the way I had. He answered her, mumbling: "I dunno. I guess, like, you know, yer *unit* holds it up."

I saw an acquaintance of mine, Dave, on a bench outside the Bookend Café, sipping an iced latte and looking cool and collected as always. Dave is someone whose vibe I've never quite figured out—is he gay or bi or straight? Or some combination of those? Or none of the above? He has an odd demeanor, where you can never tell if he's flirting or merely talking normally; if he's listening to what you're saying, or doesn't give a shit. He must be from California, he's so odd.

"Oh, hi, Aviva. How are you?"

"Hey, Dave. What are you up to these days?"

"Well, actually, I've been really busy with some new designs."

"Oh, for your skateboards?"

"No, actually, it's for furniture. But *unusual* furniture."

"Oh, really? Like what?"

"Well..." he paused. "Kind of *lovemaking* furniture."

"Say what?!"

"Furniture for enhancing the sexual pleasure of both partners. Like... fuckiture! You know how when you're having sex, and you just every now and then by chance suddenly hit that sweet spot..."

I nodded, not trusting my voice in that moment—I think it would've come out all squeaky. I was picturing Dave on his sex furniture. It was quite a nice image. Dave has this amazing body. He's a bit short for my tastes, and he's losing his hair, but he has the most sexy body, really well-built, muscular, with a perfect butt and a very nice, very large bulge that I've sneaked looks at when I've seen him out performing in tights around town on his various skateboards. (I have no idea if this guy has a real job or is just another Boulder Trustafarian, or what.) Dave suddenly said, "You know, I could use a research assistant."

I was startled. My god, now that I've started this, the men, like weevils, are just coming out of the woodwork.

"Well, when you get your prototype built, let me know and I'll...ah, take a look at your sex furniture."

"I have to think of a better name for it, though. Sex Furniture just sounds too *raw*...it makes me wince, actually, to hear you say it. Maybe Sensual Support? No, that sounds like a jock strap, doesn't it? Let's see...Erotic Consoles? Dirty Divans? Paramour Platforms?"

"Enough with the alliteration already."

"Well, if you think of any good names in the meantime, let me know, will you?" Then he looked past me and began studying a tree trunk with great interest.

At the gym, I checked the sub board to make sure Fury was teaching. Fury's the *best*. Okay, she's a bit of a freak, but in the greatest way.

I changed clothes, then went into one of the stalls to pee. I could hear a couple of college-age girls in the locker room, chatting loudly. Girl #1 said, "Hey, Jen! What are *you* here for?!"

Girl #2: "Oh, I just came by to do some weights, and maybe do the kickboxing class later!"

Girl #1: "Oh, *fun*! That sounds *fun*!"

Girl #2: "Yeah, it *is*! It's *so* fun! Have you taken the kickboxing here?"

Girl #1: "No, but it sounds *fun*!"

Girl #2: "Yeah! So, what are *you* doing? The kickboxing, too?!"

Girl #1: "No, I'm doing *NIA*! It's *fun*! *You* should do it, too!"

Girl #2: "That's okay, I'm kind of in the mood for kickboxing. I'd like to *try* NIA, though! I've heard it's really *fun*!"

Girl #1: "Yeah, it *is*! You know what, we should get Michelle and Dawn in here sometime and all do NIA *together*! Wouldn't that be *fun*?!"

I was about to gag. (Luckily, I was in the right place to do it.) I flushed the toilet, hoping it would drown them out at least until I could get by them and escape. As always, I wondered: was this merely the product of the terrible public school education in this country plus MTV, or was there something even *more* insidious going on?

Fortunately, as usual, NIA with Fury made me forget all my woes and petty irritations, allowing me to feel that the entire universe was inside me and that I was one with it—like really good sex. It's about the only time I can *almost* become one of the club of Boulder Bliss Ninnies. And since you do NIA in semi-darkness, it also allows you the illusion of feeling slinky and sinuous, swanky and svelte. Fury comes up with the most original shit, unlike those Aerobics Playboy Bunnies who yell out "inspirational" stuff like: "Get those knees up! All right! Yeah!"

Fury screams out things as the spirit moves her. Sometimes she'll just be so into the music, she'll start wailing, or hooting and shrieking, like a cage full of monkeys, or she'll start roaring like a lioness. And she's very stream-of-consciousness. "Okay, feel the basket... Feel it...you're lifting it now but uh-oh! it's just become a basket of snakes instead... Indeed... Heh heh heh!... And now you're going to put those snakes on the very top shelf of the cosmos, so if it turns back into laundry you can forget about it forever... Heh heh heh!" She's got this hilarious raucous laugh, deep and spontaneous, and everything she says and does is absolutely genuine. We have to form a big circle at the end of class, raising our arms to the center, while Fury gravely intones, "Look around you, folks: This is your

Neo-Tribe du jour."

NIA is a bit unexplainable to those who've never seen or tried it. It's a combination of aerobics, modern dance, jazz dance, hiphop, African, tai chi and yoga; all done to the funkiest New-Agey technobizarro stuff that Fury can dig up. And Fury is the most badass chick I've ever met, for a white girl. Rumor has it she used to be a heavy metal singer. Another rumor has her being a former porn star. One thing is clear: she's not going to stop partying until she's in her grave. Which I really doubt she's worrying about digging.

þ

One of my many pieces of junk snail-mail today has reminded me that I need to start making some notes for another course I'll be teaching soon, An Exploration of Nomenclature. I still crack up every time I receive mail addressed this way, to Mr. L. O'Porch. One time, I had been expecting a package, and knew I wouldn't be home when it was delivered. I'd called the company and asked them to put into my computer record that they should leave it on the porch if no one was home. About two weeks later, a new individual, Mister Leave O'Porch, began receiving mail at my address. Can I claim this guy on my next tax return?

I collect examples of real people's names that I can't believe are real. Just a few, from this year alone, are: Carl Crumbpacker, Griselda Manicotti, Gary Schmuck, Ding Ling, Prunella Scales, Tiffany Tin-Tin Talley, Candida Pappasmeer, Duane Peckerhed, Lemon Ales, Smiley Pool, Dr. Paulette Le Tarte, Ree Strange Sheck, Linda Lindamood, Slinky Pincus, Trip Coffin, Gireesh Sebastian Bembalkar, Malte von Schlippenbach, Helmut von Lippenschmacken, and Ginger Snap.

And you have to wonder about the ol' chicken-or-egg thing: I've read a novel by Francine Prose. My childhood doctor, a surgeon, bore the unlikely surname Swords. Out there are flycasters called Fisher, pastry chefs with the family name Baker, hikers called Walker, tailors who are Schneiders, and gynecologists named Dr. Bush.

6

Finally, Sunday. It was a great day, a bit hot as all Boulder summers are, but otherwise perfect. I felt really good, energetic, healthy...horny. Steven was due to arrive in a few minutes to pick up me and my bike. I was slightly hungry, but low on groceries. I foraged and found a very odd snack, a combination of the sublime and the prosaic (and what would be a severe temptation for those on the Boulder no-wheat, no-dairy diet): a bit of smelly (merely "ripe," to the French) very old Brie, and the dregs of a bag of Chex Mix, which at this point was mostly just crumbs and a lot of salt. Chex Mix is one of those foods you're really embarrassed to truly relish, like Sloppy Joes or Green Bean Casserole made with Cream of Mushroom Soup Mix, and is the kind of item I would never admit to actually purchasing, let alone consuming (hey, we can't really all eat *kale* every day).

Well, maybe with this much salt I wouldn't have to stop and pee as often as I usually do. Seriously, I have to pee more often than, like, *anyone*. I've even been to a couple of doctors about it. The first one, a man, took a verbal history, then proclaimed emotionlessly: "You have a bladder the size of a garbanzo, what can I say?" The second doctor was a woman. Also without examining me or seeming the least bit concerned about my problem, she said, equally nonchalant: "Welcome to being female in Colorado."

It's so arid here that you have to rehydrate constantly, leading to the phenomenon of virtually everyone carrying around a water bottle at all times. In fact, once when I was traveling in Israel, a New Yorker who used to date a Boulderite studied my habit for half a day, then said: "Let me guess—you're from Boulder, Colorado." In my case, it seems that it's the combination of the constant water-drinking with having a bladder the size of a Spanish legume, that's so deadly.

Half an hour later, Steven and I had gone up the canyon and were donning our helmets. (Now here's a confession of great stupidity: I never wear a helmet *except* when mountain biking, which I do only maybe once a summer—in spite of having been hit in town by two cars and a van [that's three separate incidents, not one spectacular pile-up] while riding with no helmet.) For a week, I'd been looking forward to seeing Steven in the *de rigueur* skin-tight Spandex bike shorts—but damn him, he'd showed up wearing those super-baggy nylon kind that look like the damnably ever-popular swim trunks. I watched Steven put his helmet on, thinking if only he knew French, it would be a great opportunity to make a joke: that he couldn't be from a wealthy family. In French, you're not born "with a silver spoon in your mouth," you're born "with your hair already styled."

"Race you to the top!"

"Oh yeah?" I asked. "And what do I get if I win?"

"Umm… If you win, I'll…um…tell you what the bet was about between me and my dad!" He hopped on his bike and started pedaling uphill.

"Wait!" I cried. He stopped, rolled gently backwards. "What if *you* win?" I asked him.

"If *I* win…um…I get a kiss from you." Oh my god. This guy was *so* adorable.

"Wait a second!" I realized. "That gives me no incentive at all to win."

"Unless you still want to know what my bet was!" he answered, and took off again, with me screaming at him no fair, he had a head start. Then I realized I had to pee. Damn. If I were to have any chance at all to catch up, I'd have to go *really* fast. Since there was no one around and no other cars here at the parking area, and Steven had already disappeared from view, I quickly made the decision—peeled down my bike shorts halfway, and just squatted right there. It always takes a while to get started out in the open. You have to try to fool your mind into believing that you're not hanging out with your naked ass in the wind and your vision focused carefully between your shoes, but rather that you're comfy as can be on your own toilet at home, your four familiar walls around you.

Just as I finally achieved flow, Steven came zooming back around the corner, shouting, "Hey, Aviva! What the hell happened to—*Oh*." He kindly did a one-eighty. How humiliating. Now I was going to have to start our race mortified, as well as with the handicap of his head start. He was waiting for me around the bend. I glanced at him and realized we were both blushing. Jeez, what a pair. "Okay!" he said. "You ready? We're starting...*now*!"

It was a good race. Each of us kept the lead for a little while, got tired, fell back, then had to work like crazy to catch up again. After about forty minutes' hard riding, I took advantage of Steven's momentary lead to stop again; my bladder definitely wasn't going to make it the rest of the way. We hadn't seen a single other person—very unusual for a weekend—so I squatted right where I was, next to the trail. I thought again, *Okay, the door's closed...*

I heard a high-pitched trilling sound in the distance and wondered what kind of bird it was. About ten seconds later, I had finally started peeing when, *whoosh!*, "Hi there!," this guy greeted me very peppily from atop his bike. He'd come zooming down the trail, *right next to me*—close enough that my urine probably splattered onto his tires. I heard the bird sound again. As he passed me, he whipped out a cell phone from god-knows-where, and the avian noise ceased. While still navigating perfectly down the treacherous rocky trail one-handed, he said into the phone, "How many shares?," then disappeared.

Oh well. I guess you can't really *see* anything, right? I was red from embarrassment as well as the exertion of having to pedal harder than ever to catch up. All of a sudden, I spotted Steven up ahead, standing on the side of the trail, his back to me—*Hah!*—in that unmistakable posture: legs planted sturdily, a little wider apart than normal, right arm bent at a certain angle, head tilted down just so, standing precisely in front of a tree. Why do men always have to pee *at* something?

Unfortunately, although I tried very hard, I saw nothing.

I reached the end of the trail about two seconds before he did. I couldn't help but gloat. Both of us panting hard, we collapsed against some rocks and gradually caught our breath.

"Okay," I told him. "Now you're gonna tell me what your bet was about."

"No."

"*No?!* But you promised!"

"Later..." he said, taking my face in his lovely big young hand and gently turning my head to a kissing angle. Mmm...

Just when things were getting really interesting, and amidst his nylon bagginess I was detecting something *très joli*, a few accursed cyclists showed up and started unloading picnic stuff. We got back on our bikes and started carefully back down the trail, which is harder than it sounds, since there are giant rocks and tree roots everywhere; mountain biking downhill can actually be technical. Uphill is often just plain hard—on the thighs, back, lungs.

In my rock-riding vibrato, I asked him—shouted at him—to tell me now what the bet was about.

"Okay. So, like, you already know I lost this bet with my dad, and what he wanted for winning was for me to, like, shave my head, right? The thing is, once I did it, I actually kind of liked it, so I kept shaving it."

"Uh-huh," I said. "But what was the bet *about*?"

"Our dumps."

"Ex*cuse* me?"

"You know, our...bowel movements. Our shit."

"Your *literal* shit."

"Right. So my dad is always, like, bragging about his dumps, okay? Like, how big they are, or how long, or what color..."

Oh my god, how unbelievably fucking gross. "Uh-huh..." I said reluctantly.

"So I bet him that he couldn't control what his dumps would look like. Like, I bet him he couldn't make his next dump look *exactly* like brownie batter, you know, all dark and gooey..."

Aaaaaaaaaagggghhhh! Part of my brain could hear Steven ahead of me continuing, "...so he ate, I don't know, like forty prunes and watercress soup and a bag of Fig Newtons and half a pan of actual brownies—which *I* think was cheating...," while the rest of my brain was recording the fact that I was now, quite suddenly, upside down, still attached to my bike, just about to complete, in fact, a perfect slow-motion endo. How had this new perspective come into being? I think it may have had something to do with a rock my front tire had hit wrong, but I couldn't tell you for sure. (Though I'd lay bets it was more interestingly choreographed than even this New York show I saw advertised in a photograph, *The Flight of the Lawnchair Man*.)

Pain. Pain. I knew only pain. And tried really hard not to think about what brownie batter looked like, as Steven gently walked me and both our bikes down to the car, saying extremely comforting things like, "Remember, suffering is all in your mind."

An hour later, my ankle swollen up huge and purple, my road rashes making themselves known (a hot shower was going to *kill* me for the next week), and Steven holding my hand, telling me about other interesting bets he and his dad had made in the past, we sat in the emergency room waiting for my X-ray results.

A Hispanic family entered through the automatic doors. At first I couldn't see anything wrong with them (when you're in the emergency room as a patient, you immediately start assessing everyone who comes in the door to see if they're better or worse off than you: amateur triage), then I noticed one of the little boys holding a baggie full of blood over his foot like it was a slipper sock. Strangely, however, he wasn't even crying; in fact, he seemed to find the plastic bag on his foot hilarious and his mother and older sisters were having a hard time restraining him from using it as a fun new kind of roller-skate. Guess *he'd* mastered the mind-over-matter thing.

i

Three hours later, Steven was being extremely sweet, puttering around in my apartment—getting me ice wrapped in a towel for my sprained ankle, aloe gel for road rash, ibuprofen for general aches, and crackers and peanut butter for my crying stomach. He rummaged through my cupboards.

"Let's see, what kind of tea do you want? You have chamomile,"—this incited in me an instantaneous gag reflex—"Raspberry Zinger, SereniTea… Hey, that'd probably be good for you right now, huh? Calm you down?"

"You want some too?" There's this great series: I think they have TranquiliTea, ElectriciTea, ImmuniTea, Mental ClariTea…

"Do they have MasculiniTea?" Steven asked.

"Why, do you need some?"

"Well, seeing as how there's a FemininiTea…"

"Why don't you get on their website and look it up?" I said. I've always thought these tea people ought to get really radical, and put out some truly useful ones, like how about InvisibiliTea, or PariTea. For genetic engineers, HerediTea; for lawyers, LiabiliTea. And, for certain inflexible cultures, VirginiTea.

"Do they have a website?" he asked.

"Who *doesn't* have a website?" It's like, Where in Boulder *isn't* there a Kokopelli?

"Hey, cool, you're doing, like, Yinglish!" He stared at me, impressed.

"What do you mean?" I asked, irritated at the work content that was suddenly intruding.

"You just did it again!"

"Did what?"

"And again! Wow! Totally rad! You know, like, answering a question with a question."

"I've been doing that?"

He sat beside me on the bed, looked at my ankle—"Trippy colors, yo!"—and started stroking my bare knee. In spite of my injuries, I was turned on. Or maybe it was some kind of instinctive survival reaction kicking in, where anything that isn't dolorous suddenly starts feeling unusually fantastic.

Amidst yelps (of both pain and pleasure), we made careful love. We knocked over both cups of tea in the process (scaring Baby momentarily, but I remember her lapping up SereniTea later—not that cats need that, sleeping eighteen hours a day), and I'm pretty sure we made my ankle a lot worse than it already was, but what the hell.

Oh, and the bald thing? *Yesssss!*

h

In class, trying to avoid looking directly at Steven. The students have already asked about my taped-up ankle. I am totally cool in their eyes (well, as cool as a thirty-five year old prof can be) by pseudo-casually tossing off: "Oh, just a little mountain biking mishap."

We're dissecting the humor in the newspaper headline "Elk wasn't friendly to everyone in town, woman claims." Steven exists only in my peripheral vision. I read that there's an eye disorder in which a person has no peripheral vision. That would be really strange. I wonder if those people get surprised a lot by cockroaches—that's the kind of thing you always suddenly see moving, but only in your peripheral vision. Which is another great reason to live here: there are virtually no cockroaches in Boulder (other than, strangely, in the building of my Department).

Today I introduce an interesting regional phenomenon: that the humor in the Midwestern United States, in general, seems to be lagging about five to twenty years behind. What the rest of the country has long considered passé is still touted there as fresh, novel humor. I'm going to assign my students to research this, because I personally find it really intriguing. (Then, of course, I'll be able to use their results to write up a monograph and publish it under my name.) Some of the examples I've collected for class come from shiny new bumper stickers spotted within the last year on Midwestern-licensed cars: *My kitty is purr-fect!*; *I'd rather be fishing!*; *My other car is a Porsche*; *Don't Like My Driving? Call 1-800-EAT-SHIT*; *If you drive too close I'll flick a booger on your windshield*; and on a canvas tote bag (a very Midwestern-style item), *Teaching Is My Bag!*

As assigned for today—a discussion on Humor—a couple of the students had found some nice items in newspapers (News of the Weird and tabloids are, of course, forbidden): "Cop thought was gun; mistakenly shot man holding four-inch tube of mints;" and a front-page AP news item, complete with picture—a doctor commenting on George W. Bush's infected boil: "We're not certain what caused it, maybe an ingrown hair," she said, adding that "it's not a pleasing sight. It's a large bump."

I often marvel at how desperate for material newswriters must be, to have to use a quarter of the front page for "Woman goes to Kensington Park to place rose on local shrine to Princess Di." Is there *really* nothing more interesting going on anywhere around the globe? (And that woman in Kensington Park needs to get a life.)

A student reads the local newspaper clipping she'd brought in. It's about one of the seemingly constant EcoPass (local bus pass and merchant discounts) votes, and the Boulder City Clerk is quoted: "It's been difficult. We had a group hug when we came in this morning."

Everyone laughs, then the guy in front of her brings out his item: that the editor of a supermarket tabloid was hoping to get the unethical charges that had been brought against him (for bribery and extortion) dropped, in exchange for his donating one hundred thousand dollars to the university's Ethics Department. I realize it's going to be very difficult to tease apart the Irony section of the course from the rest of it.

We were almost out of time. There was one example of humor that was proving very difficult to analyze, and I decided to assign it as extra credit. It was an overheard remark in the Safeway aisle: "See, there *is* such thing as Juicy Juice!"

Only two minutes till the bell. "Remember," I told the students in an imperious voice, "your assignments will not be accepted unless they're typed."

"Yo, nice use of the passive voice, *teacher*..." drawled a guy in back.

I attempted to wrest back my pitiful little authority. "Typed! Or else!"

"You mean, like, *keyboarded*, don't you?" asked one of the younger members of the class.

"Yeah," one of the girls told him, "that's what she means. You know, she comes from that era when they still had, like, *typewriters*."

Another girl broke in with: "Well, I get all my retro accessories at Urban Outfitters? They have the coolest clocks with, like, *faces* on them? and, like, record players?—is that what they were called?—and those *dial* phones!" She was squealing with excitement.

Yet another student joined in: "Hey you guys, I have this, like, old Mac that was like, one of the first *computers*."

There was a chorus of "Dude!" and a host of other expressions that apparently expressed admiration, but which I stopped trying to learn sometime after the term "song remake" was changed to "cover;" "previews" was changed to the illogical "trailers;" and after the birth and death of "phat."

Thank god for the bell.

Steven made sure he was the last to leave. "Hope your ankle gets better soon," he said with a wink, and slipped out the door. Hmm…no longer blushing, I noticed.

Neither one of us.

9

It was late June; I'd done four guys in two months. I needed to get my ass in gear, so to speak; only four guys under my belt (sorry) meant twenty-six left. I had ten months, so that meant…2.6 guys per month to meet the challenge. I wondered, if each month I found one normal guy plus one guy with a huge dick, would that count as 2.6 guys? Tee hee.

Such were my thoughts while doing my Nautilus circuit at the gym. There seem to be only two types of hetero guys that do weights: the ones that look like they just got out of prison (frequently true), with crewcuts or shaved heads (nice memories of Steven, though), tattoos all over, and huge, disproportionate muscles that grossly inhibit their body movements. Most of these guys are really short. There must be a mathematical law that states that the more vertically challenged an American male is, the more he will try to compensate by growing horizontally (his muscles, I mean). Apparently, no one has ever broken the news to these guys that all that weightlifting will never make them any taller. Brandon, who was 6'5" (and wonderfully endowed—he wore a size fifteen shoe and was the only white guy on his basketball team every season), didn't care a bit about weightlifting, and claimed that guys who were spending that much time developing enormous muscles all had a small-penis complex.

The other kind are these really skinny little accountant-type guys with the stick bird-legs, sweating and straining at the machines with nary an apparent effect. You have to wonder if there's actually something wrong with them, some disease that eats muscle, because they look really pathetic—they have even less muscle mass than I do, and I only started doing a few weights a couple of months ago (in a probably hopeless attempt to fight gravity in the, ahem, chest area—I know you can strengthen the pec muscles but there's nothing you can *really* do for saggy boobs. But I'll keep trying).

Men still consider the weight room their exclusive arena. They tell the counter person to change the music to hard rock (I'm sure *that* choice can't be attributed to wishful thinking) without consulting with any of the women in the room. They hog the machines—when you go to use one that's sitting empty, a guy will suddenly jump in front of you and go, "Uh, duh, uh, I've got four more sets to go on that." And they're always in the midst of a grunting contest; whoever grunts the loudest and grossest (probably even better if they simultaneously fart, too), wins—I guess. They have these inane conversations about reps, which consist entirely of numbers, bragging, and comments like "Dude—it's *all* good."

I have a blind date set up for tonight, a friend-of-a-friend-of-a-friend thing. Supposedly he's a writer, which is really cool, so I'm assuming he's a sensitive, introspective kind of guy. My contact said he's really fit, with a great body, too (but who cares about that?).

When I told Therese about it, she'd warned me, "Ave, just one word of advice: if he writes fiction and his protagonists are serial killers, just cut off the date *right then* and go home! Okay? Swear! You haven't given this guy your phone number or your last name, have you?"

I am, if nothing else, an experienced dater. Of course I hadn't.

W

Over *momos, dal bath*, tamarind sauce, *rakshi*, and other Nepalese delicacies (we met at the restaurant, my choice), I tried to keep up a pretense of interest in Bob the writer and, it turned out, hanggliding instructor. Intriguing professions, although my rendezvous arranger had conveniently neglected to mention that he was only 5'5". In my 1" heels, I was taller than he was. Another egregious omission on her part turned out to be that he was one of those divorcés who has to bitterly mention his ex every five minutes and how unfair the settlement had been in her favor. I decided that books were the only mutual interest we might have, so I asked him what he wrote. He stared at me very strangely and intently, and finally said, "I need to tell you something."

"Okay."

"About a year ago, I was in a terrible hanggliding accident. It was my fault, I admit... I know now that I must've gauged the wind wrong that day. The only thing I can remember anymore is leaving the cliff and beginning my glide... Then waking up in the hospital." He looked at me, waiting for a reaction.

"Um-hm." I checked my fingernails: no, I could wait a day or two more before filing.

"*Well*," he continued, obviously dissatisfied by my reaction, "when I woke up in the hospital, it was *three months later* than it had been when I jumped off that cliff."

"Oh, what were you, in a coma?" I asked him, simultaneously as he triumphantly exclaimed, "I was in a coma!"

He looked quite upset that I had spoiled his punch line.

"Aviva," he confided in me, leaning across the spinach fritters, "I had to relearn how to walk, talk, tie my shoelaces—everything. There are still some parts of my previous life I don't remember. I may never recall them, the docs say. But that's okay, because I'm enjoying life now. I'm dating a lot (wink)… But only women who don't remind me of my ex (frown)… And I've got the ol' hanggliding business back up and running—"

"Isn't the fact that you, as the instructor, had such a bad accident, kind of, oh, I don't know, *off-putting* for business?"

He glared at me.

"*So*," he continued pointedly, "I'm really learning how to, you know, *live* all over again. Other men can say they feel like a new man, but there's not many of 'em it's true for! Ha ha ha!"

"So, anyway…" I said, "*What* kind of writing did you say you did?"

He stopped chuckling. "Well, see, here's the *really* amazing part. After I learned how to read and write again and all that, I logged on to my computer, which of course I hadn't done for about six months, by then. And I was looking at everything, my files, folders, having to relearn how all that stuff worked, too. Then one day I noticed this huge file on my hard drive. Turned out it was a novel I'd written, that I'd finished the day before the accident."

"My god, that *is* amazing!" Now he actually did have my attention. "So, I assume it all came back to you when you saw it?"

"Nope," he said proudly. "I still don't remember writing a single word of it. None of the characters even seemed familiar, or anything. I read it, though, and I thought it was pretty damn good. Publisher thought so too. It's coming out in hardcover next month." He beamed, waiting for my approval.

"So what's it about?" I asked.

He got excited. "Okay, see, the main character is this murderer who…"

Merde! I'd just realized that, at the beginning of dinner, when we'd been going through the discussion of the origins of my name, I'd mentioned my last name.

I was doomed!
And Therese would kill me too.

õ

I *guess* he counted.

Ol' Bob the formerly-in-a-coma-soon-to-be-bestselling-thriller-writer had seemed a bit, shall we say…bobbed. That was the teeniest dick I've ever seen on an adult male. You'd think he'd have noticed something was amiss by now—what about all the crestfallen visages of previous potential paramours? Or how about the fact that a (normal-sized, never mind Tex's Maxxes) condom end hung a few inches beyond what one would expect from merely the reservoir tip. Oh, it was *hard* enough—but it was like this tiny nubbin, poking hopefully out only a couple of inches into space.

I did end up sleeping with him—partly because of the bet and partly because I was curious to know if I could even *feel* that thing; I guess I hoped it would at least hit my G-spot. The weird thing was, he seemed to get the most inordinate amount of pleasure out of it. Maybe it functioned sort of like a clitoris—the smaller, the more concentrated the sensation.

I think that while Bob was lying in a coma, forgetting how to walk and talk and attempting to forget how much he hated his ex-wife, he forgot how to please a woman, too. Or maybe he just never knew in the first place. It was quite a disappointing experience, all things considered. If I were Bob, I'd just go sign myself up for a sex-change operation to complete his current trend.

He'll have enough money soon thanks to having sold that novel.

R

I have a Fourth of July date with this gorgeous doctor I met at a Third of July party. His name is Eli, and he's Jewish, and he has one of those lovely hawk noses and bewitching green eyes, and he's tall and slender and has beautiful, delicate long fingers, and he's gorgeous…did I mention that?

We meet at the bottom of Chautauqua Park. He's remembered a blanket, the sweetie. He looks awesome in his linen shorts and polo shirt. He seems…what's that archaic and ridiculous word? *Cocksure*, that's it. I have on one of my flirtiest outfits, a tank top (with built-in support, of course) and a little flippy skirt that I live in all summer. A colleague in the Spanish Department told me this is called a *falda de vuelo*: a flying skirt.

There is *major* chemistry going on between Eli and me. I'd felt it the moment I'd seen him at the party, and he told me the same thing when he boldly came over and asked me to go with him the next day to the fireworks. Now, why is this man not taken? There must be some fatal flaw I'm not yet aware of. I hate to be so cynical, but I know it must be true—either that, or I've somehow wandered into a parallel universe—a "possible world" where the sort of stuff that should happen, actually does.

We hold hands—pure electricity—as dusk comes upon the hill, crowded with families and groups of punks (you can already smell thick clouds of marijuana, despite scattered police presence), and, here and there, lovers cuddling like I hope Eli and I will be doing soon. We find a relatively isolated spot—both of us had instinctively kept going until we were at least ten feet away on all sides from anyone else. We spread out the blanket, take off our shoes.

Eli lies down and luxuriously stretches out his stunning lanky self: fabulous contrast to the compact Bob. I have an almost uncontrollable urge to pull up his pristine white shirt, to untuck it and discover the lovely trail of dark hair that surely waits just underneath. He has a nice tan. Must be those leisurely afternoons of golf—or is that just a myth? I purposely didn't ask him one important question yesterday—he'd better not be a gynecologist; I'd be too jealous. He reaches up a hand and strokes the small of my back. "Comfortable?" he asks.

"Yeah, for right now...I'm enjoying the view." I look into his eyes, then let my gaze boldly travel down his body. He chuckles.

"You are so beautiful, Aviva," he tells me softly—great timing, great delivery. He's suave, all right. This man is a dream. How did I get so lucky?

"So are you, Eli." We move together for our first kiss. Oh my god. He tastes like sex. And he's absolutely delicious. I must taste that again—and again, and again...until suddenly we're both startled to recall we're still in public; some grandmother is screeching at her charges only about fifteen feet above us.

It's gotten darker, although you can still discern people's light-colored clothing. Eli's shirt is practically glowing—as are his eyes, in the little bit of moonlight. "You look like a wolf," I tell him, "with those adorable sharp white canines of yours... I *love* those." I reach down and let them sink into my tender fingertips. He growls, gloriously, and pulls me down on top of him. "Wait, wait," I protest weakly, hissing at him, "there's, like, someone's *granny* and a bunch of little kids right over there..."

He makes an effort to sit up, smiling sheepishly down at his shorts, which, being a light beige, are also fairly iridescing, and poking up suspiciously—and more than high enough to fill up a condom, I'm relieved to see; at least *that's* not his fatal flaw. He giggles. Oh my god, a man who giggles! Help, I'm falling in love!

"It *would* look bad, wouldn't it, Aviva, if a prominent Boulder doctor got arrested for..." he whispers, "public lewdity... I mean nudeness... I mean... Come here, you yummy thing." He pulls me back down.

I laugh into his ear. Then we both freeze, because a group of twentysomethings is approaching. "What about here?" one of them asks. Eli and I hold our breath. And hold. And hold.

"Nah," another of them finally answers. "Let's go over by that rock." The voices and footsteps move on. Eli and I both take a huge breath and start giggling.

"As soon as it gets a little darker..." begins Eli.

"I know." I cover his mouth with my own to hush him.

As soon as it did get a little darker, Eli unzipped those fancy shorts. In the moonlight I could clearly read the Calvin Klein label on his underwear. He pulled me on top of him. A condom was able to go on quickly under the protective cover of my flying skirt. As soon as I settled wetly down onto him, he inadvertently moaned really loud.

"Ssshhhhhhh!" I giggled into his mouth. "Ssssshhhhhut *up*!" I didn't dare move for a few moments, until it seemed safe that Grandma wasn't coming over to investigate. Thank god for age-related normal hearing loss. Then I let my PC muscle speak for itself.

It was absolutely, truly, perfectly perfect—the two of us *invented* sex.

Eli opened his eyes just as the first burst of color shot up and completely filled the sky above us, ruby reflected in his viridian eyes, his groan of maximum pleasure and "Oh, Aviva!" drowned out, fortunately, by the collective "Aaaaaaaahhhhhhh!" of the crowd.

"Happy Fourth of July, Eli," I whispered, smiling, into his left ear.

9

The next morning, I'm in love.

I'm floating around my apartment cleaning happily, watering plants, playing with Baby, singing loudly to one of my favorite Indigo Girls CDs: *I don't want what's best for you / Where would I be / If you found it?* A man like Eli, my god, could make me forget Alan. *And* Brandon. I'm already fantasizing about the traditional wedding we'll have. Do Jewish brides do that same white-dress deal? Well, maybe by then they'll have VirginiTea.

The phone rings, and I leap for it. Eli had promised to call today. It's Georgette, though, and I spend a happy hour yakking about Eli. She's a good friend and listens, requesting details at the appropriate moments (even though she must be envious; she still hasn't found a boyfriend), so I can blather on and on about his magnificentness. However, she's also a good enough friend to ask the question I've been dreading: "So…do you know what his fatal flaw is yet?"

"Georgette, I *swear*, he doesn't seem to have one!"

She sighs. "They always have one, Ave."

I sigh back. "I know."

"So, Ave, let me give you this guy, Jon's, phone number. J-O-N."

"But Eli—"

"I know, I know. Just do me a favor and jot it down, okay? If Eli does turn out to have something majorly wrong with him, then you can call Jon."

"But I'm telling you, Eli is perfect. I won't be needing this Jon."

"But, Ave, you're not giving up on the bet, are you?!"

"Well..."

"Ave! You can't do this! Where's that feisty spirit? What about all the women you were going to *redeem*? What about—?"

"Georgeeeeeette," I whined. "What if Eli wants to do the, you know, boyfriend-girlfriend thing? You know, that thing I haven't done for soooooooo long?"

"Well...I can certainly see the temptation in that. We all want that, no matter how much we deny it, right? But in the meantime, take down this number—just in case Mr. Perfect should happen to fall from his pedestal. Okay?" I was sure I wouldn't have to use it, as I'd fortuitously stumbled across The Man. And as for Alan, well... Uh-oh, now I was experiencing a small moment of doubt: Alan was the Einstein of Elbows, the Pavarotti of the Pelvic Bone. *But*—Alan was a slob; Eli was a Sharp-Dressed Man. Alan left; Eli was here.

But I took the number to make her happy.

The phone rang again. I immediately recognized that amber tenor, that dulcet tone.

"Aviva, hi! It's Eli."

"*Hiiiiii......*," I purred. "How *are* you?"

"Great! Listen, I'm glad I got hold of you, because I'm packing up to leave right now, and..."

"Leave?! Where are you going?" My *chuppah* came crashing down, rose petals flying away, scattering in the sudden gust of gelid wind.

"Oh, didn't I mention it last night?" he asked casually. "I'm leaving on a five-year tour of duty with this excellent organization—have you heard of them?—Doctors Without Frontiers."

"What?! Five *years*?! No, you *didn't* mention it!" I was dumbfounded. "The what? Isn't that a Peter Gabriel song?"

He chuckled. "I meant, Doctors Without Borders. I always translate it wrong. We'll be traveling all over the world, doing volunteer inoculations, that sort of thing."

"You could've told me before!"

"But, Aviva, last night was beautiful. It was *poetry*. It was...*exquisite*. Whether I'd told you or not, what difference would it have made?"

"Well..." I said. What about our wedding? What about the child I'd suddenly decided I wanted, who'd have an adorable miniature version of that hawk nose, and be the modern bearer of the awkward, multisyllabic name of some Hebrew biblical personage? "Well, when you get back," I started, then dead-ended again. When he got back, I'd be forty!

"I just wanted to tell you what a fantastic evening that was, Aviva. It was my best Fourth of July ever. I'll remember it always. Nights when I'm lying in my vine-woven hammock, fanning myself with banana leaves and watching the tarantulas creep up the wall…"

"I can't believe you're leaving!"

"I can hardly believe it either. I'm not even packed yet, actually. You know, Aviva darling, I'd try to stay a little longer, but my wife is expecting me at the airport in Addis Ababa in about thirty hours, with ten boxes full of syringes and alcohol swabs. Farewell, my sweet Aviva."

â

Browsing books at the Trident. I vainly attempt to temporarily interest myself in *Harris on the Pig: Practical Hints for the Pig Farmer*; *The Lost Finnish Identity*; *Bear Attacks: Their Causes and Avoidance* (hell, I've been waiting ten years to see a bear in Boulder County, and the closest I've gotten is a newspaper photograph); and *Farm Appliances and How to Make Them* (I can't believe DOUCHEBAG didn't think of this one first, but then what did I expect to see for the author's name, Douchebag Goth? For all I know, it *is* his book).

I look into the café to see if Jon's here yet. I've been told to keep an eye out for a "really nondescript" guy. That should actually make him quite easy to spot.

There's a man striding purposefully through the bookstore, dressed head-to-toe like Zorro. No one except me gives him a second glance. A young hippie couple near me is in the middle of a break-up. As she starts to weep, he proclaims, with a skinny shrug, "But, Cloud, I just can't find my joy with you!" I spot the guy who always brings the enormous blank-paged book. He's doing his usual thing—composing line after line of incredibly miniscule, cramped, left-slanted handwriting, with tremendous concentration. He averages approximately a million words per page. He's been at this for at least the last five years now, which is when I started noticing him. I *definitely* do not want to know what he's writing.

I glance back into the café. Still no sign of Jon, but there's a burly, walrus-mustached Harley-type dude sitting at a table staring at me. He can probably barely read Dick and Jane, but has decided to try to *pick up chicks in an intellectual coffee bar*; he's pretending to peruse a couple of enormous tomes, *Chaos and Fractals* and *Computational Number Theory*.

I decide I'd better go and pee now so that I won't have to go as soon as I sit down with Jon. I make absolutely sure the door is shut and locked—there's a trick to it that you only fully master after you've been frequenting this place for about a year. The neophytes get the door pushed in on them while they're sitting with their jeans around their ankles.

When I come out, I see a guy standing around looking lost: average height, average weight, average build, short hair (mousy brown and thinning), khakis, Rockports, oval wire-rim glasses, tan-colored button-down plaid shirt, and no earrings or visible piercings. I introduce myself to Jon, and can tell by a slight gleam in his medium-brown eyes that he likes what he sees. We get in line. I make a mental bet with myself that he's going to order a latte—no special requests, no extras. It's going to take some tremendous willpower on my part to sleep with this guy, after the entrancing Eli and those exotic jade eyes… But I'm back on this bet. I am recommitted. Someone behind me in line is confessing to his partner, "Ooooh, I *love* purple bamboo in the evening!" Is this some Eastern sexual act I should know about? But it turns out to be the name of a tea.

We sit down (Jon with his latte, me with my usual) next to two young guys playing chess on the Trident's board. They've had to substitute a small Japanese teacup for one of the bishops.

"So, Jon…" I begin. "What do you do?"

"Um, well, actually, I'm an orchidist."

Another doctor? My heart lurches at the thought of Eli. "Um, so is that some kind of subspecialty of proctology?" My graduate work wasn't in etymology, but any linguist worth their salt knows that *orchid* means "testicle," from the Greek.

He looks puzzled. "Is it? …Anyway, I've always been obsessed with pseudobulbs, you know, since I was a kid… Now I finally feel like an expert. I guess you could call me an *orchid doctor*, sure!" He gives me a big smile.

"So, is that a common euphemism? I mean, is that what everyone calls them now, or something?" I asked.

"Calls what?"

"Calls, you know, *them.*" Now I'm totally confused.

He looks equally confused. "I guess. There might be some other terminology, but yeah, pseudobulbs is the most common word for them, sure. I'd say so."

"Since when?" I ask, smiling, blushing a bit to be talking this openly about *balls.*

"Oh, since the seventeen- or eighteen-hundreds, I suppose."

"Really? How strange that I've never heard them...referred to that way before."

"Well, if you're not an orchid expert, I wouldn't expect you to know what their technical name is."

"Oh, right, of course," I respond. Imagine—an orchid *expert!* "So... what is it about, um, *pseudobulbs,* that you find so fascinating you decided to specialize in that...area?"

"Oh, I don't know...their size variation,"—I raise my eyebrows—"their storage capacity, the way they start out such little baby things and end up growing so plump and round..." he enthuses, obviously warming to his topic.

I'm growing rapidly redder in the face. I sip my drink just as Jon says, "I don't want to bore you with all this talk about pseudobulbs, Aviva—"

Pfffffffffffffft! I inadvertently spray.

"Really, we can change the subject! I'm sorry, really!"

"No, no," I assure him. "It's just, this drink tastes really weird—kind of *nasty,* actually."

I wipe up some of the mess and take my glass back to the counter. Turned out that instead of soy milk, they'd accidentally grabbed the chai carton—so, in essence, a new drink had been unwittingly created just for me: mocha chai. I don't recommend it.

"Everything okay?" Jon asks as I sit back down.

"No problem. So, you were saying...?"

"Oh, we can change the subject if you want..."

"That's okay." I don't want him to think I'm a *prude.*

"Well, I was just saying, you know, I've always been fascinated by pseudobulbs, their shapes, sizes... I can never resist touching them, caressing them..." Okay, this guy is getting a *little* too weird for me. Caressing *whose*? I can't stop visualizing his testicles. I'm getting very uncomfortable. Finally he asks, "Do you want to go see what I'm talking about?"

I nearly choke on my revised mocha. "Go...*see*...them?"

"Yeah, so you'll know what I'm talking about. See them with your own eyes, touch them..."

This time, I do choke. "Are you okay?" he asks, whacking me unhelpfully on the back. I nod, coughing, and think about his proposition. Well, after all, aren't I supposed to be the woman to finally turn the tables on the guys, for whom the conquest of thirty men while the clock ticks is but a trifle? And besides—this Jon is certainly turning out to be a lot more *interesting* than his appearance suggested.

"Sure, Jon. Shall we go?"

♫

Jon led me by the hand through his backyard in Longmont, a.k.a. Schlongmont. (Longmont is one of Boulder's myriad "L" satellite cities, where all us normal folks eventually have to move when we can no longer afford Boulder rent; among them are Lyons, Longmont, Lafayette, and Louisville. Possibly the "L" is for "loser.") Jon was guiding me toward a shed or something. *Mon Dieu!* Just what did this rascal have in mind?

Jon opened the door to what turned out to be a greenhouse. "In here, where it's nice and warm and steamy..." This guy was turning out to be a hell of a lot kinkier than I ever could have suspected—what did he want to do in here that would involve his scrotum? "So," Jon said, with a proud and expansive arm gesture, "what do you think?"

"Um...nice," I answered, wondering what kind of hot, humid sex he had in mind for us. I didn't really see much room to do it in here.

"Look," he said, grabbing a nearby plant and holding it up for my inspection.

"Uh-huh," I said. "Very nice."

"So what do you think of the pseudobulb?"

"Excuse me?"

"The pseudobulb—what do you think of it? You said you wanted to see some."

"What pseudobulb?"

"This one," he said, gently grasping a protuberance at the base of the plant.

"Wait a minute—*that's* a pseudobulb?" I was incredulous.

"Of course. Haven't you ever seen an orchid growing before?"

Oh my god. Oh Jesus. How embarrassing.

"Oh," I said weakly. "Yes, very nice. Really…nice. Yes. I'm really glad you brought me here, so I could see them in person, like you said."

He suddenly reached out and picked up a random pot and tipped it way over. I gasped, expecting the typical potting-soil-strewn-everywhere kind of accident, but to my surprise, there was nothing in there but a few pieces of bark. And an awful lot of what looked like cooked spaghettini.

"Check out the gorgeous roots on this one!" he exclaimed like a proud papa. He looked excited now, and started talking a mile a minute. "So over here, I've got mostly Oncidiums, with the occasional Miltonia mixed in—some Miltoniopsis too, species and hybrids both—and on the wall, hanging there, I've got vandaceous, see those terete leaves? I finally got a Miss Joaquim just last week; I've been wanting one forever! And those little ones mounted on the cork—see, with the sphagnum moss? Those are Epidendrums, like the *tampense* right there, and a few species *Laelias* that haven't bloomed for me yet, but by god they'd better this year or I swear I'm selling them off! On the floor here, in these big pots, I've got Cymbidiums, mostly warmer-growing varieties, of course, though I couldn't resist trying a few of the Far Eastern species as well, which—what did I expect?—haven't bloomed for me… Here, smell this standard Catt—isn't that heavenly? I think it smells just like lemon pound cake, although this one orchidist friend of mine, Paul, swears it's buttercream frosting, like they use on poppyseed wedding cake, you know, the kind with the raspberry jam layer? I had that once at my friends' Rebecca and Bill's wedding, and it was so delicious, I—"

I flung myself against him and gave him a long, deep French kiss. It seemed to be the only way to shut him up. Plus, I had gotten a little turned on—any guy who's an expert on something and is giving a lecture about it turns me on. This can even include themes like "sea cucumber respiration" or "repercussions of toad disappearance on marsh ecosystems." It's a Pavlovian habit stemming from a life cloistered in Academia. This friend of mine in Botany, Joe, gave a talk on birches last semester that got me wet within five minutes.

Jon looked surprised by my attack, from what I could see (from my fly-eye view) of his suddenly raised eyebrows, but then he started kissing me back, with almost as much feeling as he'd demonstrated for his flora. After a while we came up for air. "Are you a professional at this?" I asked, gesturing to the hundreds of plants, all the greenhouse equipment. "Do you do this for a living?"

He laughed. "No, I'm just an amateur. A hobbyist."

"*Amateur*," I repeated, giving the word its proper pronunciation. "You know what the word means, literally?"

"Fuck-up?" he guessed, with a smile.

"Lover."

"Oh, Aviva, that's exactly what I am! A *lover*!" He launched himself back at me.

We fell together under the deflasking table, rattling glass and spewing plastic tags all over the place. At one point he reached over and turned on the fogger machine. "Imagine we're in an unexplored Brazilian rain forest, viewing wild *Miltonia spectabilis moreliana* in situ," he whispered into my steamy ear as he reached down purposefully with his hand.

"Oooh," I breathed involuntarily. "Yes—*that* situ. *Wild*—yes."

"...And, oh, Aviva, I've always wanted to go traipsing through the forests of Malaysia, or maybe Borneo...or maybe *traipsing*'s not the right word; it'd probably be more like *bushwhacking*...searching for the elusive and delicate *Cirrhopetalum vaginatum*..."

"The *what?!*"

"*Cirrhopetalum vaginatum*. Of course, one wouldn't want to get too close to it—they do tend to be kind of...well...stinky, you know."

"*Stinky?!*" I reared back in outrage. "Just what are you calling *stinky?!*"

Jon finally understood, with a typical geek's slowness in comprehending a social gaffe. "No, Aviva, not *yours*! No, Aviva," he told me as he got ready to go down on me (bonking his head on the table above), "yours is as sweet-smelling and beautiful as...as...well, as the most perfect *Rhyncholaelia digbyana* I've ever seen. Only *yours*, of course," he said, nuzzling happily, his speech now beginning to slur, "...isn't green."

Mollified, I pushed his head down more firmly. That's when I noticed that right on the crown of his head, where his bald spot was, he had a tiny, intricate tattoo, in shades of orange, yellow, and red.

"What's this?" I asked, touching it gently.

"*Psychopsis papilio*," he whispered reverently.

Well, well. I guess even the most ordinary-looking guy can have his hidden passions.

ú

Date: 08 JUL 01 22:01:36
From: allpedalnowork@yahoo.com
Subject: Save me!
To: profaviva@yahoo.com

Aviva,

I was roused from my morning reveries by an incessant call from outside, "Here kitty, kitty," and went out to investigate. My neighbor (we'll call her "Zoe") was looking for her cat. I deduced, after listening intently to the cat's cries, that the cat was in fact situated well above our heads, in the tree over Zoe's home.

The cat (we'll call it "Freddie") had climbed to about 60 feet because it was afraid to go down, but we managed to talk it into coming down to a branch above the roof of the house. Freddie proved that a cat **can** back down a tree. Unfortunately, one point at the main trunk of the tree was just too steep for Freddie to try to pass.

I suggested that Zoe call a tree service, but

they all declined to take on the job. A call to the police yielded the useless advice "Lure the cat down with some food," and we were referred to the fire department, by whom Zoe was told that someone would come out right after the "Captains' Meeting."

After another 15 minutes, the situation seemed dire. Little Freddie had made some heroic efforts to come down, but these consisted mainly of voyages to higher points in the tree. Freddie was crying, and even the best scientific studies can't resolve how long a cat can hang onto a branch before fatigue and gravity set in.

The fire department had not yet arrived with its hooks and ladders, ropes and safety nets. The Captains must still have been in meeting. Something had to be done!

Having long before climbed from the top of a fence to the roof of the house to better assess the situation and provide moral support to Freddie, I now mused aloud that perhaps a rope could be thrown from the roof and over a branch to allow me to climb to the branch and reach for the cat. Zoe went into her house and returned with some rope. Alas, it was only recommended for 80-pound weight.

I asked Zoe if she had a ladder. She produced a rickety, wooden six-foot ladder, which she handed up to me. Against my better judgment I managed to balance it precariously between the slanted roof and the tree trunk, clambered up the ladder, and from the very top of the ladder was able to pull myself up to the next branch. Balancing myself on the one leg that I was able to fit in the intersection of that branch and the trunk of the tree, and hanging onto the tree with one arm, I was able to reach down with my other arm for the basket that the owner of the cat was now proffering me at the end of a very long pole.

From where I was balancing in the tree, Freddie was still about two feet above my head. Holding the basket up to the cat, I offered him a cozy space in the basket, but for some reason Freddie declined to simply let go of the tree and jump into the basket.

I reflected a moment, and then cleverly set aside the basket for future use by hooking it onto a little branch stump located lower on the tree. Still balancing on one leg and hanging onto the tree with one arm, I reached up to take hold of the wayward feline with my other hand. I didn't know before that you can pick up and grip a frightened cat with one hand, but so you can, if you don't mind your integument shredded. Then still balancing on one foot, leaning my back against a branch for balance, and maintaining my hold on Freddie in one hand, I released my grip on the tree with my other hand, reached down and picked up the basket, and stuffed little Freddie therein.

I was slightly concerned that it had required two arms and two legs for me to make it up into the tree, and here I was now with the basket in one hand and one less limb to call upon in my journey down. I wished I had thought to ask Zoe to tie the splendid 80-pound rope to the basket, so that I could just lower the basket with the rope.

Now I had no rope, **and** had to keep hold of the basket. Would the Fire Captains now have to be summoned for **me**?

NEXT WEEK—Can our hero escape the tree?
Alan

p

Waiting for Therese and Georgette to show up at the Starbuck's near campus. You can feel fall in the air—undergrads decked out in thousand-dollar outfits driving new Range Rovers, loaded up with new electronics in the back, on their way to their three-thousand-dollars-a-month condos that Mommy and Daddy in Austin, in Los Gatos, in Santa Barbara are paying for. A sparkling Jeep Cherokee pulls up so the bimbette can get her five-dollar Tiazzi with whipped cream. Her bumper stickers say *You Know You Want Me* and *Treat Me Like The Princess That I Am*.

I browse the paper for band names: Bad Religion, Guttermouth, Poison Spider, The Anti-Heroes, Bad Influence, Itchin' For An Incident, Pleasant Nightmares, Napalm Death, and Domestic Problem.

On to other sections of the paper. One employment ad says they're looking for a Youth Prevention Education Coordinator. I silently applaud—I think *all* teenagers should be prevented. Another ad reads: "Penile Enlargement. FDA approved vacuum pump/surgical." I don't know what it feels like to have a penis, but if I did have one, I don't think I'd like the sound of that. Speaking of which, I heard that men are now paying to get collagen injections to make their scrota look bigger, the way women do for that bee-stung model-lips look.

At The Ravenheart Center, there's "Finding Your Soul Path. After Death Communication. Past Life Regression. Shamanic Soul Retrieval.

Led by Psychologist and Medium." I can't even figure out what this event *is*: "Upgrade Your Mental Software. Merge With Your Future Self. Mount Baldy Institute for Resonant Viewing. Individual or Group Instruction also available."

Someone's business card in the gym the other day offered her services in the following areas: Illumination Processing, Energy Healing, Essence Guidance, and Movement Imprinting. Lolita's Market currently has an ad up for a class, Astrology For Meditators; and a completely separate ad, Meditation For Astrologers.

An ad for a bar in Denver shows a dude on a "chopper" (a word I learned in Pulp Fiction) with a scar on his face, a patch over one eye, and a T-shirt reading "Born To Burger." It reads: "The only Fern you'll find in this bar rides a '92 Harley Fat Boy. And you won't find tiramisu on the menu either. We serve real drinks and real food in a bar that feels like a bar. So when you're done with trendy, we're here." The cultural difference between Boulder and Denver, only thirty minutes apart, is as extreme as that between New Orleans and Salt Lake City.

I get up to join the line and start daydreaming about Alan. An email a few days ago, about a month after the Freddie and Zoe episode, informed me that he had moved yet again and was going out with someone new, but "of course still not having intercourse."

A guy starts to cut in front of me. I say, "Excuse me," and reassert my place.

He says, "Excuse you? Why? Whadja do?" and cracks up. What planet did this guy just wander in from—Kansas?

A kid about two or three years old has been fussy and clingy the whole time we've been in line, and the woman in front of me, who apparently owns him, is getting frustrated with his behavior. Finally she squares his shoulders a bit roughly and says to him, "What are you experiencing right now, Dylan? I want you to go into that corner and meditate, all right?"

Just then I'm distracted by a hearty "Hey, Ave!" It's Georgette, wearing an outfit that's so vintage it looks like she grave-robbed it. "How are you?" she says, joining me in line. "Excuse me," she says to the guy behind me, before I can warn her.

"Excuse you? Why? Whadja do? Huh! Huh! Huh!" She raises one eyebrow at him and turns back to me.

"Where'd *he* come from?" she whispers to me in disgust.

"Michigan or thereabouts, would be my bet."

"Speaking of bets," Georgette says, eyes shining. "How's it going? Do you think you're gonna make it?"

"*Cake,* my dear! I've done twelve already, and it's only the beginning of fall semester." I'm glowing with pride.

"Twelve what?" *Aaaackk!* It's the guy from the line, standing next to our table.

"Hey," I say to him, fluttering my eyelashes at him. "My girlfriend and I are just *dying* to know... Where are you from?"

He's so flattered by the female attention, he can hardly find his voice. "Minn-uh-*soww*-da," he finally croaks and, blushing, wanders away.

Georgette and I do a high five. "Hey," I ask her, "did you ever see that Seinfeld episode with Elaine's boyfriend doing the obnoxious high five thing every thirty seconds?"

"No—remember, I've never seen that show."

I'd forgotten again. Georgette has these bizarre personality traits, like being a non-Seinfeld watcher, and the fact that she can do math in her head.

Therese joins us. "So, Ave. How many?"

"Twelve," I say proudly. Georgette beams as well, as if she somehow deserves part of the credit.

"Wow!" says Therese.

"Yeah, at this rate, she's gonna be done way before her year is up," says Georgette.

"Maybe this is too easy," suggests Therese. "Maybe we should make the challenge harder." She winks at Georgette.

"Hey!" I protest. "You guys have no idea how much I've suffered already—and there's still eighteen assholes to go!"

"Assholes?! Ave! I thought you *loved* men!" Therese and Georgette both look astonished.

"Well, it's just…it must be some kind of physics law, like the more concentrated your men experience, the more assholey they seem…"

"So," says Georgette. "Tell us everything. Especially, tell *me* everything, since I'm still getting *nada* action of my own."

"Remind me—you guys have heard about up to what number?"

"Start with number eight," Georgette says eagerly.

"Wait, wait!" says Therese, "Do a recap first; I can't keep track of who all there's been so far."

"All right," I say with a sigh, and consult my file (of *course* I had a file; otherwise how would I keep all these guys straight? I kept it hidden in a locking file drawer, with the hopefully sufficiently boring label *MLA Conferences* on it). "Number one was Donald, you know, my friend, the telemarker. Number Two was The Persian, a.k.a. The Duck; Three was The Texan; Four was my student last semester, the bald one who shall remain otherwise anonymous to protect the guilty; Five was Bob, you know, The Writer-Formerly-in-a-Coma—"

"Wasn't he the one with the teeny dick?" interrupts Georgette, loudly. The table next to us suddenly ceases conversation.

"Yes," I whisper, and continue: "Number Six was Eli The Damned Doctor—*damn* him!—on the Fourth of July. Seven was Jon The Orchid Maniac. Numbers Eight, Nine, Ten, and Twelve were Dave, Dave, Mike and Dave—very forgettable guys I actually went to a frat party to pick up—too easy; no challenge there; I'm never going to do *that* again, for a *multitude* of reasons. But I *gotta* tell you guys about Number Eleven…"

"Who was Number Eleven?"

"Guess."

"Um… Mr. Bad Jokes? Mr. Bad Manners?" asks Therese. I shake my head.

"Mr. Kinky? Mr. Foot-Long?" guesses Georgette.

I laugh out loud, shake my head no. I wait a beat, theatrically. "Mr.

Gadgetry."

"No!" they exclaim happily. "Details!" They settle into listening poses.

"Okay," I say, "so at first it was just, you know, the usual techno-toys like the cell phone that kept ringing all through dinner, and the pager-thingie, and then he had to whip out this—"

"Huge penis?" asks Georgette. Therese's eyes widen in alarm.

"Ha ha. This device that, like, gave him real-time stock quotes or some other retarded thing…"

"No way!" exclaims Therese, delightedly.

"Yes way. Why do I—oh, never mind. Anyway, then we went to his place—"

"Woo-hoo," says Georgette. "Now comes the good part." Therese looks mildly frightened again.

"Well, but wait," I say, "first there were all these gadget thingies in his car."

"Like what?" asks Therese.

"You know, like radar detector, car alarm, negative ionizer, all these dials that lit up… CD player that looked more difficult to operate than even my VCR…"

"Damn!" interjects Georgette. "Remember when I came over and tried to help you figure that thing out?!"

"Yeah," I say. "Exactly. So, once we got to his house—"

"Where does he live?" interrupts Therese.

"Knollwood Estates."

"Where?"

"You know, that little exclusive neighborhood with all the fancy houses, like, right up next to Sanitas trail?"

"Oh, yeah. Harry and I looked at a house there once."

"Well," I say, and start giggling. "I've peed on his lawn before."

In unison: "*What?!*"

"Well, this one time I just had to go so bad, there was no way I was going to make it all the way back home… I had just done all of Sanitas, and you know how there's always so many people out there no matter what the weather…"

"Yeah, and so many dogs, too," says Georgette.

"Not to mention dog *shit*," adds Therese, then looks surprised at herself as she clamps a hand over her mouth.

"Yeah, really!" responds Georgette. "What ever happened with that last group, the FIDOs or whatever they were called, that were going around picking up dog poop?"

"Yeah, I think that was them… Friends Into Dog Oopsies, something like that?" asks Therese. I sulk quietly in the background.

Georgette responds, "Or was it ROVERs? Really Odiferous Vast Excremental Rights? Plus, have you heard that now people are using their personal Global Positioning Systems to locate doggie dumps on the hiking trails and sending the locations in to the city, to try to get stricter leash law enforcement?"

"That's one use those GPS makers probably never anticipated," says Therese.

She and Therese collapse into giggles and high-five campily. I'm being ignored—something I don't deal with too well.

Finally, Georgette asks me, "So, you got to his house and realized his lawn looked familiar…?" I'm immensely pleased to see they haven't forgotten my storyline.

"Yeah, so of course I didn't say anything about *that*. But when we got there, first he had this like really complicated garage door thing, then there was the house alarm to defuse—"

"I think you only say 'defuse' with, like, bombs," says Therese.

"Or land mines," adds Georgette.

"—*Anyway*," I continue with a *look* at both of them, though secretly I'm enjoying the semantic debate, "we finally get inside and he disappears to get us some wine and asks me to put on a CD…and of course he has one of those CD players that looks like a spaceship, so I give up on that right away and decide I'll just *choose* a CD first. So they're all on this rack-thingie that plugged in and spun around and around like at a dry cleaner's… Whatever those things are called…"

"Gee, Ave, for a linguist teaching a course on Nomenclature, you certainly are—" begins Georgette. I give her another look. She shuts up.

"So then what? Did you pick a CD?" asks Therese.

"Well, I *tried*—"

"Uh-oh," says Georgette.

"Yeah. I tried to grab this Cat Stevens one—"

"Cat Stevens?! Ave, don't date yourself like that!" Therese practically shouts.

"Well, it was the only one I recognized. Plus it would make, you know, good *mood* music. So anyway, I tried to grab it each time it came around, but it wouldn't come out—"

Therese interrupts, "Did you guys hear he's, like, some kind of extremist Mormon or something now?"

Georgette cracks up. "You mean *Muslim*! And I think he'd be considered a fundamentalist, not an extremist."

"So anyway, you two...am I going to have to break out the duct tape here, or what? So he comes over carrying two glasses of wine that had these, like, little built-in thermometers on them..."

"No way!" says Therese again.

"Yes way, and keep quiet and let me finish."

"Okay, okay."

"So he asks if I've chosen a CD and of course I was too embarrassed to admit I couldn't figure out the dry cleaner rack, so I just told him I'd let *him* pick one. He took one with no problem and put it on his UFO, also with no problem..."

"Well, yeah, but don't feel bad. I mean, it was his; he'd know how to use it. *I* wouldn't have been able to figure it out," Georgette reassures me.

"Me neither," says Therese.

I love these women.

"So then we're on the couch, right?, and we start necking and everything," I say.

"*Necking*! I *love* that word!" shrieks Georgette, then looks around in surprise at the audience she'd attracted.

"What music did he pick?" asks Therese.

"Some old classic jazz thing—you know, makeout music. And he called the rack his *Power Tower*." We all laugh. *Men.* "So anyway, we're necking on the couch and all of a sudden this light comes on—this, like, spotlight that starts changing to all different colors."

"What was it?" asks Georgette.

"It was a spotlight that kept changing colors."

"I know, but what was it *for*?"

"It wasn't *for* anything. That's just what it did."

"Jesus," mutters Georgette. "Some people have too much money."

Therese asks, "What was he, one of those Hammacher-Schlammacher kind of guys?"

"I guess."

"Is that a Jewish company?" asks Therese.

"What else did this guy have?" asks Georgette impatiently.

"Well, I went into the bathroom, and there was this special kind of CD player in the shower, and another thingie that looked like one of the old Star Trek communicators, remember those?" Therese nods while Georgette looks blank again. "Anyway, that one was sitting on its own little shelf right next to the toilet... Then all of a sudden I heard this deep voice say, 'Everything okay in there, Aviva?' I freaked. Was this pervert spying on me with one of those baby monitor things? But no, it turned out to be him talking to me via walkie-talkie..."

Georgette and Therese are staring at me in astonishment.

"...I told him everything was fine, trying not to sound too startled, and checked out the rest of the bathroom. There was this device stuck onto this normal Bic razor. I turned it on, and it made the razor vibrate really fast. Does that make for a better shave? I have no idea. Women might be able to come up with some interesting uses for that thing, though..."

Georgette nods eagerly.

"When I got out of the bathroom, he was wearing this really weird-looking thing around his neck. It looked like he had some severe medical problem he was being treated for, like a broken vertebra or something. I was concerned. I asked him what it was, and he goes, 'It's a Personal Climate Control System. Do you want one?' I said no thanks.

"So he brings out another bottle of wine and pulls out this blue plastic gadget that had a flashlight, a corkscrew, and god knows what else on it. Kind of Swiss Army meets Star Wars. I'm thinking, get me out of here. I motion to him to show me his watch, and I can't even read the damn thing. Then he flips open a panel on this thingie—"

"You're saying 'thingie' a lot," interrupts Georgette.

"—that was sitting on the coffee table and tells me the outside temperature, wind speed and direction, and current barometric pressure to four decimal places. He hangs a Personal Air Purifier around my neck like an Olympic medal. Then he asks me if I'd like to 'retire to the bedroom.' I say sure, figuring, I've invested this much time, let me just get this over with and go home. He touches this thing that looks like a joystick with a lit-up panel, and it starts saying these really cheezey things in these hokey little electronic voices, like 'Count on it,' 'You go, girl,' 'Shake it, don't break it.'

"I follow him to his bedroom and he goes into the walk-in closet, where he turns on this machine that rotates about a million ties around and around, again just like a mini-dry cleaner's rack, and then it flashes a light at him and he puts his tie on it. He takes off his shoes and puts them in this big plastic box thing, and it starts whirring—shining his shoes. He starts emptying out his pockets and comes up with this bizarre silver thingie that looks like a perforated steel kidney, and asks me what my phone number is. I still have the presence of mind to make up a fake one quickly, and he talks to his device, says 'Memo: Phone number: Aviva.' It beeps three times at him. Then he takes out this huge scary heavy steel tool and proceeds to find a nail clipper on it somewhere amongst the car jack, the pliers, and the buttonholer, and files one nail, then puts the thing away. Now he's sitting on his bed, waggling his eyebrows at me. I sigh and go over to him.

"Of course, as soon as I start relaxing, the bed starts vibrating violently. Then the headboard side of it starts raising and lowering, in about four different sections. He asks me what *settings* I'd prefer. 'Actually,' I told him, 'I'm a simple soul—how about perfectly flat?' He looked disappointed, but put it back down like a regular bed. I suddenly then experienced a moment of *extreme* trepidation, realizing that a man like this was bound to own a whole *room* full of bizarre sex toys. I kissed him, then when he got excited and was in a more malleable mood, I whispered to him that I liked sex *au naturel*, and didn't he?"

"And what did he say?" asks Therese faintly.

"He said he hadn't done it that way in a *really* long time, but if that's what I wanted, it was okay with him—'just this once.' He was a boring lover—at least, without any battery-powered aids, he was. When it was over, he made me play Zappin' WeeBots with him, these little round plastic things that move around and you try to hit each other with your colored laser, while the thing makes all sorts of weird electronic noises."

"Aviva, you poor, poor thing!" says Georgette, finally finding her voice. "I cannot *believe* what you went through!"

"It's okay..." I say with planned nonchalance, having looked forward to this dénouement since the moment I entered Starbuck's. (Timing is everything, and I admit to a love of the dramatic.) "...I kind of enjoyed the Zappin' WeeBots."

Z

I decided to go to the Jacque Michelle store, in spite of the snooty, anorexic women who "work" there discussing their pedicure plans, and the fact that there are only two dressing rooms, with flimsy little cloth curtains that allow people to glimpse your cellulite through the sides. Browsing, though, is the operative word; I can't afford to actually *shop* there. Today, though, I dared to throw my budget to the dogs for a $78 wine-colored velvet scarf.

I got in line and waited...and waited. It shouldn't be taking this long, should it? Then I saw that the woman ahead of me had thrown three huge armloads of clothes on the counter: silk skirts; rayon prints; linen dresses in white, peach, seafoam, compost, whatever. The pile was about four feet high. At first I assumed she was just too lazy to put them back and that the clerk was berating her. But then I realized—impossible as it seemed to me—that she was *buying* them all (and this is a place with a no-returns policy). One by one, the clerk was slowly ringing them up. I sighed and went to put the scarf back. As I left, I overheard the clerk say cheerily to the customer, "That'll be five thousand six hundred seventy-two fifty." Gulp. Nearly three months' salary for me. (Yeah, that's really how little they pay us. Kids, don't go into college teaching.)

I emerged into early fall sunshine at the eternally lively confluence of Vic's Café, Moe's Broadway Bagels, and the liquor store: an odd but apparently successful combination. There's always a St. Bernard or two tied to the outdoor tables, basking while their guardians feast and then shop for the most expensive wine they can find.

Well, there's always shoe-shopping. Onward to The Pedestrian Shop, home of the Dansko clogs I wear constantly. It's a different type of clerk in there; in Jacque Michelle, one tends to get kind of early Nancy Reagan. In the Pedestrian Shops they're usually college students with an Attitude.

There was only one other customer in the store at the moment, someone who, coincidentally, looked a lot like the Jacque Michelle clerks. The young employee was trying her best to look bored; however, this client was persistent—and *loud*. (And also anorexic—not that I'd noticed, or anything. Men *really* prefer women with some flesh on them, you know.) There were about thirty pairs of shoes on the floor, but apparently the customer hadn't yet found anything to her liking. The clerk sighed loudly.

I picked up a $150 Teva, put it back down. Gingerly I handled the disgusting cow-hair-still-on (dyed into a leopard print) clogs, and shuddered. Then I noticed that the customer was making a stick-insect arm gesture at one whole wall of shoes. The clerk looked in the direction of the pointing finger, and asked, "What? You want to try some of *those* on, too?" To which the woman replied, "No, I just *told* you, I already *own* all those. Now tell me, have you got this ponyhair in chocolate?"

It's known as the Aspenization of Boulder, a sad and unfortunate phenomenon for those of us who aren't so well-heeled (pardon). And since there's no rent control here, Boulder is certain to complete its course in that direction soon enough. As Christine Lavin noted; she has a song called Nobody's Fat in Aspen, in which she observes that in that glittering town, though everyone's stuffing their face with Brie and cream cheese, nevertheless no one there ever makes the faux pas of getting fat: they're all too busy being "healthy, and…wealthy."

On the way home, I pass a yard sale, which is the kind of thing I hate, but something odd about this one catches my eye. I get out of the car to investigate. Oh—I remember; I was here once, met this woman at a party I crashed with my friend Marta—it's the home of this weird Boulder denizen, a misplaced debutante (the only word for her) who ought to be living in South Carolina, daughter of some tobacco plantation owner. But instead she's a Boulderite trustfunder with a huge, beautiful house to herself, fancying herself an interior decorator as an excuse for existing. Her own décor consists of garish colors, mismatched fashion statements, and about a million framed photographs of herself. Herself with some B-list movie star; herself with an Olympic skier or two; herself at the annual Exotica Erotica Ball, thin red spaghetti-straps barely covering her emaciated yet sinewy pecs.

She has always looked like a man in drag to me, even when not dressed for the Exotica Erotica. This hallowed Boulder giant orgy-like event is held around Halloween, where if you have enough money to get in, you have license to dress and act however you please for the night, but you're *especially* encouraged to explore any closeted sexual identities you might be keeping hidden the rest of the year. Needless to say, I've never gone.

Looks like the debutante has emptied out three or four of her walk-in closets. There are chrome racks (the kind usually found in department stores) spread out all over her lawn. On each rack are about a hundred dresses. I check out the prices: four hundred-dollar range. She comes rushing over with her scary industrial-strength *man hands* stroking the silk charmeuse, and assures me, with some kind of fake accent I can't quite place, that most of these have never been worn; she just got tired of looking at them. A few of them she did wear—but just once.

This "yard sale" is about as comfortable to me as the skiing kind: when you wreck so badly, everything you were wearing ends up scattered all across the slope and the mean people on the chairs cruising above you laugh and shout it as you're lying there, dazed and stunned, face down in the snow: *"Yaaaaard sale!"*

Back at my apartment, I see that one of the cars on my street that's had a slightly dented fender for a few weeks now, has received a parking ticket for "derelict vehicle."

Another typical day in Boulder—much as I hate to admit it, it's not just sunshine, scenery, and wildflowers.

f

The brilliant fall weather is holding: turquoise sky, dried weeds the color of pure gold, no clouds, unobstructed view from below of Devil's Thumb (a wonderfully transparent euphemism for a natural rock feature that can really only be described as a stubby penis).

I'm hiking in Chautauqua Park, the Royal Arch trail, with a candidate: except, physically, everything's wrong with this one. He's squat, altogether gnome-like. His proportions (inadvertently—I know it's not his fault) offend my sense of aesthetics: short bandy little legs; long monkey arms; small, pudgy, horribly hairy hands and feet; tiny hips; hideously rectangular head. I do need to pick up the pace (not the hiking pace—I mean the *mattressing* pace. But suppose he's just *not mattressable?*).

I feel bad, because he seems to be trying really hard to compensate for his looks with congeniality. No matter what I say, he agrees. However, as Christine Lavin knows, this can be too much of a good thing. She sings about eager men making women feel "ill at ease."

"Pretty steep trail, huh?" I ask.

"Yeah! Yeah, it is!"

"Are you okay, or do you want to stop and catch your breath for a minute?"

"Oh, I'm okay! I'm fine! Unless, of course, *you* want to catch your breath? In which case, I'd be happy to, I mean, that'd be great, I'd love to catch our breath. I mean..."

"No," I say, though I'm panting, my lungs desperate and we're barely at the halfway point—I just don't want to have to sit and *look* at him until absolutely necessary, i.e., at the top, under the arch, which he damned well better not interpret as synonymous with mistletoe—or I'll have to throw him off the cliff.

There's a thought. I wonder if anyone's ever murdered someone that way before, here in Boulder? It's a long way down—fifteen hundred feet—and nothing to break your fall. Okay, I *have* to stop thinking about this.

I was minding my own business down in the lower-altitude part of the park, reading a book about bulbs—the flower kind, not the lamp kind—because I know this is the season you're supposed to plant them. Only, of course, I have no land. So I'm thinking, maybe buckets. Or, as they say so quaintly in the book, "container plantings." (But how can I possibly wait till next spring for them to bloom? Bulbs definitely do not work for those who need instant gratification.) So there I was, hanging out with the gorgeous photos that made me want to get on-line immediately and order fifty bags of tuberoses, drowsing lazily in the strong October sun, watching all the frisbee-catching dogs, and the toddlers running in short spurts till they fell down. That was when this gnome-like fellow walks over to me and feeds me this line, variations of which I can never resist: "Hi. I hope you don't mind me bothering you, but I was admiring you from afar and I just *had* to meet you." I think what happened was, I was so bedazzled by the words, I didn't even look at him.

So now I'm stuck hiking with him. Well, at least I'm getting my workout for the day. Maybe I should do him really quick at the top if no one else is around? He'd be Number Thirteen...The unlucky number; that'd be appropriate. I can close my eyes and pretend that I always have sex with my eyes tightly shut. I bet he has premature ejaculation—normally, a terrible thing, but in his case a mercy, something women give thanks for. *If* he's ever had sex before.

Suddenly, "*What?!*" I ask him. I must've heard him wrong.

"I was saying, with the overpopulation of the earth and all, it'd be selfish to have children. So I've decided I'm going to give myself a vasectomy as a fortieth birthday present!"

I look back at him. He's beaming—waiting for my face to light up in joy? I respond: "Actually, *I've* found that if one really tries, one can manage to be celibate with several people at the same time," and speed up, which quickly has the desired effect: he's too out of breath to keep speaking. I glance back and see a furrowed brow.

Ten minutes later, on the only flat part of the trail, the false summit, I absolutely have to stop, to slow my heart rate down. Mile-high hiking, even after living here all this time, still makes me feel like I'm eighty years old. I hope the Gnome has forgotten about the vasectomy business by now.

"So, what do you think?" he asks me.

"About?"

"The vasectomy!"

Putz.

Two couples are very slowly, huffing and puffing, coming up the trail. Ah, out-of-towners: they're all wearing *jeans* and various kinds of dressy leather sandals to hike in, and the women are wearing perfume, hairspray, and (now runny) makeup. I'm extremely impressed that they've made it this far; it's rare to see "foreigners" up this high on any trail. Well, mustn't let flatlanders beat us to the top. I again take the lead. "Aviva," he says behind me.

"Yeah?" I ask, without slowing down nor turning around. I hate to have him staring at my butt, but at least this way *I* don't have to look at *him*.

"Um… You have a great-looking backside. Is that too forward of me?" I grimace and start wondering how long I'd have to go to prison for pushing him off the cliff, and whether a pro bono lawyer would have enough clout to make sure I got dental floss in the slammer.

"So," I say, "what else are you doing for the planet?"

"Oh, um… You know… I recycle most stuff, and… Aviva, guess what?"

"What?" I pick up the pace even more.

"Chicken butt!"

I stop, turn around. "*What*?!"

"Chicken butt!" I stare at him. He giggles, then looks chastised by my glare. He explains weakly: "It's just something we used to say, you know, growing up."

I raise my eyebrows at him. I've always wished I could raise just one, but I've never been able to. So two will have to do. I turn around again and push for the trail's end: ah, here's the sandstone arch, finally visible.

Extreme pulmonary relief.

There are a few other people already here, enjoying the rays, sprawled every which way on the rocks. The view is fabulous—you can see all of Boulder one way, and in the other direction the Third Flatiron, covered with ant-like climbers. Further on, the brown haze envelops Denver like an anti-biosphere. I pull out my Clif Bar and try to ignore the Gnome, who grunts unattractively as he arrives and pulls himself up the last couple of big rocks. I'm glad now that there are people up here—even before the *chicken butt*, I'd decided not to add this repulsive creature to my list.

The Gnome is now feeding pieces of his Power Bar to chipmunks, for which the rest of us immediately reprimand him. How come he doesn't know the Boulder environmental rules?

"Where are you from?" I ask him.

"New Jersey, originally." Well. That explains a lot.

As the other people go back to their conversation, with a glance at me that clearly says, What are you *doing* with this loser?, the Gnome asks, "Say, Aviva, did you happen to watch Letterman the other night?"

"No," I say truthfully. "I've been living too close to the Flatirons—haven't had TV reception for years. Why?" I was surprised to hear the Gnome and I had any tastes in common, especially humor.

"Well, there was this really cool thing they did—you know, one of those stupid human tricks?"

"Uh-huh..."

"Well, this is something I just *have* to try as soon as I go back for a visit to New Jersey and see my parents' dog again... So anyway, there was this guy, and, like, the guy lays down on the floor and opens his mouth and then pours milk into his mouth, you know, from this carton that Letterman handed him."

"Uh-huh."

"So then the guy like, snaps his fingers, and his German Shepard comes over to where he's laying on the floor, and the guy, like, points to his face, and the dog leans over and laps up the milk out of his mouth."

I stare at him. He wants to *do* this? He's beaming, waiting for my approval.

"What kind of milk?" I ask, finally.

"What?"

"What kind of milk?"

"I don't know... But, Aviva, that's not the funny part. I mean, that doesn't matter. What's so cool is—"

"I know," I interrupt him, catching the eyes of the other Arch visitors, who've been listening. "I wonder if it'd work with soy, though." The other hikers laugh and turn back to the view, pointing out where they live, which campus buildings are which, admiring the reservoir. The Gnome is left staring at me with incomprehension, brow furrowed yet again.

See, I was right—we *don't* share a sense of humor.

è

Date: 19 OCT 01 00:30:11
From: allpedalnowork@yahoo.com
Subject: mouse music
To: profaviva@yahoo.com

Aviva,

I'm having a great time escaping reality here in [medium-sized beautiful Californian surfer-filled city name deleted, for the privacy of all involved parties].

Did I tell you I got into the [city name deleted] Community College orchestra and got to play Tchaikovsky's 6th Symphony with them? A major highlight for me. (They forced me to replace my violin string, though I attempted to explain to them that I've been managing perfectly well without it for years.)

Also, today I tried out for free advanced violin lessons for the remainder of the semester, playing something I learned in sixth grade (but playing it a little better this time, I hope). The assembled music faculty serving as judges did politely clap, but then the department head told me, "Thanks, see you around next year maybe," which suggests that they won't be seeing me in violin lessons this year.

Finally, only in [deleted] is there a class for $11 that gets you free tickets to top orchestra concerts if you attend a 1.5-hour lecture about the concert-to-be before attending and send written comments to the instructor after attending. Here's one of my comments I submitted re the first concert:

"The Kodaly work: As you suggested, moving and rewarding to listen to. Although admittedly not very relevant and maybe even counterproductive, I found myself during the fastest parts absorbed by the conductor's prestidigital histrionics.* Well, it only added to the whole wild whirl of the piece.

*In the Liszt piano concerto I also got a kick out of Kocsis' transforming from conductor to pianist and back again whenever the opportunity arose—it had a kind of Fantasia feel to it."

Aviva, for your further reading pleasure, following is a copy of my entire commentary for the next concert, which in the interest of saving time I have written in advance.

"My comment is simply a comment left over from the [date deleted] concert, concerning the fact that the piano solo in the Liszt concerto we heard was first performed by Liszt himself—I call it the Zeno's paradox of composition, ontological variant.

It stands to reason that a supremely great composer might be the first to **conduct** his composition, but I can't get past the incongruity that the composer would and could instrumentally **perform** it. How could a great performer be capable of composing a work so good as to be worthy of that performer, or how could the composer of a great work be such a good performer as to be capable of doing justice in performing such a great work? It seems like the creator of an immovable object being strong enough to move that object, or like Napoleon also being the most physically fearsome warrior. Or Puccini singing Rodolfo in La Bohème (I'm assuming he never did that except in the shower).

If Paganini was, as you say, the greatest violinist ever, then a violin concerto he composed and performed, although excellent work, should not rank as high in caliber as a composition as a Brahms or Bach concerto. The supreme physical talent of Paganini to perform should not be accompanied in Paganini by a supreme creative talent to compose.

The example in the same concert of Bartok's last work is much more sensible: Bartok composed at his very best while he was physically as good as dead, yet certainly would not jump into the orchestra even to try a little bongo drum solo or to hit a tambourine, at a wasted 97 lbs. lacking the strength to hold up a drumstick, maraca or even a castanet or two. [Editor's note: True.]

And Beethoven ceased at once his habit of playing all the piano, clavichord, and glockenspiel parts in his own orchestra concerts after his ex-wife, a skilled but heartlessly vindictive piano tuner and piano repair technician, once mortified him and turned his hair prematurely white when she tuned **all** the instruments' keys to middle C, which his advanced stage of deafness precluded him from discerning but nonetheless amused the audience to no end and cost Beethoven his pay for the concert. [Editor's note: False—Beethoven never wrote for the glockenspiel, finding it too expensive and esoteric an instrument to conveniently locate and stock in his orchestras. In fact, Shakespeare and Cervantes both stopped attending Beethoven concerts in disgust at his intransigence and turned to Eastern music and fiddling music, respectively, for their listening pleasure.]

[Replacement Editor's note: No, that's False—in Beethoven's earliest works a glockenspiel was prominently featured and played by a trained mouse named Hugo, who, unfortunately for Beethoven's concert routine (and unfortunately for Hugo too) was kidnapped for ransom (Hugo was) by Barbary pirates on Hugo's Nile River cruise and tour of the Egyptian pyramids and held captive for two years (sixty-four mouse years) only to tragically die in a twelve-coach pileup on his way to finally being released upon raising his ransom of twelve guineas (coins, not pigs) from Queen Isabela of Spain.]

Aviva—I look forward to your comments.
Semi-sincerely Yours,
Alan

θ

I've had my eye on this really exotic-looking guy who started hanging out at the Trident recently. I'm on my way there now, hoping he's around this evening... I have plans for the man.

In front of Jax, the usual Yuppie Huddle is in full swing. The sidewalk in front of this seafood restaurant attracts only women with sprayed hair, gallons of makeup, three-inch heels and lots of flashy jewelry; and men wearing actual ties, blazers and dress shoes. Nary a Birk to be discerned. Everyone in the Huddle is always drunk, loud and obnoxious, the women cackling and shrieking at everything the men say, and all of them refuse to cede to pedestrians trying to navigate that part of the sidewalk, forcing people to take a small, semi-dangerous detour into the road. At the corner bar, The West End, about four hundred white people are packed inside, grooving to a blasting reggae beat, "Keep Jah people free from oppression, Keep mah people free from aggression..."

Here at the Trident, right next door, are turbaned oddballs smoking clove cigarettes; underfed, hippie-owned puppies roaming the sidewalk trailing tie-dyed bandannas and pieces of dirty clothesline; whole factions of Rainbow People.

But the guy I'm looking for tonight isn't any of those, of course: he's a beautiful gypsy, a mysterious dark stranger. His name I can't wait to hear: it'll be Djembe, or Xango. His ancestors: Romanian nomads, ebony-curled Brazilian beach roamers, Sevillian flamenco dancers. He'll have just moved to Boulder from Belo Horizonte, from Malaga, from Sicily. He'll own no furniture except a futon to sleep on the floor with a purple velvet duvet and Japanese neck pillows, and plenty of African drums and Indonesian wall hangings. He'll be a loner in this world, like myself, someone without living family or mundane attachments.

But *he's* no unwashed hippie—his long curls are shining, held back with a twist of turquoise-studded raw leather, his clothes clean, quietly bohemian. Wrinkled linen. Absolutely adorable tiny black tufts of curls on his big toes, wearing those Italian toe-ring sleek leather sandals. For dinner, he'll serve me beet-and-nettle-infused organic pasta with freshly grated Asiago, and afterwards grappa and sweet Turkish coffee. He'll burn incense in citrusy scents, lemon and tangerine—and later switch to cinnamon and vanilla to set a romantic mood.

Can you tell I've been checking the man out?

There are some men who look like they could never get it up. A lot of British men fall into this category (the luscious young Prince William a definite exception.) So do many blond and redheaded men, and Far Eastern men. It's a certain look, involving a softness, a paleness, a less-than-impressive chin, a lack of body hair—an over-civilization, a weakening, of the male animal. The complete opposite look from an Israeli soldier, an Italian paisano on his motorcycle, a Greek fisherman.

Djembe, though? I know his animal instincts are still intact. He's Paco de Lucía, he's Joaquín Cortés—the ideal foil to the recent visual insult of the Repulsive Gnome.

b

He's here! I can feel already that it's my lucky night... *Lucky* number thirteen, coming up.

He's sitting next to the boisterous round table of Trident icons: the Sunday New York Times crossword-puzzlers. I bring over my mocha and ask him if I can share the table. He looks up, smiles.

"So...," I say as seductively as possible. "I'm Aviva. And your name?" The moment I've been waiting for—this is going to be music, I just know it.

"Jack. Nice to meet you...what was it, Alicia?"

Jack! *Jack?!* No, he cannot *possibly* be named Jack. "Aviva, not Alicia. And you said your name was...?"

He looks puzzled. "Jack," he says again, loudly and clearly.

"It's a nickname?" I ask hopefully.

"No," he says, still looking puzzled.

I will kill his mother—how could you give a baby with such looks-potential a name like *Jack*? "Where are you from...*Jack*?"

"Iowa. My family have been corn farmers there for three generations," he states proudly.

No, no! This cannot be! How could those dancing, roaming, hot-blooded gypsy ancestors of his have gotten stuck in *Iowa* and never found their way out? "And you?" he asks me politely.

"Me what?" I ask stupidly, mesmerized by his warm black eyes.

"Where are *you* from?"

"Oh…kind of all over the place… You know how it is… Born in New York, one year of grade school I don't even remember in Geneva, a year studying in Paris much later, another short stint at Oxford… My ancestors are mostly Russian Jews."

"Wow, that sounds so neat! I've never been further west than Colorado, myself, or further East than my home town (wink)." I can hardly hear him through the sound of so many of my illusions shattering. But the wink—the wink, I caught.

I muster up some more of my assumptions about him, and say: "Okay, I want to guess what you do. I like doing this, as a kind of game. I'm usually pretty good at it, too…"

"Okay, shoot!" he says with a beautiful smile, and brushes some glossy tendrils out of his face.

"Dancer? Musician? Wait!—maybe both?!"

He laughs, his curls jumping. "Not even close."

"Um… psychic? No, I know—artist! Painter! Traditional Healer?" He shakes his head again, smiling. "I give uuuup," I say flirtatiously.

"I sell insurance."

I stare at him. "You do not."

"Yeah, I do. Why? What's wrong with being an insurance salesman?" he asks peevishly, his face closing up.

"Oh," I say, trying to recover status quo with him, "nothing, nothing at all! I mean, that's *great*!"

I sound ridiculous, but it apparently works, because he looks friendly again. I *suppose* I can overlook the incongruity of his profession—*and* his name—given how scrumptious he is. I know his ancestors had those same curls, those same dark furry eyebrows, that same spark in the eyes.

At least, as of four generations ago.

j

Half an hour later, we're on our way to his house. I can't wait to see it. I can't wait to *feel* it—cream silk dupioni drapes scratching lightly against my bare back, that purple velvet duvet run slowly between my legs... Mmmm...

But what is this incompatible vehicle?: a beige Volvo with a dented front passenger door. I'm sure that, being the kind of person I know he is, he doesn't even *own* a car, that this one's borrowed. (But I don't ask.)

Hmmm...well, the house isn't quite as I expected, either. It's an *apartment*, for one thing. There's *furniture*, for another. And it looks like bloody *Ethan Allen*. The lights are fluorescent and too bright. I perch uncomfortably on the brown-and-yellow plaid couch and he asks if I'd like anything to drink. I ask for Merlot, and he looks apologetic. "Sorry," he says, "there's only beer...or milk." *Milk?!* When's the last time I drank a glass of milk? I'm gagging at the mere thought. Although, if he has any dogs around, I guess I could try that Letterman trick to liven up the evening.

"Um... What kind of beer?" Why am I asking this? I *detest* beer. Although, given the choice of beer versus milk, I'd probably rather drink a beer.

"Coors or Pabst."

"I'll just take a glass of water, if you don't mind."

"Are you sure? The milk doesn't even expire until tomorrow."

"Yeah, just water, please." He comes back to the living room carrying my water and a Coors for himself. "Are you...um, subletting this place?" I ask.

"No, why?"

"Just wondering." I look around. Where, oh where, are the Bali batiks, the original Raku pottery, the Senegalese talking drums? The prayer flags, the Kenyan woven baskets? "What about incense?"

"What?"

"Incense."

"Oh, I thought you said *incest*! Ha ha! I don't have any. Why? Does it smell bad in here or something?"

"No, no, of course not!"

"I could get the Glade from the bathroom."

"No, no...*please* don't. It's fine."

"Okay. Hey, wanna watch some tube?" he asks cheerfully, grabbing one of the many remotes from his coffee table. The television comes on suddenly.

"Actually...if you don't mind... I, um, I'm not really in the mood for *TV* right now." Was that a big enough hint?

"Oh! Okay. Well..." (Now's the time he should say, with a knowing, sly tone, "So what *are* you in the mood for, hmmm...?") Instead, he says: "So, no Roseanne? I have it on tape."

"Um, no thanks. Can we just...talk?" I ask him.

(Now's the time for him to sidle close to me and say, with a knowing, sly tone and a wink, "Or just, um...*whatever*?") Instead he says, "Sure! What should we talk about?"

"I don't know...tell me about your family." I'm hoping to get back to at least a *mental* place where his inky-eyed relations are still doing what they're supposed to: making merry.

"Well, my folks are retired now. They've got a time-share in Daytona. I always go visit them when they're down there, every December. I get them a tree—usually a silver one from K-Mart; that's their favorite kind and K-Mart has them cheapest—and set it up for them, dig out the old family ornaments, put up the stockings. You know, it's so amazing—we still have the same stockings that my brother and I made in grade school! You know, with glitter spelling out our names, and 'Mom' and 'Dad,' and even 'Fido,' our first poodle." I'm having a *huge* cognitive dissonance problem, trying to reconcile his appearance with everything else. "Then we sing carols out by the pool, and—"

"You have a brother?" I interrupt.

"Yeah. Why?"

"So...what's *his* name?"

"Well, actually, he has this really weird name—I mean, *different*. It's Rai."

"Rye? Like rye bread?"

"R-A-I," he spells. "It's supposed to mean 'king,' or something like that."

"Huh. Is he older or younger than you?"

"Older. I guess my parents regretted their decision to name their kids anything weird by the time I was born, and my sister."

"So they called you Jack, and your sister...?"

"My sister's Jennifer. Man, and I tell ya, I think the naming thing must've had some kind of psychological effect, too."

"What do you mean?"

"Well, like I told you, I'm in insurance. Jenny's a real estate agent. She loves it, and she's real good at it too. But Rai..."

"Yes?" I ask, slightly breathless.

"Well, Rai... You name it, Rai's done it—folk singer, trapeze artist, calligraphy instructor...that's actually why I laughed earlier, when you were trying to guess my profession."

"Uh-huh," I say dolefully.

"Right now, as far as I know, he's still somewhere in Indonesia, studying how monkeys and people live symbiotically. Before that, he spent some time in Africa learning how to build the way they do, you know, mud huts and stuff. And, let's see, before that I think it was Borneo. Yeah, he lived with the natives, in those longhouses, you know, those houses way up on stilts, in the middle of the jungle? Man, those people are still *head-hunters*, can you believe that?!"

"Huh?... Oh, actually, yeah, I did know that. So...do you guys all look alike?"

"Who, my family? Yeah—man, it's so weird—we pretty much all look like clones! My mom and dad used to joke that they couldn't tell any of us apart."

"Well. Your brother sure sounds...adventurous."

"Yeah, he is—either that, or just plain stupid! You know, Alicia, you actually kind of look like us—same curly hair, same brown eyes…"

"A*viva*," I say icily.

"Oh, right, sorry! Aviva! Sorry!" He waits until I stop glaring.

"That's okay," I say, finally.

"But Rai's hair is even longer than yours, I think."

"It is?!" I gasp. Now he's starting to look at me funny. God, why did you send me the wrong one? I bet his brother doesn't have a door knocker that's meant to look like the American flag. I bet his brother doesn't have canisters for flour, sugar, and coffee shaped like little ducks and which say *flour*, *sugar*, and *coffee* on them. I bet his brother doesn't have a cross-stitched thingie on his front door that says *Welcome To My Kountry Kottage*. I bet his brother doesn't even have a front door.

"Yes. It is," he says, staring at my hair. All of a sudden, he grabs me and presses me down into the couch, kissing me so hard I can't breathe. I struggle up for some air. "Alicia!" he moans.

I almost laugh, sober myself by thinking of his beautiful brother even now placing tiny red bananas on lacquered trays, retreating into the bushes dressed only in his curly black chest hair and a colorful sarong, silver rings on his toes, spying on the monkeys, gamelan music forever pinging in the background. If I can keep him in mind, maybe I can get feeling horny again.

"Rai!" I shout ten minutes later, when Jack's hand finds itself in a very sensitive spot.

He draws back suddenly, fingers taking leave of my anatomy.

"What did you say?!"

"Right! I said *riiiiight*! I *love* that!" I gasp, putting his hand back where it was. Obediently (the way I like my men), he starts again.

At the end, to add insult to injury, as it were, he came suddenly—without waiting for me. Nevertheless I was kind enough to rake his back with the tips of my fingernails, which made him, like all guys (and all canines) sigh with pleasure. I thought I'd wait a few minutes, a polite interval, until I brought up his omission. Meanwhile, his emission fortunately remained trapped within the condom, I could see as he rolled halfway off me, thus preventing yet more dark-curly-haired creatures from roaming this planet.

"Hey, Jack?" I whispered. No answer. "Jack?"

And got a snore in response.

Ø

Date: 30 OCT 01 23:56:45
From: allpedalnowork@yahoo.com
Subject: saving dough, saving the world
To: profaviva@yahoo.com

Aviva,
My new landlord is incredibly cheap, like me. She doesn't run the heat at all. She is thrilled that I don't wash my clothes a lot, since this will cut electricity and water use, and wear and tear on the washer and dryer. We are recycling, deluxe. House rules require us to collect all vegetable, fruit, etc., remains in a bucket on the counter. This includes water used to rinse plates. Bucket is dumped in compost pile in yard daily. The compost pile also has about 30 to 50 slices of bread in it (explanation below).
Chinese John Wayne ("CJW") comes twice a week to do fix-it jobs for the landlord here. Today he put up a curtain rod. When the rains stop, he will go up on the roof and fix the leak that began

to drip from the kitchen ceiling today. He is about 85, obviously brilliant and with a couple of Ph.D.s earned in Communist China.

CJW also brings 3 or 4 loaves of bread and assorted fruits and vegetables with him whenever he comes. He gets the food from some soup-kitchen place. One of his chores here is to take the bread left over from his prior deliveries and spread it over the compost pile.

The landlord is retired on disability. I don't know what her disability is. I had thought maybe it was deafness, as she started out shouting all the time. Then she said she was off to her AA meeting. The second day I was here she was talking about a friend she wanted to fix me up with, and casually mentioned that they'd been committed together in the past. So I figure her disability is alcohol and/or drugs.

The day I saw this room for rent was one day after my predecessor was reportedly taken away by police in handcuffs. Allegedly, he was dealing drugs and also had stolen the landlord's license plates and put them on his own car.

Current paranoid musings:

Could landlord and friend have planted drugs in former tenant's room as revenge for him having spurned their amorous advances?

Is landlord feeding me arsenic in either the filtered water or through CJW's day-old bread deliveries?

Will I be buried with other former tenants in the compost pile?

With trepidation,
Alan

t

    The aspens are all yellow now, and the leaves from the other deciduous trees, like the spectacular maples here in the Chautauqua neighborhood, are almost all gone. I'm taking a walk through here before I teach; it's too beautiful a day to actually sit at my desk for office hours. Today is Halloween, and I need to get some more men done pretty soon; I'm falling behind.

    A darling Golden Retriever puppy comes wiggling across one lawn to meet me. Every time I think I want a dog someday, though, I remember an excellent poem I once saw in a children's poetry exhibition—I forget the first part, but the last two lines will always stay in my memory: "Pees on the rug / Baby dogs." Guess I'll stick with my beloved feline. Although, in their favor, dogs don't bring you *petits cadeaux*, the way cats do—like the puked-up head and torn-off legs of a grasshopper for you to step on, on your way to the bathroom in the middle of the night. On the other hand, cats don't actively seek out, and ecstatically roll in, rotting animal remains. There was a joke handout that was going around during a graduate Psycholinguistics seminar I took, where there was this supposed map of the canine brain; the vast majority of it was devoted to "love of the putrid." Dogs also *eat* cat turds—I think that fact alone settles, once and for all, the superiority debate.

    The puppy suddenly dashes out into the road (apparently, to *greet* the oncoming car—shall we once again discuss superiority?), and I automatically grab its collar as it tries to lumber past me. It licks my hand, totally unconcerned about its near-date with *la mort*. The guy sprawled on the ancient, stained couch on a warped front porch waves his thanks at me, yells, "Dude! You're huge!"

Somehow, I've never appreciated that phrase.

I step on a business card, stoop to pick it up. It reads: *Psychedelic Gospel Convention. Donations needed for my brother's liver transplant. Matthew (one of the 12 apostles). De Ja Vu. Central Park. 420 Everyday.* Thanks to my students always talking about it, I now know the number 420 has something to do with pot.

Back in class, my afternoon stroll finished, I ask my students what the number has to do with marijuana. They all crack up and, as a group, refuse to tell me. Sigh. Just another indication, like all the waitpersons lately who keep calling me *ma'am*, that I'm getting old. I thought I still had a few years left before students would start refusing to explain their slang to me. Hell, they probably don't even call it *slang* anymore. This being a nomenclature course I'm teaching, I should inquire. But I don't want to be laughed out of the classroom.

I ask them to hand their homework up to the front of the room. There are suspiciously few assignments being reluctantly passed up. In fact, there are *three*. Out of twenty-two. I can't help it; I lose my cool and sound like a total old-fogey teacher: "Will someone please tell me why almost no one here did their homework?"

Total silence. Then a voice from a guy in the back: "Didn't have time."

More voices join in: "Yeah."

"Me neither."

"Same here."

"But I assigned this two classes ago. What do you mean, you didn't have time?" Silence again. I try, "Well, what do you do with your evenings? That's when I always did *my* Linguistics homework…"

The guy from the back answers again: "Well, you know… You watch your three, four of hours of tube—like, dude, only the shows you absolutely *have* to catch—go out for a couple of beers, cruise the web for two, three hours… There's just not much time left for, you know…*other* stuff."

i

Crashing a Halloween party with Georgette. I warned her that (if all goes well) I'll have to bail on the party at some point, so we came in separate cars. On Mapleton, for all the major holidays, there are always a few huge parties—parties so big, you don't even need to pretend to know the host's name. You just walk in, try to find a safe place to stash your coat, and start looking around for someone good to flirt with.

I'm dressed as a cat. I know, I know—*boring*. But Halloween in Boulder is always too cold to wear my authentic Japanese kimono with the little wooden *geta*. (As usual, it dropped fifty degrees since this afternoon and now it's snowing.) All the poor little Boulderite kids with their anticipation—every year they have to end up covering those little princess, ballerina, and Batman costumes with a parka and boots.

Anyway, I'm too cheap to rent a costume. And too tired and overworked to think ahead and invent a really good (warm) one. So I always fall back on the black sweater, black leggings, sexy black boots, drawn-on whiskers from a tiny stub of twenty year-old eyeliner pencil I have kept all these years for just this occasion, and two little black construction-paper triangles bobby-pinned crookedly to the top of my head. It looks nicely color-coordinated because of my dark hair. In the past, I tried to have a tail as well, but I never found a way to avoid it looking like an obscenely huge African phallus coming out of my rear, so I've given up on that part of it—I guess I'm a Manx, although whenever I tell people that, it turns out they've never heard of it. People have such weak vocabularies these days.

Therese told me that when she was living in Dallas, she was mugged for her purse on Halloween night while dressed as ZZ Top (well, as one of them). That had to have been just too weird—for the mugger, I mean. She's had an aversion to their music ever since.

Georgette, when she saw me tonight, was definitely disappointed. "Oh, Aviva—*again*?" I assure her—as I do annually—that this will be my last Halloween as a cat.

She has turned up as a fabulous-looking flapper, wearing a genuine, ancient, fringe-y thing, Cupid mouth drawn on in red lipstick, short shiny black wig. I refrain from stating the truth: that the costume was easy for her because this is the kind of thing she wears all the time.

"Aren't you freezing?" I ask.

She flips up her beaded dress to the hip, peels down her opaque black hose, and I see revealed a layer of thermal underwear. She grins.

We head off to find the bathroom, weaving through a Superman, several hookers, an Elton John, four or five other black cats, and what is apparently a giant hotdog with mustard and relish. Well, if there's a prize at this party for most original costume, I certainly won't get it. But I need to find a prize of my own tonight—a Number Fourteen. Georgette and I join the line.

A Monica Lewinsky, stain on dress and all (jeez, I can't believe people are still doing the Lewinsky thing!), emerges from the bathroom. Good, only four more people in front of us now. The thing with these big parties is, it's like at a rock concert: the line for the bathroom is so long that you have to get back into line as soon as you come out, thereby missing out on the event you came for. I examine the people in front of Georgette. There's an angel; then a guy dressed as a woman, with huge fake breasts (guess he didn't get his fill of cross-dressing at the Exotica Erotica); then a guy dressed as I don't know what (something white and red); then an Elvis. The door opens and Elvis goes in, already unzipping his white jumpsuit in combined eager anticipation of his task and inebriated obliviousness to the present audience. Georgette looks at me and we laugh.

"Can you believe people are still doing Elvis?" she giggles, then realizes her *faux pas*. "Not that there's anything wrong with…um…*enduring themes*. I mean, the classic ideas are the ones that survive, of course," she amends, reaching over and straightening one of my kitty ears.

Later, I find myself dancing with the Jolly Green Giant. I can't help but wonder about the color and size of his...appendage. Then—what is this, *penis night?*—I dance with a guy in a kilt, wondering if it's swinging free under there, as tradition prescribes. I try to look, but he never does a spin quickly enough for the kilt to ride up far enough, plus the little silver purse-thingie over that area is a visual impediment. What is the purpose of those things, anyway? As far as I can tell, they function solely to cover the genitals in case a big wind comes up. (Which happens really frequently in Boulder; what would be considered hurricane-strength in other parts of the country doesn't even merit a comment from the news stations here.)

Then Madonna (the hussy kind, not the religious kind) touches me gently on the arm and asks me in a husky voice to dance, but I smile apologetically and tell her I'm trying to find a man. She rolls her eyes, says, "Good luck, honey. I gave up on that *years* ago," and stalks off, wiggling her ass for me.

I dance with the Pope. Then I notice he has all these translucent things pinned all over his white robe; I look more closely. Oh: they're condoms, still rolled up, fresh out of their packages. A Pope making a statement, then. He seems pretty drunk. Suddenly he's grabbed by Superwoman, with huge metallic conical breasts. Hey! She stole my Pope!

An Indian is my next dance partner. No, not a "Native American," nor an "indigenous North American." This is the old-style costume: a plain old *Indian*, as in "cowboys and Indians." Faux feather headdress, faux buckskin clothing, toy bow and arrows strapped to his back. Even though the whole thing is fake, there's still something majorly sexy about the thought of him naked except for a loincloth and fringed soft knee-high boots, shuffling and chanting around a bonfire. *Damn!* It's a good thing it's time to bag another guy, with how horny I am tonight. I think part of it is just the relief of PMS being over with; I got my period a few days ago.

Speaking of which, time to get back in line for the bathroom...

When I return to the living room, my Indian has been nabbed by Darth Vader. Darth looks my way and I bare my cat claws at him/her. He/she turns back to the Indian and does a pelvic thrust disco move.

I wonder where Georgette has gotten to in all these people... Oh, there she is, next to the sliding glass door to the patio, close-dancing with Big Bird. Looks like she's having fun—although unbeknownst to her, she's getting tiny downy yellow feathers all over her expensive dress.

Suddenly my hand is grabbed and I'm pulled out to the middle of the dance floor. It's the guy from the bathroom line, the one that I can't tell what he's supposed to be—something white, with red paint on top. Kind of a white cottony material, wrapped around his whole torso... *Eeewwwww!* He's a giant used tampon!

In spite of his costume, though, he's kind of cute. Light brown hair, tall, big nice hands... Coming out from the very top of his headwrap is a long braided white cord, hanging down, which he is making swirl around and around his face as he fake-jitterbugs. Well, a man dressed as a tampon is still a man, right?

Then a vampire waltzes me away, relinquishing me subsequently—as he suddenly realizes the appropriateness of his dancing, instead, with the used tampon—to two guys dressed as the Siamese-twins-with-three-heads from Monty Python. The middle head is constructed from papier-mâché and resembles the two of them, blond and blue-eyed. Scandinavians from Siam? I start dancing with them, and soon, due to all their wild gyrations, the middle head suddenly cracks noisily at the neck, hangs for a moment by a thick thread, then falls right off. The guys freeze, stunned momentarily into stillness, then both let out a shout and go after it like a soccer ball, forgetting all about this lonesome cat.

Which is how I find myself once again with the giant tampon, who doesn't seem to be too drunk and is, after all, nice and tall, with big feet. (The vampire is nowhere to be seen, perhaps having decided to look for fresher blood.) The tampon leans over and whispers to me that he'd like to "groove with me." Man, what is the deal? Since I took this bet, I must be giving off some new kind of pheromones. Guys never actually said this kind of thing to me before.

It's getting late, and most of these other guys are probably too drunk to function properly. I wave goodbye to Big Bird and Georgette. She's never going to get all those little yellow feathers out of that beadwork.

ă

Back at my apartment, the guy and I kiss for what feels like forever. Then I open my eyes again and realize he's still wearing that awful costume. I insist he take it off. He grins, pulls off the head-wrap, and starts unwrapping the torso part, too. "That's better," I purr. He tugs the cat ears out of my hair and tosses them on the floor. Mmm...what a great kisser. Who would've expected that from an ambulatory Tampax?

We progress to my breasts. He turns out to be good at that too. Mr. Tampax has a smooth, hairless chest—he's no tribal member, that's for sure. The change is kind of nice. Whoever said that variety is the spice of life must've anticipated me and this bet.

He plays with my belly button, always a strange feeling. Once is sexy, twice weird, three times feels like it's going to pop out and unravel, like letting go of a balloon—you can imagine yourself going *phhhhhtttttt!*, flying in rapid figure-eights around the apartment, until you shrivel, peter out and come to a dusty landing in some corner.

He stands up suddenly. I whimper; where is he *going*? But no, he just stood up to achieve a better angle for undoing the top button of his jeans. There is no better sound in the world than that of a man's extremely taut zipper slowly and steadily unzipping. I once saw a movie in which heaven was portrayed as being allowed to choose only one memory forever after. If heaven meant you could only have one sound, I would have to choose the male zipper. Well…either that or Beethoven's Seventh.

He looks fabulous naked. He tugs at my tights, pulls them down to my knees, then goes for my black bikini underwear.

Then stops dead.

"What?!" I pant.

"You…you have your…your…*period!*"

"Yeah. So?"

Silence.

"Is that a problem? *I* don't mind…" I shrug.

He is mute.

"It's the fourth day—it's hardly messy at all anymore."

"Um… Well…"

I look down, see that his proudly flying flag has been lowered—completely—from its mast. In fact, it looks like it wouldn't stir in a cyclone. "Your neighbor's chicken is a duck," I mutter, disgusted.

"What?"

"Nothing," I sigh, thinking: *I should've gone home with the vampire.*

3

Date: 01 NOV 01 13:04:20
From: eatmoreradishes@juno.com
Subject: Re: FWD: FWD:
To: profaviva@yahoo.com

You guys know I don't usually forward internet stuff, but this is just **too** good!!!
...Georgette

> > Hey, all you bitchin' babes out there,
> > get a load of **this** shit!!!
> > This is an excerpt from a 1960's Home Economics
> > textbook:
> > When retiring to the bedroom, prepare yourself
> > for bed as promptly as possible. Whilst feminine
> > hygiene is of the utmost importance, your tired

> > husband does not want to queue for the bathroom as
> > he would have to do for his train. But remember
> > to look your best when going to bed. Try to
> > achieve a look that is welcoming without
> > being obvious. If you need to apply face-cream
> > or hair-rollers, wait until he is asleep,
> > as this can be shocking to a man last thing
> > at night.
> > When it comes to the possibility of intimate
> > relations with your husband, it is important to
> > remember your marriage vows and in particular your
> > commitment to obey him.
> > If he feels that he needs to sleep immediately
> > then so be it. In all things be led by your
> > husband's wishes; do not pressure him in any way
> > to stimulate intimacy.
> > Should your husband suggest congress, then accede
> > humbly, all the while being mindful that a man's
> > satisfaction is more important than a woman's.
> > When he reaches his moment of fulfillment, a
> > small moan from yourself is encourag-

ing to him and
> > quite sufficient to indicate any enjoyment that
> > you may have had.
> > Should your husband suggest any of the more
> > unusual practices, be obedient and uncomplaining,
> > but register any reluctance by remaining silent.
> > It is likely that your husband will then fall
> > promptly asleep, so adjust your clothing, freshen up,
> > and apply your night-time face- and hair-care
> > products. You may then set the alarm so that you can
> > arise shortly before him in the morning.
> > This will enable you to have his morning cup of
> > tea ready when he awakes.

I'

There's this extremely adorable, quite young guy I've been noticing. He's not my type—he's blond. Very sweet-looking. In fact, angelic. *Cherubic.* He's prettier than most *girls*. Really white skin, not unhealthy—just delicate. As a baby, my god, he must've been cute. Those blond ringlets, always askew from being mussed so often by adoring hands. I'm not sure why I'm so attracted to someone who doesn't look at all "macho." Or even vaguely Mediterranean. But there you have it.

In fact, he looks so like a work of art that I've developed an idea in my scheming, horny little brain: I'll ask him to be my model. I want to draw him. (Nude, of course.) No, but I really do; the aesthetics of him are as astounding as his sexiness, or perhaps they're what constitute it; I don't know. I just know I have the urge to draw those smooth, bare limbs. To reproduce with black charcoal an outline of all that ivory and pale rose beauty.

He's around the Trident nearly always, playing backgammon or just hanging out, shooting the breeze with his friends Z and Peggy the Dog-Walker and anyone else around, taking and giving hugs; everyone loves him. (Backgammon is not a game I play; someone tried to explain the rules to me once, but it involved way too much math.) He exudes this innocent, childlike happiness. He has a lovely smile. His lips are the palest pink; his cheekbones and jawline exaggerated, in an ascetic, feminine face; his complexion flawless, pores invisible. He should be an Oil of Olay model.

Ý

Marcel is posed with a sheet draped across his loins (that's the only appropriate word; we are after all *artistes* here), the late-afternoon Western light perhaps a bit strong on his nearly hairless pearly thighs, his ethereal curls and aquamarine eyes shining as he gazes into the middle distance, where I've asked him to focus. The object of his focus is in fact staring back at him just as intently: Baby, who is perched on top of my dresser, across the room. She is the model-watchcat. Every time he moves even a millimeter, from posing fatigue, she notices immediately, and stares fixedly at the offending body part. Once he's stopped moving it and has resumed his exact, original pose, she slowly moves her gaze back up to hold his eyes again.

"Ah-hah!" I shout. "Are you sure you don't need a break? She saw you move your bottom leg just now!"

"No, no," he assures me. "I'm fine. Maybe another fifteen minutes, half an hour."

"Okay, if you're sure... But if she catches you again, I think you'll have to break for a little while."

"Agreed," he says, giving me the most beatific smile.

He ought to be surrounded right now by apricot-wash unfinished plaster walls, antique teak floors, enormous *vases* (pronounced in the French manner, of course) holding fresh calla lilies, muted European light streaming through the arched floor-to-ceiling windows of my *atelier*... The cloth draped so artfully across his alabaster body ought to be soft linen, once naturally-dyed carmine but washed so many times as to be now nearly indistinguishable from his own pastel skin tones. But in fact, Baby is the sole artistic element here, the only one (besides my beautiful model himself, of course) that wouldn't have to be changed to make this scene *juste*.

Because the only extra sheet I had in my apartment—I was too embarrassed to just go and yank the one I use off my bed (what, and risk stray black pubic hairs raining softly down onto his marmoreal form?)—was one I found way back in my closet. It had to be from, like, the first sheet set I ever bought, when my tastes were shamefully unsophisticated, the current result being that here was exquisite Marcel looking more than a little ridiculous with half-polyester orange-and-yellow cartoon octopi patrolling his private parts (about which I must admit to a tremendous curiosity, having allowed him his modesty when disrobing for his modeling session—are they as snowy as the rest of him? Can they possibly be? Or *must* they tend toward the rose spectrum?).

And while we're at it, why is the term *private parts* plural? I remember repeatedly quizzing Brandon. "But, Brandon, how many...*things*—you know—*stuff*...discrete *objects*...does it feel like you *have* down there?" I used to ask. At first he looked puzzled, then interested in tackling the subject. What surprised me most was that he'd never thought about it before.

"One, I guess." And he assumed: question answered.

"One? Really? Not, like, *two*?"

He scowled, thinking about it. He even amused and titillated the hell out of me by unconsciously and totally un-self-consciously reaching a hand down to kind of jiggle, juggle, and weigh himself—his part. Or parts. "Okay, yeah, I guess, yeah, maybe two."

"Two? So...you're not *sure*? I mean, it could feel equally like you have *two* parts or *one* down there? Oh my god, that's so *weird*!" But I was genuinely fascinated, and wanted to settle this issue. How could there be part of your body that felt like maybe it was one thing or maybe two, and you'd even spent your entire life with this thing (or things) dangling off you? Women—we just *are*. We're *whole*.

"Two, I guess. Yeah, let's say two, whatever, fine," he'd said, obviously getting annoyed—for no apparent reason.

"Or...*Brandon*," I'd said. He looked at me warily, a look I'd always loved, out of the tops and corners of his eyes. "Could it be...*three*?"

That was when he said one, two, three, twenty, however many I wanted, but he was done talking about it. I'm still disappointed in him for that; he was a *scientist*, for Christ's sake.

Anyway... Let's face it, there's just something totally unsatisfactory about attempting to do life-drawing—or anything artistic—in a suburban apartment, and on wall-to-wall carpeting. No serious artist has *ever* had to work on wall-to-wall carpeting. This is just something I know.

Baby hasn't changed her gaze at all in the last few minutes; I guess Marcel was telling the truth. I continue sketching, reflecting all the while: men are so unconcerned about—nay, even eager to—show their nakedness. At the slightest provocation, the most wishy-washy request, the flimsiest excuse—or even no pretext at all—they whip off the shirt, drop the pants, fling the boxers to the far corners of the room, and parade around without the least inclination to hide, conceal, or protect their newly-exposed part(s). I have a hypothesis: Could men's ease be a result of the way our culture's restrooms are set up? Women pee in private (and moreover, while we're peeing, our anatomy is at its least visible), but men have to haul out their equipment for all to view every time they have to urinate, starting as soon as they're old enough to stand up—a process which starts before they can even remember.

Whereas we women know precisely how we're off from the ubiquitous and incalculably pernicious advertising images: every unwanted dimple of cellulite, every new broken capillary that has defiled our formerly pristine teenage thighs... We know every centimeter of our body, track every year's battles lost to gravity and aging, are aware of how we look in every position, every piece of clothing we own, every menstrual phase of the month. We never just disrobe happily, freely, wildly, and prance around in front of every new lover, assuming absolutely that we're perfect, saddlebags, saggy boobs, belly and all.

Oy, what a pity.

C

Have you been wondering what ever happened to my ex, Brandon? Well, he used to be someone who was going to *be* somebody, who was going to make a difference in the world, who drank freshly-ground hot chocolate with me in the *zócalos* of Oaxaca and stayed up all night discussing polytheistic societies or *The Little Prince*...but he turned into this really boring, gin-and-tonics-after-work guy with an 8-to-5 job, three kids, a mortgage, and a minivan.

One thing he ended up doing didn't quite fit the mold, however: he married this Aussie chick who had (unbeknownst to him) already slept with every other guy in the office—she was *majorly* trolling for the ol' Wallet-And-A-Penis (one who would simultaneously provide her with a green card, a new last name, and legitimacy for all the critters she wanted to pop out), and boy, did she ever find it in sweet, innocent, well-hung Brandon. *My* Brandon. Sigh.

Anyway, I did feel just the *teensiest* bit better when I heard (from a sympathetic mutual friend who used to work with him) that when all Brandon's office buddies threw him his bachelor party, they got pretty drunk beforehand and therefore decided to do something slightly ill-advised: they printed out a bunch of paper banners and hung them all around the room; interspersed amongst all the "Congratulations!" was one which read: "I'm Marrying The Office Bicycle!"

When Brandon, in the general bonhomie and ale-induced camaraderie, asked a guy pleasantly what that last one meant, that guy nudged the guy next to him and pointed at the banner, which caused the guys next to them to notice, which caused the guys next to *them* to notice, and so on. After about thirty seconds, all the (highly intoxicated) guys were paying attention. They all put their arms around each other and around Brandon, too, to include him in the club, and shouted in unison in their best imitation Australian accent, "Everyone's 'ad a ride, mate!"

S

On my way to meet Therese at the Fall Festival to celebrate—ta da!—the Halfway Point. Fifteen guys!

This challenge has kind of taken on a life of its own. I was considering it the other day, right after Numbers Fourteen and Fifteen (Marcel and one that I'm calling My Indian), and I'm afraid I couldn't stop now even if I wanted to. Is it a matter of pride, or is it (horrors) mere wantonness? I'm not sure. (If asked, of course, I'll go with pride.)

A beat-up old pickup truck cruises by slowly, apparently looking for parking. It wears a white bumper sticker with some kind of peculiar-looking drawing on it in red—a pair of glasses? A butterfly? The infinity symbol? I squint to read the lettering before the vehicle disappears: *I had a ball at the Testicle Festival!*

I'd always wanted to have sex with a Native American. They have great skin, great hair, great coloring, nice beaky noses, good cheekbones. Like tribal members (sorry) without their hirsuteness.

When a colleague in the French Department said she had an old friend coming to town and could I entertain him for an evening while she interviewed a couple of candidates for the new tenure-track position, I said yes immediately, thinking, hey, if he's hetero, within the right age range, and not particularly ugly, he can be my Number Fifteen. When she told me he was thirty-nine and Native American, I was *majorly* psyched. I immediately started worrying I'd fall in love, screwing up not only the bet but probably the rest of my life as well.

"Which Nation?" I'd asked her, pointedly using the latest hypercorrect P.C. term.

"Navajo."

"Cool," I'd answered, although it didn't make any difference to me. She'd raised one eyebrow at my response (the bitch! How come I still can't do that, even though I practice constantly?). Then I'd remembered she taught Lesbian Literature. Oh, shit. Maybe her friend was gay, too?

Ouch—I trip over a signboard. I've arrived at the first of the Festival booths without noticing. I look at the offending board: *Harmonic Self-Transformation. Alchemical Hypnotherapy. Body Alignment Technique. Cellular Release. Starr Galaxie, M.A., C.H.T.* Yep, I'm here.

Walking a bit more carefully now, I relive my excitement upon anticipating handfuls of silky, waist-length raven-black hair, to wrap my hands in and gently (or not so gently) tug as my fancy took me while we made savage (sorry) love. There was even supposed to be a full moon that night—okay, *almost* full. I couldn't help but think there was something propitious about the fact that the Halfway Guy would be a type I'd always wanted to experience. Plus, ever since the Halloween party, I'd gotten aroused every time I remembered that guy in his Indian costume. I assumed that my chances of getting this real-life Navajo dressed up like that were probably nil, but in the heat of the moment…you never knew what a guy would agree to, if a woman said it turned her on. Recall Tex, after all. But even if this guy refused to go whole-hog and wear the loincloth and headdress and everything, well, if nothing else he was probably really good-looking and I could certainly count on *at least* long black hair and let's say a turquoise necklace or two, *n'est-ce pas?* Such were my thoughts as I drove to the airport.

I spot the back of Therese's head. As agreed upon, she's sitting on the hay bales in "Speaker's Corner," an odd little setup that is not very popular, but they keep trying. I wonder if it's never very well-attended simply because freedom of speech is already so…*rampant* in Boulder. Therese is looking skeptical (I can tell this from the back of her head, I know her so well).

"Hey," I say, sitting down next to her.

"Hey," she says. "Congratulations, by the way, on the fifteen. Halfway!"

"Thanks." I smile at her. We look up as the speakers change. A short guy with bright orange pants, a red T-shirt and odd, bouncy, girly carrot-top ringlets (it hurts just to look at him) gets up and poses diffidently in front of the microphone. He needn't be so afraid, as the entire audience at the moment consists of: me and Therese way in the back, who'd picked that spot merely for its convenience to meet; a couple who've stopped there to change their baby's diaper; two or three oddballs who aren't even aware that anyone is within a one-mile radius of them; and three or four people who've walked over with some lunch from Alfalfa's across the street and are eating it and noisily discussing something, paying no attention whatsoever to the erratic changing of the guards up front (eating our own Alfalfa's deli takeout here once is actually how Therese and I originally met).

The curly-haired guy looks out at the "crowd" with fear and awe and starts mumbling something, but it's too soft to hear. After a few moments, I give up and turn to Therese.

"So," I tell her, "I had another Only In Boulder Moment yesterday, hiking Sanitas."

"What was it? Break the record for the number of dogs named Cody?"

"No," I tell her. "This guy was hiking with his Siamese cat. It was kind of draped around his shoulders. Wasn't even digging him too bad with its claws."

Just then the shy speaker onstage steps ever so slightly closer to the mike, and some of his words start to become audible. "…Second coming of Christ…be me…put my hands in the creek, little fishes come up…electricity coming out of my hands…"

Therese blinks at the speaker, absorbing this, then turns to me and asks, deadpan, "Chocolate point?"

"No," I tell her, "seal point." She nods, and we both look back at the stage.

The guy continues, a little more boldly: "…And my sister had this hamster that used to just kind of like, sit in the corner of its cage and after I put my hands on it, she said she thought it started coming out and, like, using its wheel more… And…I think I also might've, like, helped my friend's blind dog see again, so maybe I can, you know, like, heal people… um…I think I did it last night… So if anyone, like, wants to try it…?"

Therese and I look at each other and burst out laughing.

"I've got electricity running out of my fingers!" I giggle, wiggling them at Therese, "You better watch out!"

"I think I might've, like, cured a leper or something, like, maybe once!" shrieks Therese, though softly. We're clutching our sides. Oh, man. You know when Dorothy has to repeat "There's no place like home"? Well, I say this, and truly: there's no place like Boulder.

"Shall we go?" I ask finally. She nods, wiping away tears. We begin to make our way into the crowd, turning back to observe the laughing skateboarder teens who have dragged one unwilling friend bodily, struggling and cursing at his buddies, to be "healed" by the speaker, who has by now forsaken the microphone, and, bending from the waist with his hands and forearms heavily on top of the reluctant teen's head, appears to be trying very hard to effect something. Behold, though! Thanks to the skateboarders' prank, a line is now forming; three kayakers are laughing but definitely waiting, as well as two elderly women. The curly-haired guy looks surprised and amazed to see that he has attracted a *flock*, however small.

We're approaching a homeless-looking guy on a bench, dressed in multiple layers of tattered rags, sitting extremely upright, dignified and serious. In fact, motionless. As we pass the guy, he observes us desultorily, but then something on the ground seems to catch his eye fully. He startles us by suddenly disturbing his extreme stillness to whip out from under his many layers, folds, and coats—a can of Raid. He leans over, and with tremendous concentration, sprays a thirty-second non-stop stream on what appear to be two small black ants. When apparently satisfied as to their sufficient demise, he suddenly pops the instrument of death back under his layers and reverts to stone again. Only his eyes move to watch us pass, and with a great deal less interest than in the apparently trespassing members of the insect kingdom.

"That guy better watch it," Therese comments. "I don't think the Boulder police will take too kindly to people randomly spraying pesticides around. I didn't even know they *sold* that stuff around here."

"Yeah, really. They're gonna slap a hefty fine on him. They probably sell it at Target or somewhere like that."

"I haven't seen a can of Raid in I don't know how long. He must be from out of town. Hey, so is Georgette dating Big Bird, by the way?"

"Are you kidding?" I answer. "She said he didn't even merit a two-night stand."

"Well, it sounds like it was an interesting party."

"Yeah. It was."

I'm looking around at all the crap for sale: my god, the horrendously awful "Western art." This stuff is so terrible that I am ashamed just to be living in the same *state* that it's being painted and exhibited in. Today it's even more horrible because it's reminding me of My Indian.

So I'd gone to the airport to fetch him, excited already. I felt sure I'd be able to pick him out of the crowd of disembarking passengers, so I didn't bother doing anything as useless as holding up a sign with my colleague's name on it. I hadn't even asked *his* name—just gotten his flight number and time. You know the old expression, pride goeth before a fall? Well, there's a reason that expression has endured.

I waited and waited. And waited. I read exciting airport posters: *It happens at the Hilton: Business Rooms—with PowerDesk!* I waited through all the reuniting families and young lovers and corporate handshakes, all the crying babies and rumpled suits and women with faces in too-stark just-reapplied (somehow, in those tiny bathrooms—and you can imagine the angry lines forming outside) makeup. No Indian. Eventually everyone was off the flight, accounted for, and whisked away—all except for one middle-aged, short, stocky, Norwegian-looking mostly-bald blond guy in chinos, a preppy shirt and penny loafers, who was kind of standing around by himself.

There was *no way*. I approached him slowly. "You're not here for Sylvie, are you?" I asked him to be sure, knowing the answer would be no.

He brightened immediately. "I am! Are you her friend she sent to pick me up?"

My heart sank. Moreover, I was totally confused. Where was My Indian? And who was this impostor? How to be tactful about this? "Um...well...is there some mistake? Sylvie told me her Native American friend was coming to town...?"

"Right, that's me," he beamed. "Bobby McKenzie," he said, extending his hand toward me. "Happy to meetcha."

δ

I woke this morning to a large chartreuse pile of fresh cat vomit on the carpet laid out in the precise shape of the nation of Chile. (I always assign a geographical referent to them to help take my mind off how disgusting it is to have to clean them up.) The only thing worse than cleaning it is wandering bleary-eyed through the apartment first thing in the morning and stepping in it. (Then you can't even tell what country it was, either.)

It was hard to work up any excitement about having passionless gringo sex with a Bobby McKenzie when you wanted to make the beast with two backs with a guy whose name consisted of an animal and a verb. What I learned about fish-white Mr. McKenzie, in polite but dispirited (sorry) pillow talk, was that he claimed a whopping three percent Navajo blood. (Where was it hiding? I wondered. In a pinkie toenail, perhaps? Gee, there's a thought. Maybe I should've looked. Maybe he had a *wild toenail*, and my sexual experience with him could've been far more exciting than it was, had I known.) I still haven't figured out whether this whole thing was Sylvie's idea of a practical joke, or whether it's just that, being French, she's so out of the loop she has no clue.

And then there was Marcel. Marcel, whose most private part(s?), by the way, turned out to indeed resemble the delicate coloring of a just-out-of-bud *Souvenir de la Malmaison* rose. I suppose I should've guessed what the consummation of our *après-midi artistique* would be like, judging from Marcel's looks and general demeanor. He was, after all, so *beautiful*. So sweet, so gentle, so languorous… So, although I can't say for sure, because I have no familiarity with the other team, my best guess is that Marcel was the closest thing I've ever had to a lesbian experience.

Ö

In line at the Trident, with Bobby McKenzie. I have to entertain him for one more afternoon before he leaves, and it's not going to be between the sheets again. It's a lovely, mild fall day—*Indian* summer?—and we've been out biking. I've been showing him the highlights of Boulder and I even enlisted him to look for good bumper stickers while we were out on the roads. He spotted one that I loved and would even consider buying (except that I refuse to put bumper stickers on my own car), *My Cat Is Weirder Than Yours*.

Around the five o'clock rush hour, we managed to coincidentally run into a Critical Mass group, so we joined in for a while. Critical Mass, I hear, is spreading to more and more cities. Five hundred cyclists in giant packs, refusing to yield to automobiles, purposely taking back the roads from cars for hours at a time, pissing off drivers coast to coast. Of course, Boulder has its own spin on this; here, they have the Cruiser Ride and you're supposed to be on one of those old, one-speed bikes with the curved frames (and these people are tough; one speed in Boulder is grueling) and dress up in Mardi Gras costumes and get drunk before, (possibly) during, and (definitely) after the ride. We were near the end of the pack and I noticed the few police officers, present ostensibly to arrest any cyclists running red lights. Frankly, I think they were loving the fact that they got to be out just pedaling around and getting paid for it (although of course they had to maintain a serious expression, and they looked bummed that they weren't allowed to participate fully, like honking the old-fashioned funny claxons or cheering during the roundabouts). I bet they fight over who gets to be on this duty each week. Every time I see a police officer lately, I think of that one bumper sticker—what chutzpah (or stupidity) it would require to actually paste one on your car: the one that says *Bad Cop, No Donut*.

So here we are in line for post-cycling refreshment and also because the Trident is one of Boulder's landmarks to show Bobby. I suddenly realize just how many hours I was perched on that uncomfortable little seat, and excuse myself to use the restroom.

When I return, I notice there are two women at the front of the line who look like out-of-towners (we Boulderites can just *tell*). They're holding some kind of large rectangular paper thingies—origami?—and staring at them with great fascination. The barista asks for their order. They spread out the papers on the counter, adjust their glasses.

My god, they're *menus*! I didn't even know the Trident *had* menus! Everyone else in line who's a regular (i.e., everyone except Bobby, who's oblivious) is now craning forward to see the menus, fascinated. Where did they find them? Could the menus possibly be an actual relic, a historic item, perhaps left over in some forgotten corner from when the Trident was originally constructed? Are these tourists really anthropologists?

I'm distracted from this incredible incident by Bobby, in line behind me (must keep him in his place), who is asking me why I don't wear a helmet. When we rented him his bicycle, of course they gave him one and he wore it (as all the bike shops insist their renters do).

"See, the thing is," I explain, "when you live in Boulder, you bike a lot. And sooner or later, you get hit by a car. It's just, you know, a given. Kind of a fact of nature," I tell a shocked-looking Bobby.

"You're kidding."

"Nope." We advance in line. The out-of-town women are gone. And the menus? They appear to have been confiscated, but I've missed the whole scene. It will forever remain a mystery.

"Oh, come on!" Bobby says. "I don't believe you. Not *everybody*. Sure, *some* people must get hit by cars, I mean some percentage of the population, but—"

"No, really, *everyone*," I assure him. "I don't know anyone who hasn't been hit."

"Wait a minute. You've actually been hit by a car?" he asks me, incredulously.

"Yep."

"So then why don't you—how come—"

"Several times, in fact." Cool, I've left him speechless. I continue, "Actually, the last guy who hit me turned out to be a bike shop owner, so that was really convenient, you know, in terms of getting the front tire straightened out afterwards and everything."

"So then why the hell—"

"Why don't I wear a helmet?" I interrupt him.

"Yes! My god! I'd think, *especially* if you'd been hit, you'd be *more* likely to—"

"I can see why you'd expect that. I don't know, it's like… I'll try to explain." I notice I have quite the silent but avid audience by now: most of the customers at the nearby tables, the entire line, and the barista are closely following our conversation. "It's almost…a philosophical thing. I guess you'd have to live here to really appreciate it, but it's like…since everyone gets hit sooner or later, afterwards you're either dead or you're sort of, I don't know…fearless."

Just then a guy who's a few people behind us in line blurts out in this loud, arrogant voice, "Hey, that isn't true, what she's saying, dude! *I* live in Boulder, and *I* haven't been hit! Yo, and I ride my bike, like, all the time!"

Instantly, everyone else in line, plus about four or five people sitting at the tables who turn around to face the line, and the barista too, as he clangs espresso powder into the trash, all chime out in matter-of-fact voices: "You will be;" "That's odd;" "Dude, just wait;" "Your time is coming;" "It's only a matter of time, then;" "You're overdue;" "Hate to tell you, but…" It's a cacophony, but the unanimity of the message is obvious, and the guy who hasn't yet been hit by a car turns quite pale and begins to tremble. He abandons the line and exits the Trident, heading for the street. Poor guy. I wonder if he'll ever ride his bike again in Boulder.

If so, I hope he wears a helmet.

Ż

Date: 05 NOV 01 01:10:55
From: allpedalnowork@yahoo.com
Subject: but I **liked** Simon
To: profaviva@yahoo.com

Aviva,
I ask you, why can't all women be as reasonable as you?
Allow me to fill you in on an incident that recently took place and which, I fear, shall have proven to be the definitive end of a minor relationship with a woman I have been seeing for a few weeks (don't worry, I swear she wasn't as sexy as you).
Scene setting: I was at her house and she was in the bathroom doing god knows what women do that necessitates that they be in the bathroom during a large percentage of each day.
Situation: I had to take a leak, really bad. I knocked on the bathroom door and told her and she said to give her a few minutes, but I really

couldn't wait. When she is in there, she disappears for literally hours.

Options: a) I thought about pissing somewhere on her property (e.g., her lawn), but she lives in this really yuppie neighborhood and there are security lights, cameras, alarms, etc., i.e., surveillance equipment everywhere and I didn't want the cops to come.

b) I went into the basement where she keeps the litter box for her cat, Simon. Simon is a very handsome, striped orange cat whom mostly you don't see. I don't know where he hangs out all day, but he is a very elusive creature. I stood over the cat box and took out my urinary apparatus but then wondered, if I use Simon's box, 1) will the volume of my urine flood the box to the extent that the litter will be unable to absorb it, thereby overrunning said box and causing a mess?; 2) will the odor of my urine cause Simon to hereafter view me as his enemy, thus hating me on future visits? I am unsure about the ammonia content of my own urine as compared to that of the average adult male domestic feline, but decided that these were unacceptable risks, and tucked my equipment away. By now, however, we had a state of near...

Emergency: I had to urinate so urgently by now that I really didn't care where I did it, as long as I could relieve my bladder. I came back upstairs into the kitchen and moved some pots and pans in the double sink from one sink all into the other, so that one was totally clear and decided to...

c) just piss into the sink and then I could use the sprayer hose to wash it down. Why didn't I think of this before? I was so excited at the thought of being about to ease my internal pressure that I almost allowed urine to start dribbling right then. I pulled out my paraphernalia yet again and got ready but—relief was not yet to be! I had...

Another Situation: I immediately found that I was not at the right level to pee into the sink. It appeared that I would have to climb onto the countertop—which in my current state of discomfort was no easy feat—and then stand upright and urinate down into the sink. Amidst excruciating bladder pain I managed this and was just in the midst of a blissful long release when Guess Who finally chose that moment to emerge from the bathroom—where she had a perfect view into the kitchen.

I tried calmly explaining to her but she became somewhat hysterical. I actually don't understand why she got angry at all, especially when I delineated the entire situation in detail to her (plus it was her fault for being in the bathroom so long in the first place). In fact, the more I think about it, the more I believe she should have appreciated me **more than ever** because of my thoughtfulness about the potential repercussions of the litter box issues—don't you agree?

Current Status (mine inre her): Ex-boyfriend.
Alan

d

I have to stop this terrible habit. Whenever I get too bored with HPSG or left-dislocation or a number of other dull things that only Ph.D.s in Linguistics have to care about, I do this to get a dose of reality. Though, now that I consider it, that's an interesting question—truly, of the two, which one displays more irreality: the subjunctive mood in Valencian Catalan, or the on-line personal ads?

The guy who has provided me with a much-needed laugh during these wee hours, after putting the finishing touches on a difficult paper I'm to present tomorrow (procrastination doesn't end at studenthood) at what they like to very poetically call a "faculty brown-bag," has sent in his hand-picked photo which he is sure will attract the greatest number of female humans with whom to mate. In it he is standing in a trailer park. He's dressed in army fatigues and is holding some sort of automatic weapon, almost larger than his body, at an angle representative of an erection. He sports a very fierce expression and a very bad haircut.

In the text portion, where he's supposed to check off what he is looking for, it appears that he will be content with anything—as long as she's female. Any height from 4'0" to 7'0" will be fine; any weight from 80 to 400 pounds; any age from 0 to 99. But the best is yet to come: his "free verse," that little box where he describes himself. He says he feels the need to "be prepard 4 any & all emergensies" but that he's "not all ruff and tuff." In fact, he confesses to some "ood quite moments" and during these, he says he enjoys "bilding a fier."

Oh, Camouflage Man, where have you been all my life?

Another thing that cracks me up is that somehow, somewhere, someone has screwed up scanning some of the photos, so that very occasionally when you click on some guy's photo, instead of seeing it come up normal-sized like everyone else's (maybe two or three inches high), it comes up like the size of a Tic-Tac.

And then there's the guy where the photo he chose to submit was one where he cut out some woman from the picture; you can still see her arm around him, this disembodied limb around the grinning dickhead. Or even better—it's his wedding photo. Yeah, him and the (now) ex feeding each other cake on the big day—*that'll* make us want to date him.

I want to assure you that I (*bien sûr*) only look at these things for comic relief. I've never actually used a dating service or personal ads of any kind (and I don't masturbate, don't pick my nose, and I have some land in Florida I'd like to sell you...). No, but it's true that part of the agreement of the challenge was that I wouldn't use any dating services or personals; that would've sapped the bet of its lifeblood. I'm also not allowed to *tell* guys what I'm trying to accomplish—each seduction has to be legit, realized on its own merits. After those four frat boys I did, I decided I wasn't even going to use *bars*. It would've made the bet, on the whole, too easy. Nothing in those bars but buckets o' drunkards hoping to get laid. What can I say? I like a challenge. I must say, though, the bet is going swimmingly thus far.

And no help from Camouflage Man, thank you very much.

מב

At Starbuck's, perusing a newspaper while the incompetent teenagers bumble around behind the counter. "**Prince Charles tries his hand as DJ:** The Prince of Wales is now king of the turntables. Prince Charles played disc jockey Tuesday as he visited a center for homeless youth supported by his Prince of Wales Trust. The heir to the throne tried his hand at 'scratching' on the turntables while at the Centrepoint shelter in London. 'Dig that crazy rhythm,' the prince exclaimed as he blended DJ Dee Kline's dance hit 'I Don't Smoke' with 'Little Man' by Long Lost Brother. Pressing a set of earphones to his head he added, 'Are you insane?'"

I'm distracted by some sort of scene taking place at the front of the line. There's a man who keeps requesting a pastry, then rejecting it when the clerk puts it up on the counter on a plate and tries to ring him up. Everyone in line has suddenly gotten very quiet and is watching closely. The customer is a very ordinary-looking guy, not foreign or anything. Hmm, can't be a language problem, so... Alcoholic, homeless and/or slightly deranged? No, he looks too well-dressed and clean for that. Maybe he has a brain injury? That would be (professionally speaking) really interesting for me to observe. I listen in:

"No, I mean the biscuit," he says genially.

"The biscuit," the cashier echoes, with a hint of exasperation creeping in, breaking through the defenses of the corporate politeness training at last. She bends down once again into the display case and selects a scone that he seems to be vaguely gesturing toward. (This seems to be an additional problem—his pointing skills need work.) She puts it on a plate, looks at him as if waiting for protest, then puts the plate on the counter, lets out her breath in relief, and starts to ring him up again.

"No, I meant the *biscuit*," he says. You can feel the collective tension from the line.

"The *biscuit*," she says, "the *biscuit*... Uh-huh. And which biscuit would that be?"

"The one with the chocolate," he replies calmly, apparently feeling none of the overwhelming pressure coming from all the people behind him. At least half the pastries in the case have chocolate in or on them.

"O-*kaaay*," she breathes, as she bends down yet again and selects, this time, a muffin with chocolate chips in it. She's halfway back up to the counter when he clears his throat. "Yes?" she pronounces icily.

"No," he begins in a reasonable tone, "it's the—"

"*Biscuit?*" she asks, her eyes narrowed evilly.

"Right," he responds happily.

Just when it seems this scene is going to repeat forever, the man makes what must have been, for him, a supreme effort, and his right hand ends up in a sort of half-point (hunting dogs, as puppies, would've been euthanized as useless) at the cookie section, surprising everyone. "There," he says with a small sigh, "a *biscuit*. With chocolate."

(Oh: he was Canadian, I discovered by observing his license plate as he drove away.) As the man walks away smiling with his chocolate-chip cookie in hand, a college guy in front of me mutters, "Dude, some people just runnin' some *bad* software."

It's a fairly warm and sunny day out and most people in line are wearing shorts... I've noticed that more men than women in Boulder shave their legs (ostensibly for cycling). That's one thing I always loved about Alan—he's the only professional (male) cyclist I know of who doesn't shave his legs. That leg fuzz is such a turn-on. I'm really wondering about all these men in Boulder lately with shaved legs. They can't *all* be cyclists.

When it's my turn to order, I open my mouth to speak but before I get a chance, the Starbuck's girl (a different one; I think the first one is in the back finishing her nervous breakdown) suddenly barks out a Gestapo command. I'm frozen. I'm unreasonably scared. It reminds me suddenly, acutely, of when I did my requisite backpacking-through-Europe thing in my early twenties, and even though I'd learned a little German in preparation for the trip, I didn't have a clue about *Austrian* German. I will never forget the terror I felt, standing in an empty bakery salivating over the cakes in the display case, when suddenly this little old man came out from the back and shouted at me, *demanded* of me: "Grüss Gott!"

Greet God?! I'd understood the words but not the intent; I thought, holy shit, *how can he tell I'm an atheist?!* How the hell was I supposed to know that's how they fucking *say hello*?

It turns out that the Starbuck's clerk is merely overzealous with her rapid-fire stock greeting, and once I ask her to repeat it, I reply, "Soy decaf latte."

Right after I order, the little boy behind me in line points up at me and asks his mother, "Mommy, is she talking Spanish?"

च

Oh my god, I'm so mean. So I met this decent-looking guy the other night at yoga, and he seemed cool, nice, not too hippie, just right for my Number Sixteen. I brought him home, put on Gilberto Gil, and we ordered in for some vegetarian Vietnamese (food, not people). A couple of hours later found us in my bedroom, mellow, me triumphant.

Things were fine until Baby crawled out from under the bed, where she'd apparently been taking an all-day siesta. She leaped onto the mattress, did a Down Cat stretch, then sat down primly, looked at Marcus and gave a huge yawn, as if to say, *Yeah? So what are* you *going to do for me?*

Marcus shot off the bed and to the other side of the room so fast I didn't even know what was happening. I was only aware of a blur of movement and a displacement of air. Even Baby looked impressed (quite a rare expression for her). She looked at the spot on the bed where he'd been, then where he was now across the room, swiveling her head back and forth, a couple of times, then she bounded suddenly and gracefully to his feet, causing a piteous and heart-rending shriek to come out of Marcus' lungs and sundry vocal apparatus. I stared at him in amazement. He was standing all hunched over, against the wall, folded in on himself, male anatomy reduced to nearly nothing, arms hugging ribs, eyes rolled up in…abject terror?

"Marcus?" No response. "Are you okay?"

A whisper: "Just get— The— Can you...?" He gestured with one finger vaguely yet extremely cautiously—like someone trying to point out the location of just-noticed piranhas—toward Baby, who sat at his feet gazing raptly up at him.

"What? Baby?"

"Please. Aviva. Not...the time...for endearments," he whispered, almost hyperventilating.

"The cat? You want me to get the cat out of the room?" I couldn't help but smile.

"Oh yes, *pleeeease*," he all but wailed, his voice actually breaking. Shrugging, I walked over and scooped up Baby, kissing an apology on her cute little flat forehead, and put her into the living room. I returned to the bedroom and closed the door.

I patted the bed next to me, and said: "Now, Marcus, come back over here and try to relax, okay?" He remained frozen against the wall, like a Yale law student caught in a cop's flashlight beam with a kilo of cocaine. "Okay? Come on, the kitty's gone now, she's in the other room."

Slowly, slowly, he unclenched his muscles and came back to the bed, looking around warily.

"It's okay, Marcus. I promise. Hey—*look* at me! I *promise*. She's gone, okay? Um...why are you so afraid of cats, anyway?"

Over the next ten minutes he told me this hysterical hypothesis he espoused (well, *he* called it a theory; I corrected him; he got mad; he said I needed to *honor* it, regardless of what I chose to call it). He said that people currently being afraid of housecats is a function of whether their *clan* was in direct contact with saber-toothed tigers. And that this fear has been transmitted through the ages via genetic memory.

I couldn't help it, I just couldn't—I really was trying very hard to *honor* this and keep a neutral expression, but the laughter just burst through my defenses; my facial muscles were quite unequal to the task. Needless to say, Marcus was insulted and turned away, pouting.

That wasn't the mean part. What I did next was. When I noticed the tiny click of the bedroom door latch (I'd never actually had to lock Baby out before, so I'd never tested the latch—apparently it wasn't cat-proof) and then Baby jumped up lightly behind me, purring, I hugged her to me.

"Marrrrr-cus," I enticed sweetly.

"What," he said petulantly, still turned away.

"Marcus…turn over towards me, sweetie, and close-your-eyes-and-I-will-give-you-a-big-surprise…"

He did, eyes shut, finally looking mollified, his previous *moue* converted to a hopeful pucker.

"Marcus," I said, "open your eyes and…give Baby a big kissie-poo!" I pushed her fuzzy little face into his, whiskers-to-eyeball.

He screamed so loudly as he left, snatching up clothing here and there, that the neighbors came by afterwards and asked if there was a problem. The only problem was that he grabbed my bra by accident—and it was an expensive one, too. Why do I have a feeling he won't come back to return it when he discovers he has it? Maybe I could ask him to meet somewhere neutral, safely far away from Baby, to give it back to me? Say…at the Denver Zoo? In front of the panthers?

بس

Today being such an auspicious day, it damn well better improve. I'm thirty-six today, November 20. My favorite and most succinct description of the Scorpio personality I've ever come across (sorry) is "creature of dark passions." (I probably wouldn't have even taken on the challenge if I'd been something really mellow like an Aquarius.)

I had only a ten-minute window in which to hit the post office, and of course there was a twenty-minute line in there. Actually, there's *always* a twenty-minute line in the P.O.; it really is one of the most consistent things in life. When they finally drop the big bombs or launch those missiles and the national populace is alerted, there'll still be a twenty-minute line at every post office.

While waiting impatiently (I guess I'll never really be Zen, will I? But on the other hand, isn't accepting the fact that I'll never be Zen a Zen accomplishment?), I noticed an enormous plastic sign: "Please do not place small children on counter." I thought about this, the language of it. First of all, they'd left themselves a surely unwitting legal loophole, wherein one could place large-, or even medium-sized children on the counter. Furthermore, one could place one's small children other presumably undesirable places: on the very delicate postal scale, say, or on a postal clerk's head. On the other hand, where *should* one place one's small children, if one had such a thing? On the floor, where they would presumably get stomped on and/or crawl away with alacrity, thereby causing far more havoc and creating even more serious potential legal repercussions than those that would have resulted from the mere inconvenience of tolerating them for a few moments on the counter?

Momentarily extremely pleased by the workings of my brain, I thought (not for the first time): I should've been a lawyer. I sure as hell would've been better remunerated. And I wouldn't even have to be waiting in a post office line myself; my assistant would be doing it for me. *Hmmpff.* Such logic was doing nothing to improve my mood.

Just when I thought it was finally going to be my turn, and this unkempt-looking woman was leaving the counter clutching her stamps (it had only taken her fifteen minutes to decide between the Jiminy Crickets and the Romanian gymnastics coaches), she suddenly turned back to her helpful Mr. Post Office Man (who, for all she knew, might have a semi-automatic weapon concealed under the counter to deal with the errant placing of small children; she really ought to be more circumspect) and asked him in a new and excited tone: "Guess what I found in my dresser drawer this morning?"

He was totally unfazed. "What?" he asked pleasantly. This guy must be on some serious drugs.

"A ferret!" she announced, and studied him, waiting for effect.

"That's nice," he told her. "Next!" Whoa. *Very* serious drugs. I must say, I was truly impressed with the way he handled that. I should hang around the P.O. and take notes for dealing with my students.

I zoomed over to the business supply store to grab a box of staples, and the only kind they had were blue glitter. Gee, *that* would look good. My papers would look like my students'. They have this idea lately (I'm sure it comes from MTV and/or the Internet—don't all their ideas?) that they should *jazz up* everything they turn in, which means all their "professional" papers are covered with stickers and decals and temporary tattoos and god knows what. I never wanted to teach grade school, and here it's turned out that teaching in the university is the same thing.

I dropped by the public library to grab some novels, and got unpleasantly surprised by the Tourette's book re-stocker. No, this is not a joke. I think it's great that they're employing this man, but he scares the shit out of me whenever he has an episode next to me. On our very first encounter, I must've jumped ten feet when this formerly-quiet guy shelving books next to me suddenly whacked himself on the head a few times, let loose some loud and ear-curdlingly nasty curses, and viciously slammed the remaining books on his cart into their correct places before dashing himself into the wall. He doesn't have the world's best hygiene, so usually I have olfactory warning, but today I must not have been paying attention.

Driving out of the library parking lot, I almost hit one of those scuzzy teenagers riding around on one of those little trick bicycles. I slammed on the brakes, but my beneficence went unacknowledged by the Nim Chimsky look-alike and his sidekick, a white hippie Rasta on a skateboard.

A gaggle of Asian girls forced me to wait as they crossed extremely leisurely at the crosswalk near Alfalfa's. They always make me so mad, ever since I read about this unjust paradox. You know how they're always so naturally slim, so perfectly slender? Well, ironically, they actually have the *highest* percentage of body fat of all races. Now, is that totally unfair or what? Okay, I'm definitely degenerating here. I have a Ph.D. and I'm starting to sound like one of my undergrad girls. Perhaps it's time for a refreshment break.

…At the Trident. Ahhh. A mocha and the band advertisements: Pork Tornado, Limp Bizkit, Piltdown Men, Sexy Beast, Crouton Dragnet, Dick Can Dance, The WingNuts.

Then, just to interrupt my tenuous tranquility, a bunch of C.U. students suddenly wanders into the Trident, a large herd of brand-new everything: blond ponytails, J. Crew, platform shoes, cell phones, and loud, look-everyone's-staring-at-us-isn't-it-fabulous giggles. They immediately detect that the Trident is not their usual watering hole; perhaps they wandered in accidentally from Urban Outfitters next door (moo…)? They stop dead. One of them says to the clone behind her, "*Oh. My. God.* Is this, like, where we come to be, like, *deep?*" A mass of giggles, then the pack reverses itself, presumably to seek out its own kind at Starbuck's or Peaberry's.

With a big sigh, I finish my mocha and head off to campus, where the only thing standing in the way of my birthday party tonight is a faculty meeting to get through (no small thing). The Yiddish proverb comes to mind unbidden: "Don't worry—things are never so bad that they can't get worse."

ώ

Blah, blah, blah…twenty minutes into the first time all of us Linguistics faculty members have been together since—could it be? Since the Ugly Word Party? I keep visualizing those signs around everyone's necks. Lisa wearing PREPUCE, Jenny dressed in BELCH—how am I supposed to take budget and scheduling concerns seriously with that image in my mind? Am I the only one having this problem?

I realize that the faculty member who Couldn't Follow Rules has apparently not seen the light of even one more semester here. Poor sod (I can't seem to shake that Brit phrase; I like it nearly as much as the Brazilian Portuguese *coitadinho*, but whenever I try to throw *that* casually into a conversation, it falls a bit flat). But he *was* supposed to be a linguist, after all. And, if we're to be honest, we must acknowledge that we're all just grateful it wasn't us; in fact, show us his fresh corpse and we'll gladly throw it to the starving dogs—we'll even count in unison while we swing it in preparation.

The Chair is blathering on about how we'll all have to keep buying our own supplies—pens, paper clips, envelopes (this, while the football players get chauffeured around in limos from drunken catered gang-bang to drunken catered gang-bang and have more new buildings built for them—but am *I* kvetching?).

Finally something in the meeting manages to catch my attention: total silence. I look up to everyone staring at me.

"Sorry?" I say, trying to inject some British sound into the word, with its inherent dignity (and its *don't fuck with me* message). Apparently, the topic has shifted to what courses we're teaching next semester, and the Ling chair is waiting for me to confirm mine. "*Right*," I say, attempting to continue in the Anglican vein, "Morph—"

Chris interrupts me: "Hel-*lo*? What's with the retarded accent?"

I glare at him—bloody misogynist!—and am about to continue when I am attacked from another side; Ralph joins in belatedly:

"Yeah, why are you doing that?"

I glare at him, too, and think, Well, Ralph, if only you were British, at least you'd be allowed to pronounce your ugly name *Reyf*, and I continue (in a more normal voice): "Morphology and Syntax, and also—"

At which point Lisa joins in with a gleeful: "Oh, all *right*! 'My good father-in-law saw a spider monkey. And my many brothers-in-law shot it from place to place.' Gotta love it!"

Ralph adds: "'Go up killing monkey!'"

I sigh, shut my mouth, and leave them to their antics—they get up to their same old tricks every time anyone brings up the Morphology and Syntax course our department teaches. This is due to the bizarro data sets in the textbook we always use, utterances recorded in the jungles of the world by some long-dead mosquito-plagued linguists. The oddest data of all come from Australian aboriginal languages, or impossibly obscure tongues like Peruvian Cashinahua, immortalized (if you wish to call it that) in my colleagues' silly exchanges.

Jenny and Chris chime in unison: "'With my very good brother's spear!'"

And then stiff old Jane, even, contributes: "'Your brother, going along wanting real monkeys, descends. And I shoot men with many arrows.'" I look at her to see if she's done, and she finishes in a small voice, knowing she's used up her time allotment: "'The jaguar kills the little man with its many teeth.'"

Michael, who is still pretty new here and must not have had the unforgettable experience of ever teaching with the manual in question, is looking around with the most priceless expression. (Understandably, the students get the same freaked-out expression the first time they confront this textbook.)

The Chair, while not actually encouraging this long-running frivolity, apparently doesn't mind it either. She seems to tolerate it as something necessary that must be gotten through, the way women automatically ready a wad of toilet paper when they sit down to urinate.

"And also Memetic Theory," I finally finish, once the laughter dies down.

"Fine," the Chair says. "Next?"

"Um...," hedges Ralph. "I read the other day... I mean... Well... Actually..."

"Ralph," says the Chair. "If Japanese were our native language, that would be a fine beginning. However, it is not and we do not have all the time in the world." A snicker runs around the room.

"Yes, ahem," he clears his throat. "Well." The Chair eyes him sharply, and he forces himself to continue: "I heard that Indiana State is teaching Philosophy of Star Trek..." We all look at him disbelievingly. True, American universities are getting more and more like this preschool here in Boulder called *Make a Mess and Make Believe*, but still, there are limits to one's credulity. Then he pulls out his trump card: "...for credit."

There is a general outcry, uproar, and indignation (you know that Seinfeld character, the African-American lawyer, who always talks like that? Well, I thought I'd try it out.). I might even say there was *hubbub*. Hubbub, Bubba. That reminds me of this long-ago friend of mine who was absolutely fascinated by the alveolar ridge dance his tongue had to do when saying "Little Italy" or "had to edit it" fast (in an American accent, of course—gotta get that tongue flap in there), though "hubbub, Bubba" is of course a bilabial tango. My friend didn't know anything about the alveolar ridge, he just loved saying "Little Italy" over and over again as fast as he could. Alveolar ridge polkas aside, back to the dick dance that is our meeting.

Finally, one voice breaks through the loudest, Ralph's, directed at the Chair. His tone is that of a small child who's just seen his twin sister get served a bigger scoop of ice cream than him. "If ISU can teach Philosophy of Star Trek for credit, then I—"

Everyone (except Michael) chimes in in a bored voice, finishing Ralph's sentence for him: "...want to teach Verbing Nouns and Nouning Verbs." The auditory effect is reminiscent of a Gregorian chant, or probably more like the Monty Python spoof thereof (minus the punctuation of everyone hitting themselves on the head).

Michael has that expression again. I'd love to get it on film. By the next faculty meeting, this will all be old hat. Chris can't resist inserting, "Well, if *he* gets to teach Verbing Nouns and Nouning Verbs, then *I* want to be able to teach Women, Fire, and Other Dangerous Things! Lisa gets to teach that *every* time and I'd do at *least* as good of a job." I think any minute now the Chair is going to have to reach down inside herself for some latent mothering skills she doesn't even know she has, and slap one of these boys. I sigh, loudly.

Only to look up in surprise to hear the Chair actually say: "All right, Ralph, let's go ahead and put you down for Verbing Nouns and Nouning Verbs for next semester. Anyone else have anything—other changes?" Ralph is beaming so strongly I could use him instead of my SAD light the next time we have a gray day.

I am shocked, amazed, and stunned. No, but seriously; Ralph's been begging for this forever. Well, as long as I've been here. And the Chair has never come close to entertaining the idea before. And now she okays it, just like that? What could possibly be the reason for this dramatic turnaround? Because I have so much sex on the brain lately, the horrifying possibility crosses my mind that the Chair is *horny* and that she finds Ralph *attractive*. Aaaaggghh—don't make me…ralph.

Then Michael pipes up, "Excuse me, but…a whole *semester* on Verbing Nouns and Nouning Verbs? I mean, couldn't that be covered in a chapter or so, of, say, Aviva's upcoming Morphology and Syntax course?" I smile at him, but he's in trouble now. Michael doesn't know it yet, but he's just made an enemy for life: Ralph. Someone once told me a little joke: Why are academics so damn petty? Answer: Because the stakes are so damn small. Too, keep in mind the other meaning of "academic": trivial, essentially meaningless. Then Michael says something that makes my heart stop and blood freeze, something I never thought I'd hear, *the* unforgivable amongst tenure-track academics, a thing I would've expected only from the loser who Couldn't Follow Rules. "I mean, such a course isn't actually *necessary*, is it?"

I never knew you could hear a room full of people *stop* breathing.

Damn. And Michael was a pretty nice guy. Pity he won't be around anymore after this year.

ē

    Well, might as well start off my first (or is it actually my second? I've always sucked at math. It's like trying to figure out century vs. year; or how you count floors in buildings outside of America) day of being thirty-six by taking a run. Must stay in shape, after all. I have to say I got pretty sick of all those stupid comments yesterday about how I'm no longer at my sexual peak (that being, of course, thirty-*five*). Well, if one can't have an easy and gorgeous Number Seventeen, one can nevertheless go for a crisp fall run.
    There sure are a lot of runners out today. What am I saying? There *always* are. Ever since Frank Shorter, apparently, Boulder's been a genuine runners' mecca. Something about the oxygen at this altitude and the red blood cells—some kind of physical advantage. After you've lived here for a little while, you get inured to the fact that you're running the same trails on a daily basis as Olympic competitors. I guess it must be the athletic equivalent to living amongst movie stars in L.A. Here, though, when you see these famous people, everyone's drenched in sweat and dressed pretty much alike—both you and them. It makes them seem more human. However, if I'm running the same direction on a trail as they are, they blow past me pretty damn fast.
    We have Frank Shorter, we have Ute Pippig, we have Arturo Somebody. We have tons of world-famous runners living and training in

Boulder whose names I don't happen to know, because I don't follow running as a sport. I just jog occasionally to keep not too zaftig and to stay, as a German teacher of mine used to say (palpating and then lamenting his too-soft middle before going out on his nightly beer binges) "vizin ze realm of ze socially aktzeptable."

We have international running stars: short-distance, medium-distance, long-distance, ultra-long-distance. We have runners living here who can give the infamous barefoot and tire-sandal-wearing, hundred-miler Mexican Tarahumaras a run for their money (pardon). We also, here in Boulder, have runners' *cults*. They're occasionally so bizarre as to make the national papers. I remember something about an exclusive group of ultramarathoners (those for whom a whole fucking *marathon* is not enough), where the male leader supposedly reserved the "right" to "train" the new women by having intercourse with them whenever he felt the timing was *just so*.

And lately, we have more and more of one particular type of runner training all over Boulder. I see them everywhere along the bike path. They're these tiny Olympic-caliber Korean runners. They're all perfectly identical and interchangeable; in fact they even seem to be unisex. They all have thick, short, shiny black hair, and are dressed alike. They are never walking, always running. They're all the same size and shape. In fact, I'd swear I was always seeing the same person, except that for example when I'm on my bike, I see one, then five minutes later another, then another, then another, then a whole pack of them together, such that I estimate there must be at least forty or fifty of them in Boulder, if not more. I have never seen them anywhere in town *except* running on the bike path—not grocery shopping, not at movie theaters, not at coffee shops, not on campus. They never look tired. They never wear anything except spotless, perfect athletic clothes. They don't even sweat.

I have developed a hypothesis: might they not be real? Could they, possibly, be part of a grand Energizer battery experiment? Not as cuddly, perhaps, as the big pink bunny, but maybe the advertisers have their sights set on a new approach, and I'm the only one who's figured it out so far.

Ĉ

Running is also a good way to muse about things—like my birthday party. I must hand it to Therese and Georgette, who arranged everything; all except for one tiny detail at the end, they did an awesome job.

They'd invited just a few of my other women friends to Georgette's: Marta, MaryLynn, and Sarah. It was a good group, a familiar one for hanging out, although of course it usually takes "Acts of God" for us all to be able to be together at once. I was therefore quite flattered to see the whole gang.

Georgette was in charge of video entertainment. The first thing she did was get us all lined up on and around the couch and tell us to be quiet because she had the most *fantastic* video for us. We of course paid no attention through the beginning credits, instead chatting, catching up, until finally Georgette had to hush us forcibly. We all swiveled our heads around obediently to face the television just in time to see *The Saints— With Sister Wendy* written in fancy script. The video had solemn-sounding classical music. I immediately figured it must be some fabulous new cult comedy I hadn't heard about that Georgette had become privy to (although the title somehow sounded like porn). I caught Georgette's eye, gave her a thumbs-up. She returned a huge smile.

Five minutes later, though, we were still waiting for the punch line— *any* punch line. At which point I started to suspect—could it be?—that in fact this video wasn't a comedy. I tentatively broached the possibility aloud. Georgette owned up: "I found it at the public library," she said. "I just couldn't believe it was for real." At which point, the video suddenly *did* seem funny. We made some popcorn and enjoyed ourselves thoroughly, loudly and frequently commenting over and above Sister Wendy, all but drowning out the poor nun.

"High five," I said to Georgette.

Then she put on the *good* stuff: Monty Python. (Where did you think I'd acquired my excellent fake British accent?) The Dead Parrot Sketch: "'E's pinin' for the fjords!" The Cheese Shop: "It's the single most popular cheese in the world!" And a more obscure one, one of my and Georgette's favorites, A Bicycling Tour of Cornwall, in which the poor eager Asian guy fails—again and again—to properly enunciate: "*Colunuwaru!*"

We broke out the Ben & Jerry's and discussed how my challenge was going, filling in Marta, MaryLynn, and Sarah on the newest conquests. They all accused me of getting really cocky, just because I said it was going to be child's play to fulfill the bet—after all, I was right on schedule.

"Besides," I started to say, total silliness, "I can't be *cocky*; I don't have a—"

"Cake?" Georgette interrupted, in a syrupy voice. "You want cake? You'll get *cake*, all right!" I looked at her curiously. Therese shushed her.

Then Marta announced, with a sly look, that it was her turn to introduce what she was in charge of. And what was that? I innocently inquired. Why, *gifts*, of course.

Presented with huge degrees of laughter on the part of givers and cohorts: the neon sparkle light-up anal-beads-for-couples; the little red wind-up chattering plastic penis; the foot-long black rubber dildo (not only was it twelve inches long, it had a diameter of, like, my calf—what were these things actually *used* for, if anything?—Never mind, I don't want to know); Ted the Inflatable Buddy; and the Beginner's Dominatrix Kit, Including Plastic LuvKuffs.

Okay, okay, say I'm being paranoid, but what happens if the fire department has to come to my apartment sometime and stumbles upon this stuff (hidden away in a brown paper bag in the back of a closet somewhere)? I mean, Jesus, *how embarrassing*.

"Thanks, you guys. Thanks *a lot*," I said, trying and failing to suppress a smile. Just wait till one of them had *her* next birthday.

The real gifts were, of course, a lot nicer (well, I guess that actually depends on what you wanted for your birthday): various gift certificates (Boulder Bookstore, Boulder Bodywear, Bart's CD Cellar); a massage certificate, and a gorgeous orchid plant (fortunately including instructions), which looked like a bunch of purple butterflies hanging off a long twig and reminded me momentarily and very warmly of Jon, a.k.a. Number Seven.

Hugs all around.

And the *coup de grâce*, pre-arranged by Georgette and Therese: late, late at night, everyone (except night owl me) yawning, one of those ridiculous gigantic fake cakes delivered to the house, out of which came, dancing and stripping (though not singing—guess he wasn't really multi-talented), a muscly tanned dude. My Number Seventeen-to-be, my final birthday present! They'd even requested a dark-haired guy, knowing my tastes as they did. Such a cute one they'd ordered, just for me! And they'd had him bring a variety of adorable outfits to take off in front of me, as many times as I wanted (hadn't had so much fun since playing with my politically incorrect Barbies during my politically incorrect preteens)—he was paid for, for the whole night. How considerate of them!

Oh, but if only they'd bothered to inquire about the boy's *proclivities*. The man and I ended up in Georgette's guest room discussing the virtues of silk vs. leather for posing pouches, the best ways to depilate, hair gel, and the rapidity of velcro vs. hand-ties: the boy was as gay as a three-dollar Parisian.

V

I've had a weird, weird, *weird* Thanksgiving.

There I was, with Therese at Alfalfa's for our annual non-turkey dinner (Harry always refused to participate, preferring to hang out with his unmarried buddies, drink beer and heat up microwave turkey meals, which was fine with me—and with Therese, too). Here, they were having this event called Meet The Turkey Whose Life You Saved. The weather was spectacular: warm and golden, ever so slightly crisp—very much, in fact, like the baked turkey skin of non-veg memory. Everyone was sitting outside at picnic tables. There was this huge buffet set up with organic soy pumpkin pie, organic mashed potatoes, all the usual goodies—except, of course, the main dish. Instead, there was Tofurkey. Not my favorite thing, I must admit. The texture is like (I imagine) a stack of baked rubber gloves. I usually take a token tiny serving—the way I used to take only a tiny serving of real turkey when I was younger and not yet a vegetarian, because the *really* good stuff was waiting: sweet potatoes with marshmallows, warm apple pie with vanilla ice cream... Excuse me while I salivate.

So you got yourself a plateful and sat down at a picnic table with a lot of other vegetarians (or vegetarian wannabes, or those who'd been reluctantly dragged there that day by their spouses/friends [hence, Therese]/guilty consciences)—and standing at each table was your own personal mascot: a real live turkey, tied around the neck via a string collar to a leg of the picnic table, and with his/her own little aluminum pan of birdseed nearby. Everyone was surprised at just how large, ugly, and fearsome the creatures were. There was a lot of that loud, bravado laughter going on, like when you're all floating around on inner tubes a half-mile out from the beach and someone makes a semi-joke about having just seen a shark fin.

The only available seats left were the ones closest to the turkeys—with one glaring exception. I nudged Therese with my elbow, both of us holding our recyclable paper plates laden with goodies and biodegradable cornstarch implements.

"What is that woman doing sitting so close to that turkey?" I whispered to Therese.

"Where? Which table? Who?" Therese answered loudly. Too loudly—enough to attract the attention of a dredlocked guy at the table next to us, wearing a T-Shirt that said *I Lost My Phone Number, Can I Have Yours?*, who gestured magnanimously for us to sit down. I rolled my eyes at Therese but she didn't seem to notice; she was still trying to locate the turkey talker. "Oh!" she proclaimed suddenly—she'd seen.

We sat down between Phone Number and another guy whose T-Shirt said *Only You Can Save Me From My Spiritual Path*. I *loved* that one. He was even sort of cute, in a geeky, Jewish, doesn't-see-the-light-of-day-enough way. Hmmm...

"So, what *is* your spiritual path?" I asked him, at the same time that Phone Number was explaining to Therese, "Yeah, so that lady over there, right?, so she has, like, psychic connections with animals?, so, like, she's, like, *communing* with the turkey and all."

"Huh?" responded my guy to my question. Total blank look. "Spiritual path? Whattaya mean?" His eyes narrowed suspiciously. "You're not, like, one of those Jehovah's Witness people, are you?" He made a move to pick up his plate.

"No! God, no!" I said.

"Jews for Jesus? Up With People?" He started getting up.

"For Christ's sake, no!" I assured him. "A little sensitive about that, are we?! I was merely referring to your T-shirt," I said, pointing to its message.

"Do you know what she and the turkey are discussing?" Therese asked Phone Number politely. I looked at her, saw the wicked glint of humor in her eye to which strangers were always oblivious.

"Oh!" said my guy, looking down, relieved. "The T-shirt! No, it's my roommate's. Must've grabbed it by accident."

Just then a song began over the loudspeakers. The intro music seemed familiar...but before I could identify it, a whole bunch of other people did, because applause and whistling broke out, then everyone started shushing everyone else so the lyrics could be heard:

When I grow up
I wanna work at Alfalfa's
Where the cheese is dairy-free
A Birkenstock spandex necktie patchouli grocery store

More applause. Now I remembered—it was Leftover Salmon; I'd heard this song a couple of times before, but this sounded like a live version. Everyone around was laughing—well, everyone except those who actually worked here.

"Yeah," Phone Number was whispering to Therese, "She said the turkey is, like, so totally psyched about its *salvation*, you know?"

I'd have a job
Pickin' through the produce
No pesticides for me!
I'd be a working moderate-income socially-conscious Boulder hippie

"So, is your *roommate* on a spiritual path?" I asked the guy next to me. He gave me a *look*. I was about to drop the subject for good when he mumbled, "Yeah, actually he is—some Jewish shit."

And I'd drink soy milk all day long
And feast on bulgur, wheatgrass, and Windham Hill songs
Ride up on my mountain bike
Just in time to turn off my solar-powered growing lights

"You look kind of Jewish yourself, if you don't mind my saying so," I told him, hoping he wouldn't take offense. "What's your name?"

When I grow up
If I could work at Alfalfa's
How happy I would be
A Birkenstock spandex necktie patchouli grocery store

There was a more-or-less-unanimous standing ovation for the song. Then everyone sat back down again when they realized that in this, the KBCO Studio C version, there was more—a spoken part I hadn't heard before:

Folks, we'd like to have you all call in to KBCO right now and vote for your favorite product available at Alfalfa's that is not available anywhere else... I'm sure the voting will be big for the ol' spinach-flavored yogurt... Or is it frozen yogurt?... The wheatgrass lemonade... But you know, folks, it's a cultural thing... It's a thing that a community can be based on... And I think that soon people in Des Moines, hell, maybe even Detroit, will be singing this song...

Spontaneous eruption of clapping, whistles, etc. This got Turkey Talker very excited and she sprang up and shouted, "How about a round of applause for this beautiful, *free* turkey right here?!" She hugged her turkey—or tried to, but it appeared to be focusing its beak on her eyeball, apparently readying its aim to peck out the shiny orb, and she hastily desisted. There was some cheering for her, though less than for the song.

I looked at my neighbor, still awaiting his answer.

"Mordecai," he mumbled, eyes downcast.

If *I grow up*
If I could work at Alfalfa's
How happy I would be...

Mordecai looked absolutely miserable.

"What's the matter?" I asked him. "By the way," I added, thinking, *you self-centered prick, thanks so much for asking,* "*my* name's Aviva."

"It's just... Never mind."

"No, what?"

"Well... Okay, so maybe I'm just a little bit *sensitive* about...the Jewish thing." Oh, god help us, another Sensitive Jewish Boy.

"Oh? And why is that?" Expecting, of course, the usual answer: something about his mother, of course. Or perhaps something about too much matzoh ball soup, or being beaten up by the public school kids for being a glasses-wearing sissy, or having to go to Hebrew School instead of getting to play baseball on sunny summer weekend afternoons, or...

"Well, 'cause of my name..." (Well, okay, that one I'd have to grant him.) "...and also 'cause...well, this sounds kind of dumb, but...well, my roommate, he's kind of, like, this *chick magnet*, you know? And he doesn't even *care*! I mean, Jesus, the guy's a *religious nut* or something! Shit, man, he's a *dweeb*!" I was staring at him somewhat aghast; now that his floodgates were open, I was wondering how we could get them locked back up again. "Damn! If I got half the check-out looks from babes that he does...!" He finally noticed the look *I* was giving him—and shut up.

"What kind of religious nut?" I was mildly curious. Here in Boulder,

I thought I'd heard it all—but I always liked to make sure.

"You know—that numbers or alphabet thing. Or whatever. I'm pretty sure. He and I don't really talk much."

I nodded sagely. "Kabbalah. Jewish mysticism."

"Right!" He looked at me closely, suddenly suspicious. "Hey—you're not one of those religious fanatics too, are you?"

"No!" I said firmly. "Haven't we been through this already? What, just because I've heard of Kabbalah? Jeez, you *are* sensitive, aren't you?!" Was it even worth pursuing this guy?

Whilst pondering the issue, I was about to do some meaningful eyebrow-waggling with Therese, to see how she'd done, conversationally speaking, dealing with Phone Number, but there was a distraction: the manager of Alfalfa's had appeared in our midst, standing on a couple of stacked wooden fruit crates and was, apparently, in the beginning throes of a gratitude speech on behalf of not only his store, but of the Turkeys Whose Lives We'd Saved.

All of a sudden, a cacophony—pounding, crashing, you name it—came from every table at once. It was total chaos. Everyone was leaping to their feet and screaming, us included. It took a couple of minutes afterwards to figure out what had happened: the turkeys had used the lull in our collective attention to take the opportunity to jump onto the tables and begin eating—no, cramming, inhaling, *gobbling*—the much tastier vittles than those meager dry little bits laid out at their feet, intended for their sustenance. No, these guys wanted cranberry sauce. They wanted garlic roasted whipped yams with fresh rosemary. They most definitely wanted mini-marshmallows. And above all—as it turned out—what they really, *really* craved was Tofurkey.

J

But my weird Thanksgiving was far from over. As you have probably already surmised, the only way my day was going to get even odder was going to involve Pale Stolen T-Shirt Guy. And you would be correct.

So. Let me tell you about Ol' Mordecai, he of the biblical name and the…(are you waiting for me to finish that sentence with "…biblical proportions"?) Anyway. He of the biblical name. (Actually, his proportions weren't half bad.) He of the biblical name and the… quite unexpected proclivities.

So everything's going pretty much normally at first. The usual: "heavy petting" and all that, the detection of the boner… Typical stuff, portending imminent conquest, right? Well—no.

As soon as we got undressed, the weirdness started. I reached for the Biblical Boner and he recoiled as if my hand were a hot iron. Also, I noticed he seemed to be averting his eyes (gosh, another biblical phrase—his absent roommate's influence?) from my body. What was the deal? Finally, he was behaving so bizarrely, refusing to continue the foreplay we'd begun with our clothes on, that I just asked him straight out what was the matter.

"Mordecai," I began gently, "what—"

He winced. "*Morty*," he corrected. "Please."

"Morty," I began again, though I hate the nickname—for me, it belongs solely to old New York Jewish retirés in Miami with sock suspenders. "What is going on here? You suddenly seem kind of...*uninterested* or something."

"It's just..." He seemed to struggle to define an answer, then made up his mind to not tell the truth—you could see it in his face. Come on—no one named *Mordecai* could lie worth a damn. "It's nothing! Really! Nothing! Um, let's just! Just! Um! Okay!" He grabbed me, carefully avoiding looking at my body, and started kissing me forcefully, stuffing his tongue in my mouth as if he'd win freedom from life in prison if he could only get it down far enough. *Yick*.

I disentangled my vocal chords (well, folds, technically) and sputtered, "What the hell!"

"You like that?" he asked hopefully.

"Like it?!" I asked incredulously. "I—"

He took that for an affirmative and lunged at me again, tongue protruding. I managed to avoid the scary proboscis this time—akin to Darwin's hypothesized moth's, I couldn't help thinking—and attempted to maneuver his hand onto my pubic region. He jerked it back. I again tried to force his hand down to my (I love this term) *nether regions* while he was simultaneously trying his best not to go near anything female down south, and at some point in the midst of this fray, I accidentally scraped his hand with my nails, short though they are.

"Oooh, shit, sorry!" I said. "Is it bad?"

Then I noticed he was grinning. Looking happier than he had at any point since I'd yet known him—even while he was eating pumpkin pie *à la mode* (with Rice Dream). What was going on here? I looked at his hand—bleeding! "Oh my god, I'm so sorry!"

"No worries," he said, in an attempt at a Sydney surfer accent. It came off quite badly, if I must say. I decided that a break from all the attempted sexual activity, to clear the air, was in order.

"So, Mordec—I mean, Morty—what do you do, anyway?" Somehow, this most basic of questions had never come up. What had come up, on the other hand, was a boner, which in my current circumstances—those of my postulation—seemed far more à propos.

"I run the physics computer lab on campus." Proudly. Oh. So that explained the sickly look. Not a cultured appearance, then, but an inadvertently acquired one. *And*, I was thinking, *dummy, now it's your turn to ask* me... But—nothing.

"So, Morty, what do you like to do in your free time?"

"Free time?"

Long silence.

"Well, Morty, since you asked, *I* teach Linguistics."

"Oh. That's nice. I guess."

Okay, so conversation was not Mordecai's strong point. Maybe we'd better get back to the physical. I took the initiative. I started with some gentle caresses in a certain region known commonly—shall I say *vulgarly*?—as the Adam-Come-Along Area, because of the way you tickle him there. Now, this is a trick that has never failed to get results. Never—until now. Ol' Mord brushed my hand away as if it were a gnat annoying his face while he tried to determine the check-mate move for Grand Master of the World. I had to deduce that he didn't like it. How could this be?! Maybe I had, in my haste to get back to business, performed it slightly too hard? I tried one more time, as gentle as the proverbial lamb on whose ivory fluff March hopefully floats in. This time there was no mistaking his reaction: "Would you cut that out!" he snarled, removing my hand from his crotch.

"Sorry!" I protested meekly, chagrined. "I thought you'd like it." There was a long pause before he answered.

"Actually," he said very quietly, sounding slightly embarrassed, eyes focused on a cobweb in an upper corner of my bedroom, "you know what I *would* like?"

No, Mordecai, quite frankly, I have absolutely no idea. To go back to the womb? To be stroked with ostrich feathers from head to toe while I simultaneously perform Tibetan chants and fellatio? To have boiling oil poured down onto you from castle ramparts? (As it turned out, the latter was not so far off the mark.) "What?" I asked.

"Well...would you...would you....um...?"

"Go ahead."

"Would you...kind of...slap my balls?"

After this stunning request, he finally met my eyes. And, I noticed, there was some stiffening going on in his groin area...not seen since we'd first been making out, clothed.

I figured I must've heard him wrong. *Slap?* He couldn't have said "slap," could he? Maybe he said "tap"? I tried a few hesitant taps. He waited them out, looking puzzled, then grabbed my wrist, and, keeping my hand captive under his own, let loose a real sonorous spank, a genuine *whack* of the type prohibited by law as abuse when administered even occasionally to the backside of children for disciplinary purposes. Then he wailed—a true howl of pain.

I shook my hand from his grasp. "Jesus!" I shouted. "Are you all right? My god! Why did you do that?! Are you okay?!" I was truly concerned. That had to have hurt like hell.

He had genuine tears in his eyes, although he wouldn't answer my questions. I didn't know what was wrong. I cradled him until he seemed somewhat recovered, then I started noticing how good he smelled, and started stroking his curls...and I started getting aroused again. I couldn't understand why he wasn't reciprocating at all with any touching or caressing, though, and it started to really get on my nerves. I resent having to make *all* the moves. I resignedly tried again to put his hand back between my legs, and he resisted with all his strength. What the fuck?!

"Anita, I..."

"A*viva*!"

"Oh, right, sorry... Um, I guess I should tell you about...um. I kind of...it's just..." I wished the Chair were here to reprimand him in her inimitable way.

"You *what*?" I asked coldly.

"I kind of...don't like...vanilla sex." Then he sighed, hugely. "Whew! I'm glad that's out. It's always so hard for me to confess that, you know? Like, I'm always so afraid to talk about it, when actually, once I do—" The floodgates had opened again.

"You *what*?!" I interrupted. I knew I was repeating myself, but for a change I seemed to be at a loss for words. This was simply not a confession I had ever been privy to before, and certainly not at such...proximity.

"You know. Vanilla sex."

"Yeah, I heard you. I'm just not sure what you mean by it. You mean, man plus woman equals good time? *Normal* sex? You're not *into* it?"

"Right!" he exclaimed, happy I was getting it.

I was utterly flabbergasted. Why, then, had he come home with me? Why all the making out, which he had seemed to enjoy so much? Then an even scarier question popped into my mind: What *was* he into, then? Was he...*contaminated* in some unknown way?

I decided to start with: "So...what *are* you into, then?"

"Well...I like to be...you know...*dominated*. And I like pain. So if you could, you know…"

"So you're a masochist?" I asked, my spirits falling. This would never work.

"Well…I guess so. I guess you could call me that. But it's more than that, I think…you know? I mean, I find the female body, like…really repugnant. So—"

I snatched up a sheet and hastily wrapped it over my whole front.

"You find it *repugnant*?"

"Well…yeah. Maybe that's not the right word. Grotesque, really. Disgusting. I mean, all that pinkness and moisture and stuff…"

I was shocked and pissed off. I felt not only personally insulted, but as if he'd insulted all my global sisters as well. "Well, then why the hell did you flirt, and come home with me and everything?"

"Well, it's weird… It's like, I'm *attracted* to women…you know, at first. But then when the clothes come off, the only way I can have sex is if she's like, a dominatrix or into sadism, I suppose… Just not vanilla sex, that really turns me off." Seeing my expression, he said defensively, "It's not my fault! It's just how I am. I mean, there's nothing bizarre in my childhood or anything… I mean, I'd say I had a normal childhood…there wasn't anything weird with my mother or anything," he finished, just as I asked him, "Don't take offense, but—was there anything weird with your mother?"

I withdrew to the opposite side of the bed to think. I believed we were probably at an impasse, since I was not into S&M to any degree. Vanilla Sex—ha! I hadn't even known that what most people routinely did had a *name*. How odd to hear it scorned. Also, how strange to find out that someone so normal-looking was actually so…perverted? Well, so *kinky*, anyway.

Mordecai was staying quiet over there on his side of the bed, apparently giving me space to cogitate.

Finally he asked tentatively: "Um…Aviva?" If he'd gotten my name wrong again, I would've thrown him out right then.

"Yes?"

"Do you think you could just…try?"

What a concept. "You know, I'm really just not the type, Mordecai." He let the name slide this time, with just a small wince (maybe he actually enjoyed the pain of hearing his full name?)—a sign that perhaps he was desperate to compromise.

"I know, I know...but maybe just try...a little bit? I can show you..."

"Well..." I really did need to try to get a Number Seventeen, and I'd already invested so much in this one. He could sense my weakness, and rolled over toward me. I had to admit he still looked cute, and he had a nice body for someone who probably spent about twenty-two hours a day in a computer lab.

"Okay, so for example..." He put my hand on his balls. Well, so far this wasn't bad at all! "So, Aviva, can you just, like...squeeze them?" I squeezed—gently. "More?" he said. I squeezed a bit more firmly. "Um... like, a lot more?" I squeezed a little more. "No, like a *lot* more." I tried. I really, really tried. But I just couldn't make myself squeeze any harder, which, having been trained by my first few boyfriends, I knew would've hurt him. So he put his hand over mine and squeezed—hard. And screamed.

I tore my hand away. I was shaking, totally unnerved. No way—I could *not* continue. I guess I was just not meant for anything but vanilla sex (a fact which had never before made me feel inadequate).

"Aviva! That was..." I waited for him to throw me out of bed, to curse me. "...awesome!" His forehead had broken out in a sweat and he was flushed and had a huge smile on his face, much to my surprise. "Will you do it again?" He opened his eyes and saw my hesitation. "Please?"

Please or not, I still couldn't. He put my hand back on his scrotum. "It felt *so* amazing, Aviva..."

An ethical dilemma: if it really turned him on and felt good to him, did it matter if it bothered me? Maybe I could try again... My mind had pretty much convinced itself to give it a try, that the deed was in fact *philosophically* feasible. Moreover, I thought, perhaps I even did harbor some small sadistic tendency, albeit dormant, judging from the amount of pleasure I'd derived from inflicting Baby upon Marcus, a.k.a. Number Sixteen, a.k.a. the Scaredy-Cat (pardon). However, somehow the mental go-ahead signal refused to transmit to my hand, which of its own accord continued to cup Mordecai's family jewels as gently as a newborn baby's skull. "Pleeeeease..." he whispered.

But I couldn't. He then added something that startled me so much that I, ironically, inadvertently squeezed; he'd whispered: "...I'll get you Adobe Photoshop."

What the hell?

In any case, my accidental squeeze brought another shriek of pain/joy to Mordecai. Next he brought my other hand to one of his nipples, cute brown dime-sized circles. From the contortions of his wrist on my hand, I gathered that he hoped I would give his nipple a good hard twist. Yikes. No way. I tried stroking it instead. This elicited a very disgruntled look from Ol' Mord. "Come on, Aviva…please…" I tried a tiny motion, which brought the beginning of a smile to his lips, but I could go no further. "Please…I…I can get you the latest translation software!"

"Mordecai," I said, "all the translation software totally sucks."

"Well, then, I can get you…um…Excel?"

"How lame. Forget it. I can't do it anyway. I just don't seem cut out to be a sadist. I'm really, truly sorry." Having said that, it occurred to me what a bizarre statement it was. Then something brilliant occurred to me. "Hold on, Mordecai. I just thought of something that might be an okay compromise for both of us."

"Okay…I'm not going anywhere," he murmured, grimacing in pain/smiling as he dug his fingernails into his own perineum.

I rummaged around in my closet for a while, then triumphantly approached the bed—still wrapped in the sheet so as not to put him off too much with my horrid femininity—bearing (ta-da!) the birthday LuvKuffs.

With much fumbling, I put them on his wrists, strapping his arms to the bedposts. Several times I accidentally pinched his skin in the cheap, badly-made plastic forms and instantly apologized, "Sorry! Did that hurt?!," to which I'd receive a glare in response. Finally he got frustrated enough to say, "Jesus! Do I have to spell it out for you?! It's *supposed* to hurt! Duh!"

Oh. That's right. I forgot. Damn, some things are just too ingrained, I guess. Well, I do think the *duh* was uncalled for.

Finally I got the LuvKuffs locked. "Are those too tight? I don't want to hur—whoops. Sorry," I trailed off sheepishly. What, I'm supposed to keep apologizing for being *normal*?

Anyway, the LuvKuffs digging in to Mordecai's wrists were painful enough to cause a lovely erection, of which I took prompt advantage. He enjoyed them so much, in fact, that in the heat of the moment he didn't even notice that I was (egad!) naked.

I let him take the Kuffs home with him and didn't even ask when my new software would be delivered.

I walk past the new Oxygen Bar and wonder what yuppie trend is going to hit next here from California...maybe the silicone-filled faux testicles for neutered dogs who have developed a complex, to replace a lifetime of costly psychotherapy. Or Strip Aerobics? Nah...I think Boulder's just a little too conservative for that (discounting what weirdness may go down regularly in the semi-penumbra of the StarHouse or the Barefoot Boogie; get a gathering of hippies together anywhere and you're bound to encounter a lot of nakedness, has always been my observation).

A band of Rainbow Gathering types are camped out in front of the store in the cold, smoking something, and one of the guys—I think it's a guy—unabashedly asks me if I can spare "like, fifty bucks?" I shake my head, amused—*I* look rich?! Then I realize I forgot once again; I keep meaning to try out the reply, "No, sorry, but would you mind taking over my seventy-five thousand dollars' of student loans?"

I duck into the Trident, warm and hopping as usual. No sign yet of Tracy, the "poor dear" (that's how I've been remembering her) from Iowa City (well, at least it was a *city*, if it had to be *Iowa*, I'd consoled her) whom I met at one of those New Faculty things. When I first encountered her, I thought, my god, she's going to be eaten alive in Boulder. Her pale skin is going to fry here; her plain looks are going to make her disappear; and her meek nature is going to get her consumed. She was just so...

Midwestern. From the land where people pronounce "striped" with two syllables, still say "neato," and make use of the exclamation "Jeezoflip!" The poor dear.

I check the clock on the wall, look around again. Nope. I grab a magazine from the rack, National Geographic Adventure, randomly flip open to the middle of some article: "But once we no longer fear unexpectedly stepping into a deep channel, because we have already done so; once we no longer worry about getting soaked, because we are already soaked; once ice-cold feet become normal; once the sinew-bursting labor of pulling the boat becomes painless, because we are numb—then oceanic hiking becomes sublime." Oh, please. How *Boulder.*

I scan likely subtitles of interest on other covers. There's *Maximize your Search for Geospatial Data!*, but I just don't have the time right now. This morning I got a spam-email which asked me, in the subject heading: "DO YOU WANT A FREE 24-PIECE TOOLKIT?!" Where do these things come from, anyway? Are there really conscious aware people who sit around and compose and send to other conscious aware people these little unwanted messages from hell? Or is it just some computer-generated crap? We should all hope very strongly for the latter. Or at least for the monkeys-at-typewriters scenario. Because witness what poor Therese received yesterday: "SHOCKING COCKS: CAN THEY FIT??!!" (She *claimed* she didn't look at it, just deleted it.) I glance at one more magazine: *Become a Rock Star—Without Leaving the House!* Strange. Normally the Trident is strictly a *New Yorker* kind of place.

A young white guy with an enormous Afro enters the café. I mean, a real Afro. I'm not sure how he even managed to produce such a hairstyle, but I must say, it is quite impressive. Because we have so little ethnic diversity here in Boulder, I feel that people often try to create it where it doesn't actually exist. Is this an instance of (unconscious) fulfillment of the Nature Abhors a Vacuum theory? I'll have to check with some Physics colleagues, see if they've ever used this guy as a classroom example.

I'm bored. I start eavesdropping. Table to my right: two college-age guys. One is saying: "…and then I suddenly became, like, aware of, like, all the *pigeons* and all the *beaks*!"

To my left: two college-age girls.

"So like, you know how, like, you're supposed to do everything, like, mindlessly?"

"You mean mindfully?"

"Whatever. So, like, anyway…"

I cruise over to the newspaper table and grab a Nexus to kill time. "Sacred Sexuality, Private Sessions and Seminars for Individuals and Couples. Upcoming Events: Tantra Parties; All Day Tantra Bliss." Hey, this woman is getting *paid* for this! Should I…? No, let's not even go there.

"Angelspeake: How to Talk with Your Angels. Learn how your angels can work for you… with Cassie O. Peia. Certified Angelspeaker. Must call to preregister." It's a four-hour workshop. I honestly cannot believe I am in slave-wage Academia hell, after the Dantean infernal rings of the Ph.D., while random people surely inventing random qualifications are being paid big bucks to be modern-day courtesans and to hold glorified séances. It occurs to me that a linguist ought to go along to the Angelspeake thing to ferret out whether they're using Klingon, Esperanto, or Pig Latin, to make as if they're "speaking in tongues." We should send an emissary from the Department; perhaps we could get a Humanities grant to attend.

There's a weekend seminar on how to purify and bless your bathwater using magnets and pendulums (pendula?), and another on how to cleanse your new home of negative spirit with "medicine words" and sage bundles. (Or you can just pay extra and have the person do it for you.) And of course there's the usual bunch of self-proclaimed Feng Shui experts (is that a dragon in my living room?). There's also a notice about Jewish Renewal's upcoming meeting. I went once (out of curiosity and the vague, Boulderesque desire for more *spirituality* in my life) and got scared off forever by all the forced-participatory, hand-holdy, obligatory hug-your-neighbor-now, singing and dancing stuff. The evening struck me as a perfect blend of temple and the Rocky Horror Picture Show.

Someone calls my name from a table inside. I look around for the Poor Dear but don't spot her. Then I hear her voice again: "Aviva! Girlfriend, over here!" I look directly at the owner of the voice. Oh. My. God.

I must've walked right by her before. Her hair is in a million tiny braids with beads; she's wearing one of those red third-eye thingies that women from India wear (what is that called again? Oh yeah, a bindi); about a thousand turquoise necklaces with huge crystal chunks hanging at the ends, some interspersed with tail feathers from some kind of bird of prey; and her clothing is of a million different ethnicities, colors, patterns and textures, although the predominant one seems to be Nepali, like those sold next door. I wonder where she found any larger than a size two; I've never had any success.

I approach the table and she gets up and makes a motion to give me the Big Boulder Hug. Under the alpaca cardigan, her hemp tank top leaves her armpits exposed—and they're mighty hairy. I'm not sure which shocks me most: the armpits, the fact that I'm about to get the dreaded New-Ager greeting, or the fact that all this is coming from the mouse I'd dubbed the Poor Dear. My temporary paralysis does not save me from the hug, but Tracy (as is always the case with the people who give these hugs, such is their enthusiasm to bestow them) notices neither my reticence nor my lack of return-hugging.

"So, Tracy... What's new?" I ask, then inwardly cringe. Obviously, *everything*.

She says, "Oh, Aviva, I hardly know where to begin! Boulder's had such an *effect* on me! So, so..."

Don't you dare say *healing*, I think.

"...*healing!*"

Blah. "Yeah?... So what's up these days?"

"Well, the pivotal thing for me was, I found my guru! You see, I went to..."

I tune out immediately as soon as I realize she's talking about one of those quintessential Boulder events in which everyone pays a lot of money to go to some *soi-disant* retreat where they're supposed to spend all weekend fasting, getting up before sunrise, and going around unnaturally spending hours embracing everyone else with their eyes closed. You just know all the women are thinking, "I've found my soul partner in this other human being whom I feel so close to in this moment! I know we feel as one in the universe; there is no need even to speak! How spiritual!" while all the guys are thinking, "Mmm...nice tits."

I start listening again when I hear her say "...Scorpio."

"What's that? I'm a Scorpio."

"You *are*?!" She says it as if it's the most fascinating news she's ever heard. "Because, really, Aviva, you have such a *Taurian* aura, you know? I can sense something...mm, perhaps more of an Aries...I'll just bet you have a moon rising."

Hey, whatever. And I'll just bet you might be full of shit. But who am I to judge? She does look happier than me. As I've noted before, so do all hippies. So there must be something they know that we normal mortals don't, or something they're doing right that we're not. Or else it's just all the drugs.

"So…" I ask her, "what else?"

"Oh, let me tell you about this allergy testing I had done! I feel so much healthier now! I don't eat dairy, or—"

"—Wheat, or eggs." I chime in along with her.

"Oh! You too?" she asks.

"No, it's just that everyone says the same thing."

"Well, it's *true*!" she says defensively. I smile, nod for her to continue. God forbid I should contradict any of this stuff: you want to swear you've been *healed* by colored lights? By hot stone cranial placement? By eating nothing but PaleoMeal? By doing Tree Pose in a room that's heated to sauna temperature till you pass out? Fine with me—as long as it's *you* that's doing it.

"So," Tracy goes on, with renewed enthusiasm, "like, when they tested me for the egg allergy, for example, I couldn't eat any eggs of course for a whole weekend, or anything with egg in it, or any kind of poultry…"

"So how do they actually know if you're allergic?" I ask, wondering if it was a blood test or a skin-prick test, but somehow harboring doubts that it was anything so scientific.

"You hold this cup in the air, as high up as you can, and the tester puts different substances in it. Then he—well, mine was a he, my *guru*," she sighs, "pulls on your arm. When it's something you're allergic to, you lose your strength and you can't resist the pulling."

I look at her. I really think she's kidding. I burst out laughing, imagining this scene. I'm dissolving in delicious giggling, in contrast to her stony stare, and eventually my chuckles give way to gasps. I wipe tears out of my eyes. The gasps become sporadic.

"So, you're telling me…" I'm starting to realize she was serious, and this fact is in danger of setting me off again. "He puts an egg—" I start.

She blurts out self-righteously, "Well, it's not that easy! You also have to burn mugwort under your big toes in all four corners of your bedroom every day for seventeen minutes."

I whoop so loud that the manager comes over with a washrag and glares at me with the pretense of cleaning our table. Oooh-hooo, my ribs are aching.

"He puts an egg—" I try again.

"Exactly," she responds belligerently. "Well, or a feather."

"A *feather*!" I'm off again, imagining her unable to hold up that feather. Oh, the pain. "Okay, okay," I say, wiping tears again, regaining some control. "Sorry. Okay. I'm just trying to understand this, this…*procedure*. I'm curious."

She looks dubious, studies my expression, finally nods.

I continue, "So he puts an egg—or a *feather*—in a cup, and you try to hold it up, while he's pushing your arm?"

"Right." She's brightening again, now that I'm showing a genuine interest in the details.

"And you're telling me you *can't*?"

"Right! Because I'm allergic!"

"Hmmm. So, if it's that easy to test, can you try it on me, say?"

"Oh, no! You have to be *trained* to be a tester and everything," she says.

"Uh-huh... So, how come you had to wait a whole weekend without eating any eggs and stuff, if you did the test in one go?"

"Oh, well, you see, we did the test after the weekend, so that I'd be more sensitive to poultry and stuff." This makes no sense to me, but I don't say so.

"So you couldn't eat eggs, or chicken, or…"

"Right. Or even touch feathers."

"But you're wearing feathers now!"

"Oh, I know! But Swami Murkh has decided that's okay, as long as I'm not eating any eggs."

"And Swami Murkh is…?"

"My guru," she breathes happily, to the tune of *my hero*. She smiles big again. "*And* my tester, that's how I met him. He was specially trained in Santa Fe."

"Uh-huh." I start thinking of all the hidden places that feathers exist. "So…I guess you weren't allowed to, say, sleep on a down pillow?"

"Right! Swami Murkh thought of that and warned me." She looks so proud. Then she leans over and whispers to me, as if imparting some girlfriend-to-girlfriend secret, like a new way to give head or something: "He told me I wasn't even allowed to *look* at a chicken."

Your neighbor's chicken is a duck, I think. "What would have happened if you had?" I ask.

"I would've had to start the whole weekend all over again."

"Oh." Then I think of something: "Would it count if the chicken were in a movie?"

She frowns. "I don't know. I hadn't thought of that."

"Or a photo? Because, say you unexpectedly suddenly saw some scene and there were some chickens in it... I wonder if that would have invalidated your weekend experiment."

She looks a tiny bit upset.

"Or," I can't resist continuing, "What if, without thinking, you drove past a Kentucky Fried Chicken? You surely must have, at some point during the weekend, whether you were aware of it or not, wouldn't you agree? Do you think maybe it would be okay if it were on the opposite side of the road from you, but not okay if it were the same side? And would a divided highway be enough buffer, do you think? Or—suppose some bunch of guys went out and bought themselves a bucket of this KFC and then *they* drove past you on the same side of the road—"

"Stop it!" she hisses.

I pause to consider the issue. "How about chicken *hawks*?" I ask, finally.

"Chicken...hawks?" she repeats dubiously, slowly.

"Yeah, you know, like, circling."

"*Circling?*"

"Overhead. Would that cou—?"

"Enough! Enough! I get your point!"

Oh, goody. I love it when my point is gotten.

The manager comes by again to glare at me, so I miss part of what Tracy is now mumbling. Apparently some New-Age reference—sounded to me like *the eagle gets in the way*.

"What was that?" I ask reluctantly, not really wanting to hear some stolen-from-the-Native-Americans aphorism.

"Nothing," she says.

"No, I just didn't hear you."

I shouldn't have insisted. "I *said*," she informs me icily, "seems to me like your ego's getting in the way."

Ouch. "So, Tracy..." I begin, trying to move to different territory. "What's the significance of that thingie on your forehead? What's it called again?"

"Oh!" she says, touching it, her smile returning. "I totally forgot I was wearing it! It's called a bindu."

"No," I say, "Actually, I think it's *bindi*."

She continues obliviously, animatedly, "Swami Murkh likes me to wear

them. It's a sign of spiritual devotion for their women, you know…"
I ask, "And his spirituality is…?"
"Oh, Swami Murkh?! He's Hindi!"
No, Tracy, I think, Hin*du*. Sigh.

g^w

I quickly made a cappuccino—why don't they ever taste as good at home? You swear you're gonna cut down on those café bills, so you buy the three-hundred dollar espresso maker, calculating that it'll pay for itself in six months, and it never does, because what it makes tastes like crap and you end up taking two or three sips and having to go to the café later for the real thing—and logged on. And promptly sprayed out my mouthful, choking and laughing. My instant global news summaries had come up, and a typo or editing slipup was evident, involving the lack of one tiny but ultimately extremely important word, unfortunately turning tragedy into high comedy and rendering the day's headline, seen by the entire wired world, as: "Two Palestinian suicide bombers killed at least three other people and wounded 40 when they blew themselves in rapid succession in Tel Aviv's foreign worker neighborhood, Israeli police said."

Driving to campus, there was snow coating the Flatirons— frigid but beautiful. I passed a health food store with a big sign in the window advertising a sale on Horny Goat Weed.

All of which put me in the perfect frame of mind to teach a new bunch of *studnets* (while I was still a T.A., one of them misspelled it while writing his or her comments on evaluations: "us studnets think its to hard," and it's been standard amongst me and my teaching peers to refer to them as "studnets" ever since) who didn't want to be there after their winter break and would soon let me know it. Today was Intro to Memetic Theory.

To what appeared to be an entirely brain-dead class, I read aloud (from the syllabi I'd just handed out, to give them the benefit of the doubt and a small head start/advantage in case any or all of them were literally illiterate) the names of the three required books we'd be using. "*The Meme Machine*, by Susan Blackmore; *Virus of the Mind: The New Science of the Meme*, by Richard Brodie; and *Thought Contagion: How Belief Spreads Through Society*, by Aaron Lynch. Any questions?"

Two zombie guys roused themselves, one to comment: "Yo, dude, 'thought contagion'—that sounds trippy, like a sci-fi video or somethin'," while the other simultaneously asked, "Aaron Lynch? Rad! Is he, like, related to David Lynch?"

I sighed. Not for nothing I'm an excellent teacher: you have to use what you're given. "No," I said, "he's not related to David Lynch—that I know of—but that brings up an excellent example of a meme. Does anyone know—at this point—what a meme is?"

Total silence.

Then, Thought Contagion Guy: "Is it, like, somethin' from outer space, dude?"

The class exploded in laughter: nerves being expelled. I'm a good *and* experienced (and sometimes patient) teacher; I know what this sounds like.

Twenty minutes later, they were eating out of my hand.

Toward the end of the period, I gave them their first meme assignment: besides the readings, watch half an hour of TV and write down every instance of every meme you notice (a completely impossible assignment, but that was the point; hopefully about three minutes into it they'd understand that and have their epiphany about how ubiquitous memes really are).

In the last five minutes of class, I read them a few tidbits out of Blackmore to keep them laughing and on my side. (It really is true that most of teaching is being an effective stand-up comedian.) For those who had the text, I had them follow along, just to get them back into the habit (or perhaps it was their first time ever; their being in college meant nothing) of *looking at print* after what had certainly been a purely physical three weeks of debauchery, drugs, and sex. On page 80, I pointed out and quoted: "In this way the memes are, as it were, dragging the genes along. The leash has been reversed and, to mix metaphors, the dog is in the driving seat." I waited a moment for that to sink in, then asked, "Will anyone volunteer what image that immediately brought to mind?"

One girl asked, "Really? I mean, it's totally stupid..."

"No, no, *really*," I assured her.

"Well, there's like, this Gary Larson cartoon? I mean, like, a Far Side? Where, like, *dogs go to work* or something, and they're all, like—"

"Totally!" "Nailed it, dude!" About ten different studnets joined in.

"That, my friends," I told them, *avec panache*, "was a very successful meme."

"Oooooooooooh." They were all *very impressed*.

My last two items were just to keep them entertained before they walked out the door.

"Page 136," I directed. "Middle of the page... Discussion of possible sexual transmission of memes." (The things we have to do to get their attention.) "Paragraph: 'However, transmission is no longer largely vertical. So what happens to sex when memes are generally spread horizontally?'" I paused for them all to laugh, which they did with perfect predictability. Humans scare me.

For my grand finale, I went for the cheapest of laughs (strangely enough, that always works; comedians, take note). "Please consult page 139, those of you who have the text... Second paragraph." I then proceeded to point out the discussion of meme/gene conflicts, and the comparison to gene/gene conflicts between host and parasite: some parasites chemically castrated their hosts in order that the energy of the host go toward replicating the parasite's genes... Celibacy... Etcetera, etcetera. "*And*," I asked them, "to whom is this intriguing quote attributed?" I got the expected big laugh when they saw that the author's last name was Ball. I also got a few blank looks from those who probably didn't know the word "attributed" (or was it "castrate" they didn't know?).

And, like Jerry Seinfeld (minus the moolah), I made my exit on a wave of chortling and cheering. I'm pretty sure I'm the only prof routinely getting *applauded*. So how could someone as smart as me have done something as stupid as gotten a useless Ph.D.?

מ

Can I just say how extremely glad I am that "the holiday season" is finally over? I mean, I avoid all stores *comme la peste* from the time they put up the damn Xmas decorations on October first, all the way till the last Christmas carol stops playing sometime around the beginning of February—but one can't exactly go without groceries for four months. Having to hear some new jazzed-up version of "Jingle Bells" or "Here Comes Santa Claus" every five minutes, wherever I go, just drives me plain fucking crazy. I want to call in Camouflage Man to blow out the sound system.

And the Christian assumption (no pun intended) also bothers me. Every time I have to duck in somewhere to buy toilet paper and someone glazedly wishes me "Merry Christmas!," I get perturbed. Jews all have different strategies for dealing with it. Many retort: "And a Happy Chanukah to you too!" I guess we're always trying to educate, although it bothers us that Chanukah is not the equivalent to Christmas (though Christians seem to think it is), and so we also feel uncomfortable perpetuating that belief. (Aren't we just such a bunch of *sticklers*?) Some Jews I know have given up on all that and enjoy the mystified looks when they say, "And a Happy Kwanzaa to you!"

In the entrance to Ideal Market, I check my horoscope (something I of course do only tongue-in-cheek) on the second page of a free weekly.

Mine, this time, makes me think: a) maybe I should try to finish up my challenge *this week*; and b) I *really, really* miss Alan:

"How many times have you looked in the mirror and seen only that same tired face looking back? Well, sometime in the coming (and I do mean coming) seven days, (and be ready for it, baby), you're going to be startled by the reflection of your dark side. Those hidden desires are going to make themselves known, ready or not. That secret wish of yours to be a porn star, baby? Well, here's your chance."

While shopping, I notice, in the Personal Products aisle, a *kit* of some kind, a truly awful-sounding item, reminiscent of torture chambers in German castle basements. It's called *Ear Candles*, complete with pen-and-ink diagram involving fire, candles, places where candles do not belong, and, inexplicably, an aluminum pie plate à la Jiffy Pop. Why, in this era of Q-Tips, would such a thing exist? And, perhaps more importantly—who is buying it? Mordecai?

In line to check out, I become aware of several things simultaneously: 1) Everyone seems to be staring at me and what I'm buying, which, now that I examine my selections, *is* a tad embarrassing: tomatoes, cucumbers, condoms, and lubricant. (But I *am* having salad tonight!) 2) The cashier has a scary shaved head, huge "cut" muscles, and various frightening facial piercings, and I would've guessed she was gay or butch or whatever the proper term is, except maybe she's not, because she's wearing a hilarious T-shirt, of which I am instantly enamored. It says: *You think* I *look good? You should see my boyfriend naked.* 2 ½) I'm slightly afraid of what effect 1) might have on 2). 3) The guy ahead of me has the worst B.O. I've ever had the misfortune to smell. I back up, trying to maintain maximum personal distance from him without losing my place in line. My god, this is truly horrendous! He must not have bathed in months, to smell this putrid. He does look suspiciously like a Rainbow Gathering type, but this B.O. goes beyond the norm; this is approaching Seinfeldian proportions. When he reaches the cashier, they appear to be acquaintances and begin chatting. The cashier has to have superhuman powers or else lack olfactory ability altogether; she didn't even flinch as he approached.

Then she asks him, "Hey, weren't you going to work here?"

"Well, yeah, I *was*—I mean, I applied and everything. I mean, I even, like, *interviewed* and everything. But they wouldn't *have* me. Then this other friend of mine, who, like, works here? He, like, told me later that they thought I *smelled* bad. Can you believe it?"

Mais non!, I think, still desperately holding my breath about ten feet back, outrage!

There's a psychedelic hand-lettered sign up on the wall near the clock: *Feeling like the line's just too slow? Remember: The Universe wants you here now!*

Well, okay, perhaps, I think. Or maybe the cashiers are just lame.

I recall my horoscope. The challenge had been going along very smoothly; in fact, I no longer even thought about it these days. It had become as much a part of my life as my exercise routine—I went jogging, I did NIA, I did guys and added them to the list. I no longer had any doubts—*none*—about finishing the bet. I was already up to twenty-six and it was just March. I occasionally missed Alan terribly; reading his emails was great, but nothing could make up for not having him next to me physically. Basically, though, I was on sexual autopilot. It was like eating Saltines—boring, bland, and ultimately not very nutritious—but hard to stop once you'd started.

The guys were memorable in small ways only, ultimately forgettable: there was the student from Le Centre du Silence Mime School, who remained fully in character the whole time. Quite amusing—for about five minutes. (And I do mean the *whole* time—have you ever seen someone mime an orgasm?)

There was the one who—for some strange, probably Freudian reason—isn't capable of just normal lovemaking, but rather needs desperately to bury his face in your ample cleavage and cling there, alternately whimpering, crying softly, and shouting "Mama!" when he comes, as his body bucks itself to a rapid orgasm against yours. You feel about as involved in, and sexually necessary to, the scene as an overstuffed sofa cushion. Can you say *disgusting*?

There was the android dude I picked up when I went to do a linguistic consultation at IBM. He turned out to be a raving sexoholic (literally—he goes to group therapy for it) once the khakis and tie came off. The other ironies at IBM were more interesting than him, though—like the linguistically inscrutable signs I saw posted at the doors of various conference meeting rooms, e.g.: "Brio Query Explorer Release G;" the fact that the electronic security entry badges they themselves manufacture didn't work very well; and seeing "Out of Order" signs on some photocopier machines.

As IBM turned out to be an excellent place to pick up sex-starved drones, I had solicited the phone number of another, a Hindu (I made sure his name wasn't Swami Murkh). It was Badrachalam, which I had trouble remembering until he told me it sounded like "bad rack of lamb."

There was a Spaniard whom I first saw at the airport en route to a conference and for whom I felt a moment of real tenderness and what I thought could be true love, when I witnessed him in an intensely intimate moment with his aged mother: unbidden, he reached over and plucked out one of her long white chin hairs as she was ordering him to move their bags. Too bad he was a terrible lover and a premature ejaculator. He told great postcoital jokes, though. I vaguely remember something punacious about a chicken and a penis...

There was a new guy in yoga class who laughed out loud at the same time as me when my favorite teacher, Ron, instructed us to "squat, grasp your stomach, and move your chocolate pouch out of the way." In spite of our common sense of humor, I did resent the guy later, however, after I'd seen him naked and realized that his nipples were way perkier than mine. To make myself feel better, I told myself it must be a function of reverse size-proportion ratio or something.

Next was a Canadian-Italian dude who was just *trop* cool, a consultant whose entire apartment was decorated in only black, white, and chrome; and who wore only black and white designer-label clothing (I'm sure he would've worn chrome if he could), even down to his underwear and socks. I inventoried his place while he was in the shower and it gave me the chills.

And lastly, Number Twenty-Six was a guy who had demonically prickly pubes, and only when repeatedly accused did he admit to routinely shaving them to make his penis look an inch longer.

The one common denominator was that I'd told myself I would stay away from Jewish boys—no more weird Mordecais for me, and no inadvertent reminders of Alan or (god forbid) Eli, either. Although going after Jewish guys did have its clear advantages: 1) you knew they would be literate; 2) you could be sure, in advance, that they would be circumcised, so there'd be no scary surprises when the underwear came off; 3) there didn't seem to be any wifebeating amongst Jewish men—masochists they might be, henpecked husbands, yes; but sadists, never; 4) you could be sure you'd like their mothers, or at least have someone to go shopping with after you were married.

Someone interrupts my thoughts with "Aviva! Hey! What's up?" It turns out to be JoAnn, a colleague from the Spanish Department.

"Hey, JoAnn. What up?" JoAnn is cool. She loves making her undergrad studnets with the worst gringo accents repeatedly say, "I would win" in Spanish: *ganaría*.

"Actually, I'm just on my way to make some copies…after I get *this* little necessity." She shows me the Ben & Jerry's Phish Food carton in her hand. We move up in line. She suddenly wrinkles her nose. "P.U.! What is that smell?!"

"Don't ask. You're lucky. The origin of the smell has just departed… so what are you xeroxing?"

"Oh, it's this gem I dug up in the stacks the other day… Nineteen-forties… Can't you just imagine? Pretty soon we won't even *have* stacks anymore, and only people of our generation will be left to mourn the fact…" She shows me the tiny old book, cloth-bound cover and all. It probably hadn't been checked out in all those decades. *Palabras enfermas y bárbaras*: Sick and Barbarous Words. "Yep, I think I'm definitely gonna have to do a *sorry, dudes, I lost it, darn, guess I'll have to pay the fine* on this baby," she says with a wicked grin. Yeah, I sure do like JoAnn. I grin back. "What about you?" she asks. "What's the latest from the studnets?"

"Well," I tell her, as we exit the store together, "you're not gonna believe this, but this one came from a *grad* studnet." Her face forms a mask of armor in preparation. It's like Jaws: just when you think nothing can surprise you anymore…as summed up in this fortune I got in a cookie the other day: "Always think of danger when things are going smoothly," like floating along calmly on your surfboard and having your arm ripped off. "Okay," I tell her, "so this dude is in my office, right?, discussing Yinglish issues, which he's confused about…" She nods. "So 'fronting' comes up, right?—simple concept, right?—and with perfect innocence he goes, 'Um, just want to clarify here, so fronting is like, how, like, you Jewish chicks always have these big boobs?'"

"No *way!*" JoAnn bursts into giggles to the point of choking. I start pounding on her back, and she's finally forced to fend me off. Then she says, "You know I have to try to top you now, right?"

"But of course," I reply, trying to make a poker face. "Go for it."

"Okay, so you know I have this friend in Astrophysics, Youssef? So he calls me the other day and says, all serious and everything, no major preamble, 'Guess what, JoAnn. It has been discovered that the color of the universe is beige.'"

Now it was my turn to crack up. Gasping, I manage to squeak out, "What, in passive voice and everything?" which sets her off again.

"Exactly," she says, laughing, half-draping herself over me weakly. "That's Youssef for you. You know, his girlfriend told me she can't even say, *Oh look, a shooting star!*, without him going *Well, that's simply a meteor, a particle that enters the earth's atmosphere at high speed and, due to atmospheric friction, super-heats and glows. It can be as small as a grain of sand and may be of any matter, though ice and/or dust from comets is one common source.* From what she's told me, it can really kill a romantic mood."

We part, grinningly, in the parking lot.

Beige? I think. How...sedate. How demure. How boring. No way could that be true! Shouldn't it be more like turquoise or fuchsia or something? At the very least, burnt sienna. Anyway, how could it be just one single color? Surely this Youssef was pulling her leg—or taking her hair, as JoAnn had told me the Spanish idiom was. I locate my car and read the bumper sticker on the SUV next to it as *Support your local nutcases.* Awesome!, I think. Then I shake my head and re-read it the way it really is, boring, sedate, demure: *Support your local businesses.* Bah, humbug.

The car on the other side of mine is an extremely ancient beat-up thing, on the front of which is strapped, in lieu of a bumper, a weathered old piece of driftwood—to which is nailed a huge pair of antlers. A sticker on the back says *Everything Is Sacred.* Hmm. I wait for a reaction to this car. And wait.

Nothing. Perhaps I've been in Boulder too long?

As I pull out of the parking lot, a guy comes out of Ideal Market wearing a small backpack—and skipping. He continues to do so all the way down Broadway until he has to stop for the light. When it turns green, he resumes his happy locomotion. Boulder has got to be one of the few places in America (on Earth?) where you routinely see grown men skipping. (I've heard rumors that the grounds of the Dalai Lama's disciples may be another.)

Q

Got an email from JoAnn (she of the *Sick and Barbarous Words*), a forwarded collection of "English" seen on signs throughout the world. I *loved* these things. Beginning studnets assume this is the kind of great fun with language that we Linguistics professors have all the time. Nothing could be further from the truth—theoretical Linguistics is so far removed from natural language that it has very little—if anything—to do with it, and in fact much more closely resembles mathematics or computer science. It is unbelievably dry, technical stuff. Had I known what it was like before I got too far into it... Ah, well. Sadly, 'tis what all us professors say, once we're stuck. The truth is that while the outside world might hold us in esteem (well, other than the *studnets*), we'd far rather be adventure photographers, say, or hanggliders, or something.

>>"Signs" of the spread of "Inklish":
In a Tokyo hotel: Is forbidden to steal hotel towels, please. If you are not person to do such thing, is please not to read notice.
In a Bucharest hotel lobby: The lift is being fixed for the next day. During that time we regret that you will be unbearable.
In a Leipzig elevator: Do not enter the lift

backwards, and only when lit up.

In a Belgrade hotel elevator: To move the cabin, push button for wishing floor. If the cabin should enter more persons, each one should press a number of wishing floor. Driving is then going alphabetically by national order.

In a Yugoslavian hotel: The flattening of underwear with pleasure is the job of the chambermaid.

In an Austrian ski hotel: Not to perambulate the corridors in the hours of repose in the boots of ascension.

From the Soviet Weekly: There will be a Moscow Exhibition of Arts by 15,000 Soviet Republic painters and sculptors. These were executed over the past two years.

In a Vienna hotel: In case of a fire, do your utmost to alarm the hotel porter.

In Germany: It is strictly forbidden on our Black Forest camping site that people of different sex, for instance, men and women, live together in one tent unless they are married with each other for that purpose.

Advertisement for donkey rides in Thailand: How would you like to ride on your own ass?

Detour sign in Japan: Stop & Drive Sideways.

In a Bangkok temple: It is forbidden to enter a woman even a foreigner if dressed as a man.

On the door of a Moscow hotel room: If this is your first visit to the USSR, you are welcome to it.

At a Budapest zoo: Please do not feed the animals. If you have any suitable food, give it to the guard on duty.

On the menu of a Polish hotel: Salad a firm's own make; limpid red beet soup with cheesy dumplings in the form of a finger; roasted duck let loose; beef rashers beaten up in the country people's fashion.

From a brochure of a car rental firm in Tokyo: When passenger of foot heave into sight, tootle the horn. Trumpet him melodiously at first, but if he still obstacles your passage then tootle him with vigor.

The Japanese ones brought to mind some very weird memories I still hold of a Linguistics conference I'd gone to in Otsu, where for kicks I'd also wasted an entire weekend with a colleague, Lynn (no longer with our Department—didn't get tenure), traveling all the way to southern Japan. This was on the strength of many recommendations from many Japanese people and incredible-looking brochures, to go visit what was described in one such pamphlet as *A terrific and marvelous, natural phenomenon which really looks like 'Hell.'* The Eight Beppu Hells: natural hot springs buried in different kinds of muds, "blood-red" and "blue-white": spectacular abodes of crocodiles, explosion sites of volcanoes, home to exotic animals (hippos, in the photo) and a great red demon sitting atop an enormous cooking pot. We *had* to go.

So did about half the population of the islands. Whenever the huge crowds would let us elbow in and get a peek, we could just catch a glimpse of tiny lukewarm puddles of dun-colored muck, surrounded by ugly chain-link fences and look-alike touristing Japanese, the black-stockinged men smoking like fiends and happy to be out of the office, the demure-skirted women happy to be out of the house, the children wearing silly hats to protect them from the sun (no one had told us it was going to be witheringly, tropically hot), all of them snapping pictures and videotaping everything that did or didn't move. There was nothing to eat at the snack bars—either at the Hell Site or in the train stations—except bananas, or crackers with fish and/or seaweed in them, or squid-on-a-stick, or snack-packets of little stiff dried fishies with the eyeballs still in them.

At one point we thought we'd found the real booty, some kind of Japanese dessert. We bought the biggest box and proceeded to investigate its contents on the train while some Japanese across the aisle pretended not to be watching us out of the corners of their eyes. I vaguely remembered a Japanese taboo against eating in public, but screw it. Both Lynn and I were starving, neither one of us was going near any of that fish or seaweed crap, all the bananas had us terribly constipated and irritable, and the only thing we wanted on a stick was either a Popsicle or to see one of the brochure-writers' heads skewered, so we opened up that box and dug in. It looked heavenly—okay, not *totally* heavenly; I mean, it wasn't a chocolate truffle. It appeared to be a dumpling. Maybe a Japanese version of a cream-filled doughnut? Mmm...that would really hit the spot about now. We bit in, looking into each other's eyes with the anticipation of lovers. It had probably been about thirty hours since we'd eaten anything edible besides the bananas; we'd earlier passed on fabulous menu delicacies like sushi that was still alive, and raw egg floating in a cup of seaweed.

Then the horror registered in Lynn's eyes—and, I suppose, in mine too. What I'd tasted was so awful that I gagged and had to spit it out—right back into the box. Lynn did the same. The Japanese people's eyes across the aisle got huge. They looked at each other and gave a tiny shake of their heads but didn't say a word.

We were crabby all the way back to Otsu—a long, long journey when you're starving and disappointed as hell (and also *by* Hell)—where we grumblingly settled for plain rice and fishy-tasting miso soup with suspicious-looking things floating in it. Others around us were relishing octopus tentacles and parts of the sea anemone that should never have been disturbed. Vegetarian Jews were never meant to go to Japan.

We found out later that the little morsels our Occidental palates had so summarily rejected were the most exquisite choice of Japanese dessert—if they ever eat any dessert, that is, which is rare (as rare as them consuming cheese, chocolate, bread, pasta, butter, olives, Mexican food—all the great gastronomic wonders worth living for). They were sweetened fermented bean-paste stuffed inside bland ultra-processed rice dumplings. Which actually doesn't even sound that bad, but believe me, it tastes quite horrible. Especially when you're starving and expecting a frigging *cannoli*.

λ

I usually screen all my calls, but this morning I was so out of it, I just reached for the phone without thinking:

"Hello?"

"Yes-this-is-blahblahblah-we're-asking-for-your-assistance-our-community-really-needs-your-help-it's-only-your-input-we're-after-not-a-contribution-and-there's-even-a-free-complimentary-gift-so-please-don't-hang-up..."

Well, normally, that's exactly what I do, but now, of course, I felt guilty...and not only guilty, but as if this guy could somehow read my mind. It was a bit spooky. Oh, what the hell, I thought. What, is it going to *kill* me, to pay attention to some guy's spiel for once?

"Yes?" I asked.

"Yes! Thank you for taking the time. Really, just a few minutes... It's just a small survey... Really almost nothing at all..."

I cleared my throat definitively. This guy would fit right in back in *Nihon*.

The questions started out innocently enough: marital status, age, employment. However, they all had some strange common theme that I couldn't quite put my finger on (keep in mind that I hadn't yet gotten out for my double soy mocha latte). For example: *divorced* they didn't care about, nor *separated*; the only categories they acknowledged were *single*, *married*, or *widowed*. And the age question was kind of weird, too: there was a broad, all-inclusive *under 40s*, but if you were over 40 then they were apparently very interested in breaking you down into smaller and smaller, more and more specific subcategories. And they sure didn't seem to want to know much about the job thing; they had only two categories: employed or non-employed. Oh, wait, sorry, what? Oh, I'd heard him wrong. It was: employed or retired.

"Okay, then," I said, "employed." I started getting dressed and managed to complete most of it before the phone held between ear and shoulder became an impossible obstruction.

So I started pulling on a sweater and for about thirty seconds, the phone was in a no-woman's land, before I got it back up to the opposite ear, just in time to hear the guy ask in a rehearsedly tender voice: "Does the person whom you will designate know your preferences, including the type of casket you wish to be buried in, music, flowers, and services?"

"*Excusez-moi?*"

"Ah...ahem," he said carefully, "Perhaps we should move on to a less...*delicate* question. Please keep in mind that this is nothing personal, of course, just a survey, as you know... Yes, let's see here. Number five: Are you aware that you can arrange and pay for a funeral in advance of need?"

"*Funerals?!* We're talking about *funerals*? Jesus! And first thing in the morning? My god!"

"Ma'am, if you wouldn't mind answering the question... Number five, it was..."

Well...okay, what the hell. "What was it again? Am I aware that I can pay for my funeral in advance? Was that it?"

"Yes, ma'am." He sounded overjoyed that I was cooperating, now that he was into the hairy part of the interview. Jesus. What a job.

"In advance of what?" I asked.

"Excuse me?"

"In advance of what?"

"Well," he ventured tentatively, "in advance of...need."

"You mean," I asked him, "*death?*"

"Well, we don't like to..."

"You mean would I like to pay for the arrangements regarding my death previous to the occurrence of said death?"

"Ma'am, are you by any chance a lawyer?" he asked, sounding frightened.

"Maybe you guys should include that one in the beginning," I suggested sardonically. "Maybe it should say: retired, or lawyer, or otherwise employed."

"Damn, that's a great idea!" he exclaimed, sounding for the first time like a normal human being rather than an embalmed corpse. Then he gasped at his own audacity: "Oh! Goodness! Please excuse my language!"

"No problem," I said, stifling a smile, knowing as I do (ad technical nauseum) how a smile changes the frequency of the voice and makes itself known over the telephone. "Well, in any case, the answer to your question is, no, I would *not* like to pay for my *death* arrangements before I die. I would much prefer afterwards. If at all. Next question."

"Um...Yes, well, I see, well. Well, fine..."

"Excuse me, are you by any chance of Japanese descent?"

"No. Why do you ask?"

"Never mind. Sorry. I have to get going here pretty soon... What's the next question?"

"Um, yes, fine, well, it's Number seven: How much would you expect a funeral to cost? The options are: Over eight thousand; between five thousand and eight thousand; —"

I hadn't known he was going to list options, so I'd said the first (I'd thought) intelligent estimate I'd had: "Hmm, I'd guess around five hundred dollars?"

There was a really long silence on both our sides.

Finally I tried for a joke: "Well, guess I better not die, then, huh?! Can't afford it!"

"Yes, well, then, shall we just move on to one final item, let's see, Number nine: Which of the following would you choose for yourself: Burial or Cremation?"

I couldn't answer.

"Ma'am? Are you still there? Ma'am?"

I still couldn't answer.

"Ma'am? Hello?"

"Umrmghgh..." I managed, to let him know I hadn't hung up.

"Ma'am? Is something the matter?"

Was something the matter?

Finally I found my voice again: "But wait a sec... I mean, you're only giving me two options. Either/or. I mean, there's got to be something else. I mean, more choices… You know?"

He was very silent.

"You know?" I asked again. "I mean, come on. You're saying, it's this—or that. Black or white. Up or down. Yes or no. No shades of gray? Eaten by worms or burned up in flames?! There's got to be more choices than that!" Without warning, I suddenly broke into sobs.

"Ma'am? Ma'am!" He sounded alarmed but under control; surely he must have been trained in this sort of thing, considering his line of work.

"It's just," I told him truthfully, through gasps, through early-morning blubbering as my own mortality struck me for a very rare moment and thanks only to this stranger's spiel (shades of Govinda), "I don't like *either* of those choices!"

He became very silent again.

"There's got to be something else!"

He remained quiet.

"What about offering some other options, some other *services*, for those of us who don't care for options A and B? You guys could, you know, branch out, fill a business niche that's currently going untapped…"

I could hear him taking soft, measured breaths.

"You know, what is there?, there's those vultures over in Tibet or Nepal or somewhere— you put the dead person on the roof and they come and pick off all the meat overnight or something; I'm not sure what happens to the bones, though, and it's pretty gruesome to actually think about it, really, you know, the eyes and everything… And there's, let's see, what else?—Yes! There's burial at sea!, isn't there?, you know, where—"

"Ma'am," he cut in unexpectedly, but softly. "We're not *mariners*, ma'am."

"Well, you could, you know, contract with someone, outsource—"

"Here in *Boulder*?"

I said, "Well, restaurants here serve fresh seafood, don't they? They're getting it shipped in from *somewhere*, aren't they? So you guys would just be doing, like, the reverse—in fact, maybe you could even contract with the same people; I mean, their trucks would be empty on the way back, right?…"

"I think that was a movie," he said. "Was it Eating Raoul? No, maybe that was something else."

"I think it's a pretty damn good idea, myself. If I weren't working full-time already *I'd* follow up on it. Think how many landlocked people are probably dying to" (I giggled at the pun; somehow the sobs had disappeared on their own—PMS could be a major culprit) "be buried at sea!"

"Hmm. You could be right," he allowed.

"Then there's a hypothesis I heard, where if you could just shoot all the nuclear waste into the sun, it could be disposed of that way...same with all the trash and plastic and nonbiodegradables...so why not dead people! As soon as everything hit that certain point, it'd just, like, *vaporize*. Do you think that technology will be available soon? Because that might be the best way to go, you know?"

"I think that might've been a movie, too."

"Have you been listening to what I'm telling you? I don't like your two measly options, so *what the hell am I supposed to do?*"

"You know what, ma'am? It's been...uh...more than entertaining talking to you, ma'am, but I have a lot more calls to make today. If you don't like those options that are available to you, ma'am, I'd suggest you file a complaint...with your parents." He allowed himself to chuckle, and loudly. "I don't imagine the rest of my calls today are going to be as interesting and thought-provoking as this one was, and I thank you kindly for that, ma'am. And if our company obtains any solar-system rocket launching facilities in the near future, why, we'll be certain to contact you."

As he hung up, I could hear him laughing. But quite frankly, I was still extremely concerned, because, my god, no one had ever thrown my up-and-coming corpse in my face before in quite such a businesslike and nonchalant manner, and asked me how I was planning to *dispose* of it. (And I *still* didn't like either of those two options.)

Suddenly the phone rang again and, startled, I answered it.

"Ma'am, I am so sorry to trouble you again, but I completely forgot to get your address so that I could send you our free complimentary gift, as promised."

"What is it?" I asked.

"It's a free Personal Planning Guide." (You could hear the caps.)

"And what is that?"

"Well, it's a guide to help you plan your services...for afterwards."

"After what?" I asked him, just to tease him.

He sighed.

"No. No, thank you. No more talk about caskets, and flowers, and...and...*death*! This is the strangest and most...*morbid* morning I have ever had with a stranger."

"Ma'am, I'd have to say: I agree." And he rang off, laughing once again.

I couldn't help but join in.

i

I'm in my car, waiting for the light to change, and a huge series of yawns overtakes me. My yawns tend to arrive like my orgasms—sometimes surprising me, and often in multiples. Another red light... There's a mysterious force-field that governs east-west traffic in Boulder, to which north-south traffic is immune; you can go anywhere north-south in about ten minutes, but the same distance takes more than twice as long going east-west. Most residents have noticed the phenomenon. Some blame it on city politicians, some blame it on aliens (with or without crop circles), others blame it on the Hemp Initiative's repeated failure to pass.

At the next light, the license plate ahead of me is surrounded by one of those little plastic frames that are supposed to *individualize* your license plate. This one asks, along the top: *Want to go fast?* And suggests along the bottom: *Go Kartin'!* Gosh, such...*pith*. Such originality. I can't help but think: how *redneck*, how un-Boulder. (In the way that Victorian gentlewomen of yore must have frequently entertained the thought "Oh dearie me, how unladylike," we modern Boulderites frequently entertain the thought "Huh, weird, how unBoulderlike.") I then realize that the license plate doesn't start with *M* and promptly congratulate myself on my amateur sleuthing abilities: this is indeed no Boulder resident! Must be from Longmont or one of those other L places.

Finally make it into McGuckin's Hardware for my intended errand, where I accidentally get lost for half an hour in the plumbing section of the store, which covers about ten acres, I would estimate. Everywhere there are green-vested employees who are unbelievably friendly and perky, as if permanently on uppers. What does the management do to get them all to act that way? Their pockets are bulging and stinking suspiciously; all the many visiting dogs in the store know to force their guardians to stop in front of every green vest they encounter and not budge until several dog biscuits are brought forth, to the delight of all parties involved. They (the employees, not the dogs—well, the dogs too, but that's not relevant here) really are friendly and can also be quite helpful, but as every time I wander into McGuckin's I forget what I came for, due to sheer product volume overload, they are generally unable to be of assistance. I've often wondered if there could be some intriguing correlation between the perkiness and the constant exposure to the smell of dog biscuits.

While trying desperately to remember what I needed and gawking at all the alien stuff in the plumbing aisles, I pass a whole row of something labeled "Funny Pipe Fittings." I go back and take a very close look at them and I swear I see absolutely *nothing* humorous about any of them.

Finally I manage to somehow accidentally stumble out of pipes, through house paints and into gardening supplies, still without remembering why I'm in this megastore in the first place.

I'm not much of a gardener—how can you be, when you have no land? Maybe if I made more than an academic's wages, I could actually own some *terra firma*, though in Boulder it would take a stockbroker's salary to do so. But I am always drawn irresistibly, like a child, to the seed packets, with their snack-pack size, brightly colored pictures and strange, surreal common names, like a poem, a secret language. Sometimes I even end up buying some and then the packets sit around amongst my massive piles of papers for years, gathering dust.

Today, in front of me, await in all their phonetic and pictorial splendor: Japanese Blood Grass; Pussytoes; Kinnickinnick; Dutchman's pipe; Mat Penstemon (I think I dated him once); Heavy Metal Switchgrass (a new musical genre?); Dwarf Hairy Penstemon (unfortunately, I think I dated him too); Siberian Skullcap; Little Picklos (a short Greek I may have gone out with once); Dead Nettle (why bother planting it, then?); Rue (ditto); the useful trilogy of Self Heal, Fleabane, and Leopard's Bane; Greek participants in a love-triangle tragedy: Ilex, Catalpa and Pachysandra (and the father, Euonymus); the appetizing Lungwort, Spurge, and Bowel

Periwinkle; the exotic Moonbeam Coreopsis, Blue Butterfly Pincushion Flower, Pineapple Sage, and African Blue Basil; and (say this three times fast) Variegated Porcelain Ampelopsis.

Finally, I give up on whatever errand had supposedly brought me here, but not before being accosted by several more Green Vests, all trying to be *so* helpful (is it some kind of genetic failing?—not just of McGuckin's employees; I mean the whole human race) and not before capitulating to the written directives on one seed packet, a flower mix, which commanded me, on one corner, to *Be Bold!* and which also urged *Up With Reds!* Somehow, I was unable to resist the beautiful photo plus these inane exhortations and felt compelled to purchase it, even though I know it will but gather dust under copies of *The International Journal of American Linguistics* (one of my favorite oxymorons), *Sintagma*, and *Anthropological Linguistics*.

One of these days maybe I'll look into that program I've heard about, where poor, sad Boulderite apartment dwellers like me can rent some kind of little city garden space each summer to cultivate whatever they want (other than, I suppose, cannabis). Unfortunately, I've noticed that these plots have—suspiciously—the exact size, shape, and appearance of fresh graves.

I drive over to the library, park illegally in their lot, get out and walk along the creek path. In a few minutes, I startle and am equally startled by, a shirtless guy standing semi-motionless in the shrubbery. I freeze; he very slowly extends one arm toward me, then the opposite leg, then does an excruciatingly slow half-turn while looking at me out of the corner of one eye. You're always coming across random people doing tai chi around here. It's like accidentally walking in on someone who's going to the bathroom when they didn't lock the door: embarrassing and a bit frightening for both of you.

My walk is refreshing although quite chilly, and I soon head back to the car. I get home, make some cocoa, still can't remember why I went to McGuckin's, and curl up with Baby and my laptop to work on my fledgling novel (to which only Therese and Georgette are privy and are sworn to absolute secrecy under pain of death; no one else will be told I've even *thought* about writing a novel until this thing is in its second week on the New York Times bestseller list). It's going to be about a linguist who gets stranded on a desert island with her research chimp that knows sign language—I'm on page thirteen and the working title is *The Secret Life of Toothbrushes*.

?

    I've come to the Pearl Street Mall early to kill an hour or so before meeting Therese for coffee, because it's one of those perfect spring days. The sun is out, it's too early in the year to be blazingly, scorchingly hot yet, and the incredibly tall purple and yellow tulips are up and looking as regal as they do every year.
    There are guitar players here and there on different street corners; and the usual buskers, who know all the residents by sight and don't expect money from them, only from the out-of-towners (Boulder really is that small). There's the guy with the lovebird on his shoulder who throws playing cards onto the roofs, and the reggae yoga dude who squinches himself up to fit into the tiny Plexiglas box.
    Here's the Zip Code Man, a huge crowd gathered around him as usual. I smile at him as I walk past, and, as always, he somehow manages to notice this while entertaining a hundred and fifty people, and return the smile. I remember something he once confessed to me, which made me laugh: apparently he had learned the art of street performance in New Orleans. When he came to Boulder, he proceeded to do his shtick the only way he knew how, that is, very aggressively. He was immediately taken aside by some laid-back Boulder hippie who'd been totally freaked by his approach, who told him, "*Dude!* You need to *relax*!"
    Another time I asked him if he has to do anything to keep up his

knowledge, and he said yes of course, he has to *review*, like anyone would. So I asked him, expecting to catch him unawares: "Okay, so what's next to review? Quick!" and he replied without missing a beat: "Oklahoma." Another time, a few weeks had gone by without my seeing him around town. When I saw him again, I asked where he'd been, and he said he'd been to a jugglers' convention.

I pass by the usual herd of disheveled-looking teenagers near the courthouse, who live in two-million-dollar homes in the foothills, drive Hummers, and have the audacity to ask every passerby for spare change. I notice one guy holding a cardboard sign: *Why lie? I need beer.* This gets a reluctant smile from me, as it seems to be doing from almost everyone walking by. In fact, he seems to be amassing quite a collection of alcohol funds. I'd lay bets this one did well in his Psych 101 class.

On the next corner, Shazam The Hula-Hoop Stunt (or Stud? I can't tell which it is when he announces it—it sounds the same and I'm too embarrassed to ask) Man is performing. I stop and watch for a while. Mmm... I can't help but eye those suave hip movements and think about attempting to seduce him as my Number Twenty-Seven. But then I think, man, first he'd *definitely* have to lose that Gilligan hat, and those weird neon-orange nylon shorts, and he really is sort of *embarrassing* to watch... I suddenly wonder if every woman in the audience is thinking the exact same thing: okay, he's a little on the short side, and we must upgrade those clothes, and I really can't *bring him home*, and say, well, Mom and Dad, he's a *busker*... But oh, those hips are divine.

I must admit, one thing I really appreciate about Boulder is that our entertainment is so *mild*. No, I really don't want to be living in an "exciting" place like New York, where you can pay good money to attend a live performance art piece, day or night, of someone smearing their naked self with their own feces. (And then this thing would even be *reviewed*, for god's sake. In the New York fucking *Times*, for god's sake.)

I walk on, past a pillar covered with band advertisements. The Travellin' Pitas, Deep Banana Blackout, Tempa & The Tantrums, String Cheese Incident, Electric Girdle, Organ Donor, and Bodacious Barley Bake.

I get a Chocolate Fudge Brownie cone from Ben & Jerry's and sit on a bench to nosh, soaking up the sun and the general ambience. A guy passes me walking his bike (it's illegal to ride on this part of the Mall, and believe me, they *do* ticket, and it's *not* cheap). I'm unable to breathe for a moment and have to do a double-take. Jesus, he *really* looked like Alan! But no—this impostor was somehow neater, cleaner, fussier. *Plus* he shaved his legs.

Speaking of the devil (or, as they say in Spanish, talking of the Pope in Rome, there he is), got another email from him last night:

```
Ave:
   Miss you. Had a minor bike accident. Turned
out to be a sprained wrist, so no riding for a week
or so, which sucks. Said velo wreck led me to a
very odd meta-situation: watching E.R. in the E.R.
How much stranger can modern life be? (Actually,
I know for a fact it can be far stranger than that,
but sue me...it was just an expression.)
   Speaking of strange, I was in Kinko's the other
day and saw something really poignant and sad (or
is that redundant? Sorry—I'm always so aware you're
a linguist; I'm afraid you're going to ostracize
me if I misuse a word or something). There was
this old wino guy (well, they're always guys if
you say "wino," aren't they?? so was that redun-
dant??) who was kind of bumbling around inarticu-
lately (was **that** redundant??? shit) at the front
desk with this huge hand-painted (still dripping
wet paint), 99% illegible poster that I guess he
wanted them to photocopy or something; it was ac-
tually impossible for anyone to figure out what he
wanted. All I could decipher on the poster was
the word "God," written really huge somewhere near
the top. Proselytizer? End-of-the-world-predic-
tor? Who knows.
   On the lighter side of life, did you hear about
the Surprise in the Bottle? This is actually from
the Boulder Weekly, which I've been reading on-
line. In case you didn't read this particular
"piece" (ahem), here's your chance now, courtesy
of Temporarily Non-Cycling Alan in California:
   "Juan Sanchez-Marchez, a 41-year-old machin-
```

ist in Commerce City, was swigging down a 20-ounce bottle of Ora Potency Fruit Punch [date deleted] when he saw something floating in the bottle. He called his 16-year-old son, Manuel, to the scene and the two machinists investigated. Then their boss came onto the scene, and insisted that what was floating in the drink looked suspiciously like a human penis.

And sure enough, it was. A pathologist with the Adams County coroner's office determined it was a three-inch segment of a human penis, cleanly cut at the base."

Anyway, Ave, the moral of this story? Don't drink any Ora Potency (Potency!) Fruit Punch, whatever the hell that is.

Alan

P.S. I imagine this is going to do wonders for their sales.

P.P.S. I had nothing to read the other day while sitting on the "throne," so I was reading my toilet paper package (a pack of four): "If you have any questions or comments about this bath tissue, please call 1-800..."

What is **this** about? Questions? What questions would I have? Would I have to, maybe, ask them how to use it? Should I ask them for recommendations as to how many squares to use for the average defecation? And what do you think they would say if I did ask them? Don't you think they would actually hang up on me and refuse to answer? And comments? What comments? "Man, I really liked your toilet paper—oh, sorry, I meant **bath tissue**. It felt, like, really nice on my anus." What is this world coming to, I ask you?

I hit the east extreme of the Mall and turn around, but not before spotting a few bumper stickers, here where the pedestrian does not rule: *Visualize Industrial Collapse*; *Find Your Epididymus*; *Windows 95 Causes*

Tourette's Syndrome; *Haiku School*; and *Legalize Lutefisk*. Lutefisk?! What the hell is that? Is it, perhaps, the "large white people's" (to quote Garrison Keillor, humorist par excellence—even though he's not a Jew) version of gefilte fish? Consider how revolting gefilte fish is to a normal person, now imagine how much more so to a *vegetarian*.

I pass the always-packed mediocre pasta place on the way back towards the Trident, and tilt my head in confusion—didn't it used to be more to the east? I swear this restaurant moves every year or so—a block this way, a block that way—it's like an old lady getting her hair done: never quite satisfied. They also had that debacle a while back—I guess they'd always claimed their marinara sauce was vegetarian, but someone snuck into the kitchen or something and discovered the anchovies being dumped into the sauce to make it so tasty. I think there was some much-publicized vegetarian across whose lips animal products had not passed for twenty-odd years... From what I heard, when he was finally outed, the chef merely waved away the accusation with: "Hey, it's *marinara*—marinara means *from the sea*—whaddaya want, already?!" I salute the chef for his knowledge, if not his ethics.

Outside the Trident, a guy in a Cat-in-the-Hat outfit (striped trousers with suspenders, strange hat) on one of those extremely tall, two-wheeled old-fashioned black steel bicycles (which he must have built himself or stolen from a museum or something) rides past, honking one of those old-fashioned car horns attached to it: "ah-*oooooooo*-gah!" He looks very nonchalant, as do all Boulder denizens who routinely do extremely odd things to get attention.

Viz., I see, the guy sitting in the Trident decked out in full Scottish regalia: kilt, bagpipes slung over the shoulder, knee socks, the works—and no one is giving him a second glance. So, of course, I try not to either (except to notice that he has cute knees).

I spot Therese in line and join her. She's giggling over something already—ah, she's holding a Nexus. I can't wait. "Tell me!" I beg.

"Hi, Ave! Okay, but what first, what first?" she agonizes. "Okay: under Services, there's this fancy ad for *pet masseuse*, and she specializes in *iguanas*."

"No way!"

"*Green* iguanas, she says."

"Are there that many different kinds? Well, I guess there're those black, underwater-swimming Galápagos Darwin ones, but they probably aren't allowed to sell those around here; at least I hope not—"

"Jesus, Ave," Therese scowls at me. "You read too much. Okay, then there's this woman who—oh, man, you're gonna love this one!—goes around *picking up your dog's shit for you.*"

"No *way*! I do *not* believe you!"

"Look! It's right here!" She was smug; she knew she'd just won for today our long-running tacit contest, Absurdest in Boulder. The ad read: *Scoopy Doo's, A luxury pet service at an affordable price, For people who love their pets but are tired of all their crap!* Next to that it had a woman's name and phone number. And a revolting drawing of a squatting cartoon dog—with its butt facing us. I honestly could not believe this was for real. Was Boulder really getting *that* much like L.A.? Did this lady go on a walk with you and have to make conversation and everything, and then just bend down with a plastic bag when needed? Wasn't she embarrassed? Was she really so desperate to be making a living? Hell, she could always become an adjunct professor if she needed a minimum-wage-no-benefits situation that badly.

"Okay, okay," I say, "My turn...just give me five minutes with the personal ads, I'll come up with something."

"The personals! Cheating! Of course you'll come up with something *there*!"

"Well, I've got to do *something* to counteract yours! Yours was *awesome*!" I say truthfully. Therese beams and leaves me alone to peruse, after admonishing me, "But you can't use any of the threesome ones or the gay ones; that would be too much of an unfair advantage."

I agree. "Okay, got one," I say. "Here goes: 'Smilin', Happy Guy: Let's share pizza and dance the night away. I enjoy long walks and collecting rocks. SWM, 34, seeks elegant, pragmatic woman who loves to dance, for possible LTR.'"

"Aaaaaaaaaaa-ha-ha-ha-ha-ha!" We screech in unison, our hysterics as usual attracting the evil eye of the proprietor.

"'*Pragmatic*'!" Therese screams. "Must be because of all the rocks he has stacked up around the apartment."

"But wait!" I gasp, giggling. "He also wants her to be *elegant*."

"Aaaaaaaaaaa-ha-ha-ha-ha-ha!" We crack up again.

Wiping my eyes, I look through some more personals. "Oh my god!" I say. "Oh. My. God. I swear this is Mordecai! It must be!"

"Who? You *know* someone in there? Oh my god! Read it to me!"

"Okay, here goes: 'Please come my way: I don't have a lot to offer you, except a desperate clinging devotion. I'll love you right if you call me. Hit me, kick me, punch me in the eye; I'll still be your loving man as time rolls on.'"

Therese is staring at me. "You *know* this person? I'm sorry, but this guy sounds like he has a *serious* self-esteem problem. I mean, he has *issues*, you know what I mean?" She peers at me very soberly—one beat, two— then we both crack up. God, I need to do this more often—the perfect foil to those faculty meetings. But it *is* a little frightening to see that in print. Too, I'm sure it must be him. For one thing, the writer of that ad was probably Jewish; who else knows how to use semi-colons these days? Still, maybe it wasn't him—surely he would've advertised one of his best assets, the LuvKuffs?

Suddenly the guy at the next table, who's wearing a *Frozen Ass 10-20-30 Miler* T-shirt loudly proclaims to his conversation partner, "But, dude, you *know* all tri-athletes have father issues!" Therese and I exchange amused glances.

I love this town.

Just before we can get back to talking, we notice an odd-looking guy coming to all the tables, asking their occupants, very sincerely, "Are you my friend?" Negative responses do not deter him from trying at each successive table. Soon he is at ours. I see that Therese is literally holding her breath in an effort not to laugh. "Are you my friend?" he asks, looking first at me, then at her. "No," I reply solemnly, but she can only shake her head at him.

As soon as he's gone, her breath explodes in a *whoosh* and a bunch of deflated, belated giggles. She raises her eyebrows at me. I just shrug.

"So," I say, "a propos of nothing... It occurred to me the other day, when I was hanging out with Baby, just cuddling..."

"Yeah?"

"...and I suddenly realized: cats and dogs, you know?, they know *their* names—but they don't know *ours*."

Therese absorbs this. "Oooh, freaky!"

"Isn't it? And then I was also thinking: you know how cats get so startled when something sudden happens, like if you drop a glass, or someone knocks on the door?"

"Yeah?"

"Well, get this—and in a way this is really, really Zen; it *totally* weirds me out to contemplate this—they would be *no more* freaked out if an *alien* suddenly showed up than if, say, *you* suddenly showed up at my door."

"Thanks a lot!"

"No, no, really! Think about it!"

She does. "You're right! That *is* really cool! *Très* Zen!"

"Exactly! It just *thrills* me to *ponder* it, to *imagine* it..."

"Hey," Therese says to me, "Don't take this the wrong way, Ave, but...has anyone ever suggested to you that you just might think a bit too much?... No? Okay... By the way... What *did* you see in Alan, anyway?"

"You mean, speaking of aliens?" I ask, smiling.

"Right."

"And besides the sex?"

"Right. You can skip that."

"Well...it's like, he's so...I don't know. Simple, maybe. Sophisticated too, though. Complicated. Jeez, I'm really making a lot of sense, huh?... I mean, he's sophisticated *mentally*, you know? The boy knows how to use semi-colons."

"Well, he's Jewish, right?"

"Exactly," I say with a grin. "He's, you know...*educated*, and it's like he has no vices. I mean, jeez, the guy isn't addicted to pot, or cigarettes, or alcohol... I mean, come on—not even Cherry García!"

"That's pretty good," Therese says, impressed.

"Yeah," I agree. "Just the usual Boulder addiction—you know, gotta ride his bike seven days a week for seven hours a day, that sort of thing..."

"Yeah... And speaking of being Jewish," Therese says, "I saw this totally Boulder product in Alfalfa's the other day. It was called Cold Snap, and it said on the box, 'to restore righteous chi.' It's been driving me crazy ever since—"

"You mean *meshugge*," I break in.

"Ha ha. No, but seriously, isn't there some bizarre term Jews use that sounds like that? Righteous chi, righteous high? Righteous vibe...?"

"Righteous gentile."

"*Yes! Yes!* That's *it!*" She now looks extremely content, as only the satisfaction that the resolution of a TOT (Tip-of-the-Tongue state), or else a multiple orgasm, will leave a woman. "And while we're on the subject..."

"Yeeeeeeeees?" I ask.

"Well...it's kind of gross." She hesitates.

"I can take it. I think."

"Well, I saw that Seinfeld rerun lately? You know, the one with the, what's it called, the priss?"

"Bris?"

"Bris, where Elaine has to find the *mohel* and everything?"

"Oh, yeah! That one's hilarious. That guy is *such* a weirdo."

"Yeah...but have you ever thought about this: what do they *do* with that little piece of skin afterwards?" she asks me with a mischievous glint in her eye.

Simultaneously, we wrinkle up our faces in disgust and let out that universal sound of Girls Grossed Out: "*Eeeeeeeewwwww!*"

"Yeah..." I muse, "and what kind of weird profession is that, anyway?"

We think about it for a few minutes.

"So what's it really like being Jewish, anyway?" Therese now asks.

"You mean, besides the sex?"

"Ha *ha*."

"Well, okay..." I oblige, "and I'm only talking about Ashkenazi American Jews here, because it's the only thing I know, right?..."

She nods.

"It mostly feels like being part of a widespread exclusive club, which you're born into and which you remain tied to by virtue of things you have in common, like curly hair, sharp features, certain idioms and words, a particular ironic and sardonic sense of humor, the tendency to totally avoid blue-collar work, and a propensity to argue at the dinner table."

Therese is laughing. "Oh really? Anything else?"

"Hmm...Let's see. Especially, I think, we have a...I don't know, a tendency to tell the truth instead of doing that whole Pollyanna 'everything is just fine and dandy' thing. I mean, we *kvetch*, we say what's wrong if there's something wrong. That's pretty major. And it's probably a big reason that mixed marriages don't work out—the WASPs think the Jews are bitching all the time, and the Jews think the WASPs are being fake and covering up their true feelings all the time. So it's kind of a bad mix... I mean, can you imagine Woody Allen trying to fit in in Lake Wobegon?"

Therese laughs. "But, Ave, you didn't even mention religion!"

"Oh, well, *religion*..." I smile. "You know, religion doesn't really factor in these days for most Jews; Jewish seems to be more of a cultural identification. Another thing I've always found interesting is that Jews are such a small *absolute* percentage of the world population—especially thanks to Hitler...don't get me started—anyway, we're such a small percentage, especially the reform or liberal ones, the ones who are actually out doing stuff in the 'real' world... But we're way overrepresented in the arts, in literature, in Academia, in the sciences... It's interesting. A bit of a parallel with African-Americans, the way they're hyperrepresented in music, athletics, dance..."

"Hey, that's true! I never really thought about that before..." said Therese.

"And there's a really disproportionate number of Jews in Boulder, too—at least that's what I've heard. You do seem to run into a lot of them...like they seem to represent about seventy-five percent of the yogis and yoginis in town, and about a hundred percent of the meditation gurus...not just in Boulder—in the whole country. Of course, it does seem like most of the Jews I've met or heard about lately are all morphed with degrees of Buddhist: there's Jewish Buddhists, Buddhist Jews, BuJus, and JewBus, just that I know of personally..."

We look at each other, realize the conversation has somehow become serious. How did that happen?

"So," Therese says suddenly, "speaking of weird products at Alfalfa's..."

"Shark cartilage," I say instantly.

"Dong quai," she counters.

"Spirulina."

"Borage seed oil."

"Acidophilus."

"Molybdenum."

"But that's what mountain bikes are made out of!" I protest. We stare at each other for a while. "Isn't it?! The cheaper ones, at least. The kind I have."

She shrugs. "Well, it was being sold in the supplements aisle."

"Okay...whatever. Let's see, my turn... Colostrum."

Now it's her turn to stare, aghast. "But that can't be! Isn't that, like, *breast milk* or something? That's *disgusting*! How can they be selling that with the vitamins and stuff? And whose *is* it?"

My turn to shrug. "Who knows? I saw a whole bunch of those big musclemen dudes all buying cans of it, though."

She makes a horrified face, then shrugs. "Saw Palmetto," she says.

"What's that one for?"

"*Saw Palmetto: for men's prostate health*," she intones, in an advertisement voice, then giggles.

"Psyllium," I offer.

"As in, psychedelic mushrooms?"

"No, that's psilocybin. I think psyllium is, like, some kind of tiny seeds. For constipation."

"Ah. Lovely. Um...let's see...5HTP."

"Hmm... Grapefruit Seed Extract," I offer.

"What's that for?" asks Therese.

"No clue. But I saw it there last time."

"Um... Jewelweed." I raise my eyebrows at her. "For poison ivy," she explains.

"Ah," I say. "Let's see... False Unicorn."

She looks at me sternly. "Are you making that up?"

"No!" I protest. "Of course not!"

"Well, then, what's it for?"

"I have no idea! I just see the names when I'm browsing those aisles, and they stick in my head!"

"O-kaaaay," she allows skeptically. "Um... Milk Thistle."

"Good one," I affirm. "Hmm...Purple Lapacho." She stares at me. "It's an herb," I add.

"I don't believe you!" she declares.

"What?! You *challenge* me?"

"Yes! I do!"

So we have to go next door to the bookstore part of the Trident and look it up in one of their used dictionaries (a frequent pilgrimage of the many crossword puzzlers and Scrabble players in the café, but if caught in said attempted quest, one is given a sound tongue-lashing by employees; word-seekers must be infinitely discreet).

I win; we find the herb listed. Therese has to concede: "Touchée," she admits gamely. "But only until the next round."

j

Date: 22 MAR 02 00:31:42
From: profaviva@yahoo.com
Subject: bitch, bitch, bitch...
To: allpedalnowork@yahoo.com

Alan,

Miss you too. The studnets are a bit denser this semester than last; that may be the only difference. I might do a course on Split Intransitivity for the grad studnets this summer or next fall, which would be a nice change. What **is** Split Intransitivity, you ask? You don't want to know... Brandon, my ex, used to ask if it was something one would need to wear a helmet for.

Anyway, on the subject of the studnets in general, I really do fear for them and for the university as a whole, and for U.S. universities in general (and, by extension, for the country as a whole, and, by extension, for the world as a whole). I forget where I read it, but someone wrote a wonderful, scathing editorial on this topic, about how in the U.S. a generation of monsters, moral mutants, have been created: their self-esteem is excellent, no matter what they do to other people or to themselves. But that's **all** that's excellent—it's not their knowledge or their skills.

And then there's the big Spring Break (and, to a slightly lesser extent, Thanksgiving break, winter break, etc.) problem: they're given one week off, so they leave at least one week **before** that for vacation, and come back at least one week **after** that. They are absent a minimum of three weeks for every one week they're allotted. Therefore it is impossible to assign them homework, conduct classes, etc. What should be done? This problem has never been solved. I say: give the little bastards **no** breaks!

Also, I'm trying to propose a course for maybe the year after, that you know all the kiddies will swarm to, and that would be really interesting to teach: Analysis of Linguistics in Internet Chatrooms.

When T. and I left the Trident after coffee the other day, a scooter pulled up right outside and parked. A balding guy with a long ponytail was driving it, wearing sunglasses (it was a really nice day out—hey, Alan, would've been perfect for riding your bike! Don't you miss riding in Boulder? hint hint) and so were his three yellow Labs, who were smushed together, doggily happily so, in a milk crate fixed to the back of his scooter—I mean, they were also wearing sunglasses. As well as bandannas. Only in Boulder. In Texas or somewhere you know that would've been a Harley, and the dogs would've been either little yappy beribboned inbred lapdogs or else something big and mean, growling and wearing sharpened spikes on their collars.

Further news from here: it is rumored that the Promise Keepers will no longer be allowed in Boulder, but will instead have to take their scary robotic baseball-capped, "Real Men Love Jesus" T-shirted, Mountain Dew-drinking selves to Denver from now on. Hurray! What did they ever want with Boulder in the first place?

This last bit you will love (and by the way, I shall never forgive you for that Penis-In-A-Bottle article you quoth me): The other day, I walked around **all day** without knowing it wearing a sticker on my butt that said "Feel the Softness." I didn't notice it until I'd come home from a long day. The sticker had come off a new bra that I'd worn for the first time that morning—when I was taking all the tags and stickers and stuff off it, somehow I guess one of the stickers found its way from the bed where I'd temporarily put all that crap, onto the back of my skirt, while I was dressing... You can imagine the amusement I provided everyone all day long.

Sorry you missed it.

Ave

m

Preparing for an MLA conference to be held in New York this coming week. My paper is titled *The Layperson's Perception of Yinglish Syntax and Semantics*, and includes such classic examples as these from the recent Hebonics Movement (respective WASP translations follow): What do I look like, a clock?! (Sorry, I don't have the time); You should *be* so lucky! (I hope things turn out okay for you); A *doctor* she married, my daughter (My daughter married a doctor); What's the matter, the other tie you didn't like?! (Oh, I see you're wearing one of the ties I gave you); You didn't wonder if I'm dead yet?! (It's been so long since you've called).

After I read these examples to Therese, because she was curious what "this Hebonics garbage" was about, she had this to say: "You know what, Ave, maybe that's what *you* should do—to solve your financial problems, I mean—marry a doctor." I reminded her of the time when I couldn't stop obsessing over what would happen if I didn't get tenure, and had actually consulted a psychiatrist. He'd said I was *ruminating*, and offered a whole smorgasbord of adorable little sampler packs of brightly colored drugs. I'd tried to make a joke: "Isn't that what ungulates do?" His response was a completely blank look. So, I had to remind Therese, I was not about to marry any *soi-disant* professional who said *preventative* and *documentate*. No, I told her—to solve my financial problems, I probably should've *become* a doctor.

I'm hoping to earn a few "bonus points" at the conference (pathetic, isn't it? Here we are, *professors* already, and still trying to earn bonus points), and maybe be remembered by at least making people laugh a bit in the midst of these days of dry, dull papers being read by even duller lecturers. Hey, I'm not a guy—I can't wear a funny tie; I have to find a different, creative way of being noticed. There are a few women academics who resort to the cheap whore look—low cleavage and fuck-me pumps, all evidence of that brilliant mind and those long years to the doctorate entirely covered up by Victoria's Secret and Maybelline—but that's just not my style, thank you very much.

I logged on. On Yahoo News, the health headline read: "Stapling Hemorrhoids Less Painful Than Removal." There was an ad for the magazine Simplicity, geared to yuppies who for some reason want to decorate their houses to make it look as if they are poorer than they really are. They do this by purchasing extremely expensive "rustic" designer items, as advised in the magazine. Then there were the "quick click" thingies, which today I loved for their practical juxtaposition: first came *Score Points: Give Her Romantic Gifts*, secondly *Make Life Easier: When To Dump Him*, and finally *Deliver Final Blow: Send Breakup Letter*.

Last night, I confess I had a moment of weakness (no, not masturbation—I may have masturbated, but honey, that ain't no weakness) and turned on the idiot box. I channelsurfed for a while, that really late night TV: nothing worth watching and a bunch of the most bizarro ads in the universe. Like, there was one offering a "249-Piece Knife Set—Perfect for Father!" An important question springs readily to mind: who the hell *needs* 249 knives? And why 249, not 250? And why does Father need them, as opposed to, say, Mother? What will he be *doing* with them? All in all, it's a really frightening thing to contemplate during the wee hours when one should be writing a paper which is going to be delivered to a conference room of three hundred people who won't give a shit and who are all worried about getting through their own papers without a hitch and then seeing who they can get laid with before going back to the grind, and is the catered food going to be any good this time?

Just got an email from JoAnn:

```
Hey, A: Be glad we decided on Ling after all
and not med school, as many of us considered...
just heard about how med students have to prac-
```

tice drawing blood on each other before they're allowed near real patients...do ya think they have to practice gyn exams and rectal exams and stuff like that on ea. other too? I imagine they must. They can't just learn all that on those Drowning Dummies, can they?!

Let's get together one of these days soon and drink a toast to not having some rude young colleague banging around trying to find our cervix!
—JA

Jesus. What a thought! Imagine Ralph having the privilege of seeing my lovely private parts! JoAnn was right. I made the right choice with Linguistics, even if this *is* only about a hundredth as lucrative...didn't I?

There was also an email from Georgette, who, having heard about the Ugliest Words party, was suggesting a Cheeziest Song party. What an awesome idea. I procrastinated my paper for a while longer and brainstormed, putting myself mentally back into those horrible days of paisley-patched bellbottom jeans, patchouli, and acrylic-angora fuzzy sweaters (no, not the current haute couture; I'm talking about the originals, the first time around, when I was a kid and wasn't conscious of what hideous raiment was upon me). In a while I had come up with a preliminary list for (I modestly thought) first-place winners, though the prize was yet to be decided: In the Year 2525; Puff the Magic Dragon (which I could further impress people with by singing the first verse in Catalan—a never-fail party trick taught to me one giggly night by a lover, Rafael from Barcelona, after we'd gone through three-quarters of a bottle of cheap wine); Tie a Yellow Ribbon; Teen Angel; Jan & Dean's Wipeout; some John Denver; anything by Barry Manilow; anything with "shoo-bop, shoo-bop" in it; anything by Neil Diamond, the Osmonds, or the Cassidys; Sonny and Cher's I Got You Babe; some of Cher's own stuff, especially the pre-P.C. "Indian" stuff, like Half-Breed and Cherokee Nation; and Billy Don't Be a Hero. Oh, and also that one that goes "War! Huh! What's it Good For!" (and which, on a memorable Seinfeld episode, Elaine was duped into believing was the alternate title of the novel *War and Peace*).

Went out to check my snail-mail (more procrastination). There was a catalog of *bathroom fixtures. I* certainly didn't request that. Then I saw it had the previous resident's name on it; mail still comes for him—

mostly strange brochures. Nothing too scary—not bondage fetishes or anything—but moderately weird stuff like catalogs for boat motor parts, offroad shock absorbers, battery-operated flyswatters.

Let me tell you, I just *learned* a few things—like, there's a lot more soft porn in a bathroom fixtures catalog than you might think. There was a photo (*not* a drawing) of a naked woman, seen from the side, showering; a naked woman in a bathtub, from the top; a naked man (some Scandinavian model, all *buff* and everything—torso only, unfortunately) showering in some kind of James Bond kind of shower, where he was being hit by about six jets of water at once, from all sides, which would have to really hurt, but he was pretending to love it and also simultaneously soap his pits.

And there is some *seriously* hideous stuff out there for sale. Like fake-gold-plated toilet, matching bidet, and sink set, where the gold stuff covers everything in a big circle on the rim—and wouldn't that be hell to clean after a bout of diarrhea? I mean, come on, I'm not trying to be purposefully scatological here, just honest—I've traveled in India, Mexico, and Morocco; these things happen.

Or sink pedestals with little *velvet skirts* on them; or perhaps worst of all—or was the worst part of it the text that went along with it? No, both were equally horrible, *viz.* (sink with painted-on fish jumping out of a river, fisherman standing in the water): "*The Rod and The Fly (TM)* turns to the great outdoors for inspiration, conveying the mystique of the river where the greatest pleasure is to be taken with deceiving the most difficult of fish. Watery reflections and mountain shadows underscore the quiet composition rendered on a Biscuit background."

There were some hilarious *names* for things. I wished I'd had this catalog while I was teaching the nomenclature course; the studnets would've loved it. Hell, *I* was loving it. As one of my ex-boyfriends had once said about me—it was meant to be a disparaging remark; I took it as a fabulous compliment—you can never tell what might amuse Aviva. For example, none of the sinks were called *sinks*. That, apparently, was forbidden. Or gauche. Or something. Instead, they were called *lavatories*. There was one sink that was square and I suppose they thought it looked really *masculine* or something, because the name of it was Man's Lav. Man's Lav. Man's Lav. I just had to keep saying it out loud. It sounded so…*macho*.

Then there was a toilet color, *Innocent Blush*; and a toilet named *Pillow Talk Power Lite*™ (what was *that* about? Sounded like a bunch of Koreans went browsing through an English dictionary, pulling out words at random), one named *Memoirs*, another called *Portrait*, and, finally, one called *Revival*.

That last one really scared me—I don't want that stuff *reviving*! *Mon cher*, I want it *flushed* down and *staying* down.

∫

Airports are such totally weird places. They're even stranger when you're really jet-lagged plus you have a lot of hours to kill, which, luckily, I don't this time, having just landed from the relatively short flight from Denver—but seeing these little shops again makes me remember the last time I was suffering from that unfortunate combination. I think it was one of those European jetlags—you know, you haven't been able to sleep on the plane, because just as you're finally attempting to fall asleep for the first time, after hours of misery, with your earplugs and eyemask and neck pillow in place, then you (and/or the people next to you) have to get up to go to the bathroom (but no one can, because the aisles are blocked by carts during 99% of the flight), and then just as you're again about to fall asleep, they bring the stupid meals. So you're zonkered. Whacked. Or, as those funny Brits say, *knackered. Shattered.*

Then, the worst part of all, like a cruel joke: you arrive, European time, as it's just dawning there, when your body is screaming that it's had *enough* of this bullshit and it will *kill* you if it doesn't get some serious sack time, starting *now*. But!—it's early morning in London, ha ha, isn't that amusing. Not only that, you can't even check into a bloody hotel. No, you have to wander around some bloody European city with your bloody luggage, eyelids drooping to the ground, wondering, why the fuck did I want to come here, anyway?

Have I mentioned I hate air travel to Europe?

In the bizarro world of the modern international airport, we spot the Ultra-Orthodox Jewish patriarch, decked out in his usual threads, shopping in the Hugo Boss boutique; we witness Vietnamese great-grandmothers taking orders (for their all-Mexican staff) at the counters of Starbuck's kiosks for Americanized Italian coffee drinks none of them have ever heard of; we have the entirely surreal experience of trying to kill a six-hour layover while experiencing a 20-hour jetlag, browsing completely useless goods on display in completely useless shops, such as the "grownup toy" described on its box as *Three plastic fish with realistic swimming motions in a plastic aquarium!* There's the Bollywood chickette wearing so much makeup she resembles an embalmed corpse, in what must be the epitome of the shitty minimum-wage job: attempting to peddle battery-operated nose-hair clippers to business-class dot-com executives she'll never see again.

On the plane, today, there was a Moment. It had to do with what were obviously a couple of Boulder hippie types, two 20-something guys, sitting across the aisle from me and in back of an enormous Hispanic lady who was literally loaded down (and around, and above—she was taking up way more than her fair share of her allotted overhead and under-seat compartments) with about fifty white plastic bags full of junk food: packs of lollipops, packs of hard candies, packs of caramels, packs of candy corn—even entire piñatas—each item wrapped in another clear plastic bag. She must've just visited some megasuperstore in Denver and been on her way to some giant fiesta somewhere.

"Jesus, look at all that *plastic*," whispered one of the guys to his friend. "You know it's just all gonna end up in the landfill."

"Yeah, you know it, dude," replied the other. "And *I* feel guilty every time I just flush my *shit* down the toilet, dude!"

T

Date: 25 MAR 02 23:32:00
From: profaviva@yahoo.com
Subject: home is where the fashion is
To: allpedalnowork@yahoo.com

Hi Alan,
Writing you from NYC…here for a conference. Toto, we're not in Kansas anymore! (By the way, did you know there is a toilet called Toto? How I get my information, I am not at liberty to reveal.) Here, back in a "real" city, we can go to Chinese restaurants with such glorious monikers as Hung Lo and Mai Fuk.

I was met by my erstwhile East Coast-side conferencee, Penelope, who was to show me around. No offense to her, she's a *lovely* person (British accent there please), but to truthfully describe her physical self…she turned out to have those classic Brit Chick looks where she's so naturally, unadulteratedly ugly that she has unwittingly become **highly** trendy: anorexic-skinny; caved-in chest;

that vaguely heroin-addict, pale look; thrift-store, all-synthetic-fiber, ill-fitting clothing; thick, black plastic, too-big, square glasses frames; that permanent expression on her face like she hasn't gotten laid for a very long time. I.e., all the elements of what fashion moguls in America are these days, inexplicably, deeming **chic**, but what in Britain has been, lo these past sixty-odd years, moulderingly, artlessly, simply...**British**.

    Miss you,
    Ave

Date: 27 MAR 02 22:14:33
From: allpedalnowork@yahoo.com
Subject: java juju
To: profaviva@yahoo.com

Hey Aviva,

I'm getting a little sick of CA...there's just too much weirdness going on here—unlike in Boulder, ha ha. (I kind of miss the East Coast...no I don't. It was too hard cycling there; drivers were just not very courteous at all.)

What was that comment about the toilet? Are you into scatological humor lately? (Or should I say "humour," in honor/honour of Penelope?) Do they really name people Penelope in England?

So yesterday I go into this health food store near my house (well, pretty near—only 20 miles away by bicycle; I bike there and back almost every day), where I buy coffee, and I'm looking for the beans I want to grind and everything, like always, when I suddenly feel like something's just...

not quite right. I look around; everything seems the same.

It takes me a couple of minutes: you know all the little signs saying which kind of coffee is which, and the big cardboard coffee display advertisements that always stand up near a coffee section? Well, today they're **all in Russian.**

I check this out very carefully, because I can't believe my eyes—I fill a bag at my usual coffee dispenser with something written on it in the Cyrillic alphabet. Who knows what it says; it might say "fuck you" for all I know (the only thing I know it **doesn't** say is "USSR," because even the densest of Americans has absorbed over the years that that's "CCCP")—then I get my bag full of freshly-ground coffee and go up to the cashier and ask what the deal is. She's all California about it, like, Oh, rilly?

Ave, what's up with this? I know the cold war is over and everything, but...

Alan

ق

Date: 28 MAR 02 18:20:13
From: profaviva@yahoo.com
Subject: dobra den (sp?)
To: allpedalnowork@yahoo.com

Alan,
How was the coffee? Did it taste any different? Did it put you into the mood to don a threadbare overcoat, get soused on cheap vodka, write bad poetry about The State and make drunken toasts to your Comrades and the spirit of Mother Russia?
Ave

Date: 28 MAR 02 19:05:35
From: allpedalnowork@yahoo.com
Subject: re: dobra den (sp?)
To: profaviva@yahoo.com

Ave,

Da! It was great! As you can see, I'm now speaking Russki with the best of them. See what the right kind of caffeine can do?

Since you're so mysteriously into toilets these days (my guess is, you've finally gotten so [understandably] fed up with wages in Acadaemia that you've taken on some kind of moonlighting job to do with plumbing, although what it is, I have yet to ascertain—though my gumshoe techniques are sure to uncover it sooner or later), I am forwarding to you a link which is almost certain to have you jumping for (scatological) joy.

Alan

P.S. Do you plan on moving anytime in the near future?

Alan's link was a site that sold bath and kitchen appliances and there was a photo of what looked to be either some kind of Texan (because of all the doodads) electric chair, or a Teutonic torture device, and I was seriously alarmed. The accompanying text, however, described this as the "Herbeau Ligne Powder Room 'Dagobert' Wooden Toilet Throne."

I read: "A throwback to the medieval era of knights, castles, and fairy tale romance, this throne toilet with French Merovingian style (8th century) is highlighted by hand painted earthenware accessories. Its high-profile seat back with a gothic-arch top and full armrests give the toilet a majestic appearance. Inscribed on the seat back a poem by the French poet, Alfred de Musset. The musical chime 'Le Bon Roi Dagobert' with a voice reciting the Musset poem starts when you raise the lid and a bell is coupled with the flush, making a visit to the bathroom an unforgettable experience. Comes in Wood (Massive Ash Tree) with Moustier Polychrome Décor, protected by three layers of polyurethane. Comes with full set of accessories, including candle holder and ashtray. $9,367.00."

I read the poem first in French, which was hilarious. I then proceeded to read the English version, which, like all things translated from French, unfortunately rather *more* than adequately got its point across:

You who comes here in an humble posture
to unload the weight of your heavy abdomen
When you will feel your body lighter

and have deposited in the urn a modest present
Please send in the pan a stream of pure water
And on this smoking jar place like a cork
the round cover with its perfect joint
To serve as a grave to the indiscreet perfumes.


```
Date: 28 MAR 02 20:01:50
From: profaviva@yahoo.com
Subject: c'est degoutant
To: allpedalnowork@yahoo.com
```

Alan,

If/when I attain my permanent job status with the Toilet Brigade, I'll hire you to test that one personally, deal? (Don't worry, you don't have to damage those oh-so-healthy bicycle-racing lungs by trying out the ashtray, but you'd definitely have to test out the candleholder.)

I plan on staying put for the foreseeable future. Why do you ask? I would definitely miss the Boulder kind of unexpectedness, where you can just be out riding your bike through, say, Eben G., and you come across thirty guys facing west and wearing long red women's dresses, holding some kind of ritual involving the full moon, lost menses, and getting back in touch with their feminine side. Or seeing something like two people balanced on one single bike, riding along wearing Halloween costumes just for the hell of it, when it's not even remotely close to Oct.31. And then there's the Rolf Institute—not that I've ever actually **been** Rolfed, but it's somehow comforting to know it's here. Have **you** ever been Rolfed? Quite frankly, I've always been too afraid. There are various reasons for this, chief among them the following: a) they claim they even have to Rolf your **septum;** b) they make you parade around in your skivvies, very undignified! …I'd even inquired about wearing a two-piece bathing suit—what the hell difference should it make to them?, whereas lots of difference mentally/emotionally to the wearer, and they said no!!—which made me suspect there was some cult or torture mentality involved: a mental wearing-down of the "victim," like the cutting-off of Samson's hair; c) people are always **bragging** about how painful it is; and d) last but not necessarily least, the terrifying gigantic black-and-white photograph (blown up to Lenin-like proportions) of the face of Ida Rolf, hanging—nay, **looming**—over the lobby… I don't know how those secretaries can stand to work there under that stern, perpetually disappointed gaze.

Ave

u

JFK Airport, waiting to go home: the MLA conference is over with for another year. Everything went fine. My paper seemed to be a big hit. But right now, at this moment, in this waiting area, I am suddenly floored by what I see, and am reminded in the most immediate and poignant way that all the ridiculous academic papers in the world don't matter a bit—and that the world is, on a quotidian, personal level, both a far more tragic—and more optimistic—place than we realize.

Here, crammed into one of the ubiquitous, identical, uncomfortable plastic chairs, squashed between two oblivious Long Island Jewish types flashing their jewelry, wearing too much perfume, and talking much, much louder than they need to, is an earnest Asian man, very much alone, obsessively reading (while moving his lips)—unaware of the curious and occasionally piteous stares of those across from him—and now in the home stretches of a much-thumbed paperback called *What to Do About Your Brain-Injured Child*.

Y

It's just been work, work, work lately—so the girlfriends have convinced me to take tonight off and go out on the town. Although in Boulder (quite unlike my previous places of residence on the East Coast, where all-black attire, makeup, and hairspray were de rigueur) that really doesn't mean much, if you don't want it to—I mean, here, you can go "paint the town red" (gotta love those old expressions that our grandmothers tossed around) dressed in sweatpants and Birks and not having showered for two days. Which is pretty much my condition, as I'm working on another paper, this one titled *Toward New Models for Mathematical Modeling: A Model*; "publish or perish" is unfortunately no myth, and this is serious business.

Now don't get me wrong—I love a fresh linen dress and that just-showered feeling as much as the next woman—but I've discovered something interesting, too: if you get grungy enough, then that state begins to take on a sort of Zen quality. When you've had one hike, you feel grungy; when you don't have time to take a shower because too much is going on, and it becomes the next day and you take another hike, and then you have to go to the grocery store, and to all your appointments too...well, at a certain point you suddenly *lose your resistance* to the grunginess—that's what I'm talking about.

Tonight is really special in that all of us are together for the first time since my birthday—not just me, Therese, and Georgette; but also Marta, MaryLynn, and Sarah.

"So," I asked the group, at our gathering place, the Trident, "what's the plan for this evening?"

"Well," said Sarah, "there's some group playing at Penny Lane, and then there's a poetry reading at—"

Five voices broke in in outrage: "*Poetry* reading!"

"I know, I know! But it's not, like, an *open mike* or anything…it's some guy who's a friend of a friend…he's supposed to be really amazing. She really urged me to check it out. He's gonna be at Barnes and Noble."

Sarah was met with a lot of somber gazes and silence. Five, to be exact. "Well," she said, "if you all don't want to go…"

"No, no," came the reassurances, albeit somewhat wishy-washy. "That's okay…" "If you want to go check it out…" "If your friend said…"

"Okay," she said, brightening. "Cool. I mean, we don't have to stay long or anything. It's just, I told my friend I'd go and all…"

So it was settled. Not the most glamorous night on the town, perhaps, but quite the social activity for a recluse academic. I was really looking forward to it.

We arrived at Penny Lane with perfect timing, and even found one whole unoccupied table: a small miracle. We bothered quite a few colorful people as we hunted all over the room for two extra chairs to make up the deficit. By the time Therese and I found the chairs, the Penny Lane barista had come out from behind the drinks counter and was announcing, with an accompanying whine of feedback, "Ladies and gentlemen, we are pleased to introduce our evening's musical entertainment: John Kabal and his Burnt Cannoli Band!" There was a small smattering of applause (from the few hippies that weren't too stoned to notice what was going on, and from our six group members), then John Kabal took the microphone and said to the audience: "Thank you all. We also have a very special guest singing with us tonight…" He motioned to a beautiful young bindi-bedecked woman on his right, who bowed her head slightly to the audience in acknowledgment. "…Miss J. Vulvarani, all the way from Khajuraho, India!"

Again the light tinkle of applause, then the band started. The music was loud and obnoxious, and after about forty seconds I was ready to leave. When MaryLynn poked me and yelled something in my ear, I assumed that was the desire she'd also be expressing.

"What?" I shouted back at her.

"I said," she screamed, "Kabal! John Kabal! Is that a Jewish name?"

I shrugged. I thought there'd also been something suspect about the guest singer's name, but had forgotten it as soon as I'd been blasted with the "musical entertainment."

It turned out I was the only one amongst our little group who was, how shall we put this, *actively despising* the music, and ended up having to wait exactly one hour and twenty-five minutes (of course I was keeping track), until at last I was able to convince them that that poetry reading was definitely worth looking into.

So off we all went to Barnes and Noble. I half expected there to be undercover BIBA cops outside waiting to handcuff and perhaps spray-paint us (à la Fur Is Dead) and never again allow us back inside any of our favorite independent shops, instead having to frequent only Starbuck's, Borders, and Wherehouse Records for the rest of our lives. Too awful to contemplate. We'd be just like the studnets! Was this poetry reading tonight worth such a risk? I paused just outside the door to consider it, and really don't think I would have gone in after all, except that Sarah was behind me and kind of shoved me forward. Once my feet crossed the threshold, I found that I was, like a reluctant bride, committed for better or worse.

Worse, as it turned out. Much, much worse. And there was no spray-paint involved—no BIBA spies that I was aware of. But there should have been spraypaint and many other things provided—to the poetry audience. The usual: say, rotten eggs. Coffee grinds. Decomposing, maggoty tomatoes.

Grad-school-age guy dressed in the usual all black—jeans, turtleneck, DocMartens, gelled spiky hair, pale face (trying for a Goth look but not quite daring enough), too skinny but not quite enough for the Heroin Look, kind of effeminate-looking which was immediately confirmed when he began speaking: queeny Valley Girl.

The guy gets up on a little stool with notecards that have Hello Kitty stickers all over the backs of them, and he gets his butt all comfy on the stool like he's Mark Knopfler and someone's about to bring him a guitar. Then he looks at the audience—about ten people, *including* us six barely-on-time arrivals—and kind of crosses his eyes for a minute, which maybe is his way of psyching himself up, or maybe he just has a vision problem.

He clears his throat and says in this affected little voice, "Thank you so much for coming? It means so much to me? Um... I was just published in?... The New Yorker?" (A momentary lowering of the lids.) "My first poem is dedicated to?... Someone very special to me?" He blushes. Obviously this poem is going to be about his lover. Yeah, big secret, dude. "It's called?... For Larry?"

Suddenly he stands, fists balled, startling everyone. Ah, I see, this is his *melodramatic, poem-reciting stance*. And in a much deeper and louder tone, a totally different voice, what must be his *poem-reciting voice*, he enunciates:

Odious azaleas!
Similes of calabash!
From his mired candor cage:
Anus tines
Two sopranos
Mass cable ophidians.
Quasi nadir!
Uneasy papas
Okra lambdas
Torso courtiers
Get in his lean putt coach
And go.

He sits back down suddenly, as if exhausted, which is the signal to the bewildered and shocked audience that he is finished. There is a tiny bit of polite applause (though not from me).

I'm thinking: that was a *poem*?! I have a terrible, nearly overwhelming urge to laugh, and to squelch it, I don't dare meet any of my girlfriends' eyes. Finally I glance at Georgette, one of the worst risks, but I just can't help myself.

"*Anus* tines?" she whispers. A few giggles leak out of me the way bubbles rise in a fish tank.

"Mired candor cage!" I hiss back at her. "Shut *up*!" I take a glance at the poet himself, hoping *that* will kill my sense of humor, but unfortunately, the drama queen is up there *gathering strength* for his next act, staring at the ceiling, clutching his cards with one hand and the legs of the stool with the other, doing some kind of Tantric deep breathing that resembles

Lamaze. I am going to crack up. "Heeeelp," I whisper feebly to Therese. "I'm going to embarrass everyone."

"Shhh," she says. "Quasi nadir. Uneasy papas." An actual guffaw escapes me, and the poet himself loses his ninth-centimeter-dilation concentration and shoots a dagger glance my way, which causes the other four members of the audience to swivel around and give me either curious or angry looks, or both simultaneously. Finally what sobers me a little bit is Sarah's face—she who is here on a mission, and is therefore taking this much more seriously than the rest of us (somehow, even after that first doozy of a poem).

The poet manages to stop hyperventilating. He's probably had a non-ejaculatory orgasm with all that Tantric breathing by now—a bonus. He fishes out a card from his pile and Stands to Deliver. "This next one is called Matrix Five?"

Lamb, lamb, lamb!
Irregular Zambian
Billeting airwaves
Hacker queues
Species arrangement
Lunar miners
Pucker test.

I have my hand over my mouth (some sort of pucker test?) to restrain myself from snorting. I can feel I must be the color of borscht. MaryLynn leans over and gets ready to whisper something to me—uh oh, trouble's coming—her face twitches with held-back laughter, then she says (softly, deadpan) in my ear: "I particularly like how he rhymed the final *lamb* with *Zambian*"—and at last I *totally* lose it.

On my way out the Barnes and Noble exit, I see Sarah's stricken face (but I know she'll forgive me within twenty-four hours; she's a softie) and hear the introduction to the next poem, which by dint of bad behavior I have been saved forever from having to hear the rest of, which is titled "Dormer Mallet," and which as I leave is beginning:

O, veer, mentors!
Proverbial quinces
Imperious bouillabaisses
Prodigious kickstand
Pince-nez spontané.
Accordion dodger

Lifeboat surprise
Quadrate pears…
The next day, talking to Sarah on the phone (after a night of vivid dreams: golden chariots full of gay men drinking champagne and chanting in unison the Shakespeare I'd been forced to memorize in high school and which is still lodged in my gray matter in random fits and starts: "We come to bury Caesar, not to praise him! …Is this a dagger I see before me, the handle toward my hand?"), she told me they'd stayed only marginally longer than I had, and she only out of a sense of duty to her (conspicuously absent) "friend," who, it turned out, was someone she was trying to ingratiate herself with, a potential boss. Ah. No wonder. I'd begun wondering if maybe she was gay, or what. And I was really wondering what she thought of the poetry itself, as it seemed she was the only one last night who wasn't dying of laughter.

"So, Sarah…" I began. "Um…the poetry last night…"

"Yeah?"

"Well… Did you…like it?"

"Did *you*?" she asked. Oh, great.

"Sarah, I asked you first!" It wasn't obvious last night from my reaction?

"Well, I thought it was…interesting."

"Me too," I said. And that was even true.

"You kept *laughing*, though, Aviva—"

"I know, and I'm really sorry, Sarah. I sincerely apologize for my rudeness. That's why, when I couldn't stop, I decided it was better just to leave…"

"Well, that's fine, I mean, you don't have to apologize, really. I mean, the reason I'm asking is—well, you weren't offended, were you?"

"Offended? Actually, I kind of was, yeah."

"Because it was gay poetry? Ave, I'm ashamed! I assumed you'd all be liberal enough to deal with the topic!"

"No, you silly, of course not because it was gay subject matter! That, I couldn't care less about! Besides, I don't even know if you could say there *was* any subject matter. No, it's like this: you know that Seinfeld episode where Jerry's dentist converts to Judaism 'for the jokes,' and Jerry explains that he's not offended because of his *religion*; he's offended as a *comedian*? Well, I was offended last night not as a *hetero*, but as a *linguist*."

That got Sarah to finally laugh. "Ave," she giggled, "I promise: no more poetry readings. But tell me—what the hell are quadrate pears?"

"I don't know," I said, "but I would advise that you don't go eating them with a fork—I don't know about you, but I'm definitely not feeling that eating *anything* with a fork sounds the least bit appetizing anymore."

"Why not?" She sounded genuinely puzzled.

"Hel-*lo*?" I said. "A certain terrible poet from last night…? A certain terrible line from a certain terrible poem of said certain terrible poet?"

"Oh, yeah!" she remembered. "What *was* that line?! Something like…*Butt-busters*?"

I laughed. "Woman, you've been watching too much late-night TV."

"So what was it? …Buttock-stabbers?"

I hooted. "Closer! The exact quote was 'anus tines.'"

Now she chuckled. "Jesus! Are you sure? *Anus* tines?!"

"Sure? Oh, I'm *quite sure*," I said. "In fact, I think I'm unlikely to ever be able to forget it. For that, Sarah, I—no make that *all* of us—have you to thank." But I said it with a smile, knowing she'd be able to hear it.

"Hey, no prob," she said with a smile back, and hung up.

It's turning out to be one of those awesome days already. To begin with, I saw posters for bands called *Big Ass Truck* and *Orgasm Traffic*.

Then I was informed by one of the billions of weekly memos we receive at work that the new language lab liaison hired last Monday bears the improbable name Mr. Wapperflorky. How much more perfect could that be? For a *language lab*?! You'd think he wouldn't have had the nerve. It sounded like a clown for children's parties, or possibly a trained seal. I'd definitely have to go check out the poor sod soon, as well as add him to my names list.

Next, when I logged on, there were these two news headlines: "Survey: Sex Often Part of Casual Teen Relationships" and "Smoking May Speed Lung Cancer Patients' Death." Like, *duh*? What planet do these reporters live on?

I got an email from JoAnn with two more "Inklish" examples: one was a menu item in a Jakarta airport, "Chicken Mouse in Tartlet." The other was a sign written in Chinese characters and ostensibly translated to English: "Entrance and Exit for Persons and Impersonators."

Then I got back some studnet evaluations from last semester. These are always a great source of entertainment, to be shared amongst colleagues, but are definitely not to be taken seriously. Lest anyone be shocked by this, let me explain why: for every piece of feedback I get that says "Professor's too strict," I can bet one million dollars that somewhere within that same stack of comments someone else will be saying, "She needs to lay down the law more." Every bit of feedback perfectly cancels out another. For every four people in class who say they hate the book, there are four others who love it. For every three people who hated doing oral reports, there are three others who felt it "built character." In the end, all we professors can do is the best we can and get on with things. And in the meantime, we can also get a little amusement out of some of the worst of the studnet evaluations. The morons, the illiterates, the freaks: the vast majority, in other words.

For example: "The instructor failed to keep me awake." I also enjoyed: "I thawt the perfesser wasnt the write level for us. They should fire her and find some one else who nows more. Or else less. Coz some times it was to hard. But other times it was'nt hard enuf." Or: "This teacher was really mean. She wouldn't give me permission to skip class when I needed to. My girlfriend was having her belly button pierced and needed me there and this teacher wouldn't let me skip class for such an important event. You should fire her and find some one nicer." Droll as these are, it is often hard to *remain* amused for sustained amounts of time when keeping in mind that the university bases much of its decision about our jobs on studnet evaluations, including the little bubbles they fill in, usually either willy-nilly or with a vengeance, like the thwarted piercing accomplice. Sigh. "Best part: being able to look at the cute teacher. Worst part: some times the other kids bloked my view of the cute teacher."

And of course, the day you have to give them the evaluations, your precious few intelligent ones are *always* absent. I know profs who bribe their articulate ones to be there on evaluation day. There are endless scandals involving the evaluations, since the university places so much emphasis on such an obviously ridiculous source of input. There are plenty of negatively-marked sheets that, one way or another, never find their way to their respective departments. I am not one of the scandal-causers, still preferring to believe that, somehow, the majority of the stupidity will all settle heavily and out of sight to the bottom of the pile, like the disgusting lumps that form in a carton of spoiled milk.

I went out for lunch to the Hill, doing my utmost to ignore all studnets, grabbed a hummous-and-veggies bagel and then wandered westward, through the Chautauqua neighborhood. At one house, there were some construction workers also taking their lunch break. Their boom box was on—a Bach cello CD. One cute guy, kind of a moody, broody type, was sitting away from all the others, not joining in the general camaraderie. Still wearing his hard hat, he was reading and highlighting a Nietzsche paperback.

I continued on until I found a nice place to sit and eat—even if it was next to the cemetery on Ninth. So what, it was a gorgeous day, and hell, it's also a pretty gorgeous cemetery, if one is into that sort of thing. A guy—quite a good-looking guy, and in great shape, those narrow hips and strong thighs reminding me lustfully of Alan—came running by. Show-off! Typical Boulder runner—those had to be six-minute miles, and he was barely breaking a sweat. I read his T-shirt: *In Training: Bolder Boulder.*

Bolder Boulder?! Oh no! *Merde!* The challenge!!

How long had it been?

What was the date today? What *month* was it, even? I can never keep track of this stuff. Oh my god, it was May 2! Uh-oh! I hadn't given a single thought to the bet in I didn't know how long. My life had simply gone back to being...well, my life. How had this happened? Well, I guess it just...had. *C'est la vie*, and all that.

Once I got over the shock, I realized the most important question was: did I still care about the bet?

I dutifully questioned myself—and found that I *did* still care. Whether it was because I'd already put in so much "work" or whether it was just a matter of stubborn pride or because at this point I was so close to the finish line, who knows. But I discovered I wanted to Go On With The Show. Not, perhaps, with the original enthusiasm, but with enough to easily lasso (memories of Tex) the few remaining nudniks I needed to get this thing wrapped up. And then, when I'd accomplished that, well, then, I'd find myself another Alan—I mean, closest possible facsimile thereof—and get myself some *seriously* good sex for a change. I smiled to myself, then looked around in embarrassment, hoping no one was looking, wondering, who's the fruitcake smiling to herself in front of the cemetery?

So. Let's take stock here. Less than a month left. *Oy.* Who was the last guy, and what number was he, even? A fuzzy memory... Ah yes, fuzzy, indeed: it had been the pube-shaver! What number? Oh, right. Number twenty-six. So I needed four more. Four more in just under four weeks, minus one week for menstruation, so let's say about two and a half weeks, to estimate conservatively.

Pas de problème.

With a jaunty air, I gathered up my trash and headed back to work. Bumper stickers passed me as I walked along University Avenue: *New Age: Minds So Open Their Brains Fell Out*; *Spear Britney!*; *You Say Psycho Like It's A Bad Thing*.

On my walk back through campus, I paused to peruse the announcement boards. There was an expensive session of "Channeling with Oceana" in the offing (complete with glamour photo of, presumably, Oceana); a cyberaddress for on-line guided meditation; an informational meeting: "How To Climb Denali! Plan Your Trip Now!;" another for an Iron John gathering (what is the deal with that Iron John shit anyway? From what I've heard, it sounds like a bunch of suds-swilling lugs sitting around chanting, "We will *not* be emasculated by the feminists!"); and something called the "Naturopathic Medicine Forum and Pow-Wow." These were, of course, all interspersed with the usual "Make Money Fast!," tanning salons, "Cheap Beer!," ski passes, Roommate Wanteds, tattoo and piercing ads. It *is* Boulder, but they're still just a bunch of studnets, after all.

Back at work, there were Naropa Institute Continuing Education and Shambhala Center brochures in my Inbox. These things are great fun to peruse. I know I ought to be showing these two fine institutions nothing but the greatest respect, but… Perhaps if I had the kind of excess cash that many Boulderites possess in abundance to be blowing on these impractical courses (we're not talking chemistry, EMT, or accounting here), my eyes would be less apt, in their catalogs, to instantly hone in on what seem to me the most absurd wastes of money (money that for me and for most of the world would mean basic necessities such as rent, food and health care). Perhaps I'm a closet socialist. But I've learned to take it all less seriously (even without the help of these classes) and now at least I always get a kick out of the brochures.

Some of the Naropa class offerings: *Sacred Passage Awareness Training*; *Writing Like Kerouac/Sitting Like Buddha*; *Feng Shui: The Black Hat Perspective*; *Breathing Into Nature*; *Practicing Tarot for Everyday Enrichment; Equinox Celebration*; *An Exploration of Divination*; and *Contemplative Horsemanship*.

I was shocked to see that this last course title wasn't gender-neutral. I turned to the full program description: "…This weekend will provide an opportunity to experience oneself and 'other' through an equine connection. What arises in this relationship? Fear? Anger? Frustration? Aggression? Love? Empathy? Working closely with a large variety of horses ranging in color, temperament and breed, we will access our own issues of trust, self-confidence and self-esteem. Together we will explore these states and our experiences through contemplative practices of meditation, and group process. Components of the class will include haltering and leading, grooming, groundwork, and riding."

I cackled, then looked up, hoping no one would catch me laughing to myself—otherwise, so much for tenure. My take on this *horse course* was that people were going to shell out about a quarter of a month's rent to ride and brush a bunch of *different colored horses* at some local stable, then sit in a circle and talk about how they *felt* about it. Not to mention the stable owners would be getting some free grooming services. But then that was just my take. Maybe if I were wealthy I'd understand it better?

Actually, most of the courses Naropa offers seem to have the word "contemplative" in their title. They can find contemplation in *anything*. String any three random activities together, add the terms "contemplative" or "walking meditation" somewhere in the title, and you have a Naropa course offering. E.g., A Weekend Seminar in Contemplative Lightbulb Changing, Vacuuming, and Soul Journey. With Walking Meditation.

Next I looked at the brochure from the Rocky Mountain Shambhala Center. There was a little blurb from the Executive Director next to a lovely photograph of a couple of scenic buildings nestled amongst some evergreens: "Dear Friends, From the beginning we have envisioned this Buddhist-inspired retreat as a precious resource for the world community. This year our expanded programs and facilities, and the completion of The Great Stupa of Dharmakaya, bring us a step closer to fulfilling that vision. May we contribute to the lives of all who visit this brilliant mountain valley." This, along with a very vague idea I've always had about the building that sits kitty-corner from the Boulder Theater, a serene-looking shining place called the Shambhala Center—where I believe people go to meditate—contributed to give me an erroneous, naïve assumption about the kinds of programs I was about to find listed in the brochure.

What I was *not* expecting was a four-day workshop called *Golf Mind*, price tag: over a thousand dollars. "Develop the connection between meditative awareness, your golf game and life. Morning meditation at RMSC followed by golf at neighboring Fox Acres, a top-ranked private club." Or a fee of close to a thousand dollars for the guest teachings of Khandro Rinpoche on "The Path of Compassion." And plenty more offerings of compassion. Jeez, how about some compassionate pricing? When did all this Buddhist stuff become a *racket*?

A

I was sure that this narcoleptic I picked up at the Bookend Café was going to be my Number Twenty-Seven. (The poor guy fell asleep into his cappuccino next to me, splashing foam all over the place, including my table. This did wake him up, although he looked bleary, as if it hadn't been quite enough of a nap.) He fell asleep a few times during the movie we rented and also during foreplay, but I wasn't able to add him to my list, as it was his other head that fell asleep at the crucial moment, and was unable to be revived.

Then there was a guy who seemed perfectly normal and fine until the clothes came off, at which point he was more like Circus Sideshow Guy. Tattoos everywhere, which I suppose I could've dealt with, but when I saw the huge titanium bar pierced straight through his penis, I nearly fainted. I did have the fleeting thought that Mordecai ought to take up those pastimes. Surely sharp needles maiming his flesh... Anyway, needless to say, sex with *that thing* was out of the question.

I got invited to this mountain house party, one of those multi-million-dollar homes up in the foothills. I maneuvered over to the food table first, always the best tactic—gives you something to do, right off. I took some of the requisite Brie and crackers, and inadvertently tuned in to this lady behind me who was expounding at length to a reluctant (male, I noted—semi-attractive) listener about how she "should've switched to her silver chain!"

"Oh, I just *knew* it!" she was exclaiming. "I was thinking before I left the house, should I wear the silver or the gold? And I chose the gold. But now I just *feel*, you know, I just *feel* it—Oh, oh, oh, I should've switched to the *silver* one!"

Never having actually heard anyone say "Oh, oh, oh" before in conversation, I turned around to look at her. Thin in the way of beef jerky. Too tan, hair down to her butt. Mid- or upper-forties? Probably has never worked, and goes to Pilates five hours a day. And sure enough, a gold necklace (worth more than I gross in a year). Now that she had a new audience, the guy nodded quickly and made his escape. *Merde.*

I then had to listen politely for ten minutes as she gave a monologue (you *know* she was a Theater major in college) on this one particular curried cheese soufflé (sounded dreadful to me) that she'd tasted at the *last* mountain house party she'd been to, and how I *really* should've been there to try it (she *assumed* I wasn't there—so what if she was right) and how she'd just *die* if she couldn't get the recipe.

You know, I love and appreciate my independence and singledom. But I have moments, at these Boulder mountain house parties in particular, when I feel I've lost a game of adults' musical chairs. Everyone else has found a spouse, a six-figure income, and a beautiful home—a while back the music suddenly stopped, they all found their places, and somehow I was left standing all alone, looking around me, perplexed.

Most of the time, though, I'm having way too much fun to notice.

The next time someone came to the table, I copied the nod-and-escape, gladly leaving Ms. Wish I Wore Silver to her next victim. I found my way onto one of the twenty or thirty beautiful redwood decks with spectacular views. I admired the scenery, quickly made my rounds of the whole party, tried but failed to contain my house-envy, then decided the first guy I'd seen was my best bet. He was so-so attractive, not deformed in any obvious way, and no wedding ring. With Memorial Day looming so close, I could no longer afford to be picky. Nor subtle. I decided to try a pickup line I'd read in some trashy "women's" magazine in my dentist's waiting room, when I'd forgotten to bring studnet papers to grade. It had offered the very original advice, "Be bold!" (No different from the horticultural exhortation at McGuckin's, after all.)

So I walked up to this guy and said, in as trashy a voice as I could manage (being, after all, an intellectual), "Hi. I'd love to look down and see what your face looks like in ecstasy."

He turned bright red and opened his mouth and seemed to try to speak, but only a kind of half-cough, half-squeak came out. Perhaps he had no tongue? I regretted having always been too lazy to learn sign language. Then he recovered and got a kind of pleased, almost cocky expression on his face—like his wildest fantasies were coming true. Well, I suppose they were. Or maybe not the wild*est*—I don't look like a supermodel in the swimsuit issue—but maybe some of the wild*er* ones. He was all over me on the way home, talking dirty, slobbering, but as soon as we got into my apartment, I started with the Hey Baby, I'm Gonna Ravage You And You're Gonna Love It talk like I'd been advised by the magazine, and... well, I guess you could say the whole scene *emasculated* him.

Just when I was thinking I was jinxed, I did bag a Twenty-Seven. And it was actually really fun, I mean much more so than usual, because as it turned out (the guy didn't explain until several hours into it, when I was beginning to suspect illicit drugs), he was on SSRIs (a *legal* drug was the culprit) and he couldn't come—all night long. (Georgette later begged his phone number off me.)

Then I met a guy renting not one of the Chautauqua *cabins*, which is what I'd thought he'd said, but rather... We started getting intimate and the clothes starting coming off—and the clothes, and the clothes, and the clothes. We were having a cold spell, and he was wearing about ten layers. After peeling eight layers off him, I was winded. I sat back to rest for a minute and asked him what the deal was. He clarified that he was renting the *screened porch* of one of the cabins.

"Wait, you mean all *winter*?"

"Yep," he replied proudly. "It's only costing me a hundred and fifty bucks a month, plus fridge and shower expenses."

"Fridge and shower expenses?"

"You know, fridge space. And shower, two dollars every time I use it. So I try not to use it more than once a week."

Which is why I decided that even if I told him to bathe first, he might be harboring some long-term germs or something mildewing down there that I *definitely* did not want to discover. Because I didn't want to hurt his feelings too badly, I did keep chatting nicely with him as I redressed him.

"So," I asked, "where did you live before this?"

"Oh, in a *much* tougher housing market than here!"

"Where was that?"

"D.C."

"Oh, yeah, I lived there too!" I said. "Man, it *is* tough there, I remember! Apartments cost an arm and a leg... Even the group housing situations, the rooms for rent in those, were so expensive... So where did you live there?"

"Dude, I rented a hallway," he announced with real pride in his voice.

"A *hallway*?"

"Yeah, dude, for three years," he said, as I put his final layer on him: jacket, scarf, and hat. I ushered him out the door and we stood there before he left.

"What was it like?" I asked, with real curiosity.

"Well, it was the hallway between the bathroom and this other guy's room. They'd hung up a pillowcase at each end to, like, give me some privacy. I'd say I had about, maybe, six and a half feet?" I looked at him. He was about six-two.

"So what about when someone had to use the bathroom?"

"Oh, yeah, people were always having to come use the bathroom, dude! I didn't mind. They'd just wake me up and I'd sit up and, you know, let them by." Jesus. This guy was nothing if not patient and tolerant. Were the religious Jews wrong? Had the Messiah come, albeit an unwashed Messiah, and they'd overlooked him?

"And you lived there for three *years*? *Why?*"

"Well, you know—it was a good deal. It was only three hundred a month. The other people in the house—it was one of those D.C. group house dealies...there were nine of them, and they all had, you know, normal rooms and stuff...were all paying five-fifty and higher, except for the guy whose room in the basement flooded every spring—he was paying four hundred. Suckers!"

Yeah, I was thinking. And those suckers probably had things like windows and furniture and a closet and bookshelves and a bed and space to move around in. Actually, this skinflint was starting to remind me a little of Alan; maybe I should do him out of nostalgia? Then I thought again of the once-a-week shower. No, I didn't want to get a whiff of those bottom few layers, thank you very much.

"Okay, well, ciao, enjoy your porch!"

Then there was someone I met as he was getting kicked out of the public library for disturbing the peace by continually playing some kind of little portable video game. (As time was so scarce, I was of necessity becoming less picky.) "But I can't turn it off right now," he was attempting to explain to the librarian. "I've just defeated Planet Moregore for the first time!" The librarian, normally a reasonable man, was having none of it, and ushered the young man outside to let him continue his plan of mass destruction. I followed the guy outside and approached him. He proved not immune to my charms and we encountered no difficulties until it was found that he did not approve of the décor of my apartment.

"What would you do differently?" I asked him.

"Well, you know, in my place I have, you know, posters up. It makes the place look, you know, better."

"Better? What kind of posters?"

"You know...sports guys. Football. Baseball. Hoops. All of 'em. And swimsuit calendars. *Oh* yeah!" Did this guy have some kind of weird hormone problem and I was going to get arrested later for seducing a fourteen year-old who just *looked* like a thirty year-old?

"Brian, how old are you again?"

"Me? Thirty-two. Why?"

"No reason. Let's get comfortable, shall we?"

Everything was fine until there was a sudden beeping sound that drove Baby instantly insane with curiosity (and scared me to death—I thought maybe it was the fire alarm, and I was pretty sure the battery in that had been dead for years). Brian suddenly leaped out of bed screaming, "Fido! Fido! Hold on, buddy! I'm there!" It was time to feed his electronic pet.

Once we were getting back into the swing of things, Brian suddenly glanced at the clock on my bedside table and again leaped out of bed as if *he* were on fire: "Oh noooo! Is that the time?! Man, I gotta go! Sorry! I'm outta here! *Now!*" He started flying around, throwing on his clothes haphazardly.

I looked at the clock. It was 4:45 p.m. "What's the matter?" I asked him. And can't you just hang out a *tiny* bit longer, Brian, so I can claim you as Number Twenty-Eight and move right along?

"FedEx pickup is at 5:00!" he shouted as he pulled on his last sock.

"What? What are you sending? What's so important?" I followed him to the door with the sheet clutched around me.

"My laundry!" he shouted back to me as he flew down the stairs. "My dirty laundry, to Mom. And pick up my clean stuff, and my dinners for the week…in *Tupperware!*" his voice trailed off as he disappeared around the corner. And out of my life.

There was the guy who, when I asked what he did for a living, said he was a Zen Archer. Yeah, whatever. However, his aim turned out to be crucially off.

There was another man with an interesting claim to profession: he said he was in *entropy repair*. "Really?" I asked him. "So what do you actually *do?*" This was at yet another mountain house party I'd finagled an invitation to, by suggesting I bring a curried cheese soufflé, which must have made the rumor rounds—hey, I was desperate, I had less than two weeks left and three guys to go; I was doing far worse than expected.

"Oh, you know…" he answered. Well, no. I didn't. I thought about telling him his sentence needed a bit of entropy repair, but decided I'd have more success in my mission if I were nice. You can catch more flies with honey, and all that crap. Anyway, to sum up our brief, unsuccessful experience together: it was a *study* in entropy.

If you were starting to get the impression that my entire next couple of weeks were devoted exclusively to trying to nab men…you'd be right.

Then there was a caption writer for middle-school textbooks. I tried making small talk with him, but was yawning with boredom within two minutes. How much conversation can you make out of "Soldiers at Gettysburg," "Cell division," or "The layers of the earth's crust"? I couldn't bear even talking to him long enough to pick him up.

There was a Denver med student who seemed fine until we got to his apartment and he introduced me to his dog, a mutt called Foreskin. I thought, okay, whatever, but then I decided the vibes were getting just a little too weird and decided to scram when his two Siamese cats approached; he stroked them an abnormally long time and told me in a hushed voice that their names were Labia major and Labia minor.

I wasted a precious three days hanging around with this adorable foreign guy—I think he was half Jordanian, half Pakistani; or maybe it was half Syrian Druze, half Egyptian, who'd grown up in various countries—he was dark and gorgeous, in any case. He was really sweet, and hung out with me almost constantly, having just arrived in the country. He also became more romantic each day, which kept me hooked. He asked questions about all sorts of things: "I walk past dance studio today. Teacher is white man dancing hop-hip music. Is looking very silly. And all students is only young beautiful white girls. Very strange. Why is?"

"Um…" I tried. "Um, well, you see, in *Boulder*…"

Or, "Today I smoke cigarette after lunch in restaurant. They send me outside, like *servant*! Not let me have coffee with cigarette, like is normal! Why is?"

"Um…"

Or, "Today I go for walk on mountain. Is so many dogs! And all people picking up dogs' *merde*, and smiling like no problem! I would not never touch dog's *merde*! Very very dirty! Why they do?"

"Um…"

"Also, is lot of people washing rock there. Why?"

"Washing the rocks?" I ask him, certain there must be some kind of misunderstanding this time.

"Yes, yes, washing rock! With big, how you say—from ocean, is soft?"

"Sponge?"

"Yes, yes, with big sponge, is—*quitter*—"

"Removing?"

"Yes, is all removing white mark from rocks. Why?"

Oh. Climbers' chalk marks. "Um…"

Or, "Today I visit university campus, first time. For see my department, you know, for working in future. And all students, I am so sorry, you know! I feel they must being so, how you say, so not *riche*—"

"Poor?"

"Yes, yes, so poor!"

"*Poor?* The C.U. studnets—er, students? *Poor?!* How could you ever think so?" I asked, astonished.

"Because all clothing is being too small, must be old clothing, other people clothing, you know? Is all too small, all"—he touched his abdomen—"is expose to sight! No *chemise* is adequate! Also materials is not so good, you know, *le polyester*? In my country students is all dressing very good. Poor, poor university students here!"

"Um…"

"Also, Aviva, you tell me before, Boulder is famous for *cuisine* of health?"

"Yes, yes!" In my eagerness to get just one thing straightened out, I sounded like him.

"But today, I am seeing Taco Bell and Dunk The Donuts."

"Um…"

"Perhaps they are new, these ones restaurants?"

"Um, actually, no…"

He also, when introduced to my cat, Baby, for the first time, refused to touch her (I almost kicked him out at that point, but decided to make this one allowance, he being from a part of the world that inexplicably considers non-human animals "dirty"), and when she started purring as I was petting her, he blurted in alarm, "Aviva! What is this noise?! Where it comes from? It is a *rumble* noise! Aviva, what is *happen* in this animal?!"

At the end of three days, he was more than willing to get pretty hot and heavy into petting (with me, not with Baby), but when it came time to strip off the few remaining clothes and actually count him as Number Twenty-Eight, he very politely unwound himself from me, looked into my eyes, and said, "Aviva, I am feeling very, very sorry, but you know? This is to be against my religion."

And that was that.

I was seriously running out of time. This was awful. Had I done all these guys for nothing? *No fucking way.* I was going to finish this bet come hell or high water (another of those quaint expressions I love).

The next man turned out to be *perfect*. He definitely didn't look like he'd been sleeping on any porches. But when I brought him home, he went into my bathroom and gargled about ten times, then asked me if I would please not only brush my teeth, but also floss and gargle before he kissed me. I thought, okay, sure. But then he washed his hands for about three minutes, then asked me to wash mine. I started wondering what was up. What did this guy think, that he was about to perform surgery? Nevertheless, I thought, cleanliness is never a bad thing, so I complied.

In the bedroom, he took off his shoes and spent about one minute lining them up with exactitude, then he took off his socks—and *folded* them. He turned to me—who'd been watching curiously—and requested a hanger.

"Sure, what for?"

"For these," he answered, gesturing to the folded socks. I raised my eyebrows, but handed him a hanger. I watched him hang his limp little pair of folded nylon socks, then he took off his pants, folded and *creased* them carefully, top to bottom (this took about three minutes), asked me for another hanger, hung them up, then unbuttoned his shirt, took it off, procured from me another hanger, *re*buttoned the shirt on the hanger, and hung it up, making sure it was evenly spaced next to the hanging socks and pants. He then took off his Fruit of the Looms, and I watched in (decreasing) astonishment as he proceeded to carefully fold these as well. This time, I was ready with the hanger. He stood there naked, and, presumably, finally ready. (There was nothing more to take off and hang up, in any case—that I could see.)

He looked fine, completely normal.

Then he asked, "May I examine your sheets?"

"Ex*cuse* me?"

"Your sheets. To make sure they're clean," he said matter-of-factly.

Challenge or no, I made a sudden decision. "No, you know what? Just…no. *No.*" And I handed him his creased-and-folded pants, his buttoned-up-shirt, his folded socks, his folded underwear. "I'll be waiting in the living room…to see you out."

I never did find out if he had obsessive-compulsive disorder, or if he was simply an ideal candidate for Seinfeld's twelve-step "germophobe" program. If the former, hey, I'm all for advocating the case for mood-disordered individuals. If the latter, JoAnn told me later there was this awesome word in Spain to describe someone like him: *tiquismiquis*. But I could only imagine what sex with him would be like—*quick, hand me a tissue, hand me a washcloth!*—no thanks.

And the race was on again.

All the terrible stress of being about to screw up (so to speak) this bet, after doing so well the whole year, made me decide to take a break and go to yoga to remember how to breathe again. But when I got to the studio, there was a sub instead of Ron. It was some gringo dude who had renamed himself—something Indian or that, to my non-Sanskrit-specialist ears, sounded like it was at least meant to make you think so.

"Hi everyone," he said in a near-whisper, his voice matching his emaciated appearance, "my name is Vajiya." There was a smattering of helpless giggles from all over the room, surprising from this well-mannered audience: his name rhymed with *vagina*. "I'll be your teacher today. I have just returned from studying in India, at the Iyengar Institute." That probably explained his gaunt look; we'd heard from the other teachers how studying in India was wonderful, even mandatory, but a real trial—what with the inevitable stomach bugs, the heat, and the Indian students swiping your yoga props right out from under your nose and then proclaiming innocence.

You could tell the guy used to be kind of cute (before he lost fifty pounds). At the end of class, I felt much less stressed and invited him out for a coffee. He asked me if I wanted to come over to his place for an herb tea instead. I figured, that was evidence of two contradictory things: 1) wimpiness, because of the herb tea—what hetero guy actually drinks herb tea by choice?; 2) machismo, the opposite of wimpiness—inviting me over to his place just like that. These two things canceling each other out, I didn't know what to think. I decided to hope for the best, and, as my Hindu Bad Rack of Lamb had put it, play it by the ear.

At his apartment, looking around, I was once again stymied: it was the first time I'd been presented with apparent evidence that contradicted a hypothesis I'd developed ages ago, and which was really, by now, a theory. This being that *no hetero man has both cats and plants of his own volition.* What I mean is, maybe an ex-girlfriend left him with some—that's fine. But if he went and decided on his own to get a cat, *and* houseplants (one or the other is okay), then he is not hetero. (I suppose there needs to be some kind of footnote in there about him taking *care* of them, too.)

But Vajiya (did I really have to call him that?) had a lot of flourishing tropical plants, plus a cute little fluffy gray kitty named Jane—and, confusingly, he was also starting to put some moves on me.

"So...these are *your* plants...and cat?" I asked him, inanely.

"Yeah, I *love* plants! I love the, you know, *nurturing* aspect of taking care of them, and watching them grow, put out new leaves and everything. And Jane—I couldn't *live* without *Jane*! It was terrible being in India without her. I spent so much money calling my friend to ask how she was doing, because I actually couldn't get on email much there at the Institute."

"And did you... Where did you get her?" I just couldn't rest till I'd gotten to the bottom of this. The death of a theory is a very serious thing and must be investigated thoroughly.

"Jane? Oh, I was *dying* to have a kitty for*ever*...I finally got an apartment that allowed pets, so I could get one. I went to the Humane Society and picked out Janie here...must've been about...let's see, four years ago now! She's the love of my life, aren't you, Janie girlie?" He picked her up and cuddled her under his chin.

My theory was shot—assuming, of course, that this guy *was* hetero.

As it turned out he was—have you ever had sex with a yoga teacher? It was...how shall we say... Exhilarating. Vigorous. *Strenuous*. I can't even remember how many different asanas we did—or is it blasphemous to use the term in this context? I could imagine that the next day, how shall we put this nicely, I was certainly not going to encounter any problems with my digestion. Or, as the French say (not mincing words), *ça aide le transit*. The only off moment was toward the end, when we were bent over backwards together on one of those Swedish exercise balls, and it sprang a leak, letting out a loud *hsssss* and terrifying Janie, who made a leap about five feet up onto the tie-dye sheet being used as a curtain. I started laughing really hard which caused my oh-so-limber yoga teacher to pull a muscle somewhere in his, as he called it, "groins." Which made me laugh even more, not exactly earning me the undying affection of Mr. Vajiya.

It wasn't too long afterwards that I thought I had a Number Twenty-Nine—at least, he seemed just dandy all the way up until the moment we started disrobing. Then he happened to say something which was the verbal equivalent of the fatal flaw: "Man, this sure is working out a hell of a lot better than the time I accidentally called that maid service!"

"You what?" I was still, at that point, unconcerned, tugging off my leggings, which were being a bit stubborn.

"Well, see, there was this ad in the paper? You know, like Merry Maids or something like that? And it said 'we'll provide every service for you with a smile.' And it had this picture of, like, three sexy babes holding feather dusters or something, and *winking*, I swear! And they were sandwiched between, I mean the *ad* was between—ha ha!—all these other ads. I think it was in the Boulder Weekly or Westword or somewhere like that, these ads saying, like, 'topless and totally nude,' 'full body massage for masculine muscular release by leggy blonde at your place,' you know, that kind of thing."

To his credit—the *only*, infinitesimal amount of credit I *will* give him—he was blushing when I looked up at him, my leggings swinging, cat-toy-like, from my hand.

"And you called this ad *why*?" I asked him.

"Well, you know… I thought it was, you know…"

"No, Todd, I don't know. Tell me."

"Well, *you* know. An escort service, like."

I put my leggings back on while listening to Todd protest, "But I didn't *do* anything! In fact, I ended up having to pay seventy bucks to get my apartment cleaned! Aviva, don't…*go*!"

Which left me with only one week to find two more guys.

J

Two days later, I met and had dinner with a guy who had the most *gorgeous* hair: silky, glossy, dark chestnut, stick-straight to his shoulders. He looked exactly like Jackson Browne—it was uncanny. I asked him about it, and he said, yeah, ever since he was a teenager, total strangers had come up to him and asked for his autograph.

He was even about the right age—I'd recently seen an article about Jackson Browne, something about how he was into environmentally correct politics and such, and there was a current photo. He'd aged well, just like you'd expect. Still gorgeous after all these years. Or was that a paraphrase of someone else's shtick? Well, the right era, in any case.

I was *so* hot for this guy's hair. I would kill to run my hands through it. "What's your name?" I asked him. "And it'd better not be Jackson, because I won't believe you."

"Nope. It's Sandy."

"*Sandy?!* That doesn't suit you!"

"Yeah, well, I was blonder when I was a kid." He smiled, and I suddenly didn't care about arguing about his moniker—or anything else.

That evening, after a wonderful dinner of sesame tofu and salad that he'd prepared and after smooching in his living room for just a couple of minutes, Sandy went into his bedroom "to get more comfortable," saying he'd be back out in a moment. I was left pre-Jackson-Browne-hair-assault on the couch, my fingers itching to stroke, to fondle, to play, contemplating the oddness of his comment. Was he going to (please god no) come back into the room wearing a negligée and falsies?

He returned. We were in semi-penumbra, having not turned on any lights since the sun had set during dinner, so it took me a moment to focus.

"Aaaacck!" I gasped, falling over on the couch, until I caught myself with one elbow.

Sandy was bald. As an egg. As a ping-pong ball. As the head of a penis. And grinning.

"Jacks—I mean, *San*dy! What happened to, um, to your..." (there didn't seem to be any way to put this in a more subtle manner) "...*hair*?"

"Aviva. Come here, darlin'." *Darlin'?* Somehow, that sounded fine when I was imagining that by some divine gift, I was going to be allowed to experience a night of love with Jackson Browne by proxy, but *this*... "I want to show you something." He ushered me into the bedroom (on the way, I took a fearful peek up at his shining beacon), where in the shadowy recesses I could just make out...

"Aaaacck!" I gasped again, this time fortuitously being caught by Sandy. There in the corner, dark and gleaming, like a raccoon poised to attack, was Jackson Browne's hair.

"Aviva...Elvis," said Sandy, going over to the hair and picking it up—it was on a wig stand. He brought it near me, and I couldn't help it, I flinched. "Elvis...Aviva."

Je ne comprenais pas. I stared at him. "*What* are you talking about?"

"Introducing you." That grin again. I realized now, it was much cuter on Jackson than on Sandy.

"*What?*"

"This is Elvis." Sandy stroked the head with tremendous affection, the hair that five minutes ago I'd been dying to get my own fingers into. This thought now made me want to ralph my sesame tofu.

"You *named* it?!"

"Not only that," he said, "this is *Elvis VIII.*" I looked at him yet again in incomprehension. "Kind of like Henry the Eighth. Except without all the wives. Ha ha!"

Apparently, he could tell from my expression that I still didn't get the picture, so he led me to the patio door and slid it open. We were looking out on his backyard, and he flipped on the porch light. "Aviva, toupée science has come a long way. This—" he shoved Jackson in my face; I recoiled—"is state-of-the-art, human hair." Human hair? Oh my god! (And visions of Auschwitz.) On the other hand, I had a sudden, impossible hope that, by some miracle, it actually *was* Jackson Browne's hair. "It's not a *rug*—ha ha! And so...it doesn't last forever, you see. Every year, I have to get a new one. These..." He gestured to the backyard, where I could now make out little white crosses all in a row, like a military graveyard, or like Stephen King's pet cemetery, each cross labeled in permanent marker: *Elvis, Elvis II, Elvis III*, etc. "...well—you see." And he sniffled, a sad little sound.

I explained to Georgette on the phone later that night: "So it didn't even matter that other than that...ah...*idiosyncrasy*, he was benign and I had found him attractive up till then. It was just impossible to get back in the mood. No, that's not quite it. What I mean is, it was impossible to get in the mood with bald Sandy, when what I had wanted was Sandy with the Jackson Browne hair."

"What if he had put the hair back on?"

"No, I think just knowing it was fake..."

"But it *wasn't* fake! Like he said, it was *real*," Georgette said in a teasing voice.

"Ha ha. You know what I mean."

"Yeah, I know. Hmm. I'd have to say, Ave, one of your weirder ones."

"Oh no. Not at all. You have *no* idea."

"You'll have to fill me in. What could be weirder than Jackson Browne and a toupée cemetery?"

"Believe me..."

"You know..." Georgette mused. "Did he say toupée? Because it wasn't. Isn't the definition of toupée, like, a *patch* of hair or something? He was pretty nervy calling that a toupée. Girlfriend, that was a whole *head* of hair!"

"Tell me about it!"

"Well, Ave...you've got, what? Three or four more guys? And five days? Think you're gonna make it?" She chuckled.

I was startled. Had I miscalculated? "Hold on a second." I went to get my notes and did a recheck. "No, no! Jesus, Georgette, you scared me. It's *two* more guys!"

"Oh, well, in that case... Two guys, five days... No problem, Ave. Shake that booty!" I could hear her chuckling as she hung up.

I called her again, two days later, panicky. But I only got her machine. I scream-whispered: "Georgette! Help! I've got a guy—well, I think so—sort of—in the bathroom right now—oh, *merde*, Georgette, where are you?! He's—well, he's like that Pat character, remember that androgynous creepy guy or girl or whatever? I'm desperate in terms of timing, but please please call and tell me I'm not *this* desperate—"

I hung up quickly as Dale came out of my bathroom. Dale was a dead ringer for the infamous Pat of the old Saturday Night Live. I'm always curious in these cases: did their parents name them something that would work with either gender because the kid already looked androgynous—I mean, even more so than the average baby? Or did the kid become more and more androgynous over time because of the gender-neutral name? Maybe, if nothing else, I could end up using Dale for research in this area.

Obviously, this situation did not portend a happy ending. Look how far I'd fallen as time had caught up with me: from my good friend Donald, to Doctors Without Frontiers, to guys who rarely emerged from their greenhouses to inhabit the social sphere, to, finally, a candidate whose gender I was having trouble even determining. Thank goddess (as they say here in Boulder, and possibly appropriate given the specimen before me) the phone rang and Georgette, who was grouchy because she'd been sitting leisurely on the toilet in her bathroom with a new issue of Gardening Today, quickly talked me back into sanity.

"I mean, come on," she urged, "do you really want to get close enough—I mean *physically* close enough—to actually have to determine whether this Pat—"

"Dale," I interrupted.

"—is a male, or maybe a hermaphrodite?"

"Well, I could make sure it stays very dark," I ventured tentatively.

"Ave," she remonstrated, "trust me. There is still the...ah, unavoidable *tactile potential*."

"*Ewwwww*," I said, the movie The Crying Game coming, unbidden, to mind.

Exit Dale.

Enter Trey, on whom I wasted about four waning hours. He was at a table outside the Trident, entertaining people with photos and tales from the last Burning Man. He was planning on going again this coming August. It would be his fourth time—lifer status in my eyes, I who'd never been and probably never would go. He was looking for people to accompany him, and ideas for what kind of theme to cultivate or service to offer this time. He wanted to be, as he put it, *really unique* this time.

I sat down next to his wide-eyed, young, dredlocked disciples. I was simultaneously amused and disgusted by the photos. I figured I'd try picking up Trey after he was done recruiting here; he was good-looking, although not my type. He was that sun-bleached-blond, constant-UV-exposure, sinewy lean rock-climber type. (And me with my penchant for dark bookish Jewish boys. Oh well. The time for preferences was *long* over.)

Trey was talking about his favorite site from last year, which had been a trio of six-foot-plus blond women—Viking women, essentially, or Amazons, what have you—stark naked, giving men haircuts. The only catch: the only haircut available was a completely shaved head.

Then there was the cement truck, which during the whole week never once ceased spinning to provide the refried bean filling at The Burrito Brothers' site, and fed, as estimates have it, well over five thousand people—or up to thirty thousand, if you count those who went back for seconds and thirds or more. There was the Burning Man newsletter, *Piss Clear*. And the Bicycle Parts Man, who brought unimaginably massive quantities of random, unmatched cycle pieces, dumped them unceremoniously onto the desert floor along with tools, and let people construct their own interesting-looking self-powered vehicles, to later return to parts or to keep forever, as desired.

And of course, every afternoon there were the group mud fights, which preceded the group showers, which preceded the Bare Titties Bike Ride. And the mechanized traveling sofas built by frat boys-*cum*-engineers-*cum*-Burning Man refugees, painted banners across the back proclaiming "Naked Women Ride Free!," which trolled the sands, their occupants drinking iced beers from attached coolers, as comfy as Harry and friends watching their Thanksgiving football game. I had to smile at that photo, knowing how much Brandon and his college buddies would've loved that one. Then I had a sudden terrible thought and was stricken with anxiety: maybe that *was* them? I took a closer look. Nah, the guys in the photo *were* college-age. Whereas Brandon and his buddies by now were scrambling to pay for a new three-car garage and to keep their kids in Pampers and…and…well, whatever else you have to keep kids in. I looked again at the photo; maybe I *would* go to Burning Man this year. Not because I wanted to. But because I *could*.

After the youngsters took off, vowing to "*be* there, dude!," Trey asked me whether I wanted to go, too, and I hedged and told him that, well, my overall take on the event was that it seemed extremely full of color, drugs, and naked flesh. He raised his hand for a high-five: "*Yeah*! That's *it*, dude!" Oy vey. I guess I won't go after all, the desire to flaunt my freedom notwithstanding.

I did try to pick up Trey, but he hemmed and hawed and looked away, toward the mountains, and kept gazing up there while he whispered, "Sorry, I, I... I have kind of a...problem."

"What sort of problem?"

"Shhh," he said, looking around us, then back at the Flatirons. "Well, I've gotten it checked out, even though I don't really trust docs, you know, Western medicine and all that...so I've even gone to a couple of alternative practitioners ... Even a hypnotherapist..."

"What's wrong, Trey?"

"You know... Don't make me say it."

"But I don't know what you..." He was barely hinting.

"Aviva, I can't...you know. *Do the nasty* anymore." I didn't know what to say. I looked him over again. Young, healthy, nice body...

He snuck a peek at me, saw me appraising him. "Yeah, dude, it *totally* sucks!"

"Um...yeah. And they don't know why?"

"The only thing the docs can come up with, I mean, that they think is wrong, is maybe...well...too much pot." He bark-laughed, an ironic little yelp. "Dude—I mean, talk about poetic justice, you know?"

I left Trey there, shaking his head at a powerful and mystifying universe.

The next day, yet another freaked-out call from me. "Georgette, you are *not* gonna believe this!"

"Tell, tell!"

"Okay, woman, are you ready for this?"

"How the hell can I know if I'm ready until you say it?"

"Okay, okay. It's just, this is *so* good..."

"Come on already!"

"Okay. Georgette, I have encountered...*The Dreaded Pencil Dick*."

There was a gasp on her end. "*No!*" she shouted.

"*Yes!*"

"Oh my god! Details!"

It had been awful, really—I mean the actual moment of, shall we say, *revelation*. As a woman, you hear all your life about The Dreaded Pencil Dick, and each time that you fortunately don't encounter it, you breathe a huge sigh of relief. Or rather, you start breathing again, because you've been holding your breath until *it* was revealed, praying it's not going to happen. It's like a reverse lottery. It's merely one of the several Russian Roulettes that befall us poor women when the zipper starts coming down. We start holding our breath at that point and we don't stop until the underwear comes off and we (hopefully) see something in the normal range of length, width, and color.

"So let me hazard a guess, here," she broke in at one point. "You did not, ah, *consummate the act* with this less-than-manly specimen?"

"That is correct, my friend."

"But Ave! You are *so* running out of time!"

"Georgette! Come on! Would *you* have?"

"Of course not," she said laughing. "Tell me, was it *really* like a pencil? Or more like a *magic marker* or something?"

"An official number two," I said. We cracked up.

"Yeah," she mused. "Tall and lean has always been my favorite physique for a guy…but I guess that's not a good thing when applied to the *whole* physique."

"You know what, Georgette? I'm trying really hard to see this in a positive light. Like, for one thing, it's the worst thing that could've happened, and it finally happened, you know? I'll never be dreading seeing the worst again because now I've seen it."

"Yeah, I understand what you mean. Because, in a weird way, I'm jealous. Because it's happened to you, you know? But *I'll* always still be dreading it."

"Exactly!" I enthused. "And then, too, I'm also trying to see it in this other positive way, like…like it was this *rare sighting*. You know, like seeing a quetzal flying around in its native habitat, or…I know! It's like finally coming face-to-face…well, not face-to-*face*…with the previously-only-rumored-to-exist Yeti. Except *that* would've been more fun."

There was a guy I scared away (well, okay, *offended*) when he told me his last name. It was *Yesburger*. I'd never heard it before, and it simply struck me funny. (As a linguist, my ears are exquisitely tuned to language;

I can't help these things.) I wish he hadn't run off; I wanted to ask him if he'd ever been in the military. I was imagining him as a superior: *Yes, sir, Yesburger!*; or what kinds of scenarios might present themselves if he worked at a McDonald's…and I just couldn't stop giggling.

You're probably wondering where I managed to find all these candidates in such a short time. I couldn't believe it either. I'd never before been able to pick up so many, so quickly. Maybe I was putting off some kind of special pheromones, letting them all know that I was as available (or desperate) as I'd ever been. It certainly wouldn't have been possible if Spring semester hadn't been over and my grades dutifully turned in. It also helped that it was, by now, the beginning of the weekend of the Boulder Creek Festival (annual harbinger of the Bolder Boulder, on Monday), so there were literally thousands of people outside enjoying the beautiful weather. I'm sure it had nothing to do with my miniskirt. (Well, okay, it wasn't really a *mini*skirt. It was as short as my thirty-six year-old thighs would let me get away with. I liked to think of it as the miniskirt of a *woman of a certain age*.)

There was another one I offended because his idea of foreplay involved pretending to be a tiger. When he started approaching me on all fours, growling and pawing, I fell into helpless giggles and…out the door I was ushered. Who knew guys had such fragile egos?

Or fragile anatomy: there was a good candidate, but Baby made an unfortunately-timed play attack (*I* knew it wasn't a real attack, but try telling *him* that) on his swinging testicles from behind as he was, ahem, getting into position. Offers to put Baby into the other room were refused—I think because the guy was just so embarrassed to have screamed ("like a girl" came to mind, but of course I didn't say it) and instantly lost his erection. Actually, it probably was best that he left—because I never did fix the latch on that door, and my sweet kitty would have been able to just sneak back in and take another swipe at her fascinating new toy.

Baby ruined another possibility for me, by bringing into the room (where I was busy entertaining a strict vegan/Buddhist type, one who felt very strongly about never killing any living thing, not even a mosquito) a semi-decapitated, recently-alive bat. She dragged it in from the porch where she'd apparently plucked it out of the air while we were nuzzling, then she proceeded to tear off its wings. As we were still oblivious, she went back out the slightly-ajar sliding door and found a praying mantis, which she brought in and ripped some of the legs off of. Busy, we didn't notice. Out she went again, to murder a vole. She removed parts of its abdominal region, ate some of the organs—then noisily vomited it all up. This was the sound that finally alerted us that something was happening besides our steamy *tête-à-tête*—that, in fact, other *têtes* were being torn off around us. We looked over to behold one proud feline and a great deal of carnage. And very, very shortly thereafter, it was just me and my cat, and my cleaning products.

With less than forty-eight hours remaining, I attended the Boulder Outdoor Cinema. This is a fun event where they show repeats of classic and/or campy movies on an outdoor screen downtown, everyone has to bring their own seating, and you're given a silly nametag upon entering. I was assigned (and was highly unappreciative of) *Miss Piggy*. I made one small change, with a pen in my purse, to *Ms*.

"Tonight," a pimple-faced teenager at the mike was announcing when I arrived with a metal folding chair stolen from my Department, "there is going to be a Creative Seating Contest!" Well, I thought, looking down at my chair, which was going to be killing my *tuchus* fifteen minutes into the movie and have me sitting on the ground for sure, that definitely leaves me out of the running.

However—I am proud to announce that I, Aviva Goldberg, took home the winner of the grand prize of the Creative Seating Contest. The movie was *There's Something About Mary*, and the guy next to me had let out the usual moan of pain and grabbed for his privates during the zipper scene—but he'd done more than that; apparently looking for comfort, he'd flailed out blindly and made a grab for what he must have expected would be my arm or shoulder or hand, me being just a woman in the dark next to him. But by then, that hard metal was indeed causing agony and I'd relocated to sitting, swami-style (brief memories of a very sexy asana with Vajiya) on the ground, so the guy's hand collided perfectly with my right boob. When he realized what it was, his moan got louder—whether from embarrassment or sexual excitement, I will never know. But he politely disconnected from my anatomy and introduced himself.

Number Twenty-Nine, in the nick of time, was Thomas the Toilet Man. Yes, my prize (and prize-winner) had been enjoying the evening's visual entertainment seated atop a genuine (detached) commode of the white porcelain variety, which he had lugged at great hernia-inducing peril from the back of his Mazda to the Outdoor Cinema site, several blocks away. And the bonus, in his eyes at least, was that while he'd known that some sort of seating was a necessity, the fact of a creative seating contest was completely unknown to him, and this, according to Thomas during Postcoital Bliss Conversation, made his win doubly sweet. And *I* made it triply sweet. Did I follow? I did. What I did not tell him was that he'd just fulfilled the penultimate requirement in a contest of my own.

When he left my apartment, giddy with excitement about his "triple win," *I* was giddy with excitement about my chances to now complete the challenge—which, to my astonishment, had been looking less and less likely. I kissed him goodbye and slipped him a rolled-up magazine, which in the darkness he must've chosen to interpret as porn or something, because he excitedly whispered, "Wow, thanks, Aviva!"

"You're welcome, Thomas. G'night!"

It was the toilet catalog.

1

I honestly don't know what went wrong. I *still* don't, even from this vantage point of several months later. All I know is what I experienced, and what I, as a trained scientist, observed: with only one last day stretching ahead of me, suddenly, men evaporated. Where there had been a plentitude, there was now a scarcity. Where a surfeit, now a deficit. Etcetera. Of course I don't mean men were gone altogether—I mean, just for *me*, they'd vanished. I only saw married men, too-old ones, too-young ones (and I did even fleetingly consider a few of those, I was so desperate—but I didn't want to wind up in jail and be unable to practice sound dental hygiene), and gay ones. Where had all the *candidates* gone?! Could this possibly be what Mae West had meant by "A man in the house is worth two in the street"?

Having spent the entire day out looking for just that one man, I was weary and feeling uncharacteristically low. I couldn't believe it: all that craziness, that *weirdness* I'd been through this last year, and I was *going to lose*. And not by three, or four, or ten. Oh, no! I was going to lose by *one*.

Inwardly kicking myself now for all the days and even weeks in the past year I hadn't even thought about the bet, I felt as if someone's grandma were shaking her arthritic finger in my face and admonishing me in her quavery voice about the squirrel working to store away acorns while the something-or-other squandered the summer days…or however the hell that went. (I was the something-or-other.) Bummed as I felt, I managed one brief moment of mirth when I imagined that granny's shock at exactly what type of nuts I *had* been squirreling away. I'm sure I'm mixing all the metaphors by now, but who cares.

The sun was about to drop below the Flatirons (this is what we get instead of sunsets). More determined now than ever, I spent two final hours roaming around. Guys wearing babies on their backs, guys wearing babies on their fronts, guys pushing strollers, guys holding the hands of cute little kids… And equally inappropriately for me, guys holding hands with other guys, until at last I called it quits.

I'd done a good job—okay, not an *excellent* job, as I'd intended and always fully expected of myself in any and every situation—but still, a very good job. I'd just called it too close at the end, but nobody ever had to know what a bad something-or-other (non-squirrel) I was. I wouldn't admit to my foolish planning, or rather lack of planning…

Oh, but *merde*! Georgette already knew how close I'd been calling it! I recalled her laughter when she'd hung up the phone, saying, Ave, get out there and shake that booty. Well, maybe I could convince her not to tell the rest of them. Can you say "not bloody likely"?

Oh well. So that was it. *Finis*. Actually, I was kind of glad Georgette already knew. I really didn't want to deceive my friends about anything major.

It was quite late, and I moped around my apartment and desultorily cleaned. The place was a disaster. I hadn't had time lately to do anything but chase guys around. I didn't want to do it for a living, but…it was a fun place to visit. Someday, the next time I had a real, serious, down-and-dirty girltalk session with Georgette, I'd have to tell her how ironic it was that you could have so much sex and yet end up so unsatisfied.

While I did the dishes, ran the vacuum, and started tackling the enormous pile of laundry (the very bottom of which, quite frankly, I hadn't seen in months—maybe I could FedEx it all to Brian's mom?), I thought about the whole year, the whole experience. I never did take losing well; I've always been truly competitive. It started when I won the spelling bee in second grade and it hasn't let up since.

What had I learned this year?

That guys happily admit to having as their Significant Other someone who genuinely believes she was abducted by aliens and taken aboard their

UFO.

That only a guy is capable of being so generally clueless and illiterate as to accidentally telephone Planned Pethood when told to look up Planned Parenthood—and not to realize there was some kind of mix-up until ten minutes into the conversation.

That you should always turn down the volume on your message machine, especially when expecting a call from one of your girlfriends, especially when you know you're going to be seducing a candidate at the time you're likely to get said phone call, and especially when you've previously told said girlfriend all about the candidate you'd be seducing.

That you shouldn't bring any of those interestingly-shaped, colorful little funky new kinds of battery-operated mini-vibrators in your carry-on luggage—you'll get stopped in the X-ray area, and being asked to explain to a male right-off-the-boat-foreign security guard what it is can ruin your whole day. Also: when you have male company over, to make sure these items are put away somewhere *well*—i.e., where your darling cat can't get to them, drag them out and fling them across the floor. (P.S. It gets the cat *really* excited if the vibrators accidentally turn on.)

"Pat"-type androgynes excepted, I think I'm really lucky I decided to do this challenge now, in my generation, I mean. Because I look around me, and the high school guys I see—and this is just for an average night out on the town, say a weeknight—are wearing black nail polish, have both ears pierced, wear lipstick and blush, large fake-cowrie-shell necklaces, and mincingly tote a tin Superman lunch box as a purse.

That the famous Boulder skinny-dipping place up the canyon, which I thought might be a great place for me to pick up guys (seasonally, of course)—because I could *pre-view* them—turned out to suck, because every time I went there, I saw only fat old men sitting cross-legged with (strategically placed) second-hand paperbacks.

That there seems to be a correlation between hirsute balding men and the desire to eat pussy (NB: this does not correspond well with lesbianism; warrants more investigation).

Ah, *girls*...I'd say we've come rather far from the days of Laura Ingalls, when being naughty involved switching your pink hair ribbons for your blind sister's blue ones when Ma wasn't looking. Ladies, Little House on the Prairie this ain't anymore.

Nevertheless—I thought, as I glanced at the clock, stroking Baby thoughtfully—I still *lost the bet. Merde, merde, merde.* I really, really hate to lose—did I already say that?

I peeled that final layer of dirty clothes off the bottom of the closet, tossed it into the washing machine and gazed at the water as it filled, lost in my reverie of what I could have, and should have, done better. The machine's clanking as it started its Loud Cycle jerked me out of my musing. That's when I noticed a piece of clothing bubbling up to the surface: a black shirt with white lettering showing through as it got wet. *Lettering?* I didn't own anything so crass as to have lettering on it. No Nike exhortations, no Budweiser slogans for me (I know—a paradoxical sentiment from someone who so adores reading other people's T-shirts and bumper stickers). I fished it out, dripping, and turned it right-side-out: *Only You Can Save Me From My Spiritual Path.* What the…?!

Oh—now I remembered! Good ol' Mordecai. I had to smile at the memory—I guess I was *able* to smile, now that enough time had elapsed since our little…escapade. Mordecai—after whom I had sworn off Jewish boys. When had that been? Oh, of course! Thanksgiving; the Tofurkey debacle. But wait a sec—if I had Mordecai's T-shirt here, what had he gone home in? I certainly didn't remember him walking out of my apartment bare-chested; that would've looked too memorable, what with that pale, underexercised bod of his. All I could think was that he must've accidentally grabbed one of my black T-shirts that were lying around; I had a lot of them. And of course he *had* evinced signs of T-shirt kleptomania...

I'd loved the saying on his T-shirt, but he'd hardly even been aware of it. Whose did he say it was? His brother's? ... Oh yeah, his roommate's. He'd also said some weird things about his roommate; what were they? I couldn't recall everything, but I was pretty sure he'd said the guy was good-looking, but religious, and a serious Kabbalist. Poor Mordecai...he was jealous of his roommate, wasn't that it?

I started to drop the shirt back in, but then I had a sudden hunch. If Mordecai's roommate was indeed another nice little Jewish boy, then... I looked at the underside of the tag: sure enough, precisely what I was expecting: in permanent marker, some Jewish mother had recently written her grown son's name and address, as if he were a nine year-old on his way to summer camp.

I was off to return myself a shirt. (But I'd wait till it was freshly laundered.) Grinning, I dunked it back into the suds and closed the lid. Yes, I know I'd said I'd sworn off Jewish boys, but tough times called for drastic measures.

One *petit* problem: by the time the dryer finished, it was twenty after midnight. I had to hope that, like myself, *Joshua Nussbaum 3633 28th St #206* was a night owl. It's an interesting thing, how many creative types are night owls—and how many Jews are creative types. Kabbalists aside, as I don't know any personally (yet!), think of all the Jewish writers, musicians, and artists out there, throughout history...there's even a very funny example right here in town: a Jewish-owned pottery studio called Let My People Throw, which is open daily, but only from 6 p.m. to 2 a.m.

Are you thinking what I was thinking? That I had *one last, little* chance? Yes, indeed. Religious wasn't going to stop me—after all, he wasn't a Catholic priest, right? The only things I hadn't figured out yet were: what to do if they were asleep, and what to do if Mordecai answered the door.

Armed with a fluffy, clean, folded T-shirt, I drove to the address so conveniently provided by Joshua's mother, mentally thanking her, wherever in the world she might be (hopefully not living with him).

Excellent! Lights on in the apartment. I knocked, held my breath, praying (feeling, it must be admitted, slightly sacrilegious) for it not to be

Mordecai who answered the door. And my prayers were answered!

Well—in a way. What I got was the most gorgeous guy I'd ever seen. Now, Alan has the most fantastic body I know, from all that hard-core exercise, but although I find Alan infinitely appealing and endearing, he's not *handsome*. His teeth are crooked, his nose too; in fact, all his features are sort of...*original*. Together, they make up a not ugly face, but definitely not a classic one either. He does of course have that animal sex appeal, which I think mostly comes from his pheromones, or just from the chemical interaction of him and me, maybe.

What I saw before me now was what I swear I would've assembled as The Perfect Guy: okay, so we start with about 34 years of age; oh, about 5'11 and 3/4"; can't see the body too well (too many clothes), but that's okay, it seems fine; let's add the dark, curly, shoulder-length hair; Mediterranean olive complexion; penetrating big brown eyes; sharp, hooked beak of a nose; sensitive, shapely lips; soft, silky beard—well, that could go, but in fact it actually looked great on him.

"I....I...," I stammered, staring at him; I'd lost the ability to speak.

"Yes?" he asked, still not opening the door fully.

"I...ah...Is Mordecai in?"

"No, I'm sorry. He doesn't live here anymore."

"Oh! He doesn't? But I came to..." I held out the folded T-shirt by way of explanation.

The guy looked at the shirt and his face showed delayed recognition, then confusion. "How did you...? Look, do you want to come in for a minute?"

"Thanks," I said, stepping inside, trying not to smirk, thinking, yep, that's it—gimme about two hours and yeah baby, *wrap it up, I'll take it—* when I finally got a good look at him, full-on, head to toe, and two things registered: 1) this guy was really, truly, *incredibly* good-looking, the likes of which I had never laid eyes on before—and as you know, I had laid eyes (and other things) on quite a few men; 2) I had *no fucking chance* to win the bet.

Because those clothes he was wearing? Well, they consisted of very plain black pants and shoes, and a perfectly plain, long-sleeved, button-down white shirt. And as I stood gaping at him, he shyly ducked his head to place upon those beautiful curls—*and peyes,* I now noticed; they'd blended in with the long hair—a black hat. At any moment, I expected nine more identically-dressed (but not possibly as good-looking) men to jump out from a dark corner somewhere, form a dancing circle with this one, and all joyously shout out some lyrics regarding the imminent arrival of Meshiach.

The man was Hasidic. He was Orthodox. Or Ultra-Orthodox, or whatever the correct term was; I wasn't one to know. I *did* know enough that not only was he *not* going to be frolicking and toasting the end of the challenge with me over champagne at dawn (okay, knowing me, it'd be more like orange juice, and at noon), no—this beautiful creature was not even going to be *shaking my hand*.

"I'm Joshua," he said. I swear he had a way of making his eyes purposely melt, like when you've eaten all the chocolate in the house on a PMS binge and you're reduced to putting baking chocolate in the microwave for thirty seconds.

"Aviva," I answered, attempting to gulp down all my shock and disappointment. I recalled now Mordecai's words: *My roommate actually* is *on a spiritual path—some Jewish shit… a chick magnet—and he doesn't even care!… What a dweeb!… Some kind of religious nut… If I got half the looks from babes that he does…*

"Um…here you go, Joshua," I said, handing him the T-shirt, trying to sound less bummed than I was feeling.

"Thanks," he said. "I'll mind my own business and not ask how you came to be the bearer of this." He smiled.

"Yeah, that'd be best. So, Mordecai…?"

"Yeah, he moved out a couple of months ago. We didn't have much in common anyway." He excused himself and took the shirt into another room. The bedroom? I wondered, and couldn't help but picture him there, disrobing, or wearing something other than those somber clothes… When did he ever wear that T-shirt, anyway? To work out? To *bed*? I stifled a moan.

I was feeling unbelievably aroused, knowing I couldn't have this guy. I think I finally understood what was meant by all those Catholic-girl fantasies—the more forbidden the act, the greater the potential for steaminess if you actually do something. Oy. If I didn't know better, I'd think I was having a hot flash.

"Could I open a window or something, Joshua?" I was tempted to shorten it to Josh, but I didn't know if that was *allowed*. Man, all this forbiddenness was really something. I was getting hotter and hotter. I was s*oaking*.

He came back into the living room, went to a window, and had to strain to open it; it was an older building. I could see those muscles outlined along each side of his back—I don't know what they're called—and I don't care—through his white shirt. Were those *tzitzis* peeking out from under there? *I am going to implode.* What nerve, someone this good-looking, being this religious! It's just not right. It shouldn't be allowed. Oof, and here we are again, back to forbiddenness.

"Thanks..." I said weakly.

"Where are my manners?" he asked suddenly, noticing I was still standing. (Maybe he'd noticed because I was kind of *swaying* by now, my knees soon to give out. It probably looked like I was davening.) "Would you like something to drink? Juice? Or coffee? That's what I was just having—there's some already made."

"Um...I hope you don't think I'm rude, but..."

He raised his eyebrows—beautifully arched, heavily furred, dark brown eyebrows that nearly met in the middle. I continued, "...Why are you drinking coffee this late at night?" And why have you invited me in, me, a *woman*, not kosher (pardon) if you are Ultra-Whatever you are?

"Oh, I'm always up this late. I'm a night owl." *Bingo.*

"Do you work at night, or...?"

"Not necessarily. I'm just up, regardless."

"So... Mord told me—"

"*Mord!* He must've *loved* that! *Mord!* Ha ha!" He snorted when he laughed. I loved it. I wanted to kiss his beaky nose. I wanted to make him snort some more.

"Yeah, well, he wasn't too thrilled with...anything. Anyway, he told me you were a Kabbalist. Can you tell me something about that? I've always thought it must be really fascinating..."

"He told you that?" Joshua looked surprised. "I'm not."

"You're not?" Now *I* must've looked surprised. "But...he said you were." What a lame conversation.

"Hmm... I don't know why he'd..." Joshua was frowning, thinking. Suddenly he snorted again, laughing. "Oh, yes I do! One time he just kept bugging me, he was hanging around literally *all* day, asking these kind of disparaging questions about my religious studies...he just would not leave me alone. And I knew he hated people who were into 'mystical stuff,' as he put it. So finally I told him I was, like, really heavily into Kabbalah, just so he'd quit bugging me. And it worked!" Joshua was laughing, but stopped when he looked over at me and realized I was stricken. "What's the matter, Aviva?"

"I'm sorry—you're probably feeling the same way about me, then—here I am, asking you questions already about your religious stuff…"

"No," he said so softly I almost didn't catch it, "I don't think it would bother me if *you* asked me all *kinds* of questions."

Wait a second—if I'm not mistaken, this guy just *flirted* with me. Surely *that* isn't kosher! I blushed, which embarrassed me. I looked down to hide it, then peeked at Joshua. He blushed too—at least I think he did. It was pretty hard to tell, what with the hat and beard and all. "So," he said, after a pause, changing the subject, "what brings you to return clothing so late at night?"

"Oh, I'm a night owl too. This time of night, for me, feels like other people's seven p.m., if you know what I mean."

"I know exactly what you mean," he smiled.

"So…do you mind actually telling me about your religious studies? Even if it's not Kabbalah, I mean?" I asked with a smile of my own.

"Certainly. But please—sit down with your coffee. Be comfortable." I did and I was. "First of all, know that while Kabbalah interests me greatly, I respect tradition far too much to begin studying it yet—you know, don't you, that men should not approach Kabbalah until they reach the age of forty?"

"That's right, I think I remember hearing that at some point…"

We spent several very relaxed hours talking and getting to know one another over uncountable cups of coffee and between frequent trips to the bathroom to pee. It was so great conversing with him, I had completely stopped caring about him not working out as my Number Thirty. Joshua told me that he had always felt deeply, albeit privately, about Judaism, and that after a lot of contemplation, he was now preparing to enter rabbinical school. He still wasn't certain it was right for him, but after much deliberation, had decided that the only way to know was to try it. For several years, since his mother's death and on the advice of his aunt (who had a much heavier and more religious hand in his life than his mother ever had), he had been dressing like this, to "attempt to ward off all potential advances of a feminine nature," so that he could devote himself entirely to his studies in a serious manner. And, he concluded, it worked. Really well.

"Wait a second," I said. "Hold on—you mean you're *not* Hasidic, or

Orthodox, or whatever?"

"No. I wouldn't say that I am. Not really. Just very serious about my studies."

I didn't say anything, although my heart had begun to pound very fast, and I didn't think it was *entirely* due to all the caffeine I'd consumed. Also, my brain was going a mile a minute, calculating *whether to...*

"Why?" he asked. "Does it matter?"

I gulped ...*tell him the truth?*

I'm still not sure what made me confess; perhaps the feeling of surrender that I'd had as soon as I'd seen him, as if my usual defenses wouldn't work. Any normal Jewish boy, sure. Give me your run-of-the-mill Reform *rabbi*, even! But not someone wearing the dreaded black-and-white. Or maybe the urge to avoid prevarication came from the aura of religiosity, or simply from the soulfullness I found in those intense and beautiful eyes in front of me.

I took a deep breath. "Joshua," I began slowly, "You probably won't believe this, but... A year ago—*exactly* a year ago—some girlfriends of mine thought it would be kind of funny to propose, well, a sort of *challenge...*"

I told him about the fireworks with Eli; the Texan who ordered sacred cow at a vegetarian restaurant; Reza the Persian; Tiny Dick, the Writer-Formerly-in-a-Coma; the forbidden delights of sleeping with my bald studnet; exotic-looking, should've-been-his-brother Jack; my model Marcel; the SSRI Superman; the Mime; Thomas the Toilet Man; the impotent Burning Man; Todd who wanted merry maidens but got dust-busted instead; the screened-porch dweller; the misfiring Zen Archer; the yogi with pulled groins; the toupée cemetery; and as many others as I could think of. Pointedly, I did *not* tell him about any masochists or anyone taking home a gift of plastic handcuffs, in case Joshua had ever had occasion to divine anything of his roommate's boudoir persuasions; I didn't want Joshua to know for sure about me and Mord, even if secretly he suspected—that would be just *too* embarrassing.

He stared at me, unblinking, when I finished. After a few seconds, I couldn't meet his piercing glance anymore, and I looked down. He still hadn't responded in any way to my strange tale. Finally, he cleared his throat. "Aviva," he said softly. "Is this all true?"

"Yes," I practically whispered. I wasn't ashamed. I was more like... humbled by his beauty, still. And by his (damn, isn't there another word?)

soulfullness. It was so quiet. Other than the coffeemaker percolating in the kitchen, and the occasional helicopter going by, reconnoitering for the upcoming race this morning, it was as silent as those first few moments after walking into a classroom at the beginning of a new semester, when prof and studnets appraise each other, all contemplating the long four months ahead in one another's company.

After a while, I dared a glance up at his face. And was taken aback by what I swore to be the beginnings of a smile playing at the very corners of his mouth. But I couldn't be sure, because of the beard.

"And you didn't make it? Your bet?"

"That's right. Twenty-nine."

He shook his head slightly, then without a word, he disappeared into the bathroom. Yet another pee break. We'd been averaging one every half-hour. I had been quite surprised and pleased to find I was in the company of a man whose bladder seemed as weak and tiny as mine; it made things so much more egalitarian.

He seemed to be taking a long time. Maybe he had to go number two? Did people that good-looking actually have nasty bodily functions? Another helicopter flew over, lower and louder this time. I glanced out the living-room window and realized it was getting light out. Jeez, it must be *dawn*—we'd been up *all night* talking.

And what a pleasure it had been, truly. I regretted nothing.

Joshua came back into the living room—and I gasped. He had shaved off his beard. His clean face was grinning at me wickedly, and more handsome than ever.

"Come on, Aviva," he said, glancing at his watch. "You've got about…an hour and a half to make your bet, by my calculation." He held out his hand to me, his bare face gleaming in the early-morning light, his nose appearing sharper than ever. "And I've got a week before I begin rabbinical school—enough time to start growing the beard back."

I gasped again. I honestly could not believe what he was suggesting. "But, but… But Joshua, what about…?"

"What about what?"

"You know…your studies…and everything."

"Remember—I told you, I'm not Hasidic, I'm not Ultra-Orthodox. Not yet, anyway. I never *have* been. I just dress this way. I'm not a virgin either, so don't worry," he said, laughing (and snorting). "And I'm not a *Pencil Dick*, and I don't need *tiger foreplay*, and I haven't been in a coma—that I know of, anyway—and…let's see…I don't wear a toupée… What else?"

I got up to join him, heart pounding, crotch already *extremely* wet from the hours of staring at him and fantasizing—when suddenly something struck me. I stood paralyzed by the thought.

"Oh, shit! Shit, shit, shit, merde, *merde*!" I shouted. Then: "Sorry for the swearing."

"Shhhhh, you'll wake the neighbors! What is it, what's wrong?" he asked.

"The bet! The goddamned—oh, sorry!—bet! I'd forgotten! It's one of the rules: It *doesn't count if I tell the guy about the bet.*"

We stood looking at each other, about four feet apart. Neither of us moved for about thirty seconds.

Then, suddenly, we both started giggling. Cracking up, laughing so hard, we were clutching our ribs, doubled over. Slowly, we made our way towards each other, crab-stepping our way a little at a time until we found each other bodily, grasping onto each other, our hilarity gradually subsiding as we began to feel body heat take its place.

"Aviva," he said into my mouth as he began to learn how to kiss me, "you know, you don't *have* to tell. *I* won't."

And so it was that as the starting gun went off outside the bedroom window for the Bolder Boulder's A Wave (the fastest, leanest dudes around), I was having the most delicious orgasm and feeling only the *slightest* bit guilty that…I'd cheated on the challenge. But it was such a *tiny* cheat, really. Such a small bending of rules, in the overall scheme of things, that I hope—nay, I'm *sure*—I will be forgiven. Hey, everyone's human, right? We can strive to be perfect, but we can't actually *be* perfect. So let me not, ever again, mention this one *très petite* transgression.

♱

"Georgeeeeette," I said in a taunting voice on the phone later that day, a couple of hours after the final wheelchair racers had finished the Bolder Boulder course, "guess whaaaaaat."

"There's no way. No fucking way. You did *not* make the bet. You didn't have *time*!"

"Oh yes I diiiiiiiiiiiiid," I singsonged again.

"Okay, quit with that irritating voice, first off."

"Yes, ma'am," I whipped back, happy and cocky and *bien baisée*.

"Details."

"I seduced a rabbi. A rabbi with razor cuts. A beautiful, gorgeous, young…well, rabbi-*to-be*, if we must get technical about it. About an hour before the starting gun." I smiled sleepily through the phone line at the memory of Josh's fine hands, his eyes, his thick curly hair, his still-slightly-bleeding small facial wounds.

"Girlfriend. Ave. I don't know what to say. *I. Am. Impressed.*"

ə

I spent the next couple of weeks feeling strangely bored, unable to concentrate on much of anything and not at *all* in the mood to start preparing my next round of courses. It was as if something were missing. I guess I was feeling sort of (okay, you *must've* been expecting this)...anticlimactic.

My girlfriends and I toasted my victory by going to Ben & Jerry's and each eating a brownie covered with Chocolate Fudge Brownie ice cream and then topped with hot fudge, and a little whipped cream *para variar*, as JoAnn said, who was invited even though she didn't know what we were celebrating. (She said she didn't have to know; if we were going out for chocolate suicide she would ask no questions.)

On one of my hikes during this aimless period, I was annoyingly perpetually stuck about fifty yards behind this couple who felt the need to pause every so often to do the several-minute Boulder Soul Hug and gaze deeply and meaningfully into each other's eyes. I figured, that very phrase *gaze deeply and meaningfully into each other's eyes* was probably running through both of their minds while they did it, along with some really smarmy music in the background—instruction from some crappy New-Age Kama Sutra video they'd just watched, full of naked people prancing around wearing fake butterfly wings and mispronouncing "lingam" (yeah, I've seen the stupid thing too). It was nauseating. I hated being the unwilling witness to so much sheer *oozing* and *feeling*—it was like accidentally walking in on people having sex.

On another hike, I saw what I thought was, from a distance, a woman pushing her baby up the Sanitas Valley trail in one of those Baby Jogger things. She was cooing to it and bending down and fussing with it every so often. But when I got closer (I going downhill, she coming up), I saw that, to my tremendous surprise, her baby was actually an extremely overweight bulldog, a gigantic grinning neckless wonder, an overinflated beachball with tiny, useless appendages, strapped in and greatly enjoying its ride.

I went to Moe's for a bagel sandwich and they had a new box up near the cash register that said "Suggestions for God." I used to know a woman who had this way of saying, very sarcastically and very loudly, "*Niiiiice* one!," and when I saw that box at Moe's, I really, really missed her voice saying that.

I noted two very cryptic bumper stickers on the same day. The first was *Tranquil and serene until he runs out of supplies*, and the second said simply, *Girls can tell*. I loved them both, without a clue what they meant.

I found myself one afternoon attempting to calculate exactly how many total hours I had spent, in my lifetime, taking tests (and keep in mind: that's starting at age four, nursery school; all the way through qualifying exams and dissertation defense for my Ph.D.). When I started pondering all the other things I could've done with that time, I began getting *really* depressed and had to quit thinking about it.

Therese cracked me up by telling me about a scene she'd witnessed where this weird guy requesting Nubian goat milk had to be "escorted" out of Alfalfa's. I said, damn, the guy had to have been *really* weird to get thrown out of Alfalfa's. She laughed and said, "Indeed, he was a *rather marginal character*."

One evening, at the Trident, I was taking notes (in what I thought was a sly, discreet manner) about a woman at a table near me, for my novel-in-infinitesimal-progress (I was up to page fifteen). After about half an hour I noticed that *she* was also taking notes about *me*. I got so freaked out, I had to leave immediately.

I got an email from JoAnn, who said she'd been trying to get a friend of hers to go to an AA meeting, but the guy didn't want to go, because he "feared the step where you have to apologize to all those you've wronged in the past." When JoAnn asked the friend how he knew about the step if he'd never been to AA, the friend had replied, "Duh, Seinfeld."

In other words, it was back to my life as usual.

!

The phone rang as I was just finishing up washing dishes. I dried my hands quickly and ran for it; it's a pain in the ass to have to erase the message once it starts recording. You have to play back, or at least start playing back, a message in order to erase it. You also have to listen to the stupid mechanized voice going "Tuesday...One-fifteen p.m. You have one. New. Message. And. Five. Old. Messages." (Some of my colleagues in Phonetics swear they were motivated to get into the field of computer voice recognition *entirely* by their irritation with those voices.) This means that screening calls while you're home makes you feel twice as guilty, since you have to listen to the message that you "weren't there for" twice. So why don't I get a new machine? Two reasons: 1) they don't pay me enough to be able to afford it; but especially 2) it took me three years to figure out how this one worked.

"Aviva?"

This voice, I recognized instantly. That nasal, breathy, allergy-laden and damned sexy baritone, every Tay-Sachs-prone and myopic gene perfectly reproduced, all the way from the shtetls.

"Alan!! Oh my *god*! It's been forever!"

"Yeah. I mean, I guess. Um. Yeah." Phlegmatic and awkward as ever.

"So how *are* you?! What are you *doing* these days? Are you still racing?! What are you *doing*?!" I asked, so excited to hear his voice I didn't know what to talk about first.

"Well, actually, well, that's kind of why I'm calling, you know. 'Cause I'm kind of, um, here. Now. In Boulder, I mean. Um. I moved back here. Um, yesterday. I'm even renting the same room as before—isn't that amazing? The guy's even giving me the same deal as before! How lucky can I get, huh? And um, so, um, I wanted to know if you wanted to... you know...um, watch a video or something? Or anything. You know. I mean, at your place. Or my place. Or whatever. If you want. You know. Want to?"

The smile spread like a windblown gust of summer fire in Sunshine Canyon—from my face through my belly, all the way down to my crotch, where it stayed a while, gully-jumping and burning ever hotter; then back up to settle goofily and cozily—and *oy*, what a perfect fit!—around my semi-jaded heart. Challenge, I'd wanted? Well, you couldn't get much more challenging than Alan.

I could feel that Rocky Mountain High recommencing already. Maybe it was time to finally take the plunge—and put that bumper sticker I'd been keeping in a desk drawer all year onto my ancient used Nissan. Somehow I knew that together, Alan and I (but especially Alan) would be doing our best in the future to keep Boulder weird.

Acknowledgments

The memory of my maternal grandparents, who truly valued us and the arts: *amen*. My brother, who works too much. My mother. Sanjay, who eats popcorn with a spoon, and ice cream with a fork, and is capable of putting onions and hot chili powder on *anything*: for love and support, and all the "donkey jobs." Appa for constantly inquiring whether the book was finished, Amma for her awesome cooking. Rebecca and Bill, for friendship and support; and for masa boats, risotto, and Leave O'Porch. Also Rebecca for ZZ Top; and in fond memory of the Shoe and the Harmonica, the hedgehog, the white mouse, and the encephalitis. Ann, a sister of the soul (but not a "soul sistah;" that's different), for her support, shared writerly and Mood Monster miseries, "Elvis," and for being a part of my life—please don't ever stop. Joel Schwimmer, for character inspiration, friendship, lust, and portions of some Alan emails. Michelle, for her gifts to me of shiatsu, and not giving up on me. Also for the Nubian goat milk. Kandace, you sweet thing. Jay. Jason and Colleen, for Oxford and for helping me live through Tourette's Farm. Rafa, por la amistad, la risa y la música. Josep M., for inadvertently helping me realize I'd rather write a novel than a dissertation. "Kavulya," good photographer, good Scrabble player (though not quite as good as me), great thighs: for our long existentialist talks and our Scottish accents. Rolando y Yoyi. Gustavo, fellow banishee and partner in crime to the Acupuncture College: gracias por siempre hacerme reír. Sara: everyone should have such an enthusiastic reader. Ahoova: beautiful woman, beautiful heart. Brent, for love, seven years and seventeen fourteeners. Kendra, great dancer, great soul. Jenny, for the kale comment. Matt—מר מתוק—for his green eyes and a fiery Fourth. Kurt, for fond memories of his (real) Jackson Browne hair. Paul F. and his assistant, Shannon F., both of whom believed in this book; Paul didn't even flinch when I asked him (but the getting-an-agent books *told* me to ask!) what would happen to my manuscript if he died. "Roberto" S., former "studnet" who promised to buy the second copy of my book if I mentioned him here. Eric, for Ganesh, character inspiration, and the Nepalese words. David R., a.k.a. The Zip Code Man: it was educational. Dave W., for the celibacy comment. Abu and Panda. Payman, for fun and the Persian name and proverb. Lisa, for what happens when the Scorpio soul wobbles. Jamey, for the fortune cookie. Peggy, for the sock suspenders. Z, for the backgammon lessons. Skateboard Dan. Antonia, for the Russian coffee incident. Youssef, for the shooting star. Ron, most excellent yoga teacher. The guy who woke up from a coma to find he'd written a novel: a story so good I couldn't possibly have made it up. Thanks, dude. Halfie, Jazz, and Random: beloved animolecules. My musical muses—they must be; I played them (by putting on their CDs and by bringing out my own guitar) nearly incessantly—Silvio Rodríguez, Counting Crows, Sarah MacLachlan, Joni Mitchell. Chocolove, for their 77%-cacao bars. Christine Lavin, for her music and her Attitude. Leftover Salmon. The Trident, for great decaf soy mochas and space to write, even if the music is a little too loud for an HSP. And all the Boulderites who graciously or unwittingly participated in (the inspiration for) this novel.

About the author

Jala Pfaff writes, paints, plays the guitar and teaches Spanish in Colorado, where she lives with her husband, three cats, and two Golden Retrievers sweeter than raspberry jam. Her work has been published in *The Rose & Thorn* and *Slow Trains*. She holds a Master's degree in Hispanic Linguistics. *Seducing the Rabbi* is her first novel.

If you enjoyed this book, the author and Aviva are thrilled! More fiction, including a sequel, is in the works.

For writing excerpts, other interesting stuff, and to keep updated about forthcoming books by this author, please visit **www.jalapfaff.com**.